THE CRYSTAL WARRIOR

J Jeffreys

Published in 2009 by New Generation Publishing

First Edition

Glossary

Anari	The 'first comers', a group of 18 tribes that live in central and southern Anaria. Smaller in build than the
Anant	The 'second comers' or 'strangers', a group of 8 tribes that live in the north of Anaria.
Decan	A ten day period.
Centad	A period of ten decans
Season	A period of three centads. About the same length as an earth year.
Tarn	Three seasons or an Anarian year.
Secutor	Lightly armoured gladiator with sword and small shield.
Retaari	Net and trident gladiator with little or no body protection.
Torc	An embossed metal disc worn at the chest, secured by leather straps, showing tribal allegiance. The more precious the metal the higher status a warrior has.
Tag	Beggar

Prologue.

"Who sounded the alarm?"

"Where's the attack coming from?"

"How did they get into the city?"

Cries of alarm and fear resound through the castle. No one knows what is happening, only that the alarm has sounded.

"Summon the guard. Wake those off duty." The Lord has appeared and takes charge. "Spymaster.... Spymaster. Report."

"The Kush are attacking, my Lord. They are in the city... to the south of the castle."

"How... How did they get past our guards?" But no one knows the answer to that. "Take my Lady and our son. Now! Get them away from here." Lord Menethes orders several of the milling warriors and they obey him immediately. "The rest of you come with me. We must meet this Kush attack."

The Lord and a large group of his warriors march from the castle. Horses will be no good in the city streets.

Liam watches them from the window of the Lady's parlour. Sarah is getting dressed as quickly as she can. Judith enters and hurries over to Liam.

"What's going to happen to us?" She is frightened and grips his forearm in her terror.

"The Lord has ordered you taken to the Port," he tells her briefly. "Now be useful and hurry Sarah up."
He strides to the door. Five of his men are ready, waiting outside.

"Are the horses prepared?"
Saul nods.

They are only waiting for the Lady.

At last Sarah is ready and Liam hurries the women down the back stairs and into the courtyard.

"Where is Dom?" Sarah demands when she sees only horses waiting. "Where is my son? We can't leave without him."

"He has already gone, with Dolan and his men," Liam explains. "Two small groups stand a better chance of slipping past than one large."

He does not tell her that the Lord ordered it so in the hope that the Lady's party would distract any waiting assassins. The heir to the Lorddom will always be more important than its Lady.

They ride out of the castle and head for the North Gate. Liam knows that Dolan will leave soon after. They canter down the main street and there are Kush waiting for them.

Fifty of them and only thirty in the Lady's guard.

The Kush warriors don't even ask for surrender, they attack. One of Sarah's maids is dragged from her horse before any one realises what is happening and her throat cut.

"They're going to kill the women," Nye cries in disbelief.

This is unheard of. This is not right.

Is there to be no ransom?

"Protect our Lady," Liam shouts. They dismount, the women huddle against the wall of a house as the Menethes warriors stand between them and the Kush, swords fully empowered.

They will die protecting their Lady.

More warriors enter the narrow street and Liam's heart sinks. There is no hope now.

"It's Deri," Saul cries as the newcomers fall on the Kush.

2

Liam hurries forward. "Get the women away," he orders as he strikes at a Kush warrior.

The Menethes blood is hot and they want revenge.

The fight is fierce but swift.

Liam leans back against the wall. He is tired.

"We saw your escape from the castle battlements," Deri explains. "We could see the Kush ahead of you."

All the Kush are dead.

Eight Menethes died too.

Deri and Elon join Liam, they will protect the Lady. The others return to the castle.

"Dolan said he would wait as long as he could by the standing stones," Japhet tells Liam as they part. "Good Luck."

"Good hunting," Liam replies.

They make it safely out of the city by the north gate and disappear into the darkness. The attackers were helped because there was only light from the smaller moon Hathor, a fact that now helps Liam and his small group in their escape.

Liam wonders where it is best to make for, the Port as his Lord ordered or to the protection of the Toth?

What if the Toth are under attack too?

For a while both paths will lie in the same direction so he leads the group north, towards Menethes Port where it all began only two tarns before... Two tarns... six seasons... only six *years* ago.........

The great ships strained at their mooring ropes as the tide began to turn. The creaking of the wooden hulls and the slapping of water against stone added to the noise of the busy dock. Tired sailors were busy securing the boats for the night before going ashore in search of food. Only one ship was still unloading, a pirate ship from the Isles, its crew already scaling the rigging to ready the ship for sail. Two ramps had been lowered to the quayside and slaves were carrying barrels and sacks aboard up one whilst new slaves were unloaded down the other. It had been a bad journey and most of them were unsteady on their feet, sick looking. One stood out amongst the rest. A tall man, his dark hair cut short in contrast to those around him. He stood erect and looked around with interest.

"A pirate!" the Port Master said. "That's asking for trouble."

The Castle Steward, who had come down to oversee the unloading of this final batch of slaves, shrugged. "He is destined for the Gladiator ring, that will knock any rebellion out of him," and he went back to his lists, marvelling at the stupidity of the man. Would pirates have allowed one of their own to be taken? He sent the slaves in different directions depending on the lives and occupations they had been given. The Steward looked up as the tall man approached.

"This one can go straight to the Port gladiator school," he said and passed on.

Soon there was a group of five waiting to go to the school. Not all would be gladiators, one would be a cook, another a swordsmith. They stood apart from the slaves waiting to go the castle or to the market and were only guarded by two warriors. But most didn't think of escape.

Where would they escape to?

Better to work hard and earn one's freedom.

Become a free man and model citizen for the Lord.

The one destined to be a cook looked at the big man and asked him his name.

Rebus, son of Ragnar of the Pirate Isles. He knew that was his name.

So why did he say Liam?

He stared around him with interest, conscious that the Port Master was watching him uneasily.

No chance of escape here.

The wharves were crowded with hungry sailors leaving their ships for the comforting glow of the Port inns. Merchants in their homespun working clothes were haggling over prices for the last of the imported goods, wines in casks, anonymous foodstuffs in rough sacks, finest glassware carefully packed in wooden crates. And the ever-present tags, looking for an opportunity... an unseasoned merchant, an unguarded purse.

Liam breathed in the salt laden air. It might be a long time before he smelt the sea air again. A bird screeched overhead and he looked up as a grey-white bird with a long wingspan swooped down on a barrel and carried a large fish away in its talons. An irate merchant leapt about waving his arms and shouting curses at the thief but the bird soared effortlessly into the deepening pink of the sky and screeched its own curses back.

Liam frowned. He couldn't think of a name for the bird.

He looked around. The ship, the jetty, the port... all had an unreal air as if he were dreaming. But he could feel the skin of his forearm beneath his fingers; feel the pain as he pinched himself. It was real. But he still had the feeling he was going to wake up soon and find himself... where?

He could no more remember where he was from than the name of the bird.

Seagull.

Images of the Pirate Isles rose unbidden in his thoughts as the guards ordered the slaves to move. He knew he had family there but he couldn't summon up their faces or remember where he had lived or how he had lived.

Raids on the Arak, the Nedjha, the Oroka.

They were just names. Names that didn't seem to mean anything.

The ship that had brought them to the Port began to move away from the stone jetty, propelled by its oars. Liam glanced back at it then turned away and followed the rest of the slaves. They were swiftly marched past warehouses and the Port Master's office, past the quayside brothel and up a sloping road that ran towards the Harbour Gate set in the west wall of the town.

The training camp was outside the Port nestled in the shadow of its east wall. The group marched through the Harbour Gate and down the main road that ran through the centre of the Port. They passed the Port castle, little more than a round tower behind high walls of sombre grey stone and here the group split into two. Those whose destiny was to go to the Castle turned left and disappeared with their escort through the arched gateway with its raised portcullis. The rest of the slaves carried on through the town towards the main market square. Here another batch of slaves was separated off to go to the slave markets. Five were now left marching up the hill towards the East Gate.

Everywhere shops were beginning to close, rolling up their gaily-coloured awnings and clearing away goods displayed on tables outside. Only the inns, of which there seemed to be a fair number down the warren of side streets off the main thoroughfare, were opening. Crystal lamps were being opened and hung outside, throwing shafts of artificial sunlight into the narrow alleyways. Already the nightlife of the city was beginning to emerge out of its depths into its shadows. Thieves and pickpockets skulked in dark corners waiting for the drunk or the unwary and whores stood leaning against walls also waiting.

Liam averted his eyes as one whore, no more than six or seven tarns, called out in a high pitched whine to one of the guards. Then he was roughly pushed to one side by the same guard as the cry went up "Make way for the constable." The whore vanished back into the stone undergrowth of the town as a portly figure, resplendent in a blue jacket with the badge of a horse, wheezed towards them. Four men carrying a hurdle closely followed him. A foul stench arose from under the rough sacking that covered the litter and Liam turned away sickened. He wasn't the only one.

One of the guards raised his hand to his nose.

"What's to do?" he asked the red-faced official. "Suicide?"

"There are better ways than throwing yourself into one of the old Quarter middens," the constable panted and he pulled back the sacking to reveal a raw weeping mess that had once been a face.

"Midden worms," whispered the cook to Liam and he shuddered.

"Do you know who it was," the other guard asked and the constable nodded as he covered the acid drenched corpse once more.

"Ferel the Goldsmith," and both guards nodded as if that explained everything. "I have men out looking for his wife who seems to have disappeared," continued the man, "but which of her paramours would have the nerve for murder..." he shrugged and signalled to the stretcher-bearers that they were to continue on.

"Good hunting," called the guard as the grisly cortege passed down the main street. The slaves hurried on towards the East Gate glad to leave foetid air behind them.

It was late evening now and the sun was low in the sky ahead of them. The high walls cast long shadows and Liam shivered as he stepped from the dying sunlight into the chill dampness of the Gate approach.

"You're late," one of the guards on the gate said as they approached.

"Ran into a storm," their escort told him.

"Already? Getting earlier every year," and the sentry signalled them to wait. The slaves were again pushed to the side of the road by their guard who once more wielded the large sticks they were carrying with more show than actual harm.

Liam looked around as they waited. Warriors patrolled the high walls and the Gate was guarded too. But if wherever they were being taken was through the Gate it must be outside the Port. Escape might just be possible then. And he began to watch the patrolling warriors closely, noting what weapons they carried, how often they looked out over the walls. It all seemed quite lax. Perhaps coming back to the Port to steal a boat might be a possible option after all.

A group of trotting horses approached the Gate and Liam was amused to see how the warriors on duty stood a little straighter and strode more purposefully as they went about their patrolling. As the horsemen got nearer Liam quickly counted fifteen warriors. Not ordinary warriors these though. The silver discs at their chests, embossed with the head of a horse...*torcs*, flashed in the dying rays of the sun and they held themselves erect in their tall saddles. They might have the same long hair tied back in a 'tail but the long braids on one side of the head were easy to see.

Elite. He remembered the name easily.

An older warrior in the centre raised his hand to the Gate sentry. He glanced briefly at the slaves, indifferent to their existence. Then his eye fell on Liam. For a brief second they looked at each other. The man's eyes narrowed. He seemed to recognise Liam and then he was gone, through the gate and into the free world.

"Is that our Lord?" the cook asked in awe of so many powerful men passing within feet of him.

"No," Liam said before their guard could answer. "That's his Spymaster."

"Very good, Pirate," the warrior said. "And where have you seen such as him before... on a raid perhaps?" He prodded Liam with his stick and told them to move on.

Liam rubbed his side where the stick had bruised him. "There hasn't been a raid on your lands for over twenty-five tarns," he growled, pain making him less careful than was perhaps wise and he clenched his fists in anger as the humiliation of his position finally became too much for his soul to bear.

"Only because the Anant are too strong for you," the guard barked back and he raised the club again. "Now move on."

Liam fought to control his rising temper. He glared at the guard wondering if it would be possible to overcome him and escape. But there were too many warriors around. He forced himself to turn away and begin to walk after the rest of his fellow slaves.

But it was very difficult.

"There'll be trouble with that one," the gate sentry said, to the second guard on gate duty, as they passed. "You mark my words, Orf, that's one pirate destined to end up in the mines." Then he forgot all about the unfortunate slaves as they prepared to close the gate for the night.

The group moved on in silence. It was as if the other slaves had been unnerved by Liam's challenge to the authority of the guards. They eyed him nervously and inched away but Liam didn't care. He had finally overcome the rage that had coursed through him by thinking about the Spymaster. The man had known Liam and somehow Liam had known him although he was quite certain he had never seen the man before that day. Now, how could that be?

He pondered the question carefully as he walked the mile or so along the walls towards the Gladiator training camp. But no matter how many different ways he thought about it, he could find no answer. He found he could remember raids he had been on far to the south. But he could find no recollection of seeing the Spymaster on any of these forays into the lands of the Anari.

He was forced to abandon his thoughts as the wooden walls of the camp neared and the gate was opened to allow them in. The guards began to bark orders at them. Two of the slaves went with one guard to the right towards a cluster of buildings. The remaining three, including, Liam were herded towards an inner compound also surrounded by a wooden wall built of huge pointed stakes. They passed through a small doorway into an enclosure. There were several wooden huts round the perimeter and Liam regarded them with interest. But they were set back from the fence so that it was impossible to climb onto a roof and escape. He turned his attention back to the compound. Apart from the huts there was only a tall wooden stake in the middle of a large open piece of ground. Obviously the training ground, Liam thought but what was the stake for?

A man emerged from one of the larger huts and came over. He was carrying a tankard and every so often he would stop, take a drink, and then carry on towards them.

"You're late," he grumbled, finishing his drink as he came to halt in front of them. A large bunch of keys hung from his belt and Liam eyed them speculatively.

"Ship ran into a storm," their guard explained once again.

"This it then?" the man said. "What am I supposed to do with this sorry bunch?" Without waiting for a reply he turned round. "Follow me then," he ordered and walked towards a hut on the other side of the compound. He unlocked the door and reached up to empower the light inside. It was a storeroom and the walls were lined with shelves piled high with all manner of goods.

"I am Eoin," the man said as he took down three shirts and then three pairs of trousers all made from the same rough woven material. "I'm the Assessor here. At the end of the initial training period I get to say where you go... to the main Gladiator school at Menethes Prime... the markets to be sold on to other Lords or to the mines if you fail to please me. And be warned... I am very hard to please."

He handed them the clothes and told them to get changed. Liam stripped quickly. It was too cold to stand around. He put on the sleeping cloth first; a simple square of linen fastened round the waist with ties, then the trousers. Not laced at the side like the leather ones he

11

had just taken off but gathered at the waist with a short piece of rope. The trousers were rough and itched and they only came down to mid calf. Then he put on the shirt, which had no lacing at the neck, merely a rough T cut into the material. There was barely room to get his head through. If he were to escape he would need to find proper clothes. These would clearly mark him out as a runaway slave.

Eoin carefully locked the door behind him and they followed him back across the training area to a hut next to the one he had originally emerged from. Liam suddenly caught the smell of food and realised he was very hungry. He couldn't remember the last time he had eaten.

"In," Eoin said curtly and they followed him into the brightly lit long hut.

There were about sixty men, all dressed as Liam was, sitting on benches at three long tables. They had wooden bowls in front of them and were busy eating. No one looked up from their food at the new arrivals. Eoin pointed to a table at the front where a slave was busily dishing up from large cooking pots. Liam picked up a bowl and queued behind the other two to get his meal. He was given a ladleful of brown stew that almost filled his small bowl then a yellow slice of something that Liam had no name for. But everyone was busy dipping it in the stew and eating it so he did the same. Room was made for the new arrivals at the very bottom of the table, farthest away from the pots of food and the only source of heat in the room, a small brazier half full of red fire-crystals.

Liam stared for a moment at the yellow cake-like slice he had been given. It wasn't bread, he reasoned as he ate. Perhaps some kind of potato cake or ground meal. Whatever it was it had been fried and had a brown crust top and bottom that sandwiched the yellow, rather bland, cake inside. For a brief second he wondered why it was so important to him to know what it was, then he put it out of his mind and just enjoyed the food. There was no spoon to eat the stew with and he had to eat it with his fingers, mopping up the last of the gravy with the yellow cake. Everyone ate in silence. The only sound was that of the Assessor Eoin talking to two men at the head of the table. Then he left and almost immediately heads turned to look at the new arrivals and people began to talk.

The two men at the top stood up and went to get more food. Once their bowls had been replenished they call out several names and others went up to get more. When the pots were proclaimed empty a groan went up and Liam wondered who decided who was called for more. He asked his left-hand neighbour and was quickly told that it was the trainers. Work hard, please them and you might get more food, he was told.

"Why no spoons?" he asked and he was rewarded with a pitying look. Spoons could be fashioned into weapons he was told.
To use to escape?
His neighbour laughed. "No, to kill yourself with. That is the only escape possible."

"Who talks of escape?" One of the two men Eoin had spoken to had come up behind them and had been listening to them. Liam's neighbour suddenly cringed back against the table.

"No one, Mica," He was terrified of the man and Liam watched with undisguised interest. This Mica had some sort of power over his fellow slaves. Obviously there was a hierarchy even among the lowest of men.

"Why shouldn't one think of escape?" Liam ventured to ask. He needed to know how things worked in this place if he was to make a successful attempt at freedom.

Liam suddenly found himself being thrown against the back wall of the hut. The attack was so unexpected and sudden that he had had no chance to defend himself. Mica had his hands clenched round the shoulders of Liam's shirt. He slammed into Liam and leant against him, pinning Liam to the wall.

"If one tries to escape all in his hut are punished. It is difficult enough to live here without some idiot messing it up for the others. No one escapes. The only way out is to get promoted or sold. Understand?"
Liam nodded and allowed his body to sag slightly. Satisfied that the newcomer had learnt his lesson Mica moved back slightly and Liam brought his knee up. Mica gasped and doubled over in pain and surprise. Liam clasped his hands together and swung them at the man's head. Mica staggered back against the end of the table and then fell to his knees.

"I only asked because I am new here," Liam said eyeing the rest of the slaves warily. "If I don't know what the rules are I might break them without meaning to." He hoped his reasonable tone would stop anyone else from picking a fight with him. "I don't want any trouble," he added, carefully watching the other slave Eoin had been talking to.

Two slaves helped Mica to his feet but he pushed their hands away angrily and took a step towards Liam. "That's enough," the second man said and Mica gave him a venomous look before turning back to face Liam.

"I'll see you on the training ground, Secutor," he said as he started back to his seat and Liam knew he had made a serious enemy.

"Secutor?" he asked the man who had been his neighbour at table but he hurried back to his seat without answering. Liam picked up his bowl that had been knocked to the ground and looked around. As he had found earlier no one was willing to even look at him. He realised he was rapidly getting the reputation as a trouble maker and common sense told him if he was ever going to escape back to his home on the Isles he was going to have to appear more co-operative. He would have to try very hard to settle to the life of a trainee gladiator and not create too much trouble. He looked around. What was he supposed to do now?

"Put that on the table up there and then come with me." The second man the Assessor had spoken to was still standing close by and he wasn't looking pleased.

Liam followed him to the end of the hut, picking up a Tanis leaf from the bowl at the end as he passed and beginning to chew it. "Lord Ammon," he prayed silently, "grant me good digestion, good teeth and a good night's sleep."

"My name is Clem," the man said. "You're in my group for training, which means you'll be in my hut. So if you've any plans to escape I'll be the one stopping you." He opened the door and Liam shivered as the cool night air hit his bare arms. "They haven't issued winter clothing yet," Clem said noticing his discomfort. "You'll get used to the cold."

He led the way across the training ground towards one of the smaller huts and Liam wondered if he should ask one of the many questions that were running round in his thoughts.

"Why did he call me Secutor?" he asked finally.

"That's what you are to initially train as," Clem told him. "Eorin was sent to Prime, so we're short a sword-man in our group." He looked critically at Liam. "And I get you." He stopped just outside one hut and turned round to Liam. "So let's get one thing straight. What Mica said is true. If you try to escape we all get punished... so no one escapes." He shook his head. "Where would you escape to? Your clothes would instantly give you away as a slave and your hair would give you away as a pirate. And trust me, your lot might not have raided here for tarns but people have very long memories. There might not be much left of you to return here for punishment." He opened the door to the hut and went in. Liam was shown a mattress on the stone floor and given two blankets. This was where he was to sleep.

Several times during the night Liam woke with a start, his heart pounding. He knew he had been dreaming but he couldn't remember about what or why it should have frightened him so. His hands were clenched into tight fists and it took him several minutes to relax enough to straighten his fingers. He lay there taking deep breaths and listening to the sound of the slave in the next bed snoring. He couldn't get back to sleep.

He didn't dare go back to sleep.

The black horses of Osiris were waiting for him there.

He wrapped the blankets round his shoulders and crept between the sleeping figures. He opened the door to the hut as silently as he could and stepped out into the cold night air. He leant back against the wall and took a deep breath. He found he was shivering only partly because of the chill. Seconds after Liam had left the hut the door opened again and Clem stepped out. He seemed surprised to see Liam.

"I thought you might be doing something stupid," he said.

"Couldn't sleep."

16

"You'll get used to it," Clem said. "Unless you're very good you'll not be transferred from here before spring and no one would think to escape in winter. So the sooner you decide to start doing what they want the easier it'll be for you."

"And for you?"

"Of course. Life here is hard enough without making things more difficult for yourself. You'll learn that soon enough. Training starts tomorrow. Do everything they tell you to do, don't annoy anyone important and you might just survive."

"Is Mica important?" Liam asked and Clem gave a low laugh.

"He likes to think he is. But we're all only important until someone more important comes along. You'd do well to remember that."

"Thanks for the advice." Liam stared up at the fading stars. It was almost light. He thought Clem had gone back inside and started when the man spoke.

"Do you have family on the Pirate Isles?"

"No, there's no one. My family died of plague a season ago." Only three hundred days yet he could no longer remember what they had looked like.

"Then what have you to go back to?" Clem asked. "I'm told life is hard on the Isles..." Liam nodded. Wasn't that why they needed to raid... To survive? "Then train hard and get to Prime. Life is easier at the Gladiator school there. You can earn great rewards at the games... even your freedom. And life is much easier in Anaria. Why go back?"

Liam shrugged. It was difficult to explain.

"Think about it," Clem advised and he started to open the door. Liam put out a hand to stop him.

"Can you really kill yourself with a spoon?"

Clem nodded. "Someone sharpened the stem to a point with a small piece of flint and then leant against a wall," he said.

"Things can get that bad?"

Clem looked at Liam steadily. "Things can get that bad," he said. "The trick is not to let them." And he went back inside.

Liam thought about his arrival at the Port and the feeling of unreality that had followed him from the quayside. He remembered the Spymaster and the murdered man. "This is real," he thought and he considered all that Clem had said. Then he went back into the hut and his bed. If training was to start that day he was going to need all the rest he could get.

II

The most senior secutor trainer was Dolph. He taught them the basics, the thrust, parry, block, attack, defence. They used roughly hewn wooden swords that could give a painful clout if a trainee wasn't careful. Liam quickly learnt to be careful.

Most of the trainers were former gladiators themselves who were no longer quick enough to fight in the ring. As the late summer evenings slowly shortened into long winter nights the trainees would gather around the crystal fires and listen to tales of Games visited and fights won and lost on a whim of the Gods.

"The Toth hold the best games," they were told. "He provides the best food and accommodation even for the lowest gladiator. But that's as it should be, he is the richest Lord."

"And the worst?" someone asked.

"Darg is one of the poorest Lords, but he does his best. Mersin has the worst gladiators and has little interest in the Games. Toth is more likely to give a losing fighter his life. He is well seasoned and has seen a lot of death. Jirdhan will give you your life if you have fought well; Orin is the hardest Lord to please. A lot die at the Orin Games who might not have otherwise."

Liam listened in awe at the list of famous names that fell from the trainers' lips. Garet, Gyrwen, Tomas, Maneto and, the most famous of all, Ximenes.

"Lord Ramses owned him, father of the Lord now. He was Anarian but he defeated the best the Anant had to offer," Dolph told the spellbound trainees.

"What happened to him?"

"Earned his freedom, of course. Became a very successful trainer for the Lord and died quite a rich man."

"All of which," reasoned Liam as he lay on his uncomfortable mattress later, "is designed to make us train hard, be loyal little sheep and maybe... just maybe earn our freedom too. In a hundred tarns... if we don't die first."

The trainers told them about the glories of the Anant games but they did not mention the Anari games. It was Clem who informed them about those, one night when the cold made sleep impossible and even lying down fully clothed in the winter issue shirts and trousers did little to relieve the shivering.

"The Toth don't go to the Anari Games so most of the Anant Lords follow him. Our Lord being half Anarian does though and since there is little love lost between Anant and Anari, the chances of living, for an Anant gladiator are not good," he said. His words sent even more of a chill through his audience.

"When are the next games?" Col, the best retaari in their group asked.

"The next Anant games are to be held here at Menethes Port in a season's time," Clem told them. "Sometime during the second centad of spring... it depends on the weather exactly when. They were to be a tarn later but that is the time of the Sed festival so they were brought forward. The next Anari games are to be a small part of the festival. If the Gods are smiling on us there won't be any fights."

Liam wondered what a Sed festival was but was too embarrassed to ask. There seemed to be so much that he was ignorant of. When he eventually fell asleep he had another of his frightening dreams but for the first time he remembered what it had been about.

He was somewhere high looking down at hundreds of tiny specks of light. It was like looking up at the night sky except he was looking down and the lights seemed to be arranged in regular patterns and straight lines. As he continued to watch the lights moved away to be replaced by patches of darkness with only an odd speck or two of light. Then the regular pattern came back with more straight lines running off into the distance. The strange thing was he didn't feel all that frightened. Not then.

The real fear came when he woke up and he once more experienced the cold sweat and pounding heart of other nights… other dreams.

But he remembered this one and he couldn't understand why he should be so terrified of lights.

But he was.

It was too cold to do any training, the ground was frozen mud and thick ice had formed where the driving rain had left puddles. The trainees sat huddled in their huts, wrapped in blankets, only venturing forth for first-meal or supper.

"Training is preferable to this," grumbled Liam. At least then you had the chance to get warm. The only thing to do in the hut was to sit shivering and watch your breath issue out in clouds of steam.

He blew on his hands in a vain attempt to stop them from freezing and then sat with them under his armpits, gently rocking back and forth.

"It's not usually this cold," Clem said. "This is exceptionally bad. Being close to the sea it's usually much milder."

"Be thankful we're not at Prime," Oser said. "I hear they're snowed in down there."

Clem nodded. "That's why they have an indoor training area at the school there."

"We could do with something like that," Liam said and Clem laughed.

"Here? This is only a minor camp, to weed out the no-hopers. Our Lord isn't going to spend more money than is necessary on this place."

"Don't need to spend money," Liam said, thinking fast. "The hut where we have first-meal would be large enough. Push the tables back... a hut at a time could have an hour training before midday and another later."

"At least it would be a chance to get warm," Oser agreed.

"And relieve the boredom," Seth pointed out and the mute Heb nodded vigorously. They all looked eagerly at Clem.

"I could suggest it to one of the trainers," he said doubtfully, "...at supper tonight... perhaps."

"Why not now," Liam suggested and Clem reluctantly stood up, pulling both his blankets round his shoulders.

"No one takes my place near the fire," he warned as he opened the door and quickly stepped through. In spite of his haste there was a rush of even colder air into the hut and instinctively the remaining five men inched closer to the inadequate fire.

Clem was gone over an hour, which Liam took to be a good sign. It didn't take long to say No. When Clem finally returned it was with good news. The trainers had moved the tables against the wall of the big hut and finally decided there was enough room for small groups to train... two huts at a time as Liam had suggested.

"And we have been selected to be first to train," Clem finished. "So let's go."

The dining hut served well as a makeshift training hall and, whilst it was only for two hours a day, it did relieve the boredom and go some way to combating the dreadful cold. Eoin, the assessor, would often come in to watch or to talk to the trainer on duty. Liam had the strong feeling he was pleased with the arrangement. It allowed him longer to judge the abilities of each trainee.

Liam would have felt quite happy, as happy as it was possible to be in such a place if he hadn't got the idea into his head that he was going mad.

It was the only explanation.

The Gods were trying to drive him insane. He had heard tales of men driven to destruction by the Gods and it seemed that he was to be one such poor soul.

His dreams were becoming more and more vivid and as a consequence he was remembering more about them.

Things that didn't make sense.

Things that terrified him.

He was afraid all the time now, not just when he woke up, but actually during the dream. He would feel his heart beginning to race and his hands to shake and he would struggle, not always successfully, to wake up. The same dream had occurred several nights in a row.

There is a girl, a naked girl lying on a bed. But it is like no other bed he has ever seen and when he lies on this bed, next to the girl, it feels soft and warm, like no other bed he has ever lain on.

The girl is soft too. So vivid is his dream, he can remember how clean she smells, not like the whores that the trainers are allowed to bring into camp. And her skin is so soft; he can remember the feel of her, the taste of her.

But it isn't right. None of it is right, because when he looks out of the window next to this soft bed there is only one moon in the sky. And when he stands up and tries to go to the window to look out he can't move, because he knows that if he looks out he will see something that will terrify him. So he turns back wanting to lie with the girl again but she is gone. He calls out her name.

Emma.

But it is a name he has never heard before. And that makes him afraid.

A girl he only knows in his dream.

On a bed he only knows in his dream.

And that window.

He knows what he will see if he looks through the window and it terrifies him more than anything.

A blue sky.

And everyone knows the sky is pink.

So why does he dream of a world where the sky is blue?

The Gods were tormenting him. It was the only explanation. Driving him mad because it amused them to do so.

In spite of the cold Liam went out of the hut and leant against the wall looking up at the night sky, as he did most nights. It usually gave him a strange comfort to look at the sky, as if the answer lay in its blackness. But that night the constellation of Horus, by which he could steer a ship home, was disturbingly covered in clouds coloured blood red by the Nestor sun that inhabited the winter night sky. Eventually, when the cold became too much, he went back inside and tried to sleep again. Clem and the others had become used to his nocturnal wanderings and rarely woke up or noticed he was gone now.

The winter continued to be unusually severe. Training stopped completely and the groups stayed huddled in their huts in the increasing gloom. The white light crystals wouldn't recharge properly because of the intense cold and the trainees had to sit for most of the time in semi-darkness. The second centad of winter slowly passed into the third and eventually the long looked for thaw arrived. Outdoor training would soon start again.

One morning, as Liam and his group finished their hour in the training hut, Eoin marched in and ordered them out onto the training area. The other trainees were being roused from their huts and herded into the centre of the training area too. They stood huddled in their hut groups wondering what was happening.

Word soon got round. Someone had broken into one of the storage huts and stolen blankets and clothes.

"Stupid," Liam said. "Anyone with an extra blanket would be spotted right away."
Clem gave him a hard stare and then pulled his own blanket tighter round his shoulders.

"Maybe someone wants to escape," he said and Liam realised Clem suspected him. He quickly shook his head.

"Not me. It's too cold."

Several off-duty trainers entered the enclosure, grumbling at having to break into their rest periods as Eoin ordered a hut by hut search for the missing items. Liam watched as they entered his hut. He knew what was going to happen even before one of the trainers emerged and shouted to the Assessor. Liam turned towards Clem and shook his head. The hut leader stared at him, his face expressionless and then walked towards the hut as Eoin called to him. They went inside for a few minutes and then Eoin emerged alone, carrying the missing clothes and blanket. Liam found himself surrounded by four or five of the biggest trainers as he was manhandled backwards towards the centre of the training ground. His shirt was roughly pulled over his head. The cold air hit his warm body immediately and he shivered. He found himself being pushed against the stake, his hands bound above his head and tied to it.

"You all know the penalty for trying to escape," Eoin said loudly so all could hear. There was a silence and Liam wondered what was happening, what were they waiting for? "Begin," he heard Eoin say and a second later he felt something touch his back.

So numb with the cold was he that it took him a moment to realise that he was being whipped. Then the realisation hit him as the rope hit his back again and this time he felt a searing pain as the skin of his back split and began to bleed. The rope hit again and then again. Liam ground his teeth together in an effort to stop himself from crying out. He wasn't going to give them the satisfaction. He quickly lost count of how many times he had been struck but after a while he couldn't feel the touch of the rope. His back was a mass of pain and burning and he began to lose concentration. He didn't lose consciousness but he felt as if it was all happening to someone else, he was standing someway to the side, observing. He even thought he could see Eoin raise his hand and say "enough", ordering everyone back to the huts, there would be no more training that day.

Liam wondered when they would cut him down but no one came near him. He was left shivering, tied to the stake, slowly becoming colder. At first he welcomed the cold. At least it numbed the pain from his bloodied back but then he stopped shivering and began to feel sleepy. It would be so easy just to give up and close his eyes. Then it would be over, the pain, the humiliation and the hunger. He could sleep and forget everything. He had the feeling that this time he would not dream.

He knew if he closed his eyes he would almost certainly not wake up again but it didn't seem to matter. The temptation to shut his eyes became too much and he felt himself falling. Only the ropes around his hands stopped him from hitting the ground and not even the pain in his wrists, as the rope bit into them, could keep him awake. He felt himself slipping into the dream world again and this time he was too cold and sleepy to feel afraid. He almost welcomed it....

III

It was the day they had found the sixth body, but only the second one The Department had dealt with. Liam Maguire and his new partner, Dave Russell, had been to the scene, viewed the body and taken some photographs, ostensibly of the scene but in reality of the crowd. It was the Commander's idea. Perhaps the killer would come back to see the crowds his handiwork had excited. It was a long shot though.

Liam shivered. He was sitting at a small desk near a window and there must have been a draught. He was definitely feeling cold. He shivered again and then put on the thick coat that was draped across the back of his chair. He looked out of the window briefly but there was only another building and another window too dark to see into. He turned back to the pictures he was studying.

No, not pictures... photographs.

"It isn't going to be this simple," he said aloud and the man sitting at the desk next to his looked up and then went back to his own work. "Whoever is mutilating and then killing these women isn't going to be stupid enough to let himself be spotted like this."

"Maybe we'll get lucky," the man said and Liam studied him as he sat hunched over his desk. He had the same colour hair as Emma.

"Of course he does," Liam thought mentally kicking himself for being so stupid. "He's... her brother." He studied the photographs in front of him. He had the feeling that he had been doing this for some time, an entire... *afternoon* and it had only succeeded in giving him a bad headache. He wanted to leave the stuffy room and get some fresh air but for some reason he found himself unable to get up and walk away. It was as if something was tying him down to the chair. His legs felt like they had turned to crystal and in spite of the coat he was still finding it very cold.

The door opened and two more men came in. Liam had to think for a moment before he could put names to them... Beaudelain, his old partner and Bolkonsky. To his dismay they indicated they wanted to talk about the case and Liam found himself becoming increasingly uncomfortable as they sat there. He was feeling cold one minute and then hot the next. If he didn't leave soon he was going to pass out.

"Truth or dare?" Beaudelain asked as Liam ran from the room. The others didn't seem to notice him leaving. They carried on talking as if he was still there and he found he could hear them even when he had left the building and was standing in the street. It was even colder outside and he leant against a low wall taking in deep breaths of icy air and watching his breath steam out in turn.

"I have to get home," he thought and he began running down the street.

His neck felt stiff from bending over the desk for so long and after a while he stopped running and began to stretch his neck forward rotating his head to try to ease the stiffness. He stopped suddenly and looked up at the dark sky. There was something wrong... something terribly wrong with the sky but it took him some time to realise what it was. There was no constellation of Horus with its bright eye star that could be used to navigate back to the Isles with. He looked round quickly and spotted the moon. But it was too small to be Ra and totally the wrong colour to be Hathor.
He smiled.

"Very good," he said to the strange white moon. "This is the most vivid yet. But I will not be driven mad by it, though Ammon himself appear and command it... So you can take it all away... I'm not playing your games anymore. I'm a Pirate. I don't believe in you." He shivered, partly from the cold and partly from the strangeness of the tall buildings.
Strange but somehow familiar.

"I don't believe in you," he shouted again but nothing changed. The white moon was still in the sky, there was an unpleasant metallic smell and taste to the air and he found himself running to catch a *bus* because he didn't want to miss it and have to wait in the cold for the next one. "I shall just enjoy whatever happens and not be frightened," he decided and began to think of the girl Emma. Thoughts of Emma occupied him for several minutes.

"Oh God, her brother." She didn't want him to know about their affair. Liam found himself nodding. That was as it should be. She was unmarried... not exactly against the law, hadn't he intended marriage? But frowned on nonetheless.
Or was it?
He had the feeling that such things were treated differently here.
But where was here?

He must have spoken out loud for several of his fellow commuters looked at him as if he were a little mad.

"Little do they know," floated into his mind but he ignored it. *"There's nothing wrong with Emma, she is all right if you like that sort of thing."*

"Shut up and go away."

"Is that any way to talk to me, after all I've done for you today?"

"Like what for instance?"

*"Well, I got rid of your headache for one and.....
I have arranged for Emma to come round and cook you
something special."*

"You arranged...? I don't remember that."

"Why should you."

The voice in his head retreated and there was
only Liam again. "It's only a dream," he assured
himself, but the strange voice had unnerved him. The
Gods were cleverer than he had thought.

He found himself outside a large building, big
enough to be an estate house perhaps and he knew that
his home was inside. He hurried in and up the stairs
eager to reach his room. He knew once he was inside he
would start to feel safe.
Emma would be there and she would make him feel safe.

Emma was there, he knew that as soon as he
walked through the door into his flat and the aroma of
beef stew hit him. She had a glass of red wine ready for
him but as she walked down the hall from the kitchen
towards him with the glass in her hand the welcoming
smile faded, to be replaced by a wary look in her blue
eyes. Something about him must have been frightening
her and he made the effort to smile. But the wary look
didn't go and he became irritated again.

"Everything is keeping warm in the oven," she
told him. "You just have to dish it up when you're
ready."

He realised that she intended leaving and he
didn't want that. Emma had to stay, surely she was the
whole point of the dream... she was to him anyway,
whatever the Gods may think. He told her he didn't want
her to go, taking the glass of wine from her and kissing
her hand. She was every bit as pretty as she had been in
his earlier dreams. If the Gods insisted that he play their

game then he was going to enjoy himself to the full and that meant keeping Emma with him.

He pursed his lips and gave her the 'little boy lost look' that usually made her smile. At first he thought it hadn't worked because she pulled her hand from his grasp and told him he looked ridiculous. But she smiled as she said it and then went into the tiny bathroom and started to run him a bath. He took his coat off and went into the bedroom to hang it up in the... *wardrobe.* He started to undress, sitting on the edge of the bed to take off his shoes and socks. He kept his eyes firmly on his feet. The room was unnervingly different from anything he could remember before. The clothes were so different too. So many strange clothes but they still couldn't keep him warm.

After a few minutes he heard the water being turned off and Emma came into the room. She climbed onto the bed behind him and began to rub his neck. After five minutes of doing this and waiting for him to speak she finally broke the silence with a quiet "Bad day?"

"Mmm," but whether this was an answer or just a response to her touch he didn't know.

He stretched out full length on the bed and pulled her towards him. He took her in his arms, but this was no prelude to lovemaking; he just wanted to hold her. And she seemed to realise this, laying her head on his chest and stroking his arm with her hand. They lay like this for some time, not talking but listening to each other. Then she abruptly sat up and told him to go and have a bath whilst it was still hot.

"If you're very good," she told him with a sly grin. "I'll come and scrub your back for you," and with that she disappeared in the direction of the kitchen. He knew he should be shocked at her attitude but he couldn't be. He took off the last of his clothes and then went into the bathroom and slid into the hot water, almost relishing the pain of the hotness as it hit his skin. Almost immediately he began to feel better as the heat began to work on his tired aching muscles and neck. He had been feeling so cold and for the first time since it had all started he began to feel warm and comfortable. He closed his eyes and sank deeper into the water.

When he opened them again Emma was sitting on the floor resting her chin on the edge of the bath. She handed him his glass of wine.

"Do you want to talk about it?"

He sat up slightly and sipped at the wine, sighing he began to tell her about the latest murder.

"It was cold, I had a bad head and I snapped at your brother," he finished and he knew all of this had happened even though he couldn't remember it happening. He stood up at got out of the cooling bath and she wrapped the towel round him encircling his body with her arms and kissing his chest. She was much smaller than he was and the top of her head barely reached his shoulder. He looked down at her. He really was very lucky to have met her. He was right; she did make him feel safe. She smiled at him again, almost as if she had read his thoughts.

As he got dressed into a pair of clean trousers and an old blue jumper that had seen better days he could hear her in his tiny kitchen humming to herself as she worked. The smell of the food was making him hungry, the bath and the wine had worked their magic on him and for the first time he felt warm and relaxed.

He could feel himself waking slowly, sluggishly and he had the feeling that it was unusual. There was a persistent ringing sound and he struggled to wake up and answer the phone. "Truth or dare, Liam... which is it to be?" He couldn't identify the voice. A strange feeling of loss swept over him and he hurried into the kitchen where he could hear Emma making tea. She put her arms round him, hugging him tight.

Liam stroked her hair and held her.

"You have to go to Kendal," the voice on the phone said.

The lights.

That's what the strange lights meant.

He was going to fly north.

He hated flying.

Liam closed his eyes trying hard to sleep but his fear of flying and the erratic buffeting of the aircraft made it difficult.

He tried to remember why they were flying north but he couldn't.

Were they following Emma...? No she was following him.

He had lost something and had to find it. But what?

And why was he so sure he would find it at his old home?

None of it made sense.

But when did dreams ever make sense?

He moved his body trying to get more comfortable in the cramped seat. The pilot's voice broke into his thoughts. He seemed very faint. "Wake up."

"Is Emma all right?" he asked sleepily, trying to force his eyes to open. It was very important he find Emma and make sure she was safe.

"Who's Emma," the voice said. "Have you been leaving the compound after all? Sneaking off to visit the Port Brothel, eh."

Liam opened his eyes. He was in a bed in the camp infirmary. "No," he groaned. He didn't want to leave his dream world. He had to find Emma, make sure she was alive.

   "Back hurting still? I can give you something for that. You're one very lucky pirate... friends in high places... nearly died of the cold." The apothecary's voice faded in and out of Liam's mind. He closed his eyes, ignoring the sound and tried to find the dream world again.

But it was gone.

He needed to find something... Emma perhaps.

   But the Gods were still playing with him and had taken their world away from him for now.

Well he could wait. He was a Pirate; he knew how to be patient.

IV

"Another hour or so and you'd have been stiffer than the post," Clem told him. He had been allowed out to see Liam who was recovering slowly. His back was healing well although he would carry scars from the whipping to the end of his days.

"I don't understand what happened," Liam said. "The Apothecary said something about having friends in high places?"

Clem nodded. "A message was received from Prime... from the Spymaster himself... asking for a report on your progress. Eoin nearly had apoplexy and ordered you cut down immediately. Then they brought you here."

He looked round at the small room Liam was in. There was only one bed in it and the mattress looked twice as thick as the ones the trainees were expected to lie on.

"I expect the food is better too," he remarked, with a little envy colouring his voice.

Liam laughed and eased himself carefully into an upright position. "Did you and the others get into trouble?" he asked. Clem grunted. "I didn't take those things," Liam added. It was important to him that he was believed.

"We know," Clem said. "They were so badly hidden in your mattress that we'd have seen them as soon as we woke up."

"Then someone must have put them there to get me into trouble whilst we were training."

Clem shrugged. "Don't worry about it," he said. "We've got the fire back and rations were never even cut. There wasn't time."

"But they might try again," Liam said and Clem gave him a hard stare.

"That's up to you," he said but he refused to be drawn further on the subject.

"Why should the Spymaster show an interest in me?" wondered Liam. "I don't know him." Then he frowned. That day at the port, he had felt some recognition, something had passed between them. It was very puzzling. He leant back against the wooden backrest and closed his eyes.

"You're tired," Clem said immediately and stood up to leave. He hesitated for a moment. "Word in the camp is the Spymaster might be considering you for one of his spies. Gladiator training is good for making you think fast... just what a spy would need."

Liam pulled a face. He didn't like that idea at all. "I might try and escape," he said but Clem shook his head.

"It seems that he was very surprised that you had tried to escape. Seth heard Dolph say that the Spymaster had said it was highly unlikely that you were planning to escape." He looked at Liam with a curious expression on his face. "Why would he think that?"

Liam had no answer to that and he lay on his bed pondering the question for some time after Clem had left. He had thought about escape often but he had never been able to come up with a satisfactory plan. He suddenly realised that he had always come up with excuses why he couldn't do it... it was too cold, he would be recognised as a runaway, he needed supplies. The more he considered it the more he realised how weak his excuses had been.

"The Spymaster must know me better than I thought," he muttered to himself as a slave brought him his supper. It was the cook that had marched from the

Port with him but Liam didn't recognise him, he was too wrapped up in his own thoughts.

Liam was sent back to the camp only a decan after the incident and immediately began training again. Training continued to take place in the hut whilst the weather was bad and this meant that the huts rarely mixed other than at meal times. Liam brooded for a further decan, looking for an opportunity. On the tenth day he decided that it was not going to happen and he would just have to take matters into his own hands.

At supper he pushed past the queue of men waiting patiently and entered the hut. Mica was at the head of the line and Liam marched straight up to him. He said nothing but hit the man squarely on the jaw. Mica staggered back and Liam hit him again. The man's nose broke and blood poured down onto his shirt. Liam hit out again and again until Mica could no longer stand. Then Liam took hold of his shirt at the shoulders, just as Mica had done to him on his first day in camp, and rammed him back against the wall. He leant against Mica and stared down. One malevolent eye stared out from the bloodied and swollen face. The other was closed tightly shut amidst the rapidly darkening flesh.

"You ever come near me and mine again," Liam hissed at him, "and I will break you in two," and he shoved Mica away and watched dispassionately as the battered trainee slowly sank down the wall to the floor.

Liam walked to the tables at the front, picked up a bowl and helped himself to supper. Without looking at anyone he sat down at the head of the table and began to eat. Clem quickly joined him and they ate in silence.

For the first time in a long while he had a good night's sleep, undisturbed by dreams.

The bitterly cold wind eased, the days gradually lengthened, and the Priests announced the beginning of the spring season. There was an air of expectation in the camp. The assessments would soon be announced.

Eoin marched into the big hut as they were all eating first meal and stood in front of the serving tables with several sheets of parchment in his hand. Everyone had stopped talking as he had entered and there was an excited tension in the air as they waited for him to speak.

"I'll start with those going to Prime," he said and they all strained to hear the names as they were called out, each praying his name would be included in the first list.

When he had finished reading his lists, Eoin left quickly and for a moment no one said anything, then everyone began talking at once, congratulating or commiserating with their nearest neighbours. Liam was to go to Menethes Prime and the main gladiator school there. There were fifteen trainees going in all. Five had been held over for another tarn at the Port and the remainder were to be sold.

"At least no one has been sent to the mines," Liam remarked at what was his last supper at the Port school. Clem grunted. He was one of those who were to remain there for another three seasons. He strongly suspected he was being singled out as a potential slave-trainer and had been grumbling to Liam about it for most of the day.

Liam listened, not entirely sympathetically, and then pointed out that, if that were the case, at least Clem would never have to risk his life in the ring.

"Never win my freedom either," was the muttered answer to that. Liam laughed at him. He couldn't really summon up enough sympathy for Clem when he was so excited at the prospect of seeing a new place and meeting new trainers and trainees.

The ring held little fear for him. He had enough confidence in his own ability to feel sure he would succeed and earn his freedom. The only annoying cloud in the sky was the fact that Mica had been promoted too. But he wasn't overly worried. He could handle Mica.

It did not occur to him to wonder why his attitude to his captivity had changed so much since his first days in the camp. It was enough that he was to be promoted. He hadn't had any disturbing dreams for decans and he had all but forgotten the vivid dream he had experienced when he had nearly died. It was enough for him that he was alive and about to experience new adventures.

And that the Gods seemed to have forgotten about him.

It was four hundred and ninety miles from the Port to Menethes Prime and for the most part the fifteen trainees walked. It took them nearly three decans but they were in no hurry and walked at the pace of the wagon carrying the food and blankets. This was a long wagon, slow and cumbersome, needing a team of eight oxen to pull it. The guards could sleep inside it at night, a few privileged trainees slept underneath. Liam found he was considered important enough to warrant a place under the battered cart.

He found the journey interesting. The immediate land around the port was cultivated and the domain of many prosperous looking farms. Further out from the Port the countryside became wilder; the farms more spread out and poorer looking. After the first few days there were hardly any dwellings to be seen and other travellers on the road became fewer too. As they came within about thirty miles of Prime the land once again took on a more prosperous air and became more populated.

Liam viewed everything with a Pirate's eye. Not that he would ever think of attacking Menethes land. The Pirate Lord had long ago ordered that there should be no more raids on Anant lands and so there were none. It was a pity though, Liam couldn't help thinking as they neared the towering walls of Menethes Prime in the centre of a particularly rich cultivated plain. There was just so much asking to be taken. The Menethes Lorddom seemed to be a rich one.

As at the Port the Gladiator school was outside the main walls of the city, to the South and it was nearly dark when they at last reached its gates. This School was much more substantial and had tall stone walls around it. Inside, to one side, were rows of huts, neatly arranged in blocks. Liam could see at least two training areas in the open and there was a large building, or collection of buildings, on the left that might possibly be the indoor training area. It was difficult to see in the fading light. He looked around with interest. Gladiators, only identifiable from the trainers by the slave collars they were wearing, were gathered in groups talking or walking back towards the huts slowly. There seemed to be a much more relaxed atmosphere compared with the port school.

Liam was assigned to the eagle hut. He would know it because there was an eagle painted on the door and the fifteen trainees stared across to the group of huts. Best go there now and introduce yourself, he was told. It was nearly suppertime and he would be shown where to go.

Liam quickly found his hut and entered. There were sixteen beds arranged in two rows at one end and some rough wooden stools grouped around a brazier, half full of red fire crystals, at the other. There were three men in the hut when Liam entered, deep in conversation around the fire. As soon he entered they stopped talking abruptly and stared at him.

"New trainee?" the tallest one asked and Liam nodded. "I'm Gwydyr the greater," the man continued. "I'm in charge of this hut. Your bed is the fourth on the right," and he pointed vaguely in the direction of the end of the hut and then turned back to his companions.

Liam found his bed and felt the mattress. It wasn't much thicker than those at the Port but there were three thick blankets, which boded well. Liam stretched out and closed his eyes. He was tired after the long march. He listened with only half an ear to the drone of voices from the three at the end. He heard the door open and someone come in. Two new voices joined in the low conversation. Liam opened his eyes. He recognised one of the voices.

But it wasn't possible.

He sat up and turned to face them. One of the newcomers was smaller than the rest of the group, Anarian in build but he had blond hair and Liam knew if he looked closely the stranger would have blue eyes, just like his sister.

It wasn't possible.

The Gods had sent dreams to torment him but they had been just that… dreams. They hadn't really existed. The people in them hadn't really existed.

It wasn't possible. It couldn't be.

They were only dreams.

But the man standing by the fire warming his hands was David Russell… Emma's brother.

V

David Russell stared across at Liam and said something to the others. Then he walked over and sat down on the bed next to Liam's. Liam could feel his heart pounding in his chest and he realised that he was holding his breath.

"Hello," David said, smiling slightly. "I'm Finn. Are you newly arrived from the Port?" Liam could only nod, so great was his relief. If the man had said his name was David he wasn't sure what he would have done. "And you are?" Finn asked.

"Liam," he said and his voice sounded weak even to his own ears.

"It's supper time," Finn said. "I'll show you where to go. I'll show you around the camp tomorrow, if you like."

"Isn't there training?"

"Not tomorrow, Callum was killed in training yesterday, it's his funeral tomorrow."

Finn stood up and led the way across the compound to the group of buildings Liam had seen earlier. They queued up outside one of them and Finn told him it was the Refectory. He pointed out the Infirmary, the dormitories where the trainers lived, and the workshops where the swordsmiths, carpenters and all the workmen necessary for the successful running of a Gladiator school, worked and lived. There were even stables to house the horses for the mounted Gladiators.

"How many trainees are there?" Liam asked as they reached the head of the queue and were handed platters of bread and meat, cheese and fruit and a mug of ale. There were even spoons and skewers to eat with.

"Between two and three hundred," he was told, "it varies from season to season. There are about two hundred and twenty here at the moment."

They sat down at one of the tables and were soon joined by others from their hut. Finn introduced each one as they sat down until there were a group of eight sitting with them. They all looked curiously at Liam and Gwydyr raised his eyebrows at Finn who gave a slight shrug.

"Still hungry?" he asked when Liam had cleaned his platter. "There's more if you want."

Liam stood up and went towards the serving tables. He had the feeling that the others were discussing him and when he looked round it was to see nine pairs of curious eyes suddenly look anywhere but at him.

As he got back to the table he was in time to see one of the others hand Finn a few small coins.

"Who says one man can't make a difference?" grinned Finn as he put the coins in a small pouch.

"Double or nothing?" the other trainee said and Finn shrugged.

"There's one born every minute," he sighed.

Liam finished his second helping of food and contemplated his empty plate for second or two. Then he went back to the serving table for a third time.

"Yes!" he heard Finn say and he looked back to see another small pile of coins change hands.

"When you two have quite finished," Gwydyr said.

Liam held out his plate for more.

"Better than at the Port," he said to the man standing next to him, also getting more food and the man nodded, his mouth already full of bread. Liam recognised him as his neighbour at the very first meal he had had at the Port, the man who had been so terrified of Mica.

When he returned to the table it was to find that a powerfully built man wearing a leather apron had joined them. He was introduced as Timon and he was the blacksmith's assistant. Liam regarded him curiously. The right side of the blacksmith's face and neck was badly scarred. It looked as if it had been badly burned and Liam wondered what kind of fire could burn a man's face like that and yet leave the rest of his body seemingly untouched. For Timon's muscular arms, visible below his rolled up sleeves, showed no sign of scarring. Liam sat down to eat again and he slowly got the distinct impression that the others were anxious for him to finish and leave. He ate quickly and then stood up. One of the others stood too. It was the young trainee that had lost so much money to Finn.

"I'm Paul," he said. "I'll come with you. We've been paired for training."

"You're a Secutor too?" Liam asked as they carried their dirty platters to the large baskets by the door and Paul nodded.

"I'll give you a few tips," he said. "There are a few tricks you need to look out for."

As they left together Liam glanced back. The others at the table were already in deep conversation with the blacksmith.

Emma.

Finn looked at Liam in the moonslight streaming in through an unshuttered window. He was sitting bolt upright in his bed. For a second night running he had woken Finn in the middle of the night.

"Another dream?" he asked. "I wish I could have such dreams."

Liam fell back against the straw filled bolster. "You can have this one with pleasure," he said. "It's not a dream; I've been riding the dark horses again."

"Why? Is she short and fat with more hair on her face than old Colm?" Finn laughed and the trainee in the next bed told him to shut up, people were trying to sleep. "Perhaps you're dreaming of your future mother-in-marriage," Finn whispered as he turned over, pulling the blankets up to his neck.

When Liam got up the next morning he was tired and his head ached. He pulled on the leather trousers and rough grey shirt and sat for a long time with his head in his hands. At first meal he was silent and morose. His dreams were disturbing, frightening.

Was he going mad?

Why did these daemons torment him?

Paul and Gwydyr the greater sat down with their bowls and eyed him speculatively. When Finn joined them a little while later Paul raised an eyebrow.

Finn shook his head. "Shouldn't be long now though," he muttered. Liam pretended he hadn't heard and went on calmly eating the porridge.

"Well, that's good news," Gwydyr said quietly. "Now do you want the bad?"

"Go on," Finn said.

"Timon has been sold, along with some others."

"Who to?"

Gwydyr shook his head. "Just another Lord, that's all I know. They went last night, ten in all."

"Any more of ours?" Paul asked glancing round to make sure another table couldn't overhear them.

"All of them. All ten."

Liam realised that something was going on. But whatever it was he wanted no part of it. It probably involved escape and he wasn't about to risk another beating like the last one. He went for a second helping of porridge and when he returned to the table the conversation had once more returned to the mundane concerns of trainee gladiators.

Well that was just fine by him.

A Gladiator's life is fighting. Training fights, practice fights, non-lethal fights as trainees and finally mortal fights at the big games. A gladiator must be fit, his mind and body honed to perfection, his fighting skills at their peak in time for the games. And so life is practice and more practice. Against secutor, against retaari, against armoured horse and rider and against unarmed gladiator too. For anything is possible once a fight begins, once the wagering begins and a gladiator must be ready for anything. There is single combat and there is paired, which most consider the more dangerous because a gladiator must then put his trust in someone other than himself. It is a hard demanding life but the rewards for success are great. Failure is an ever-present fear, accidents and death a fact of life.

"You all gave Callum a good send off," Red Declan, the secutor master said. "But I have less than a season to get you into shape. Make champions of you at the next Anant games." He looked around at his squad of trainee secutor. "Who knows, some of you may be good enough to be champions at the Sed games in three seasons time. Remember that when you think you're too tired to carry on. When all you want is a warm bed and a willing woman. Any man who becomes a champion at the Anari games at Kush Prime automatically gets his torc and with a torc comes...?"

"Freedom," the squad shouted in unison and then went back to their training with renewed vigour.

Liam wanted that torc. To get it he would have to kill.

Still he wanted it.

So badly he could taste it.

So badly it hurt.

So badly he dreamt of it at night.

And woke shouting a name.

Sean.

After four decans at the camp, Liam felt he had settled in well. The training was hard but he was good at it and didn't receive half the knocks or injuries that the other newcomers got. Most of the training was done in one of the two indoor arenas.

The start of the spring season had been particularly cold with a north wind blowing through the camp. Not even being in the shadow of the city's walls had protected the school from the strong wind that found its way into every hole in the walls or crack in the shutters to make the trainees' life comfortless and depressing. The biting wind seemed to make everyone short-tempered and the trainers became harder to please. Even amongst the trainees themselves fights became more common as remarks that would once have been laughingly shrugged off took on the role of deadly insult. Injuries in training became more common and more serious. It was a bad time for all.

As the first centad of spring neared its end the wind dropped and all gave a sigh of relief. Perhaps now training would get back on schedule for the games in a centad's time.

Liam spent the second period training with Finn, secutor against retaari being a popular event. When the Secutor Master arrived and called a halt to training it was to announce that several of the secutor trainees were now good enough to use real crystal swords.

"Suitably fixed so you can't kill each other," he said and there was a titter from the assembled trainees. "But make no mistake they can still give you a good jolt, so be careful."

Most of the trainees left eager to get to their supper before the threatened rain appeared and Liam found himself being called to help put away the training equipment.

"That will teach you to be faster away in future," laughed Pius. He was a Slave-trainer and his status wasn't much above those of the trainees. It made him a little more ready to share a joke with the trainees. By the time they had collected the discarded wooden swords and stacked them neatly, folded the nets and put the tridents in their racks the rain had started. Liam made straight for the refectory. The smell of food was too strong to resist and training always made him hungry.

The groups training in the other hall had finished before Liam's and there was a long queue for the food. It stretched out of the refectory and people had to wait in the rain. Liam saw Finn and Paul, blankets covering their heads and he waved to them and indicated that he was going to go back to the hut for a blanket. He hurried through the rain along the first ranks of huts towards his own. Something was lying in the mud at the side of one hut and some instinct stopped him from passing by. He couldn't see clearly what it was because it was in the shadow of the hut. He stepped forward cautiously to get a better look.

It was a body. That much was clear. Liam went up to it and stared down. The man was lying face down in the mud and there was a spreading pool of blood under the head. His throat had been cut. Liam continued to look at him dispassionately, noting the blood at the back of the head. He had been hit from behind and his throat cut when he was lying helpless on the ground. Liam didn't need to touch the body to know who it was. He recognised the man easily.

Mica.

There was a squelching sound and Liam half turned to see what it was. He raised his hand as he sensed rather than saw the thick piece of wood, already bloodied, swinging towards his head.

"Liam can't have done it."

"Why not?" Red Declan watched as the Apothecary examined Liam. He had already pronounced Mica dead. Not that it took much to see that. "Well, why not?" he repeated looking up from his own examination of the scene to look towards the crowd that had gathered to watch the proceedings. He wasn't sure who had made the pronouncement but he could guess.

Finn stepped forward. "Liam has been training all period. He stayed behind to clear up."

"So?"

"It was raining when he left the training hall." Finn pointed towards Mica. "The ground is dry under the body, therefore..."

"The man was killed before the rain started," Declan finished for him. He nodded. It made sense. No wonder the spymaster wanted this one for himself.

"But Liam did threaten Mica," someone in the crowd said.

"So?" Finn snapped. "A lot of people would have liked to see him dead. He was a bully and liked to deliberately hurt in training, that didn't make him very popular."

"This man didn't kill anyone," the Apothecary said standing up from his examination of Liam. "One blow knocked him senseless. It couldn't have been the other one who hit him... not unless he then cut his own throat. This one," he pointed to Mica, "was knocked to the ground and whilst he was helpless someone pulled back his head and cut his throat. It is just possible he could have hit his attacker from where he was lying." The Apothecary turned back to Liam. "But his attacker would have had to be bending over him and therefore the blow would have hit him on the front or top of his head. And, as anyone can see, this one has been hit from behind." He indicated to his assistants waiting behind him that they could lift Liam onto the hurdle and carry him to the Infirmary.

"When will he come round?" Declan asked. "He might be able to tell us who hit him."
The Apothecary shook his head.

"Could be an hour, a day, a season. You can never tell with head injuries. A blow that dazes one can kill another. He may never recover."

Declan had seen enough head injuries in his time as a trainer to know the truth in the Apothecary's words. He turned back to the crowd and ordered them all back to the huts. It was going to prove very difficult to find out who had murdered Mica if Liam couldn't identify him. Finn was hanging back trying to catch his eye. Declan waved him over.

"Well, what now?"

"It might be an idea to put a guard on Liam... just in case," Finn suggested and Declan agreed.

"Six from your hut," he said swiftly. "Two each period, excused training until he's recovered." Finn hurried away to organise it.

Liam was carried to the infirmary. For some reason his arm was hurting, a sharp stabbing pain that wouldn't let up. And his head was hurting. Oh, that must have been a rough bottle of wine. He would have groaned out loud, but his mouth was too dry. Classic symptoms, he should know better at his age.

"Are you going to lie there all day?"
Liam forced himself to open his eyes. Subdued lighting... nice.
It took him a moment to focus his eyes. Paul was offering him a cup of water.

"Who hit me?" he asked and Paul looked puzzled. Liam realised it couldn't be Paul. He was wearing the wrong clothes. He was wearing clothes from Liam's dream.

"I'm dreaming again," he thought and this time he was excited by the prospect. "Fine... but how did I get here?" He raised his eyes upwards as if addressing the Gods themselves. "Play fair with me," he said. "I need to go back a bit and find out what happened."
He closed his eyes and waited.

VI

"Wake up, Sleeping Beauty, we're nearly there."
Liam opened his eyes slowly and shook his head to try and wake up. He had only been asleep for a few minutes and he felt irritable and tired. His head was throbbing... another headache.

"You've been asleep nearly an hour."
It was his 'other self '.

"What?" he muttered, sitting up in the seat? "You're back, where've you been?"

He looked around him; his mind still muddled with sleep. He was back in the dream world but this time it felt much more real than before. Almost as if it was really happening.

Liam found himself in familiar territory once more. He knew the place well. It was as if he had never been away. Somehow he knew it had been four years since he had come down this lane, four years since he had last driven through the rusty gate at the end of the track leading to the cottage. The cottage, his home for nearly seven years. It looked the same, except someone had painted it since he had last been there. The front door was now a dark green; he had preferred the natural dark wood. The porch light was on. The clematis that grew over the porch still needed cutting back. The main stem was almost as thick as a tree trunk. It twisted its way up the brick wall between the house and the garage then across the entrance of the open porch, under the window that had been Liam's bedroom. It continued across the front of the house, sadly neglected. Loose tendrils that hadn't been tied to the wall or threaded in with the rest of the stems hung down across the ground floor windows and he had to duck under the growth over the porch to approach the front door.

It felt strange to be coming back after all this time. So much had changed for Liam, yet here nothing had changed. Time had almost stood still.

"I know this place," he thought as they approached the front door. Inside he would find... someone... someone important to him. But he couldn't remember who it was.

He walked through the front door towards the kitchen where a young girl of about fifteen was waiting. As Liam approached she held out her arms. Surprised he hugged her and held her close. She had glorious red hair but even though it was tied back he couldn't see her face. When he tried to see her face she turned around and walked away.

"Oh, I'm so glad you're here," she said. "Now we can play truth or dare again."

He found himself struggling to remember her name. He buried his face in his hands and began to plead with Gods to help him.

"There is some purpose to all of this," he said. "I don't think you are trying to force me out of my mind but this is all too confusing." He was shaking his head, trying to clear his mind and make sense of the thoughts crowding into his head.

"Judith... your name is Judith," he cried and the girl laughed.

"Don't be silly, that's my mother," she said. "I'm Sarah."

He closed his eyes and concentrated. Judith was... his wife.

No.

Judith had been his wife.

Emma. Had he asked Emma to marry him? He had thought about it.

Emma was on her way there. She would come to the cottage later, perhaps tomorrow. Sometime tomorrow she would come to the cottage and... what.

Liam let out an angry cry of frustration.

"You're tired," the red-haired girl said immediately. "Mother said to put you in the spare bedroom," and Liam found himself sitting on a small bed in a tiny room. But at least he didn't have to share it with anyone.

"They do themselves proud in this strange world," he thought as he closed his eyes.

Liam woke with a start. He had fallen asleep on the bed and had been dreaming about being in hospital. That had been the first time he had heard his 'other self '. He shivered. He didn't feel any better for having slept. His eyes felt heavy and he could feel a headache developing. He got up and wandered downstairs, stretching his neck, trying to make it less stiff and hopefully ease the bad headache that was beginning to pound away inside his head. Liam looked out of the front door. It was dark and it had been snowing heavily. There were several inches of snow on the drive in front of the house. Liam was confused. He was sure he couldn't have slept all night and all day.

It was as if the day was unimportant so the Gods had passed over it.

He stared at the closed kitchen door at the end of the hall. When he walked through the door he knew Emma and her brother would be in the kitchen telling them...what? Judith would make them a drink, tea or coffee, and then Emma would tell them what had happened to Sean. He took hold of the door handle and hesitated. He didn't want to go in. In there was frightening. More frightening than a world with blue skies and only one moon. If only he could remember what it was without having to go in.

He turned the handle and pushed on the door.

Something important was going to happen soon.

"Let's get on with it," Liam said impatiently and he realised that there was a strange atmosphere in the cottage and it was coming from Judith or Sarah. "It's not fear," Liam thought. It took him a moment to put a name to the emotion both women were experiencing.

It was excitement.

A nervous exhilaration.

Both of the women were keyed up in some strange way that Liam couldn't understand. But it had something to do with what was about to happen.

If only the Gods would hurry up.

Judith was giving Sarah an appealing look, but Sarah only shook her head. "I think it's time we told Liam what's going on," Sarah said, looking at her watch. "They'll be here soon."

As if on cue the backdoor behind Judith opened and a tall man entered. He was distinguished looking with long dark hair flanked by grey tied back in a ponytail. It made him look like an ageing hippy from the previous century. He was obviously surprised to see so many waiting for him. He glanced questioningly at Judith, who moved towards him and laid her hand on his arm. Liam knew instinctively that this was Sarah's father. Who else could it be?

It was also the man he had seen at the Port amongst the warriors. It was the Menethes Spymaster. The man that had taken such an interest in Liam.

Liam began to shake his head. None of this was making any sense any more. How could the Spymaster... and

Dave Russell be here in the dream world and in the real world?

"And Paul too," he thought. "I don't understand. What is going on?"

There was a strange yellow glow and he felt himself falling... He tried to stay awake but it was too difficult. So much easier to just give up and wait for the Gods to finish what they had started.

He knew they would in their own time.

VII

His arm was hurting, a sharp stabbing pain that wouldn't let up. And his head was hurting. Oh, that must have been a rough bottle of wine. He would have groaned out loud, but his mouth was too dry. Classic symptoms, he should know better at his age.

"Are you going to lie there all day?" A familiar voice, but he couldn't quite remember the name. "Drink this, it will help."
Liam forced himself to open his eyes. Subdued lighting... nice.
It took him a second or two to focus on the cup in front of him. He sipped at the clear liquid doubtfully, then smiled as he realised it was just water. He looked around and began to take stock of his surroundings. He was in a small room with shelves stacked high with blankets... a storeroom

Liam was staring at the wall ahead of him, trying to think, trying to clear his head and stop his racing thoughts. He hadn't woken up. The Gods had continued to torment him. He had felt so sure he was about to wake up. Why had they changed their minds?

He was staring straight at the blank wall when it suddenly opened. It hadn't swung inward or outward. It must have somehow slipped sideways into the wall. Whatever it had done, it had done it totally silently.
The Menethes Spymaster stood in the opening. He glanced at Liam lying on the bunk.

"I've bought someone to see you," he said, pushing Emma into the room. Through the open doorway Liam could see two more men, armed with crystal swords. They gave off an eerie blue glow.

He stood up and went across to where Emma was standing. She was wearing a long grey woollen dress over which she had on a leather garment. It was like a waistcoat at the top, laced tight over the breast with a three-quarter length skirt to the back and sides. The front was open to reveal an expanse of grey skirt. It took Liam a full minute to recognise what she was wearing. Her clothes were an exact duplicate of those found in Anaria. The resemblance was uncanny.

"Those clothes..."

She didn't appear to hear him but instead was looking intently at the wall where the door had been.

"I have to get out of here," she muttered, more to herself than to him. "I'm not staying here." She wouldn't look at him but stared at the floor, then went back to searching the wall.

"What's happened?"

But still she wouldn't talk to him.

She took something from a pocket in her waistcoat. It was a long silver tube, about five centimetres long, closed at one end. Holding it up to the wall she began tracing the outline of a door roughly where it had been.

"What is that?"

"It's a key. They all have one."

She had traced down the right side and started down the left. About two thirds of the way between floor and ceiling Liam heard the key buzz. The open end flashed a yellow pulse and, as silently as before, the door opened. One moment it was there, then it was gone, leaving an opening that Emma quickly stepped through. She turned and looked back at Liam.

"I don't expect you to come," she said, a little sadly and she turned away.

He didn't understand why she had said that but he followed her out and the door shut silently behind them. They were in a long corridor of dull grey walls that curved away about two hundred meters ahead of them. Liam looked behind him. The corridor went straight for as far as he could see.

"Not a full crew then?" he observed after passing several empty rooms.

She didn't reply but darted forward to yet another open door.

Steps, leading up and down.

"Which way now?" he asked. But he already knew the answer... down... into the very depths of the building they were in. Except he knew it wasn't a building they were in, just as he knew what he would find when they reached the bottom.

"How did you get the key?" he asked and she gave a low laugh.

"The man in charge of all this was explaining to me the benefits of becoming his mistress when he got called away... some sort of emergency. I merely influenced him to forget his key when he left. The other man was sent to take me back to the cell."

Influenced him.

Of course! Emma and her brother had been investigating him... she was Psi division... he remembered now. For some crazy reason they had thought he was a telepath. It was his other self who was the telepath... not him.

"You were using him as a way of hiding your abilities. But for some reason you've stopped now."

He looked at her suddenly concerned. If she could hear him then so too could their captors. Which meant they were probably already on their way. He tried hard to put up blocks, as his other self had taught him. In his case he used the image of stars and flying through space. He was beginning to understand now why it worked for him.

Emma smiled.

"I use music," she told him. "Something with a lot of noise, like cannons or bells is good." She sat down on the stair and looked up at him. "I do need to get away from here. *I* don't want to go."

Liam nodded.

"Okay, but we'd better be careful. They've probably discovered we're missing by now." As he passed her he took hold of her arm. "I'm sorry," he said. "It's all my fault. I said I would protect you and I can't. But I will get you away from here. I promise."

She didn't say anything but reached up and stroked the side of his face with her hand. "It's only truth or dare, Liam... not life and death."

He couldn't make her understand how important it was... How much he cared for her. And it was life or death. Wasn't Sean dead? Wasn't she dead too?

"Impressive, isn't it?" he said, looking across the open expanse to the tower of pulsating yellow crystal that stretched from the bottom of the chamber, about four floors below them, up as far as the eye was able to see. They had climbed down as far as they could and had then started in towards the centre, finally arriving at the very core of the ship. The chamber they had entered had a diameter of about a thousand metres, the central tower of yellow crystal being about five hundred metes across. All around the walls were a series of walkways and connecting ladders and inset into the walls, row upon row, were individual cubicles, each containing the blurred outline of a human figure.

"How many?" Emma gasped.

He thought for a moment.

"I think about ten thousand," he said but he knew it was his other self that possessed this knowledge, even though Osiris had been strangely silent.

"Ten thousand." She was staring about her in awe. "How many times has he been?"

"Only three times," Liam said slowly. "This is his last visit so he's taking as many as he can. There's the problem of dispersal at the other end. Too many at once would cause comment."

He turned and walked along the walkway. A short distance in front there was a ladder going all the way down to the bottom and Liam began to descend. He waited patiently at the bottom for Emma to join him. He was going to direct her towards the tower of yellow crystal in the centre. It was the power source and the controls to send them back home should be somewhere nearby. But, instead, he found himself staring at one of the chambers containing a human being. He knew the person inside... it was...

"Liam, you have to see this," Emma was calling to him excitedly and he moved towards her, his hand coming to rest on a small column of white crystal. On the floor, where she was standing, was a mosaic of golden tiles with a pattern at the very centre of dark blue or black tiles. "It's a bit like the eye of Ra," she said in wonder, bending down to trace part of the pattern with her finger.

"The Ra," said the Menethes spymaster. "It is the symbol of ... what you would call the King of the Gods." He looked at Liam. "Step away from the controls, please. We are expecting our Lord."

One of the warriors with him moved towards the column with his light sword active. Liam stepped back slowly, carefully considering if it would be possible to overpower the man.

"Lord arriving," the warrior by the controls said and where Emma had been standing only seconds before there pulsed a yellow-green light and the Lord Menethes and Sarah were standing on the dark blue eye of Ra. He was carrying a small case, which he handed to a warrior. Seeing Liam and Emma standing before him he glanced at his Spymaster and for the first time Liam found he could hear their conversation. It was very faint but he could hear them.

"Why is he here?"

"He woke up, my Lord."

"How?"

"We don't know. Shall I have him processed again ... or send him back?"

"Sarah wants him to come... you choose, Spymaster. It's your wife he enjoyed!"

Liam knew he had the choice to stay or go back home. But there really was no choice.

"I want to come with you," he thought as strongly as he could and the Spymaster's eyes narrowed with surprise. He regarded Liam with a speculative gleam and then nodded. Liam found himself flanked by two guards, being escorted towards an empty chamber.

"She was as good as dead. Leave and enjoy the rest of your life."

He could hear Osiris as clearly as if he had been standing next to him.

"No. I promised Sean."

"It was only truth or dare. It didn't mean anything... remember?"

"A promise was made... I have to keep it."

"But you won't remember... But if I can't dissuade you... Then goodbye and good luck."

Osiris had gone. Liam entered the chamber backwards and leant against the rear wall. It felt surprisingly warm. He was conscious of a green glow and then nothing.

He opened his eyes slowly aware that the hard chamber wall had been replaced by a softer mattress.

"Is Emma all right?" he muttered. It had been Emma in the chamber... it had been for her that he had stayed? He felt pressure on his arm as someone took hold of his wrist and felt for a pulse.

"No, they're dead," someone said and Liam opened his eyes quickly and let out a howl of despair. "Didn't think you were friends," the Apothecary said. "There are some friends of yours outside wanting to see you. Do you feel well enough to see them?"

"Of course," and Liam sat up. Immediately his head started to throb and he groaned. "What hit me?"
The Apothecary looked into his face and studied him closely.

"You must have a very hard head," he said. Then he went out of the small room and Finn's head appeared round the door.

"Are you up to seeing us?" he said and Finn and Paul both came in. Paul sat on the edge of the bed and Finn leant against the wall smiling. "You look a bit better than you did yesterday," he said.

"Is that how long I've been out?"

"You came round in the middle of the night but were delirious so they gave you something to calm you down," Finn said and Liam stared at him as if seeing him for the first time.

"I know you," he said and Finn laughed.

"I should hope so," he said. "We're paired for training."

64

"No... I mean I know you... from before. I remember..."

Paul and Finn didn't seem to know what he was talking about. They said nothing but just stared at him. He looked at the pair of them and suddenly wondered if he really was going mad.

Had the Gods finally managed it after all?

Finn smiled sympathetically.

"About time. I was beginning to think it would never happen."

VIII

"The trainee, Liam, is shaping up well," Red Declan told the Spymaster. "His swordplay is excellent; he has the makings of a champion. And he has recovered well from the blow to the head."

The Spymaster was sitting at his desk in his small office. A pile of red fire crystals in a brazier was glowing in the corner to the Spymaster's left. Declan stole a glance round the office. The walls were lined with bookshelves full of books haphazardly piled on their shelves. Other cabinets had locked doors on them, but one was open slightly and Declan saw row upon row of neatly labelled drawers. When the Spymaster looked up briefly and saw Declan's gaze he closed the door and locked it with a small key from a bunch hanging from his belt. He didn't need to find the right key Declan observed; he knew which one it was.

"Why are you so interested in this trainee?" he asked when he had finished his report.

The Spymaster looked up again from the document he was reading.

"Thank you," he said shortly. "Keep me informed of his progress," he added as the secutor trainer left.

He looked round as a door behind his desk opened and a tall woman came into his room. Expensively dressed in a scarlet velvet gown with fur trim, Lady Sarah Menethes, wife to the Anant High Lord, smiled at her father happily. She knelt at the side of his chair and, taking his hand in hers, put it to her lips.

"Thank you for finding out about Liam for me again," she said quietly. "I'm grateful, Father."

He stood up and took her hands in his. "You know if I could get him out of there for you I would. It is I who should be grateful to him, for taking such good care of you."

Sarah sighed and then frowned. "Are you sure there is nothing you can do. It is such a dangerous life. I would hate for anything to happen to him. It would be my fault. I have been uneasy since you told me he had landed at the Port."

The Spymaster squeezed her hands gently. "It is not your fault. But I can do nothing. He is one of those our Lord is taking a particular interest in; he has such high hopes of a champion in the next games." He shook his head. "Otherwise I might have..."

Sarah smiled suddenly. "Perhaps I should ask Galen then."

The Spymaster was horrified at her suggestion. "Child... It would not be right for you to ask such a thing. No man wants his Lady to show an interest in another man, least of all a lowly slave and a gladiator at that. It is not seemly, it is not right. It is not..."

"What is not?" Lord Menethes asked as he entered. He bowed his head towards his bride of only a few seasons. "Are you instructing my wife again, Spymaster? She cannot possibly remember everything at once. You must take it more slowly."

The Spymaster inclined his own head in agreement and then watched, his face impassive, as Lady Sarah went over to her Lord. Surely she would heed his warnings.

With only the briefest of glances at her father Lady Sarah slipped her arm through her husband's and kissed him on the cheek.

"My father tells me I must not ask you about Liam," she said softly.

"Liam? Oh... that gladiator. Don't concern yourself with such as him." Lord Menethes was ready to dismiss the matter, but Lady Sarah persisted.

"I'm worried he might get hurt... or killed. It's such a dangerous life. He took good care of me when I was little. It seems ungrateful..."

Lord Menethes laughed. "How like a woman to care about even the most insignificant..."

Lady Sarah twisted one of the buttons on his shirt with her fingers then placed her hand flat on his chest just above the torc. "I'm sorry," she whispered dutifully. "I was wrong to bother you."

Lord Menethes shook his head slowly. "No, it shows what a tender heart you have, and I love you for that. I will have Gerran check on your gladiator's progress. If he shows promise he will survive. If he does not show promise he will be sent somewhere else. Will that satisfy you?"

"Thank you, my Lord," she said as he slipped his arms round her waist and pulled her close to him. He kissed her on the lips, a long demanding kiss that spoke of passion and need and possession. He pushed her away from him when he had finished. "Run along to your mother, my Lady. I have business to discuss with your father."

She gave him her most elegant curtsey. She had learnt fast the ways of this new world. But once outside the door she paused a moment to catch her breath and steady her hands. She put a tentative finger to her bruised lips and hurried away to find her mother. There was something she had to discuss.

Lord Menethes waited until the door had closed behind his wife before turning back to the Spymaster.

"Are the last of the slaves ready to be transported?" he asked briskly. Any trace of the besotted Lord had vanished with his Lady.

"Yes, my lord. But I thought it better to do two journeys. The next lot should be arriving soon. That girl is amongst them. We had some trouble adjusting her mind but I think everything has worked now. The last load will arrive in late summer."

The Lord nodded curtly and opened the door to leave.

"The gladiator?" the Spymaster reminded him.

"If he has potential keep him in training, if not transfer him."

"To where?"

"The mines, of course. My Lady is showing too unhealthy an interest in this man. I must find some way of taking her mind off him. By the time you get back her expectation will be well advanced. That should keep her occupied. She will soon forget this gladiator." The Lord left and his Spymaster leant back in his chair and sighed. There were times when...

But no... he had chosen this life and there was no going back now.

He put away the report he was reading and locked the cabinet. He began to hope his Lord's optimism would bear fruit. A child would occupy Sarah. It would also make her situation secure. She was too like her mother, he decided. She did not seem to realise how precarious life was. He wondered if he had done the right thing, bringing them here. . But Judith was very lovely. And when he had learnt there was a child, he knew he had to risk it.

At the thought of his own wife he stood up and left his office. Smiling to himself he walked the stone-floored corridors to his rooms. He was behaving like an old fool. Neglecting the Lord's business to spend an afternoon with a woman. But he felt in need of pampering and Judith was very good at cosseting him, making him feel young again. He could spare a few hours and then he would have to tell her he was leaving again. His mind came full circle back to the problem of that girl. It should have worked, he finally decided, as he reached the door to his rooms. But just in case he needed to be at the port... just in case.

He entered his sitting room and, as he had hoped, Sarah was there taking tea. Judith looked up as he entered and smiled. She poured him a cup.

"I told Sarah you wouldn't be long," she said, holding out the cup to him.

"And will you get Liam transferred?" Sarah asked impatiently.

He sighed again, would she never learn.

"If you persist, my Lord will have him transferred to the mines," he told her shortly. "Leave well alone. He is happy where he is. He has a chance to earn his freedom. Leave be."

Sarah looked at her mother. They both felt guilty about Liam. If it hadn't been for them he would still be on Earth, free, with his new girlfriend. The spymaster saw the look on her face and smiled sadly.

"Foolish girl," he said gently. "He doesn't remember you. None of them remember Urth or their lives there. Forget him. He is happy where he is. Trust me."

Sarah nodded slowly and rose to get him some more tea. As he watched her the spymaster felt content. At his time of life, to have a woman willing to be his wife and to have found a daughter and seen her settled in so illustrious a position. "I must a done something very good in a previous life," he thought contentedly.

"So who is the girl, Emma?" Gwydyr asked. The only other one among them with the height and breadth to pass easily as Anant, his slow lumbering ways hid a quick mind that had made him the natural successor as their leader when Timon had been sold on.

"My sister," Finn replied. They were sitting at a table in the refectory eating their evening meal. In spite of being an unappetising plate of last season's potatoes and leeks boiled together Liam had eaten it with an obvious enjoyment and gone back for more. "No one will bet with me any more," Finn remarked as Liam wiped the plate clean with a slice of rye bread. "Pity, you were a good source of income."

Liam frowned.

"I seem to have large gaps in my memory. There are a lot of names I have no faces for or faces with no names." He smiled and shook his head in amazement. "Flying through the air. Can you believe that?" Then he shrugged. His memory was almost complete; it would have to do. At least he no longer thought he was going mad, or worse, possessed by daemons.

"You worked for a Government Agency, anti-terrorism but the Department was called in when the wife of a high ranking Euro MP was murdered. It was unusual but...I had become your partner some time before..."

"You were investigating me," Liam said. "Because..."

"We're telepaths," Finn said. "I am... was a member of Psi Division. But it was Emma who spotted you on the *bus* and I was sent to see if she was right. You had me fooled but she insisted so she engineered a meeting with you and a dinner when you might feel more relaxed…"

"That was why I felt so angry and betrayed," Liam said. "She used me…"

"No. She got into a lot of trouble for getting… so close. She really liked you. We both did. Even if you were a bit moody at times," and Finn grinned at him.

Liam started to chew a Tanis leaf, pushing it carefully round his mouth with his tongue. He began the ritual prayer then stopped. It didn't seem right somehow. He swallowed the leaf and began to think carefully.

"How many of us are there?" he asked at last. They fell silent as someone walked up to the table but it was only Paul. He sat down and began to eat.

"This stuff is actually beginning to taste good," he complained. "It's worrying."

Finn waited until another trainee, Gwydyr the Lesser, had gone past to the next table before answering Liam.

"There's no way of knowing, for sure," he said. "There are twenty three of us who remember. Or at least who admit to remembering. Twenty of those came from the last shipment. Timon reckoned something must have gone wrong, for so many to remember at once. But as to how many there were in that shipment or how many…"

"Ten thousand," Liam interrupted.

"How do you know that?" Paul asked.

"I don't know." Liam frowned. "I have no idea, but I do. He averaged about three thousand on every trip; the last one was unusually large. And he made about three trips over about five tarns."

The three men stared at him horrified. "You're talking… over fifteen thousand people," Gwydyr said.

There was something at the back of Liam's mind but it wouldn't quite come into focus. He shook his head. "I can't remember any more."

Paul finished his food and looked round. "I'm almost tempted to get another plate," he said.

"Where on..." Finn hesitated. He had almost said *Earth* and that was not a wise thing to do. "I don't know where you lot put it all," he said instead.

Paul laughed. "Sword play is hard work. You retaari don't know you're born, you have it so easy."

"Ha, swordplay," Finn retorted. "It takes real skill to use net and trident."

They continued the friendly banter as they walked out of the refectory. The evening was theirs to do with as they wished. The four of them sat on the wooden stairs that led up to the trainers' dormitories and warmed themselves in the late sunshine.

"The gladiator master has allowed in the whores," Paul said. "We could go dice for a couple." He didn't sound all that enthusiastic.

Finn chuckled. "Gord's dice are loaded," he said. "Not a lot, just enough to give him the edge."

"The... When I think how much I've lost to him." Paul's voice was an indignant squeak.

"A fool and his money..." Finn said with a superior air. He grinned again. "Did that sound pompous enough?"

"Definitely," Paul agreed.

"I've been practising."

"It shows."

Liam sighed. Did these two take nothing seriously? It seemed Gwydyr agreed

"When you two have finished your *Laurel and Hardy* impersonation," he said shortly.

"Who?" Finn asked with a look of complete innocence on his face.

Liam picked up a rag ball that some of the trainees used to kick about and threw it at Finn. He caught it easily and tossed it to Paul who threw it back again. Finn made to throw it back at Liam then thought better of it. He began idly throwing it in the air.

"I *am* worried that Emma might be here and being treated like that," Finn said and for once he sounded serious.

"I doubt she would be treated like that," Liam said but Gwydyr was nodding.

"Most of the female slaves that Lord Menethes brought with him have gone to brothels. It's the way here. There's an imbalance," Gwydyr explained, seeing Liam's puzzled frown. "For every hundred females born there are over three hundred males. That's why warriors don't tend to marry until they retire... why Spymasters don't usually take wives and why there are such a large number of brothels... a small number of females can satisfy a large number of men." He shrugged and looked apologetically at Finn. "That's just the way things are."

"Even if she is somewhere else," Finn said, "How could we hope to find her. We could escape and get back to... *Earth* and leave her here on this dying world."

This was the great secret that the trainees who remembered had discovered and which they had been anxious to discuss out of Liam's hearing the first night he had been at camp. Timon, the blacksmith, was convinced that the planet was being pulled out of its orbit and nearer to the red sun that inhabited the winter skies.

"We don't know for sure Timon is right," Paul said quickly, looking round anxiously to see if they could be overheard. "He could be mistaken."

"No," Gwydyr said decisively. "Ask anyone. The winters are getting longer, the summers colder and there are movements in the land where there were none before."

He looked up at the sun, now rapidly sinking below the walls of the camp, shielding his eyes with his hand. "We are getting further and further from the sun and closer to the Nestor sun each time we pass it."

Liam suddenly stood up and turned to face them. He closed his eyes and frowned in concentration. There was something.... if he could just remember.

"I think our Lord intended to make her his mistress," he said and he looked anxiously at Finn to see how he would react to such news.

Finn's face was sombre. "That's better than... the alternative. At least she will be well looked after and rewarded."

But Liam wasn't convinced. "Why do you avoid saying Earth all the time?" he asked swiftly changing the subject.

"Haven't you seen the reaction you get?" The three trainees were amazed. "It varies in intensity but the basic reaction is the eye of Ra." Gwydyr put his finger and thumb together to make an oval shape and placed it against his chest roughly where his heart was. "It's to ward off evil spirits." He lowered his voice. "All those who were worth saving were brought here by the Gods thousands of tarns ago. The chosen ones, the Anari. Then came the Anant, the second-comers. And those of us left behind were the damned, the daemons. Ruled over by the Evil one... Osiris, the Daemon Lord. Mothers use the threat of Urth to frighten their children into good behaviour."

Liam took a deep breath and let it out slowly. He wanted to tell the others about his other self but he didn't dare. It was obvious now what... or rather who... his other self had been. "At least now I understand why he needed me," Liam thought. "It would have been impossible for him to occupy one of the warriors without being sensed and they would have thought him a daemon and probably tried to kill him…Or leave him on Earth again."

The other three were looking at him curiously and Lim gave a weak smile, wondering what he could say to allay their suspicion.

"Here's a miserable group, Declan," Old Colm, the retaari master came towards them with the secutor master. "And us bearing such good news, perhaps we should leave them to their misery. What do you say, Declan?"

The secutor master's reply was little more then a grunt. All four trainees had stood up at their approach. It did not pay to be slow to show respect to these men. It could mean the difference between life and death.

"You three," Colm said, pointing to Liam, Finn and Paul, "are to go to the games, after the festival to Ammon, in two decans time." Colm smiled at them. "Don't let me down, will you?" He walked away without waiting for their thanks. He had others to reward and disappoint.

Declan lingered for a moment, looking Liam up and down as he paused.

"Don't worry," he said as he turned to leave. "You're not expected to do any good. Just observe, learn a few tricks and breathe in the atmosphere."

Liam watched both trainers walking back across the yard. They stopped at other groups and there were yells of delight or groans of disappointment.

"Good," Paul said with undisguised satisfaction as they made their way back to their hut. "Might be able to recoup some of my losses…"

"Maybe you should borrow Gord's dice... if he's not going," Finn suggested. "You might stand a chance then..."

Paul threw the rag ball at Finn and, laughing, the pair raced off towards the hut. Liam sighed.

"Don't worry," Gwydyr reassured him. "They can take things seriously when they need to."

Later as Liam lay on his bed, unable to sleep, he thought about the conversation they had had and wondered again exactly what it was he had brought with him from Earth.

The festival to Ammon was the second of six festivals held each tarn. It was a major celebration because Ammon was the principal god of the Anari and now of the Menethes. The Gladiator trainees did not leave the school for the procession but they were allowed onto the school walls to watch as the Lord Menethes led the procession into the city from the temple. The Retaari Master Colm stood on the walls with them. It was his turn to stay behind with the slaves but Declan had gone into the city early that morning intent on securing a good view in the main square.

"So what happens at the Festival?" Liam asked as they waited. Finn shook his head, he didn't know. But Colm had heard the question and turned round to answer.

"The Divine Ammon who lives in the Temple and is tended by the priests comes forth from his inner chambers and is carried by them for all to see." He glanced behind him to see if anything had yet come into sight. Satisfied that the procession hadn't yet begun he turned back to Liam and continued. "Lord Menethes, as Pharaoh's deputy will lead the procession, clearing the way for the God. They go into the city through the South

Gate and then once round the walls, back to the gate, then up the street to the main square where Lord Ammon will be entertained and fed with the choicest food that can be prepared." Colm looked around again. "There is entertainment in the smaller squares and along the streets. But Lord Ammon's pleasure must come first. If he is pleased, then it should mean prosperity for the tribe for the coming tarn."

"And is he easy to please?" Liam asked.

Colm shrugged. "It is hard for anyone to say. In the second period, once the sun has cast its shadow at the feet of Lord Ammon, the priests will take him back to the temple where he is bathed and dressed in clean clothes and then taken into the main temple hall where all must come and worship him. That can take all night and part of tomorrow in a big place like Prime. But once all have been to the temple the God usually gives a sign to the High Priest that he is pleased or not and it is announced in the main square." Colm saw Liam's disgusted face and laughed. "He is the King of the Gods... All should worship him... even pirates like you."

He turned back to face the road. "Make the most of the holiday, trainees," he said over his shoulder. "Once the Festival is over everything gets back to normal. And that means rigorous final preparations for the games, even for those not going."

He looked as if he was going to say more, perhaps one of his lectures on training and discipline but at that moment someone shouted from further along the wall. The procession had come into sight.

To Liam's surprise the cavalcade was on foot. Even the High Lord was walking. At the head of the line, he cut an impressive figure in a richly embroidered tunic of white and gold. A circlet of gold was on his head and it glinted in the early morning sun in stark contrast to the Lord's dark hair. The road passed quite close to the school walls and there was a good view of the procession.

Several ranks of priests followed the Lord Menethes; each row more richly dressed in embroidered tunics than the previous one. The crowd lining both sides of the trackway below began to cheer and shout. They pushed forward as if to join the parade but were prevented from doing so by the line of warriors between them and the priests. Then Liam got his first sight of what all the fuss and noise was about. Eight priests were carrying a gold litter on their shoulders, rather like pallbearers at a funeral. Elite warriors flanked them, their torcs polished until they threatened to outdo the morning sun in brilliance. The warriors walked proudly, their heads held high, backs straight. This was why they were Elite, they were chosen. Chosen to guard the God and his representative on Anaria.... Pharaoh or his representatives, the Lords. Even among the Elite there was a hierarchy.

"I'll settle for just getting a torc," Liam thought as he raised his eyes to look at what the priests were carrying on their shoulders.

What Liam saw almost took his breath away.

If the gods truly existed, did they look like that?

The statue had been cast from a red coloured metal which he thought might have been copper and it was dressed in a similar tunic to the Lord, although this one was even richer and appeared to be entirely covered in gold embroidery. As the procession passed by where the trainee gladiators were standing Liam saw the material was actually made from spun gold, with an embossed pattern just visible.

What had caused him to gasp was the sheer size of the thing.

If it was life-size then the Gods must have been well over seven feet tall with powerful shoulders and thick arms that ended in three wickedly sharp claws on each hand. Liam looked across at the statue's head that was only slightly lower than his own. Then he felt someone tugging at his sleeve and he realised that everyone was beginning to kneel as the god passed so that no head was higher than Ammon's. He quickly knelt but continued to gaze at the face as it slowly went by.

So this was what the Nestor looked like...a leonine face...a memory stirred in his mind, half remembered.

Was that what had been inside him?

Liam looked at the back of the statue, now several feet further down the road and couldn't help the sudden shudder that flowed down his body.

"We'll make a convert of you yet, Pirate," Colm said, mistaking his horror for fear and awe.

More ranks of the priesthood followed behind, more warriors. Then temple attendants carrying huge amphora and covered baskets, cushions, rugs, parasols. Everything that a God might want during the day. Nothing was left to chance. The prosperity of the Lorddom depended on pleasing the God.

The rest of the day was theirs to pass as best they could but as the bells tolled for the end of second period Colm announced that they were to be allowed to go to the temple if any one wanted to. Liam decided to go. Anything was better than more hours of staring at the walls.

The Temple surprised him. He wasn't sure what he had expected. Something on the lines of *Saint Paul's*

Cathedral in London perhaps or *Notre Dame in Paris*. But the sheer size of it amazed him. It wasn't just a temple; it was a complex of religious buildings, workshops and dwellings.

It was situated about four miles outside of the main city walls. Originally surrounded by mud walls, which were still evident in sections, a new stone wall was being erected and as the column of gladiators neared the main gate Liam could see wooden scaffolding leaning against the wall and piles of stones waiting to be cemented into place. In places the old wall was crumbling, the weather had taken its toll on the ancient fortifications. On either side of the road, for the last nine hundred yards, tall stone pylons flanked the road, eighteen in all. The road continued straight through the gate towards the temple, which was the only thing visible to the gladiators as they walked the road amidst the crowds, all intent on paying homage and pleasing the God on His day... A huge stone pyramid.
Finn smiled at Liam and raised an eyebrow... Impressive... Familiar... he seemed to be saying.

The mass of people pushed forward through the gate and up the wide avenue towards the pyramid. Liam heard the Retaari master shouting at them to stay together, he didn't want anyone making a mistake and angering the God. He ushered them together, a large group of thirty or more.

The avenue was about a mile in length and it was crowded with those anxious to make their way to the temple. It was difficult to make any progress; there were so many people. Liam realised that everyone must have come from miles around, not just from the city. After an hour of shuffling along at a snails pace movement stopped completely and the crowd fell silent. Liam looked around him. What happened now?

There was an air of expectancy.

A stillness.

As they waited patiently.

In the distance, from the direction of the pyramid a horn sounded. A single note sounded out clearly across the waiting multitude and Liam found himself kneeling down where he stood as everywhere around him people did the same. As he knelt Liam glanced ahead and saw that the avenue opened out into an enormous square in front of the temple. It was filled with worshipping people, all kneeling, their faces raised towards the pyramid. A low moaning sound came back towards him and the people round him took up the cry.

A three note keening that rose then fell.

Over and over again.

Liam found himself joining in. It was a very simple thing to do.

At the head of the crowd, in front of his temple the statue of Ammon gazed down from his dais over the throng. Liam found himself staring mesmerised at the tiny figure, made almost insignificant by the distance. He was becoming very warm; the chanting was making him feel dizzy.

Suddenly he was wide-awake. His whole body felt as if it had been hit by lightning, there was so much energy running through him. He felt himself being lifted from the ground and flowing towards the temple and the figure of Ammon. He closed his eyes for a moment. When he opened them again the feeling of flowing towards the temple was still there although he could see that his body wasn't moving.

As suddenly as it had appeared the feeling was gone. He was left standing, amidst the group of kneeling worshippers.

He wasn't alone.

Others were standing. Warriors, Elite, the Gladiator masters. Just in front of him Declan spread his arms wide and let out a deep sigh. Liam knew exactly how the man was feeling.

It felt so good to be alive. He felt so full of energy. He could have taken on every gladiator in the world and won.

He threw back his head and took a deep breath.

There was so much life in him at that moment his whole body was tingling with its intensity.

Declan turned round and stared at him with some surprise.

"You feel it?"

Liam nodded. In the distance a trumpet sounded.

Declan turned back towards the temple.

"The Gods are pleased," he said and he looked at Liam once more. "Now the festival can really begin." He was grinning. "Stay close," and he edged his way through the crowd towards Colm. "This one's with me," the Secutor Master said and Colm grinned.

"And you said you were too old," he laughed.

Declan shrugged and raised a hand in farewell to Colm and started walking towards the city, Liam following close behind.

"Where are we going?" Liam asked after a few minutes.

"To enjoy the gift the Gods have given us," he was told. "It's not given to all, enjoy it while you can."

Other warriors, who greeted Declan as an old friend, soon joined them and Liam found himself accepted in spite of his lowly status in the scheme of things.

That day of Festival there was no rank.

"So what exactly did you do?" Paul asked.

Liam groaned. "I don't really remember, but if my head is anything to go by, it must have involved ale... a lot of ale... and women. I seem to remember a lot of women."

He took another spoonful of the thick porridge provided for the first meal and shook his head.

"You must be bad if you're off your food," Finn observed.

"Where'd you get the energy?" Paul continued. "It was late when we got back to camp. After all that kneeling and praying, I was shattered."

Liam tried to remember. The feeling of incredible energy that had sustained him through a night of revels was a dim memory.

"I feel like death," he said. "I'm going back to bed."

He stood up slowly and walked towards the refectory door. Gwydyr watched him closely as he walked away.

"He even looks like them. Has the same build. You say your sister said he wanted to be here. Are you sure we can trust him?"

"Yes, I think so." Finn was quick to reassure the others. "When the time comes he won't want to be left behind. He's a survivor."

Gwydyr the greater scraped his bowl clean and helped himself to Liam's.

"It might be as well to find out where Timon and the others have gone. If any are at the next games, you two know where they will be?"

Paul and Finn nodded.

"We are stuck in this camp," Gwydyr continued. "Our only hope of finding the ship might lie with them."

They nodded again. They knew what they had to do.

They finished their meal and left in a group to go to their respective training areas. The Secutor Master finished his own meal and left soon after.

IX

"I don't remember ever being at Menethes Port," Paul said. He shifted his heavy pack onto his other shoulder and stretched up to ease his aching back.

"You must have some memories," queried Finn. "I remember being there clearly."

Paul shook his head. "No, all my memories are of the gladiator camp, right back to when I was a boy. Strange... but I remember *Earth* at the same time."

They were marching in a column three wide and ten deep behind the Lord and his warrior bodyguard. Liam was a row behind them. It was some credit to the training that they had undergone that they had walked the twenty or so miles from Prime in three hours and did not feel as if they had done more than stroll to the nearest brothel. At least that was what the gladiator masters kept telling them.

The road, little more than a dirt track ran alongside a small stream and the column leader ordered a twenty-minute rest to water the horses. Liam threw down his pack and gratefully stretched out, his head using the pack as a pillow.

"We should be at the Highway soon," Paul said as he untied his cup from his pack.

"The what?" Liam asked. He had no idea what Paul was talking about.
Paul held out his hand for Finn's cup.

"Ra's Highway. It instantly transports our Lord from Prime to the Port."

"You mean I don't have to walk all the way back to the Port," Liam said. He hadn't relished the prospect of the long walk back when he had already done it once that season.

"No." Paul grinned. "The gate is about two hours ride from Prime." He stared at Liam. "Don't you know anything?" and he walked down towards the stream to fetch them both a drink.

"Obviously not," Liam said, sitting up beside Finn to drink his cup of water. "But at least we shall be able to sleep in beds tonight."

Finn groaned. "Right now that doesn't seem much of an advantage." He slapped at the back of his neck with his hand angrily and inspected the flattened smudge. "Midges! What do these things eat when I'm not around?" He wiped his hand on the grass.

Paul sat down the other side of Finn and handed him a drink.

"I think the Highway is similar to what took us up.... that day," Paul continued.

"I've never heard of it..." Liam said suddenly excited. "But perhaps it's how they reach the ship."

Paul shook his head. "They only run in straight lines between the major cities. Wherever...." He paused as the Retaari master walked close by checking on everyone's condition and offering good-humoured advice on blisters and sore feet. Paul waited until he was well passed before continuing. "Wherever it is hidden it won't be too close to a city or big town."

"These Highways," Liam asked. "Where else do they run?"

Paul wasn't sure. He only knew what Timon had told him before he had been sold on to another Lord.

"He said there was one between Toth Prime and Secund. And another from Toth Secund down to the Kush lands, but where after that..." He shrugged. "I think they have to run in straight lines so they are quite limited. Why?"

Liam looked thoughtful. "I just wondered who built them, that's all," and he fell silent, absorbed in thoughts he didn't want to share.

Paul turned back to Finn who shrugged. Liam could be a moody daemon when the fancy took him.

The Gladiator trainers began to move among the resting men urging them to their feet. They were anxious to be on the move again, there was still a way to go and they wanted to be at the Port before nightfall. Finn got up, then turned to help Liam who was still sitting. He had a strange drawn look on his face that puzzled Finn.

As the Retaari Master went past Liam suddenly stood up and called out to him.

"Sir ... Sir, can you settle an argument for us."

Old Colm turned to them, smiling.

"As long as I don't have to say Secutor are better fighters than Retaari, I might."

Liam smiled too. "No Sir, but we can't agree on who has the lived the longest and how old they were when they died."

Old Colm thought for a moment. "Well it must be Methuselah. He is definitely known to have lived for three hundred and twelve tarns. Of course the oldest men still alive are Pharaoh and Lord Toth. They were born on the same day over two hundred and thirty tarns ago." The retaari master chuckled. "There is supposed to be a prophecy about the Toth. Must be why Pharaoh hates the Lord so much, he's certainly aged better than old Kush."

Finn was still staring at Liam who could obviously see something in the trainer's words that had escaped Finn. And from the indifferent look on his face, Paul too.

"Thank you," Liam said but Finn got the impression the Retaari master expected them to ask more questions but he couldn't think of anything to ask.

"What prophecy?" Finn asked at last.

"Haven't you heard that one?" Old Colm's tone was scathing, but not at their ignorance. Such was the rivalry between Menethes and Toth that no opportunity to take fun at the Toth's expense should be missed. "At his birth, his mother had a vision of a Toth Pharaoh. This reign would usher in a golden age of peace and prosperity. Load of nonsense. She said it would be the hundredth Toth Lord so that would our Toth's great great grandson since he's the ninety-seventh. Still, he's said to take it quite seriously." Colm started to walk away then he turned back to face them, still chuckling. "The Gods are supposed to fall and we shall have a forgotten god as Ra once more."

He turned and walked away, down the line of still sitting men, urging them to their feet.

"If an hour here is approximately the same as on Urth," Liam began.

"And there are thirty hours to a day, three hundred days to a season," Finn continued.

"Three hundred and twelve tarns is nine hundred and thirty six seasons," Liam said.

"Oh *hell*," Paul said.

"Netherworld!" Liam and Finn spoke together.

"We might not have a world to go back to," Liam said quietly and he picked up his pack and resumed his place in the column.

"How did you know?" Finn whispered about three miles further on. Liam was marching at his side now; Paul about two rows ahead.

Liam thought about the question for a moment.

"I don't remember clearly," Liam said guardedly. He wished he could tell Finn the truth but it was something Osiris had once told him. He shrugged.

"It suddenly occurred to me when we were talking back there."

Finn nodded. He was about to say more when the Retaari Master rode alongside.

"No talking," he ordered. "Save your breath for the march."

The column moved off. In the distance Liam could see they were heading for a low hill with a squat stone building on the summit. As they neared the base Liam could see why the column had been halted. The last of the Lord's elite were only just entering the building. Whatever was inside must work slowly for it had created a queue. Paul made his way back to where Liam and Finn were waiting.

"This could take a while," he said. "They have to blindfold the horses." They sat down in the shade of a tree and waited for their turn. Liam asked Paul if he knew why the Menethes and the Toth disliked each other so much. They were both Anant after all. Paul didn't know but one of the other trainees sitting nearby was able to tell them a little of the history of their Lord.

"When the last Anant Menethes Lord died without a son, Pharaoh gave the Lordship to an Anari Lordling, our Lord's father, marrying him to the female heir, and giving him the High Lord's ring," Namoth told them. "All the Anant Lords felt this should have gone to the Toth and they weren't too happy about it. As well, Pharaoh gave Toth land to our Lord to give him a route to the Anari lands. It caused a bit of anger, I can tell you."

"So what happened?" Liam was finding the impromptu history lesson extremely interesting.

"The Toth is supposed to have laughed and said he agreed with Pharaoh, he was too old to hold such a high office."

"I thought they were the same age," Finn remarked dryly and the man sitting next to Namoth laughed.

"Exactly. Then he sent his army to the border and said he was measuring the land in case it shrunk anymore."

"So how was the matter settled?" Liam asked.

"Pharaoh offered an Anari Lady with lands adjacent to the Toth as a bride. He'd been a widower for as long as anyone could remember but he accepted the lands and took the Lady for five seasons, sending her back after this time."

"Can you do that?"

Namoth shrugged. "The great Lord Toth seemed to think he could and who's going to argue with him when he has as large an army as Pharaoh's and the backing of six other Lords"

"That's not the only problem though," his neighbour said. "The trouble is Port Menethes is built about a mile inland from the coast, on the edge of a tidal river estuary. Ships wanting to dock or leave can only do so when the tide runs in their favour, but it is a safe harbour which is why it is the preferred port for most of the spice ships from the south."

"So?" Both Paul and Finn couldn't see what difference that made.

"Port Toth is fifty miles to the north," Liam told them. "It has faster roads from the port but it is more difficult to dock there, particularly in a winter storm."

"Spoken like a true Pirate," Namoth said. "The first spices to the northern markets command the higher prices, so the two ports vie with each other for the trade. It doesn't make for friendly relations between the two tribes."

"The Anant Lords don't like having to bow to an Anari High Lord," his neighbour said. "That's the real problem."

Old Colm started to shout at the trainees to come forward. It was their turn to enter the Gate. They walked up the incline towards the grey building at the top. Liam wasn't sure what he had expected but certainly not such a nondescript building. It was quite small and he found himself standing outside in the dying sunshine as he waited his turn to enter. The hilltop commanded a good view over the surrounding countryside. To the south he could just see the distant walls of Menethes Prime, about an hour or two's ride away and the flat farmland that lay in between. A few strides would have taken him to either side of the grey walled building with its domed roof and given him a view of the equally prosperous farmland stretching away to the north.

He found himself becoming apprehensive as the column neared the Gate. If Paul was right and it was similar to what had transported them onto the spacecraft then he had passed out when he had used it and he didn't like the thought of what might lie ahead.

"Just remember to keep your eyes firmly closed," Colm said. "The Gods don't like us to see their lands."

All too quickly Liam found himself inside. Again he hadn't known what it would be like but he felt vaguely disappointed. The room held nothing more than two roughly carved pillars of cream crystal in the centre, about half the height of a tall man and nothing more. The walls were of grey stone, bare with no decoration of any kind. There were no controls to be seen, nothing like the small column he remembered from the ship.

"How does it work?" he asked the gatekeeper standing at the side of one column.

"Just walk through," he was told. "This way for the Port and from the other side for Secund. Simple."

Liam took a deep breath and, closing his eyes tightly, stepped between the columns of crystals. For a moment he felt the fleeting sensation of extreme cold, then it was gone.

"You can open your eyes now." Finn's voice seemed to be coming from a long way off but as Liam opened his eyes everything began to feel normal again.

"Have we...?" he began to say and Finn nodded.

"Come and look outside," he said. They walked out of an identical grey building but the view outside was totally different.

In the far distance to the west it was possible to see a narrow strip of sea sparkling in the sunshine. About an hour's walk to the north Liam could see the familiar high walls of the Port. The port warehouses and the brothels were just visible outside the walls, between them and the quayside. To the east, also outside the main walls, was the gladiator camp. Situated in the very centre was the port castle surrounded by its own high wall. The north road sent out a branch towards the East Gate and then continued on its journey to Port Toth.

"Most of the Menethes Land is on a peninsular." Namoth had remembered Liam's interest earlier. "That's why we needed Toth land otherwise we'd be cut off from the Anari." He pointed to the east of the Port. "There are the camps of the other Lords," and Liam saw row upon row of tents neatly set out in separate groups. Long banners on tall poles fluttered in the breeze above them. "We should pass quite close," Namoth continued. "Look out for the symbol of two coiled snakes... that's Toth."

But the only symbols to be seen were that of the boar and the wolf. The legendary Lord had not yet arrived.

The participants in the games were treated better than Liam had been the last time he had been in the camp. They were given beds in the main compound outside the inner enclosure where he had been trained and the food was definitely an improvement.

After supper Liam went in search of Clem. It wasn't difficult to find him. He was still inside the wooden palisade with the trainees. He didn't look any different from the last time Liam had seen him at the end of winter. Now he had a Menethes slave collar about his neck instead of a plain one but so did Liam and now he had slightly better quarters and better food.

"Does Eoin still take supper with you?" Liam asked. He hadn't seen the assessor at all since they had arrived.

"Eoin's dead," Clem said. "Not long after you left. Went to bed after supper as healthy as anything … next morning… gone."

They talked for a little while longer discussing the merits of Eoin's successor and the prospects for the Menethes at the forthcoming games then Liam made his excuses and went in search of his bed. For some reason coming back to the Port school had depressed him.

"All of you will sleep now," Colm ordered as Liam returned to the hut where supper had been served. "The fights we're interested in might not start for a few days but you're still in training so you'll need to get as much rest as you can. Training fights will start at first light…" Colm bared his teeth in a savage grin as they all groaned. "Anyone too tired to fight tomorrow will have me to deal with." He looked round at the faces of the trainees, most of who hadn't been to a Games before. "Don't worry, you'll have plenty of free time too. You'll get to see some of the other contests."

"Should be fun," Paul said as they made their way to the dormitories. "I have some money left over from the festival. A little careful gambling and I could make a nice profit to take back to Prime."

Finn merely grunted. Liam had the feeling he was unhappy about something but he was too tired to care. It could wait until morning.

As he settled down to sleep he realised that when he had been at the Port before he had believed himself going mad. Now he relished the possibility of another dream. Another encounter with Emma was just what he needed to take his mind off the approaching fights.

X

There were to be two decans of games, not just gladiatorial contests, but wrestling, throwing spear and discus, running and jumping, horse racing and much more. If it could be wagered on then it was in the games. The gladiator fights did not start until the fourth day and the trainees were free until then to watch the rest of the contests.

Paul and Liam went to watch the horse racing. They stood in amazement as huge sums of money were waged by Lords and warriors alike on the outcome of the races.

"Finn should have come here to find a blacksmith," Paul muttered under his breath, but although they both scanned the area where the horses were tended between races there was no sign of Timon.

The horses raced round a large circular track laid out on the plain to the south of the port. Inside this track the other events would take place, areas marked by white chalk showing the arena for each event. Tiered wooden seating under the shade of a huge awning had been built down one side for any of a better sort who might attend. Others had to stand at the side of the track behind hastily erected picket fencing or ropes strung between metal stakes.

"Those are the rings for the fights," Paul said pointing to circles of rope laid out in front of the wooden seating.

"For the gladiators?" asked Liam, curious. This was where his future lay.

"And the wrestling. Same rules, put a foot on the rope and you're out, step over the rope and you're out," Paul told him.

They watched as one horse passed the finishing line several lengths ahead of the rest. A small cheer went up and there were a few whoops of delight and demands for payment of wagers. Clearly the winner had not been the favourite.

"Our Lord seems to be doing well," Liam observed as an unknown man, by his dress and ring a Lord, grimaced and handed a small purse into the Lord Menethes outstretched hand. Menethes laughed and stood up. The three tiers of seats in front had been left unoccupied and he now used these as steps to reach the ground.

"Come, Benjamin," he said turning to the dejected Lord. "You'll take refreshment with me, to show there are no hard feelings. Who knows, your luck may change this second period."

The pair, flanked by Menethes warriors and two or three from the unknown tribe proceeded to walk towards the tents where refreshments were being served. Liam knew that their Lord had a private tent so that he could retire when the mood took him and it was probably to this that he intended to go now. His path would take him passed where Liam and Paul were standing and Liam found himself bowing as the group went by. He glanced up and for a second found himself staring into the Lord's deep brown eyes, The Lord frowned for the briefest of moments and then was gone, striding towards the tents.

Paul looked at Liam and raised an eyebrow.

"He knows you?" he asked.

"I did question his authority briefly," Liam said. "He's probably not used to any one doing that."

"When?"

"In Judith's kitchen." Liam groaned.

Judith's kitchen....Sarah.

How could he have forgotten Sarah?

They were both here… on Anaria.

He suddenly felt dizzy.

So much that he had forgotten came flooding back.

His wife, his stepdaughter.

Feelings and emotions he had forgotten.

"Are you all there?" he heard Paul ask.

Liam straightened up.

"I've just remembered a few more things."

Paul nodded sympathetically. There wasn't a lot else that could be said.

"Look," a sudden inspiration took hold of him. "I won some money at dice last night. Why don't I treat us to some decent food? Anything will be better than our normal rations."

Liam rubbed the bridge of his nose; he could feel a headache coming on. For once the last thing he felt like was food.

"You can buy me a tankard of ale," he said.

Paul laughed. "I'll buy you a half tankard. We're in training, remember?"

They started to walk back towards the port, passing the tents where refreshments were laid out for the Anant lords and their families. Liam could see, some distance ahead of them, Lord Menethes standing outside his private tent arguing with someone. As they drew closer he saw their Lord was arguing with his spymaster. Paul moved away a little so that their path would not take them too close, but Liam was curious and edged closer as they neared the angry Lord. The last time he had seen the spymaster had been at the Port but the man had shown an unexpected interest in Liam's welfare and that made Liam curious about him in return. He slowed his pace a little, but still remembered to bow his head. It was not difficult to hear what was being said. The difficulty would have been to avoid hearing, the Lord was so angry he had forgotten caution and was almost shouting.

"Those damned idiots," Liam heard him say. "Can you do nothing?"

The spymaster made an apologetic but nevertheless negative gesture with his hands.

"I have tried everything I can think of," he said.

A woman came out from the tent and laid her hand on Lord Menethes arm. Liam held his breath but he quickly saw it wasn't Sarah.

"Aren't you going to join us, Galen," the newcomer said. "This is a time for you to relax and forget the cares of Lordship for a few days." A look of sudden concern crossed her thin face "I do hope there is nothing wrong with your Lady. It's always a dangerous time, when there's an expectation."

Lord Menethes smiled and took her hand from his arm. He held it to his lips.

"My good Lady is in excellent health, I thank you for your concern, Lady Darg. No, the problem this time lies with.... a hunting dog. My favourite bitch. She has been ill diagnosed and now it is too late." He gave the spymaster a long hard look. "It will have to be put down. To save any further suffering."

Liam could see the spymaster become uneasy at this, upset almost.

"I'm sure I will be able to do something," Liam heard him say. "I'll put her away from the rest ... of the pack. She won't upset anyone."

Menethes nodded. "Very well, but if it proves too difficult, have the bitch put down swiftly. Don't let her suffer unnecessarily."

The spymaster bowed, but the Lord had already turned away and re-entered the tent. The spymaster hurried away, not noticing the trainee gladiators loitering nearby.

"A lot fuss over one hunting dog," mused Liam as he watched the spymaster disappear between tents.

"Oh, I don't know." Paul pulled on his arm and they resumed their trek back to the port and the nearest inn. "I sometimes think these Lords care more for their animals than they do their people."

They entered the city through an open gate, unchallenged. It was after all a time of festivity and for once no one was at war with anyone else. One could relax one's guard a little. They walked along a narrow street next to the outer wall, passing several large taverns but none would satisfy Paul until, in a little side street running away from the wall he finally raised his hand and announced this was the one. Liam looked around trying to decide what had made Paul choose this over any of the others they had passed.

Like most such establishments it consisted of only one room open to the street, the living quarters and storerooms above supported by three thick columns of stone. The rough wooden table covered with sacking that served as a bar looked solid enough as did the tables and benches for any customers. But Liam could see nothing that distinguished it from any other tavern, unless it was the aroma of the food that came from the back room. He had to admit that it did smell extremely good.

They sat down at a table towards the back and Paul ordered two half tankards of small ale and some food from a slave standing behind the bar. When the food arrived Liam found he was hungry after all and he began to eat the rough bread, sliced tomato and soft cheese with olive oil drizzled over. As he ate he felt vaguely uneasy. There was something not quite right but he couldn't work out what was troubling him.

"This food," he said at last.

"Mmm good isn't it?" mumbled Paul, his mouth full of cheese.

"Yes, but… It doesn't seem right." Liam wasn't certain what he was trying to say. "Wouldn't you expect something different? There's not much in this world that's different."

"The power crystals are different," Paul pointed out. "A very efficient renewable source of energy."

That was true, Liam conceded.

White crystals for light, blue for the swords, red for heat and presumably cooking. But what else was different.

"Nothing," he said. "It's as if someone just plucked up everything he needed to create a world from... home... and dumped it here. But, I mean, take those tomatoes you're eating. They weren't introduced into...." He lowered his voice to a whisper. "*England* until about five hundred.... seasons ago. And what about potatoes? The same with them."

Paul sighed. Liam would be fine for days and then something would set him off and he would suddenly feel the need to find reasons, explanations. It could be very tiring.

Liam looked at him apologetically.

"Sorry. It's what I was trained to do, find answers. It's a hard habit to break."

He rested his elbow on the table and drained his tankard. "It's just that, if it's a case of parallel development, then fair enough. But if someone else has been going to.... home... as well as our Lord, there could be another way to escape."

Paul nodded slowly as he thought about this. It might be worth mentioning to the others and Timon if Finn ever found him. He ordered and paid for two more half tankards.

"That's the last of my winnings," he said, "so make it last."

When Liam raised an eyebrow Paul explained that he had arranged to meet Finn here in the middle of second period. "There's always an inn called Ra's Solace," he explained. "It's a popular name."

As if he had heard them Finn chose that moment to enter. He was followed by a stocky man with a badly scarred face on the right side.

Timon.

They came over and sat down. Liam noticed Timon sat with his back to the wall so the scarred side of his face was away from the rest of the room. The slave brought over two more tankards of ale and a bowl of dukkah, spiced nuts and seeds. Finn took a handful and lent back idly eating.

"So," Timon began, "how are the games going. Is it worth my time to bet on any of you?"

Liam used the last of his bread to mop up the oil on his plate.

"Not these games," he said. "Maybe the next."

Paul laughed. "Another three seasons and Liam will be bigger than an expectant mare."

They all laughed at this, even Liam. But he felt uncomfortable in Timon's presence and stood up.

"I'm sure you have a lot to talk about," he said. "I'll leave you to it."

He knew Timon was probably right about the danger they were all in, he was probably right that the only answer was to find the spaceship that had brought them there and escape before it was too late and he was probably right that they should work together on this. But Liam couldn't help the very strong feeling he had in his gut that the answer lay elsewhere. And he couldn't help the feeling he had that he belonged there. He didn't want the planet and its entire people to be destroyed. He wanted to find an answer that would mean it was saved. Then he could stay. Unlike the others who remembered earth he didn't want to go back. It was a thought he wisely kept to himself.

"I think you should stay and hear what has happened," Timon said quietly.

Liam frowned but sat down again as Timon ordered another round of drinks. "I do quite well for a slave blacksmith," he said and Liam heard an undertone of bitterness in his voice. "My new master, the Lord Darg, has discovered I have a talent for making fine jewellery. He takes most of the profit, but I get some."

He waited until the slave had brought their drinks and moved out of hearing range before beginning his tale. What he had to tell them was alarming.

The Lord Menethes sold ten slaves including two seasoned blacksmiths to Lord Darg, at the beginning of the season. At first all went well. The slaves settled in under their new master and proved to be hard working and reliable. One of the blacksmiths, it was discovered, had a talent for producing fine jewellery and the Lord seized on this as a way of making money. For his was not a particularly large or prosperous Lorddom and he had an expensive wife. Then disturbing whispers came to the ears of the Lord. The other slaves in the castle began to shun the new arrivals, calling them strange. They did not mix, they kept to themselves too much and then one was heard to utter a terrible word.

Urth.

"It was Robert," Timon said. "He never can stop saying 'where on *earth*'. Damned fool."

The Lord, fearful the new slaves were planning to escape, had had a watch set on them and so all was discovered. The Reeve questioned all the new slaves, then the house steward did so too, under the eye of the Lord.

"He sent for the priests who after a lot more questions decided the best thing to be done was burn the lot of them."

Paul and Liam stared horrified at Timon, calmly sitting there.

"And did he?" Paul asked.

Timon looked at them both gravely, then his face broke out in a twisted grin.

"The priests went away satisfied," he said. "But whatever he burnt it wasn't nine daemons from ... that place. Our Lord is too short of money to waste it like that."

"And you, weren't you questioned?" Liam asked.

Timon nodded. He had been examined for hours by the priests but had finally managed to convince them that his shunning of other company was due to his face, nothing else.

"Fortunately my work for the Lord had kept me busy so I didn't see much of the others," he added. "Although I'm not sure my Lord is entirely convinced of my innocence."

"We're going to have to be a damn sight more careful," Finn said, draining his tankard.

Liam stood up. "I'm going to watch the wrestling." He looked at Timon. "If you are suspect it won't look too good if we're seen in your company. If we are to find a way home it'll be in the Menethes camps that we find it. Not spread out across the country... or burnt to a crisp in some priest inspired bonfire." He nodded curtly to Paul and Finn and walked out of the dim bar into the bright sunshine.

"You'll have to excuse Liam," Paul explained. "He's the only one of us who actually wants to be here."

"Even knowing the world is doomed?" Timon was amazed.

"I don't think he believes you."

"Oh he does," Finn said. "It's just that...."He shook his head, he couldn't explain.

"Maybe we should forget about him," Timon said as he left them outside the inn to return to the Darg camp.

XI

It was the final day of the games and the Menethes had done well. Out of a possible ninety champions the Menethes' athletes accounted for thirty-eight. It had been a successful games, the weather had been fair, not always to be guaranteed these days, and there had been no serious injuries amongst the athletes. A most successful games. And the final contest to be decided would also mean another champion for the Lord Menethes, for the last contest, a gladiatorial fight, was to be between two Secutor from the Menethes camp.

Finn and Paul went to the arena early, they wanted to secure a good view of the contest, and Finn was anxious to see Liam. As trainees he and Paul had not been expected to win their fights and, as trainees, their lives had therefore been guaranteed. But the final was different. If Liam didn't put up a good fight or failed to please the crowd, and the Lord, his life could be forfeit. Finn wasn't sure if Liam realised the danger he was in and so he was anxious to arrive early and warn Liam.

"I can't believe he got this far," Paul said. "Have you had a bet on him?"

"Of course," Finn grinned. He had got very good odds from Rebus who was the unofficial bookmaker for the trainees.

"What did you bet on?" Paul asked. Finn seemed to know Liam extremely well and had already won a tidy sum since Liam had joined them at the school... most of it from Paul.

"Gotard," Finn said. "He's a seasoned gladiator, just missed out on his torc at the last games, he must be favourite to win."

Paul nodded, pleased with the answer.

"Good, that's who I've put my remaining sou on."

Finn smiled as he leant against the wooden barrier surrounding the arena.

"But I got good odds because I also bet the fight would last at least two hours."

"Two hours!" Paul's eyes narrowed as he stared at Finn scanning the field carefully. "Two hours... Save me a place." And he ran off in the direction of the Menethes camp, examining his small purse as he went.

The sun rose higher in the sky as they waited for the contest to begin. Soon the crowds began to arrive, fresh from another Menethes victory in the wrestling. Some of the Lords with their ladies arrived, seating themselves on the raised tiers of seats. A light breeze sprang up and began to ruffle the deep blue canopy high above them.

A man next to Finn jostled his arm and apologised, the crowd were getting restless. A cheer went up as the Menethes warriors began to clear a path through the crowd and Lord Menethes and his Lady proceeded to their seats. Finn watched with interest as the Lord helped his Lady up the steps. He had only met Sarah briefly and the memory was not a clear one but she appeared tired. As she sat down she leant against her husband and he smiled down at her and took her hand in his.

"Liam won't want to leave her behind," Finn suddenly realised, "but there's no way we could hope to take her with us." Perhaps it would be better to leave Liam out of their plans as Timon had suggested.

Paul reappeared at his shoulder, a broad smile indicating a success of some sort.

"Haven't missed anything have I?" he said, a little out of breath and Finn nodded towards the canopied stand as the Lord's party settled itself in their seats. As they did so the two gladiators appeared. Finn realised there would be no opportunity for him to talk to Liam; the gladiators went straight to the arena in front of the stand. Neither had shields, Finn noted, and only the protection of simple leather strapping round the arms and upper torso. Liam, as the most inexperienced fighter knelt first to pay homage to the High Lord. He did so briskly, springing up vigorously from his knee and, turning to face the crowd, raised his sword high above his head. Gotard followed suit and as he raised his sword a huge cheer went up from the crowd.

"Liam is going to find it hard," Paul said. "The crowd is behind his opponent."

Finn nodded. Would being the crowd's favourite work for Gotard or against him? As favourite he had more to prove and the crowd would be less likely to forgive if he lost. That could work in Liam's favour Finn thought, as the two gladiators took up their stations at opposite sides of the rope circle. If Gotard felt under pressure he could make a mistake.

The seasoned gladiator didn't show any sign of nerves as he stood, feet planted firmly apart, waiting for the fight Marshall to lower his staff at a signal from their Lord.

The point of the staff dropped to the floor as the Marshall stepped back over the rope and the two gladiators began circling each other warily, swords held out in front. Gotard was the first to strike, a light blow that Liam easily parried. The swords met again as the two contestants tested out each other's strength. Another meeting of swords and the two men began circling again. Gotard attacked suddenly, a flurry of heavy blows that

Liam managed to parry, but he was forced backwards towards the boundary.

Finn leant forward against the wooden railing holding back the crowd, gripping it tightly as he willed Liam to fight back. But he could see that Gotard had age and experience on his side and, Finn suspected, superior strength, for Liam was only a trainee. He wasn't used to the gruelling endurance needed for these contests. They could last for hours, continue until one or both contestants collapsed and could fight no more. And in these later rounds such a collapse could mean death if a Lord wasn't pleased by a performance.

Finn gripped the wooden barrier again as tightly as he could.

"Don't step back any more," he muttered. "You're almost on the rope now." Liam took another step back. It seemed as if some instinct had warned him because he risked a glance down to find the rope. Taking this for a loss of concentration Gotard pressed home his attack but Liam dug deep into his reserves of strength and, bracing his arm, swung aside the stroke, side-stepped to the left and left his opponent lurching perilously close to the boundary. But Gotard was too old a hand to be brought down so easily though and quickly regained his footing, He turned once again to face Liam who had backed away a little desperately trying to catch his breath and find a second wind. The brief respite seemed to have done both gladiators some good for they returned to the fight with renewed vigour.

They had been a full two hours in the arena, with no break for breath and the sun was well passed its high point. There was a little shade from the blue canopy on part of the arena and both gladiators, hot, tired, and thirsty after their long fight were standing in this part of the arena looking at each other wearily. The Marshall looked towards the stand and the High Lord for a sign to stop the fight but Lord Menethes shook his head.

"A torc for the winner," he shouted.

Gotard grinned and advanced towards Liam who retreated into the sunlight. He was on the defensive now, his strength nearly gone. The swords were not fully empowered, there was no danger of serious injury, but they could still deliver a painful jolt that left muscles aching and exposed skin red and sore. Gotard struck, renewed by the promise of the torc. Liam parried, then went down. He had had enough.

The Marshall put his staff between the two gladiators to stop the fight and looked up at the Lord. Lord Menethes hesitated; the crowd seemed to be holding its breath. The only noise to be heard was the rustling of the canopy high overhead. Then the Lord raised his hand. Liam lay on his back, momentarily too exhausted to move. He had closed his sword as soon as he had fallen and Gotard now did the same. He came over to where Liam was lying and offered him a hand up.

"You fought well," the man said. "It was a good contest."

Liam stood up and bowed to the victor. Underneath the leather strapping he was running with sweat. All he wanted now was a long soak in a cool bath.

Lord Menethes came down the steps towards where they were standing. Someone handed him a round metal disc as he descended and he held this in front of him as he walked through the crowd towards the arena so that all of them could see Gotard's reward. As he reached the kneeling gladiator there was a loud crack. One or two in the crowd looked round to see what it was. Both Liam and Finn immediately thought of gunfire, but there were no guns on Anaria. When it became clear that there was nothing to see the crowd turned back to watch the presentation.

Gotard stood up and took the torc from his Lord. Lord Menethes turned to the secutor master to order Gotard's collar removed.

"We cannot afford to lose such a good fighter," he said. "Perhaps he would like a position in the Port guard," and Gotard beamed with pleasure and stammered his thanks. Liam was kneeling, his head bowed in the Lord's presence. He now raised it, looking past the Lord as he heard a soft creaking sound. He listened for a second and heard it again. Fear gave strength to his legs and he quickly rose in spite of the glare from Declan. Lord Menethes was also surprised by this disrespect and about to order the Gladiator Master to teach the trainee some manners when the soft creaking became a loud groan and he turned instead with alarm towards the stand.

Someone towards the back of the crowd, near the stand, screamed and started to push forward. The push became a stampede as the cry went up.

"The stand is falling." The Menethes warriors immediately surrounded their Lord protecting him from any danger. Within seconds the mass of people in front of the stand had thinned and Liam was able to see it clearly. It was leaning crazily to one side, a support underneath must have given way and some of the seating had fallen through to the ground underneath. Liam hoped no one had been seated at the back; they wouldn't have stood a chance. Even as he looked the remaining seating began to tip slowly to one side throwing the seated people onto the seats in front.

"My Lady."

Sarah.

Liam heard the Lord's anguished cry and immediately ran towards the stricken stand scanning it as he did so for the familiar figure. He quickly spotted her about halfway up clinging terrified to her seat. She was not far from the central stairs and since these appeared solid enough he ran up towards her without a thought to the danger. Even as he drew close he could see the collapse of one end of the stand was causing a domino effect and the whole structure appeared in danger of going.

"Sarah," he shouted. "Come on."
She didn't seem to hear him but stayed where she was. As the seat where she was sitting shuddered she let out a cry of terror. Liam stopped on the steps level with where she was. He was a big man. His weight might be all that was needed to send everything crashing to the ground. Sarah was several feet away from him, her eyes closed tight.

"Sarah," he shouted again and this time she seemed to hear him for she opened her eyes. "Come on," he repeated, holding out his hand to her. For a moment he thought she was going to refuse to move but then she began to slowly inch her way towards him. The structure shuddered again and she screamed and stopped moving, gripping the wooden seats tightly.

Liam shouted to her again but she was too frightened to move. He thought for a moment then decided to risk putting his weight on the planks. He put one foot forward and found it was possible to reach Sarah's wrists. He pulled her towards him, stepping back onto the central stairway as he did. There was a loud roar and the end section of the stand began to fall. Liam picked the terrified girl up in his arms and ran down the steps to the safety of the ground. He didn't stop until he was some distance away. He sat Sarah down on the trampled grass and then collapsed to his knees, exhausted.

He looked back towards where, only minutes before, the Lords and their families had been enjoying the final day of the games. At first he could see nothing for the entire edifice was covered in a cloud of dust. Only as this began to settle did he see the shattered bones of the right side of the bank of seats. By some miracle the central stairs and the left side were still standing undamaged and those people who had been sitting in this section were now clambering over the seats to reach the ground.

Liam looked back at the collapsed part and wondered if anyone had been hurt or killed. He could see wicker hurdles being hurriedly brought from the city. There must have been some casualties then.

"You saved my life," someone said quietly behind him and she touched him lightly on the forearm. He turned his head to look at her and her solemn face broke into a smile as she realised who it was.

"Are you hurt, Sarah?" he asked. He wasn't supposed to be able to remember her but he was too tired and too relieved at her escape to recollect that fact. Wearily, he got to his feet and helped her to stand as the Lord Menethes surrounded by his bodyguard hurried up to them. He took Sarah by the arm and ordered a carriage. She was to be taken back to the castle. The physician must be sent for immediately. Only once Sarah was being helped into the carriage and almost on her way back to the castle did Lord Menethes look at Liam. He said nothing but gave a curt nod of the head. Then he turned and left to supervise the care of the wounded, see to the burial of any dead and order his spymaster to find out what had gone wrong. He was after all the High Lord and had his duty to do.

Liam watched as Sarah was helped into the carriage. She looked back and smiled briefly at him, then was gone. He looked around and wondered what he should do. There seemed to be enough people milling around and seeing to the injured. Should he stay and help or would he just be getting in the way?

His dilemma was solved by the Secutor master marching past with a train of gladiators in his wake. He was taking them back to the gladiator school; there was nothing they could do here. Liam fell in line at the back, trying to spot Finn or Paul but he couldn't. They must have already gone back. Hopefully someone had thought to heat up the water in the coppers; a hot bath was the only thought on Liam's mind as they marched back.

XII

"We were close to the stand," Finn said, as Liam and several other trainees sat in stunned silence in the large communal bath. "When he realised what was happening Colm shouted at us to pull those who had fallen already away from the stand. There must have been about ten or eleven bodies, just lying there. They were just lying there." He shook his head slowly as if he still couldn't believe what had happened, what he had seen. "Some of the warriors pulled the metal rods from the barriers," he continued, "and tried to shore up the seating, otherwise it would have gone straight away, no one would have got down." He was staring straight at Liam, but his eyes were unfocussed, his mind reliving the horror. "The ground just opened up. There was a long rift running right under the stand, nothing could have stayed up. Nothing." He was shaking his head again, "Nothing," he repeated.

"What happened then?" someone prompted.

"There was a cry that it was going and we all starting running from under it. I picked up a lad, can't have been more than ten seasons old and just kept running. I thought Paul was right behind me." This time Finn looked straight at Liam. "I thought he was right behind me," he insisted, but the haunted look of guilt didn't leave his eyes, "but when I looked back I couldn't see anything, there was just all this dust." He ducked under the water for a moment then covered his face with his hands to wipe the water from his eyes. "Does anyone know how many were hurt?" he asked.

"I heard it was up to five dead and four injured," Ranulph said, climbing out of the bath and wrapping himself in a coarse cotton cloth. "They're saying Tuni's back might be broken."

"By Ammon's coat, I pray not." Gwydyr the Lesser made the sign of Ra and they all echoed his prayer.

"I don't suppose we'll know for sure until the wreckage has been cleared," Finn said. "We should do that. They were our comrades. It's the least we can do."

One or two of the trainees looked aghast at this. Liam sighed. The last thing he wanted was to get out the warm bath and go back to the arena. He stood up and reached for a towel.

"Finn's right." he said. "I hope someone would do it for me. We should show respect, see they're treated right."

There were a few grumbles but most followed Liam's lead.

Lord Menethes listened patiently as the Spymaster concluded his report on the previous day's tragedy.

"And how many were killed?" he asked. "Has the final count been made?"

The spymaster consulted the sheaf of papers he was holding.

"Ten fell from the stand," he said. "Five were killed outright; two look set to die in the next few days. The rest should make a full recovery. Of those who went to pull them out two died. One was Colm, the Retaari master, the other a trainee. Two gladiators were seriously injured, one has a broken back, he won't see the decan out and the other could lose a leg. We should know in the next few days." The Spymaster looked up from his papers. "We were very lucky. It could have been a lot worse."

Lord Menethes got up from his chair and strode to the table to pour himself another glass of wine. He turned suddenly to the Spymaster.

"Are the Gods angry with me?" he asked.

The Spymaster shook his head. He had no ready answer to give.

"At least your son is strong and healthy, considering how early he was," he said at last. "If the Gods were truly angry with you..."

Lord Menethes smiled.

"Yes," he agreed, "and born as the sun rose on a new day ... a good omen I think." He frowned for a moment at the thought of his Lady. "That gladiator."

"My lord?"

"You said they would remember nothing and yet he remembered her. He called her Sarah."

The Spymaster sighed. He too had noticed this and had been pondering the question.

"I think it may be because he is a telepath, my Lord," he said. "Look at the problems we had with the girl. It may be something similar."

Lord Menethes thought for a moment.

"There was another telepath wasn't there?"

"Yes, my Lord." The spymaster consulted his papers again. "The other one carried the Lord Ramses's youngest son to safety. The boy, Hugh, had a broken leg."

"Good.... Good. They should both be rewarded for such bravery."

The spymaster was puzzled. "And....?"

"Give them their freedom, a torc and assign them to the castle guard," Menethes instructed, "and keep your nose on them, Spymaster."

The spymaster bowed and smiled at his Lord's wisdom.

"If there is anything to be found out, my Lord," he said, "be assured I will smell it out."

"So why are we singled out for reward?" Finn asked.

They were sitting on the wooden steps that led up to the dormitories, enjoying the late afternoon sun. They had often sat there with Paul and it seemed fitting somehow to sit there on the day he and the retaari master had been cremated. Liam was nursing another bad head. But they had done Paul proud, given him a good send off the evening before.

"Ra knows," Liam growled. "Remind me never to mix sweet wine with grade ale again."

"You said that last time," Finn remarked dryly.

"Just because you never drink..." Liam rested his head in his hands and groaned again.

"I've never felt the need to make myself ill for pleasure," Finn said.

Liam looked up as Finn stretched out and lay back on the steps with his eyes closed. Liam realised he knew very little about the man who was fast becoming his closest friend in this new world. He never discussed his past and since Liam had stopped having the dreams, they no longer talked of Emma either. And yet Finn had listened patiently when he had finally told Finn everything... of meeting Osiris and everything they had done together, of Judith and the breakdown of his marriage, of Sarah and...

"Oh Ra!" he exclaimed and Finn sat up and stared at him with a frown.

"What...?"

Liam silenced his questions with a shake of his hand.

"I called her Sarah. In front of our Lord, I called her Sarah and asked if she was all right."

They both sat there in silence for a moment, deep in their own thoughts.

"Why only us?" Finn asked at last. "Why not any of the others. After what Timon said..."

"Perhaps he thinks I remember because I'm a telepath," Liam said slowly, his thoughts coming together as he spoke. "Which makes you suspect too."

"Why should being telepathic make the process break down? Besides that wouldn't explain about the others remembering," Finn pointed out.

"I don't think he knows about the others. I think Timon's Lord and the priests hushed it up," Liam said. "I get the feeling that they really don't know how the process works, I don't think they built it or the spaceship that brought us here. Either someone showed them what to do or they learnt by trial and error."

"What makes you think that?"

Liam shook his head, he wasn't sure.

"Some residual memory of Osiris's perhaps," he said. "But I know I'm right...

I am assigned to the Lady's guard, you to...?"

"The Spymaster's," Finn confirmed.

"And since the Lady is the Spymaster's daughter, both duties will keep us very much under the Spymaster's, or our Lord's, watchful eye." Liam gave Finn a long cold look. "We are going to have to be very careful." And for once Finn had no clever remark to make.

Neither of them wanted to end up as fuel for some priest-inspired bonfire.

XIII

"Liam."

Lady Sarah crossed her Parlour floor in a smooth gliding motion and took his hand. For a brief second Liam remembered Emma tripping in the long skirts, then the memory was gone. He moved away from Sarah and she frowned.

"You do remember me, don't you?" she asked.

Liam glanced quickly round the room. They appeared to be alone but someone could have been listening from the bedchamber.

"Liam?"

He turned back to Sarah.

"Yes," he said a little impatiently. "I remember, but it's best no one realises that fact."

To his horror Sarah suddenly rushed forward and hugged him.

"I'm so glad you're all right."

He pushed her away quickly, concerned that someone might come in and see them.

"I've no wish to lose my head," he explained as she looked at him with a look of reproach in her eyes. Surely she could understand that. "If someone saw us, they might think... it wouldn't look…"

She laughed at him.

"If you listen to rumours I've had affairs with half the men in this castle." She shook her head and laughed again. "Come. I want to show you something."

She opened the door to her bedchamber and chuckled at him as he hesitated. She disappeared into the room and Liam could hear her talking to someone. After a minute or so she emerged carrying a bundle of fur.

"Isn't he just perfect," she said and Liam realised the bundle of fur was in fact a baby. She brought him closer to Liam and pulled back the fur wrap. "Isn't he beautiful?" and she held him out for Liam to hold.

"I don't..."

"Go on," she said. "He won't break."

Liam sat down and took the baby carefully. He couldn't remember ever having held one before.

"What's his name?" he asked.

"Dom. I said Dominic but my Lord said that wasn't an Anarian name. So we compromised on Dom. But he's Dominic to me."

"You had a ...*teddy bear*... called that," he said

"So I did." She smiled at the happy memory. "Fancy you remembering that."

"Indeed."

So wrapped up in their reminiscences were they, neither of them had heard Lord Menethes enter his Lady's chamber. Lord Menthes looked coldly at Liam.

"Shouldn't you be training the guard or something?"

Liam stood up carefully and handed the baby back to Sarah. He bowed and walked out of the room.

As he pulled the heavy door to he heard Sarah begin to speak. There was something in her tone that made him pause and then decide to eavesdrop.

"I asked him here for a progress report on my guard," she snapped.

"Then you should have received him in the presence of others. Your maid, at the very least." The Lord's tone was cold and venomous. "If you have no thought for your own reputation, at least consider that of your son. He is my heir only because he is my son. If your behaviour casts doubt on his parentage..."

"My Lord!" Sarah's voice was as cold as the Lord's. "We both know the source of these rumours." Liam heard the rustle of her dress as she crossed the room to the Lord. "If I had had affairs with all those the gossips say, I wouldn't have time to eat... or sleep. It's getting beyond a joke." Sarah's voice took on a softer, more reasonable tone. "But you are right... these rumours do threaten... your... son,"

"We are in agreement about that." The Lord was sounding calmer now too.

"Then you will let father deal with the matter?" Sarah was more assured and confident now. "It has to be so."

There was a long silence.

"Very well." The Lord was much louder now and Liam clearly heard the heavy tread of the Lord's booted feet coming slowly towards the door. Liam walked away quickly before he was caught eavesdropping.

He hadn't understood what he had heard but ...

"She seems to be able to handle him," Liam reflected as he entered the stable yard in search of those of the Lady's guard on duty,

Lady Sarah had insisted that Liam be made Captain of her guard and the Lord had not questioned that. Liam soon found out why.

Most of those in the fifteen strong cohort were close to retirement age, the rest raw recruits. The Lord would not spare any of his elite. Those he did spare were assigned to the young Lordling's guard.

Liam, ex-gladiator, ex-slave was the fittest fighter there.

However, six of the guards were retired gladiators themselves. They were used to discipline and since nearly all of them had seen Liam fight in the recent games, they had great respect for his abilities. The recruits would soon be knocked into shape by Liam's training programme. It was the thought of the four remaining warriors that worried Liam. Seasoned warriors wouldn't take too kindly to taking orders from a puffed up gladiator. To his surprise it proved less of a problem than he had thought and they readily accepted Liam's captaincy. It didn't stop them grumbling at the training he put them through in their off duty hours nor did it stop them offering advice if they thought he was wrong, advice that Liam sometimes took.

"Why should we want to be captain?" Saul explained one day as they were eating their main evening meal in the Great Hall. "At least we get time off. You're on duty all day every day."

This was true. At least in the early decans it was. But by the time the height of summer was passed and the time of the Anant Gathering approached Liam felt confident enough in his men and their fitness to appoint Saul as his deputy and allow himself some free time.

Liam finally managed to catch up with Finn too.

"Where have you been?" he asked one evening in mid summer. They had met outside the castle walls as Finn had suggested and strolled down to a small tavern in the town.

"Here and there," Finn said in an off hand way and he gave a tired smile. Liam raised a questioning eyebrow at which Finn grimaced. "Let's just say I've met some interesting people among the low life of the port and from amongst the Tags. At least they pass as Tags," he added.

"Sounds like you're having fun," Liam observed.

Finn considered this as he sipped at his drink and nodded.

"It's... been interesting." But he would say no more on the subject. "Have you heard any mention of Emma at the castle?" Liam shook his head. It wasn't likely that their Lord would keep his mistress at the castle, right under Sarah's nose.

"So what's the truth about our Lord's broken nose?"

Liam frowned. There was no truth. Their Lord had been sporting two black eyes and a decidedly bent nose for nearly a decan but it was simply a case of their Lord having had too much to drink and falling over in his rooms. "There's nothing sinister in it," Liam reassured him.

"So are you going with our Lord to the Gathering at Toth Prime?" Finn continued but again Liam could only shake his head.

"There are no plans for Lady Sarah to go."

"Pity, they say the food at Toth Prime is excellent since the Lord took a new mistress. And it's likely to be a lively time."

"Why?" As far as Liam could see the Gathering was just an excuse for the Anant to get together, flex a few collective muscles and worry the Anarian Pharaoh a bit.

"Our Lord is going to ask for Tribute," Finn said. "From the Anant."

"So?"

"So the Anant never pay Tribute," Finn explained. "In five thousands tarns they have never paid it. It's always fallen to the Anari to pay it."
Liam was becoming confused.

"They pay their tithes. Pharaoh gets his due."

"No," Finn said patiently. "Tribute. Enormous ships filled with slaves and grain and gold. Tribute to the Gods. They sail to the Blessed Isle and that's the last anyone sees of these ships or those on board. Until the Gods demand tribute again, of course."

Liam's mind was already racing ahead. He had never heard of the Blessed Isle. But things suddenly began to slip into place.

"That's where the *spaceships* will be," he said excitedly. "I told you the Menethes couldn't have built them. If we could get on board one of the Tribute ships..."

Finn looked horrified.

"Are you mad? No one ever comes back from the Isle. Besides if..."

He broke off as a slave brought them more drinks and a bowl of spiced nuts. Liam poured himself another beaker of wine and filled Finn's too. Finn dropped his voice to a whisper.

"If our Lord did get a ship from there then it must have been with someone's permission. They're hardly likely to let us just stroll in and help ourselves." He took a handful of nuts. "The ship our Lord used must be nearer than the Isle and if anyone knows where it is hidden the Spymaster does. I intend to find out where it is."

Liam was surprised by Finn's violent outburst. It was almost as if he was afraid of something.

"Are you scared?" he laughed.

"All I know is what they say about the Isle," Finn said. "It is where the Gods live and any who anger the Gods risk death at their claws. Men hunted down like animals and torn to pieces, women dying trying to give birth to monstrous offspring…"

125

"You don't believe any of that nonsense do you?" Liam laughed again. It was ridiculous.

"I ask myself what it was exactly that you brought from ...Urth... I don't know what lives on the Blessed Isle, but I know I don't want to mess with it." He threw some money on the table. "I have a really bad feeling about this," he said, walking out.

Liam stared after him. Since Paul's death Finn had become quieter, less ready... or able... to joke about everything. In spite of his previous annoyance at their continual banter Liam missed the old Finn... and Paul... more than he cared to admit. The old Finn would have laughed at such ignorant superstitions.

But as he finished his second beaker and drank Finn's untouched wine he began to wonder again what exactly he had brought with him from Earth.

Liam was to go to the Gathering after all. He was to be part of the Lord's guard in place of Japhet who had injured his arm in practice.

"Our Lord doesn't trust you with his Lady whilst he's away," Saul said and they had all laughed.

"That's enough talk like that," Liam snapped. "There's enough stupid rumours going round without adding to them."
Saul opened his mouth to say something more but the look on his captain's face made him change his mind. He shrugged. If Liam couldn't see what was under his nose, then he wasn't going to be the one to tell him.

Liam settled the duty rota before he left. He was quite confident that Saul would manage everything in his absence but he wanted everything to run smoothly nevertheless.

"Keep an eye on Pol, he has trouble staying awake on night duty," he instructed Saul. "And young Nye is lovestruck; you won't get much work out of him unless you keep on his back." He had one last look round the training yard, trying to remember if there was anything else.

"Go on," Saul urged him. "Don't keep our Lord waiting... and Liam."

"Mmm." Liam paused at the archway through to the stable yard.

"Have fun."

"Fun?"

Saul shook his head sadly.

"It's a great opportunity to try out some different women. You do remember what they're for, don't you?" Liam chuckled.

"I'll do my best," and he marched through the archway to the waiting horses.

"Rile a few Toth if you get the chance," Saul called after him. "They're too puffed up by far."

Liam raised a hand in acknowledgement and mounted his horse. The Lord had not yet come down from his room and the horses were getting restless in their impatience.

At last he appeared and mounted his horse.

"We're not expected for seven or eight days," he shouted. "Let us ride hard and catch the Toth unexpected." He raised his hand and the band of warriors surged forward out of the castle gates into the main avenue heading north towards the Highway and the Prime gate.

Liam felt a surge of excitement flow through his body. It was a great day to be alive. The future promised so much.

They left the horses at the stables at the bottom of a small incline and walked up towards the grey building.

"First time?" the warrior standing next to him asked. Liam thought his name might have been Elon but he wasn't sure. He shook his head.

"Second," he admitted.

"Nothing to it," the warrior continued. "Just close your eyes... if you're afraid."

The warrior had a smile on his face and Liam wondered if he was the being made the point of some joke. He frowned and tried to read the man's thoughts but Elon turned away and went through the open gate into the building. All too quickly Liam found himself inside.

Elon had walked up to the columns and without any hesitation passed between them. There was a flash of creamy yellow and he disappeared.

"Go on." The warrior behind Liam was getting impatient. Liam glanced back, then took a deep breath and stepped through.

"I told him to close his eyes." An amused voice.

"He's not out cold, just a bit dizzy." A concerned voice.

"I did tell him." The amused voice again, almost laughing now.

A third voice interrupted them.

"Our Lord is anxious to be away. He won't be amused by any delay. Get him on his feet by the time all are through."

Liam opened his eyes and tried to stand up. Hands caught his arms in a tight grip and he managed to stay upright.

"The Gods don't like us seeing their domain," Elon said, a little apologetically. "Don't worry. You won't remember anything. No one ever does."

He helped Liam outside into the fresh air and almost immediately Liam began to feel better. By the time all the party were through from Prime he was almost back to normal.

"No hurt feelings," Elon said, mounting a waiting horse. "It was only meant in fun." He had obviously mistaken Liam's silence for injured pride and Liam found himself forcing a smile.

"I'm not that experienced at such travel," he explained. "It was just a little disorientating."

"You'll be doing it again in a few days time," Elon said. "From Toth Secund to Prime."

Liam kept the smile firmly fixed on his face.

"I'll remember to shut my eyes then."

Elon urged his horse forward to take his place at the Lord's side. He looked back over his shoulder at Liam.

"If there is a chance at Prime," he called. "We must share a jug of ale."

An overture of friendship.

"I'd like that," Liam said and the man inclined his head before turning back and joining the Lord's guard.

Liam mounted his own horse and positioned himself towards the back of the group. It hadn't been anything Elon had said that had caused him to open his eyes. At some point during the journey, a journey that had only taken a few seconds, he had had a conversation with an old friend. That was why he had opened his eyes. To see what the old friend had looked like. But Osiris, or whatever his name was, hadn't physically been there and Liam had suddenly found himself subject to the tallest, fastest, longest roller coaster ride ever built.

And he had never liked those, even as a boy.

He urged his horse forward still trying to remember what they had talked about but he couldn't seem to recall any words. He had sensed surprise in Osiris's thoughts though, which didn't make a lot of sense. He sighed and turned his own thoughts back to the journey and to controlling his horse.

Six days of fast travel with little time to rest and even less time to eat saw Liam at Secund Gate. This time he kept his eyes firmly closed and did not sense any presence but his own. Toth Prime was four hours ride from this Gate. The High Lord's party breasted a rise and then started down towards the city. As he reached the top of the rise Liam reined in his horse and gazed down at the impressive city.

No wonder the Toth had such a high opinion of themselves.

The city was large, even for a Prime city and its buildings were neatly laid out in straight intersecting roads. There was a large open square to the front of a hill and all roads seemed to lead there. The castle itself was built on the large flat-topped hill, enclosed with high walls, slightly to the east of the centre.

All Liam could see of the castle itself was three square sections built around courtyards surrounded by a ditch and then high walls with round towers set at intervals. Between the walls and the outer walls he could see cattle grazing and cultivated fields of different coloured crops.

The city walls were almost identical in design but higher and thicker. Red and gold metal plaques of coiled snakes decorated the Gate through which they entered the city. The High Lord's entourage rode towards the square down a wide avenue lined with tall graceful trees. People stared at the riders as they passed with undisguised interest but Liam couldn't detect any hostility.

They were all Anant after all.

A wide block paved road had been cut into the side of the hill and wound its way up towards the castle. As he rode down the dusty road that crossed the open area between the outer and inner walls Liam could see patrolling warriors walking the walls keeping a wary eye on the arriving visitors. He rode through the huge stone archway in the walls and across a wooden bridge over the wide dry ditch. Now he could see clearly that the middle section of the castle was a storey higher than the two outer sections.

Excited at the thought of finally seeing the legendary Lord of whom he had heard so much he rode across a gravel training area in front and into the main courtyard of Toth Castle.

XIV

Liam was feeling hungry. He had been running errands for the Lord all day, in spite of the heavy rain, carrying messages to the warriors garrisoned in the town and so had had no chance of food during second period. Cold and wet, it now looked as if he were set to miss his supper too.

"Great Hall's been cleared," A servant told him as he entered the castle through the main door. "You should have gone round to the kitchen," she added as she eyed the mud he had brought in. The floor rushes in the large entrance hall had obviously just been changed and she was none too pleased.

"Sorry," he mumbled, looking round quickly and wondering what was best to do. Servants were putting new light crystals in what looked like new holders on the walls. They sparkled in the light unlike some of the other holders that were hurriedly being polished by more servants. They all looked harassed as if they had been caught unawares by the Gathering. Then Liam remembered the rumours that had swept through the warrior ranks when they had arrived. The Toth's new mistress had just taken charge of castlekeeping and looked set to transform his castle as she had done his kitchen. All the Menethes were anxious to see her but so far no one had even caught a glimpse of this famous young woman who had such very high standards.

The servant, brushing up the last of the old rushes, must have taken pity on him. She told him to go through a door at the far end of the Great Hall; it would take him straight to the passageway down to the kitchens. Grateful that he wouldn't have to go back out in the rain he went through a large set of double doors on the right and entered the Great Hall.

He had expected to find it full of warriors telling stories of the wars and the deeds they had done in their time, impressing the raw recruits with tales that Liam knew would have become exaggerated and embellished with each telling and each season that had passed. But the hall was silent and empty. He looked around, impressed in spite of himself at the tall windows either side of the hall. There was a large central fireplace designed for a wood fire and several smaller braziers for fire crystals dotted around the edge of the room. The top quarter of the windows, above a walkway that ran the length of the hall on either side, had stained glass in it, depicting an array of hunting animals and this motif was echoed in the highly coloured floor tiles that were visible. The lower portion of the window had high quality glass that Liam knew was very expensive. Not for the Toth the cheaper thick glass with its many imperfections. Two rows of three stone pillars marched down the hall towards the far wall and its raised platform with the High table on it and small rooms beyond. Liam turned back slightly. Behind him, above the door he had entered, there was a minstrel's gallery that continued along the front wall. As he walked slowly across the tiled floor, uncertain which way to go, the high ceiling caused his footfalls to sound louder than he would have liked. When he had entered two servants had been gathering up the last of the old floor rushes and they now carried them out of a door at the far end of the back wall.

"That must be the door I want," Liam thought and he started across the brightly tiled floor towards it.

Halfway across he paused. The hall wasn't so empty after all. A young woman was standing in front of the great hearth gazing up at a large tapestry above it.

Curiosity made Liam stop and look at her. He had not seen her before but he knew who she must be. Expensively dressed in the best damask of blue and gold, her long blonde hair loose save for two side plaits tied back, it could only be Lord Toth's new mistress; the young woman who had transformed the Toth kitchens into something that rivalled those of the Pharaoh and now looked set to do the same with his castle.

She had her back to him and didn't appear to have noticed him. He wished she would turn round so he could get a good look at her. The Menethes had said a great deal about old men and children, particularly when there were any Toth around. But instead of becoming annoyed most of the Toth warriors had merely laughed back.

"Wait until you see her," they said. "When your Lord is as old as ours he won't be able to satisfy such a mistress. Your Lord couldn't command such a mistress now."

They seemed excessively proud of their Lord and Liam wanted to see why. But she was still lost in her own thoughts and hadn't noticed him.

He was just going to have to make her notice him.

He coughed politely.

"I'm sorry to disturb you, but I was..." he began and she turned slowly to face him. Then he stopped.

He forgot what he was going to say and just stared at her.

It couldn't be.

It was.

Emma. Taller then in his dreams and her hair was a darker shade of gold than he remembered.

But it was her.

She was staring back at him looking puzzled.

Hesitantly he took a step towards her and she dropped her gaze, a little embarrassed.

Just as Emma would have done.

He took another step towards her.

"Emma?" Another step. "Emma, it is you."

Now she looked again at him and gave her embarrassed smile.

"I think you have mistaken…"

He covered the remaining distance between them in three strides and lifted her off her feet as he held her tight and kissed her on the lips. She wriggled a little but he held her tightly.

"Emma, I never thought to find you here…" he muttered as he buried his face in her neck and kissed her throat. "How can you be here?" and he hugged her tightly to him again.

"Emma!" Lord Toth's angry voice echoed across the Great Hall and he felt her go rigid with fear.

Liam lowered her gently to the ground and turned to face the irate Lord.

"Go to your room," the Lord ordered angrily.

Emma glanced briefly at Liam then ran passed the Lord's bodyguard and out of the hall.

"Take him."

Liam found himself surrounded by three or four Toth bodyguards being hustled across the Hall. To his surprise they didn't take him out into the courtyard and beat him nor did they drag him down to the dungeons, which were probably somewhere under the castle, and throw away his key. Instead he found himself in a side room, firmly held between two warriors as they waited for the Lord to join them.

"Go".

He could hear their thoughts surprisingly clearly.

"My Lord?"

"Go. I wish to talk to him alone."

The two warriors let go of Liam and bowing their heads left the room. But not before they had given their Lord's back an extremely puzzled look.

Liam found himself being scrutinised by a pair of cold blue eyes and he stared back. He wasn't sure what was the best thing to do. Show defiance or humility. Each Lord seemed to react differently. In the end he chose a middle course.

Not too humble.

Not too defiant.

But she had been his first.

He looked at the Lord who had made Emma his mistress with undisguised interest.

Taller than Liam by an inch or two.

Broader in the shoulder.

Seasoned.

In Earth terms most would have said early fifties. But there was something about his eyes that spoke of great age.

So this was the great Lord Toth.

Poor Emma. To be mistress to such a cold hard Lord.

"You are a telepath."

A cold, unemotional voice.

Liam nodded.

"Yes, Lord."

"Strange... not weak exactly..." Lord Toth was considering him carefully as he spoke. "The others must think you weak, but you are not.... It does not matter."

Suddenly without warning Lord Toth attacked him. Liam barely had time to draw his sword before he was borne down by the Lord's incredible strength.

Surely it wasn't possible. The old man couldn't be that strong.

Liam was forced further down until he lost his balance completely and sprawled on the floor. The Lord's sword was at his throat.

Liam looked around him. Everywhere was black. As he looked down he realised he could see his hands. He held them out in front of him and slowly turned them over. They looked normal.

There was no blood.

So what had happened?

Where was he?

"Show me the girl. Show me Emma."

The voice came from behind him. He turned slowly and saw Lord Toth standing some feet away.

"I knew her ... before."

"On Urth, not here."

"Urth. You know about Urth."

"Show me."

It was a command Liam found impossible to resist. He began to remember.

The first meeting at the bus stop. She steps back and bumps into him. An accident.

A few days later she is waiting outside the office for her brother.

"If I'd known you worked with Dave I'd have been more careful." She had nice smile, a nice laugh.

"You've missed him, he left early tonight."

"I was late."

He offers to walk her home.... at least as far as the bus stop.

"I know a good restaurant, near here... If you haven't already eaten?" he asks tentatively, suddenly shy in her presence.

"I'd like that."

She blushes then smiles up at him shyly.

So different from Judith. He likes that.

A few days later she is waiting outside the office again.

 "You've just missed Dave."

 "I know. I wanted to thank you for the other night." She holds up a plastic bag. "I thought I could cook you a meal. I'm quite good. As long as you don't mind sharing the table with a lot of students."

He has a better idea. She can use his kitchen.

A little hesitantly she agrees.

She is a very good cook.

Lamb steak with stilton mash, roast vegetables, a delicious dessert of wafer thin shortbread, strawberries and cream. All the things he likes. And a bottle of his favourite Merlot.

He doesn't think to ask how a student could afford such luxuries.

Afterwards she tidies up. He stands next to her as she washes up and gently touches her hair.

He kisses her and she doesn't push him away.

 "Will you stay the night?"

 "No... I can't.... you don't understand."

He is puzzled. They were getting on so well. It felt so right.

She blushes and stares at the floor.

 "I shouldn't ..."

He picks her up in his arms.

 "I won't hurt you. I would never hurt you."

He carries her into the bedroom.

 "You weren't married... how can this be right?"

The Lord's angry tone resounded in Liam's head. It echoed in his mind and became a crescendo. It felt as the floor was tipping, the walls crashing down on him. Liam swayed and cried out.

And it was gone.

He was standing between the two warriors staring into the Lord's angry blue eyes.

"Take him to the kitchen and feed him. I will inform the High Lord I do not want this.... this gladiator running loose in my castle." The Lord sat down heavily in a chair as Liam was roughly pushed from the room and across the hall towards the kitchen.

As he sat in the kitchen waiting for his food he found he was shaking, but not from fear. He didn't understand what had happened.

"It's called a Reckoning," Finn informed him the next day. "Master Telepaths do it to get at the truth. Get inside your head somehow. You're lucky you didn't know and try to resist. It has been known to break a man's mind"

"He almost did that, all right." Liam was still shaken by the experience. "So I must kick my heels in the town for the rest of the Gathering because the great Lord Toth doesn't like...." He stopped suddenly. He hadn't told Finn about Emma being the mistress they had heard so much about, just that he had seen her. "... my face," he finished lamely. He sighed apologetically. "But it was Emma, I'm sure of it."

"You should make the most of it," Finn said, thinking deeply. "Our Lord's paying to have us to stay in an inn and the food's good. What are you complaining for?" He looked serious for a moment. "How can it be Emma, Liam?" he asked. "I thought you said she was meant for the Menethes..."

"It was her." Liam was certain. She looked the same, talked the same, smelt the same. "She even blushed the same," he said. He remembered something else, something important. "He mentioned Urth."
Finn didn't seem surprised.

"Lord Darg sold Timon and the others on... to Lord Toth. He must have said something." Finn sighed with annoyance. "I haven't been able to find out where they are. We're getting more and more spread out."

Liam agreed. That had been worrying him too and now there was Emma to include in their plans. If they ever found a way to escape from Anaria it was going to prove very difficult to find everyone.

"What do you think she was doing in the castle?" Finn's sudden jump in thinking startled Liam and he had to think fast.

"I think she was working in the kitchens or something," he said. "She was supervising changing the floor rushes."

"In the kitchens. She'd like that," Finn said. "But she didn't remember you?"

Liam shook his head.

"I have to report to the spymaster at midday," Finn said. "Maybe I can get to the kitchens. Maybe she will remember me."

But when they next met Finn could only report that although he had hung around the kitchens as much as he could over the remaining five days of the Gathering he hadn't seen Emma once.

On the day of their departure, as they mounted their horses before dawn, waiting for their Lord to begin the journey home Liam wondered if he should have told Finn about Emma.

XV

The Menethes were the last to leave. Liam once again sat on his horse impatiently awaiting his Lord to emerge from the castle. It was still an hour before dawn and the only light was from crystal lamps on the walls surrounding the courtyard. One of Anaria's moons was still in the sky but a blanket of cloud obscured it. Liam felt cold and damp. He was anxious to be off. The Lord planned to have firstmeal in Toth Secund and Liam could feel his stomach complaining at the delay.

The heavy wooden doors studded with the Toth symbol of the twisted snakes opened and Lord Menethes emerged closely followed by his Spymaster. Both men were wrapped in thick cloaks against the early morning cold. That period's duty elite surrounded them as they walked down the steps to their waiting horses. The Lord was clearly angry. His mouth was a thin pursed line and even in the gloom Liam could see the telltale twitch of a muscle in his cheek. It was a sign Liam had come to know well.

"He insults us." Menethes snapped. He was making no attempt to lower his voice and Liam could hear every word clearly. He had no doubt that anyone inside the castle would be able to hear as well.

"He's an old man," one of the elite pointed out. "He can't be expected to…"

"He was out for the Ramses who left earlier than this." The spymaster said. "No, he means to insult us."

Lord Menthes pulled on his riding gloves and mounted his horse. The spymaster and the elite did the same. The Lord raised his hand in the now familiar gesture and Liam tensed up as he prepared to urge his horse forward.

There was a moment of confusion as the Lord lowered his arm and walked his horse forward slightly towards the steps and the main door. Liam strained in the gloom to see what was going on.

"He insults us further by sending out his whore," someone close to the Lord said and a murmur of disapproval went up.
Emma.

Liam looked round for Finn. He should have been among the Spymaster's men at the back. As his eyes adjusted to the gloom he saw Finn standing up in the saddle trying to see. Liam turned back in time to hear the Lord order silence.
It was Emma.

She walked slowly down the steps and stood on the bottom step. She looked nervous. The Lord reined in his horse and it snorted and tossed its head.

"It too wants to be off." Liam thought. He wondered if Emma was afraid of the horse because she stepped back up several of the steps at its sudden movement. For a moment the Lord just looked at her and then to Liam's surprise he dismounted and went over to her. They were speaking too quietly for Liam to hear what was being said. For the first time he wished he were a better telepath. Those at the front who could hear what was going on would surely be telling the rest.

Lord Menethes called to the Spymaster to join him and the three of them walked together across the courtyard and up steps to the battlements where there was no danger of their conversation being overheard. Liam sat on his horse watching them. Emma seemed to be doing most of the talking. From the wild movement of her hands it looked as if she was trying to persuade the Lord to do something. Something that he was obviously reluctant to do.

"What do you make of all this?" Liam's neighbour was watching the discussions with undisguised interest.

"I have no idea." Liam admitted. "You'd have thought there was nothing left to talk about after the last few days."

After a while the order came through to dismount.

"You can take the horses back through to the stable yard." ordered Manon, the Elite captain.

Liam felt quite pleased with himself. He had heard that.

After handing his horse over to one of the stable lads Liam looked round for Finn but there were too many warriors milling around for him to see. Most of the Menethes seemed to be heading for the kitchen in search of food so he followed them. He had no doubt Finn would do the same and he would be easier to find once everyone was occupied with eating.

There was quite a crowd of hungry warriors crowding round the doors to the kitchen and Liam almost decided to give up any thought of food. It was going to take a long time to get any. Then he heard a familiar voice raised above the noise of the clamouring warriors.

"You will get out of my kitchen now," the voice demanded. "If you want food then you must form a quiet orderly line. Otherwise I will have these doors shut and you can all go hungry."

To Liam's surprise Emma was quickly obeyed. Hunger must have prevailed over Elite pride, Liam decided. But she was right. Liam quickly found himself in a fast moving line and soon had a bowl of steaming porridge. He joined a second line as he stood eating and by the time he had finished the porridge he was being offered a freshly baked roll with butter and either a slice of goat's cheese or a dark spread of some kind.

"What is it?" he asked suspiciously.

"Blackberry preserve." the old woman handing out the rolls told him. "Our Lord likes it on his rolls in the morning." Her tone implied she thought it too good for the likes of him. But she gave him a generous serving when he decided to try it. "If you want a private place to eat it, the woman added quietly, "you could go through to the gardens on the other side of the stable yard."

Liam was puzzled. Why had she suggested that? Unless... Liam thanked her for the roll and looked around for Finn. He was just finishing his own roll and cheese and Liam concentrated on him.

Concentrate... ... Only on him.

Concentrate hard.

Follow me.

Finn turned his head, a look of surprise on his face. When he saw Liam he raised his eyebrows. Liam nodded and walked through the archway into the main courtyard and then through to the stable yard. At the far end there were a pair of heavy wooden doors, which were clearly locked, but a smaller door inset into one of these was open and Liam walked through it into the training area of Castle Toth.

A large gravel drive swept away to the left and joined the main road down to the outer walls and on to the town below. A little way to Liam's right there was a stone wall with a wooden door at the end. It only extended about a quarter of the distance down the side of the training area. The rest of the distance down to the inner castle wall was separated off by shoulder high bushes with paths leading in at intervals.

Through one of these openings Liam could see trees and flower beds...The formal gardens of Castle

Toth that were so famous. Although other Anant Lords had copied the idea none had managed to produce anything so large or beautiful as the Toth.

Liam was about to walk down to the nearest opening and get a better look when the door in the wall opened and Emma appeared. She smiled when she saw him waiting and he quickly walked over to her.

"That's a nice welcome," he said softly and she blushed.

"I thought my Lord had had you dealt with," she explained. "I am merely glad to see you are still alive," and she went an even deeper shade of pink.
Just as Emma would have done.

"You haven't changed," he said laughing at her. "Whatever they've done to you, you're still the same," and he looked around to see if he could see Finn yet.
She walked down to the opening in the hedge and gazed through at the gardens. Liam stood just behind but his gaze was solely on Emma.

"My Lord's mother had these gardens designed," she told him. "When she was first married. She was a Ramses and her father was High Lord. When he died Lord Toth was made High Lord and he felt powerful enough to put her aside and make his mistress his First Lady."

"What happened?" Liam asked, wondering why she was telling him this. There were other far more important things to talk of.

"The other Lords protested at the insult to the Ramses and they appealed to Pharaoh. He outlawed the practice of taking second wives if first was barren and, since my Lord's mother had done no wrong, she became Lady Toth again."

"So the story has a happy ending."

She indicated that they should walk back to the little door in the wall and for a few seconds they walked in silence. As she pushed open the door she stopped and turned staring up at Liam.

"Do you know me?" she asked, throwing him into some confusion.

Liam nodded.

"Very well indeed."

She looked up at him with a furious scowl on her face and he stepped back suddenly afraid. He hadn't meant it to come out like that. That wasn't what he had meant to say. The implication of his words had clearly angered her and he immediately regretted his impulsive remark.

She reached up and touched his face gently.

His head was full of images of her on Earth.

Their nights together.

"These thoughts are shameful, monstrous."

Those were not his thoughts.

He realised what she was doing.

But even as he sensed her presence she was gone.

"That is not me," she said angrily, turning to go through the door she had emerged from earlier. "You do not know me."

He quickly took hold of her arm to stop her walking away.

"What they did to us made us forget. It takes a while to remember," he said. "I know you don't remember me. But you are my Emma."

He was certain of it now. Who else but Emma could have read his mind like that? There were no female telepaths on Anaria. It ran through the male line.

"And I can prove it," he said.

"How?"

He looked back towards the stable yard and nodded towards Finn who had just come through into the training yard and was looking round for Liam.

"Finn...Here," Liam called out and Finn turned round and began to walk towards him. His face broke into a grin as he neared them.

"Emma."

She turned angrily to Liam.

"This is your proof," she said contemptuously. "You asked him to say that. You planned it..."

"Enter his mind," Liam said.

"And what will I find there?" she demanded angrily. "More thoughts like yours of lying with a girl who is clearly not me."

Finn looked shocked.

"I'm your brother.... I'm David."

Emma began to shake her head. She was clearly having trouble believing him.

"I.... I don't remember you," she said frowning up at Finn. "I'm sorry... but..."

She sighed and shook her head again. She looked across at Liam and then back to Finn. "I don't remember either of you," she said, a look of deep sorrow crossing her face. "I wish I did. I feel quite lonely at times."

She held out her hand to the side indicating they should enter into the area enclosed by the walls. Another garden, but much smaller than the formal gardens beyond the hedge. She led them to an area of grass where a blanket had been spread out with a covered tray in the middle.

"I thought you might still be hungry," she said, removing the cloth to reveal more rolls and a bowl of preserve.

"Liam is always hungry." Finn laughed as Liam sat down and immediately took a roll and broke it open.

"Finn," she said suddenly, a look of pleased surprise crossing her face because she had remembered his name. "I may not remember but you seem very familiar."

Finn took hold of her hand. He began to tell her of their life on Earth, about their parents, their house where they had lived and finally about a dog she had had.

"He was the smallest thing I'd ever seen," Finn laughed. "But you insisted on calling him Goliath. Said he needed a big name to live up to, otherwise he'd always be small."

Emma laughed too. "And what happened to him?"

The smile vanished from Finn's face as if someone had pressed a switch and suddenly turned it off.

"He died."

She stared up at Finn and for several minutes neither of them said anything. Liam wondered if they were somehow in telepathic communication or was she reading his thoughts. Liam felt vaguely uneasy and he wasn't sure why.

Emma was the first to break the silence as she stood up and took hold of Finn's hand.

"I feel I should know you," she admitted. "I don't remember you but you do seem.... familiar," and she suddenly slipped her arms round him and hugged him.

Finn lifted her off her feet. It was the happiest Liam had seen him in a long time.

"I've been looking everywhere for you. But in the Menethes lands…" he said putting her back on the ground. "How did you get here? When?"

Still holding hands they sat down near Liam, totally oblivious to his presence.

Finn had a lot of questions and Liam could see she was embarrassed to answer some of them.

"At least she has some shame," he thought. Then he mentally kicked himself.

It wasn't her fault.

The Lord was to blame.

She explained as best she could that she had no memory of how she got to be on Anaria. Her earliest memory seemed to be of Menethes port and the spymaster trying to help her.

"It was terrible," she said. "There was so much pain. I couldn't keep them out and the spymaster couldn't do anything. In the end Lord Toth put blocks in place for me and so I came here with him."

"So what do you do at Toth Prime?" Finn asked at last.

Emma glanced at Liam sitting across from her. He shook his head. He hadn't said anything.

"I... do this and that," she said looking at the ground. "I have transformed the kitchens. The food is at least edible now."

Finn laughed. "Yes. I can imagine you doing that."

"And I am trying to find someone to mend the tapestries. It's not easy. The Ladies complained so about the cold."

She chatted on about the problems she was encountering and Liam was amazed how cleverly she answered Finn's questions without telling him the truth.

Then he tensed up at something she said. For his mind had wandered a little from her inconsequential chatter and he almost missed it.

"If you remember ...*Urth*..." She had lowered her voice. "Then do you know a blacksmith, Timon by name? He remembers that place."

"Timon." Liam leaned forward eagerly. "Do you know where he is?"

"Of course." she said. "He's our blacksmith."

"Of course he's their blacksmith," Finn repeated and Liam laughed.

"So near and we didn't know," he said. "Can you get a message to him?"
She nodded.

"Tell him..." Finn thought carefully. "Tell him we've had no luck so far but we're still hopeful."
She frowned at his comment, then looked quickly from Finn to Liam and back.

"He wanted to know about the accident at the games," she said. "But everyone I asked didn't know..."

"Tell him Paul was killed," Finn said.

"Paul." She reached out to touch his arm. "He was a friend of yours?"
Finn nodded.

"I'm sorry," she said softly. She suddenly twisted round and looked up at a first floor window. Liam followed her gaze but could see nothing there. "Your Lord is preparing to leave." She said. "I'll take you back through the castle, it's quicker."

They stood up and followed her through a heavy metal door into a large room. It clearly served as both sitting room and bedroom, for there were two comfortable chairs and a table as well as a large bed. Everything in the room, even the walls seemed to be coloured a shade of blue.
Emma chuckled.

"That's why it's called the Blue Room," she said. Then she stopped suddenly and turned to Liam. "You asked if there was a happy ending. There wasn't. The Lady finally gave birth to a son, my Lord, but she never really recovered and died when he was quite young." She opened the door into a dark corridor and led them down it. Another door at the end of the corridor led through to the main entrance hall. "Everyone in the castle believes the Blue Room to be haunted." Emma said. "But I've never seen a ghost."

As they neared the great door Lord Menethes and his spymaster appeared on the stairs closely followed by Lord Toth and his spymaster. Liam and Finn bowed their heads and Emma gave an elegant curtsey.

Lord Menethes said something and laughed. Lord Toth just looked annoyed.

"Things must have gone well," Finn muttered. "I'd like to know what was discussed."

"I have to go," Emma said and she walked across towards Lord Toth. Liam watched as she gave another most elegant curtsey to his Lord

She stayed down until he had passed and Lord Toth took hold of Emma's hand and helped her to her feet.

"He's laying claim to her," Liam thought. "Making sure I know she's his," and he felt a sudden surge of anger. A servant opened the door and the two Lords went out into the sunshine. Lord Menethes' horse was waiting for him.

"I did you a good deed the day I sold her to you," the Lord said as he mounted his horse. "She will keep Osiris from your gate if anything can."

"And I thought he had sent her to plague me with her ceaseless questions," Lord Toth replied, bowing to the High Lord.

Liam hurried away to find his own horse. He was livid with anger and dislike. He had an intense desire to strike the arrogant Lord.

He didn't appreciate Emma.

He didn't deserve Emma.

How could she bear lying with an old man like that?

If it took him the rest of his life he was going to save Emma from that Lord's clutches.

"I will take her from him," he vowed.

The Menethes warriors mounted and the Lord signalled the advance. Lord Toth was still possessively holding Emma's hand. Liam glanced down at her as he passed and she gave a slight smile of recognition. She dared do no more.

Liam looked round for Finn but there was no sign of him. Annoyed, Liam was forced to keep his thoughts to himself. He badly wanted to talk to Finn but it seemed there would be no opportunity until they halted for the night.

They were well beyond the Secund Gate, almost within sight of the Great Forest before the Lord finally decided to make camp. By the time Liam had settled his horse for the night and collected his meagre ration of the food they were carrying he felt tired and irritable. But he still needed to talk to Finn about Emma. He had forgotten to ask her about the name Sean, which kept appearing in his dreams. He knew that Finn, now he had found Emma, would stay in contact so he forced himself to walk in search of his friend instead of stretching out by the fire.

Liam noticed the spymaster watching him as he searched. One of the Spymaster's guards came over to him.

"If you're looking for your friend," the warrior said, "he's gone to the Toth."

"Why?"

The man shrugged.

"Our Lord ordered it so." and Liam had to be content with that.

He suddenly felt very alone. First Paul and now Finn.

At least he had his thoughts of Emma. They couldn't take those away.

Nor his hopes.

XVI

Liam unsaddled his horse and, leaving a simple halter on, let it loose in one of the stable fields. Carrying the harness on his back he trudged to the stable yard and left it for the slaves to clean and store away. He was glad he didn't have the task. It had been an exhausting journey back to Menethes Prime and the Lord had not spared either horses or men in his haste to return. Neither Lord nor Spymaster had been forthcoming on their talk with the Toth Lord. And although all the warriors had discussed what had happened at great length, it had been speculation not fact that had fuelled their discussions.

Tiredly Liam walked the busy streets towards the Castle. It was market day and the stallholders were winding down their business as darkness fell. The nights were drawing in.

"It'll soon be winter again," Liam thought. The second he had spent on this world and he wondered if all the winters were as bad as his first. "It will be pretty bad if the summer was anything to go by," he muttered. Yet everyone was saying what a good summer it had been.

Liam entered the castle through a side gate. Unlike Toth Prime the Menethes castle was not set in extensive gardens and although Lady Sarah had a small walled garden where she liked to sit, most of the open space in the interior was taken up with busy courtyards and training areas. The gate Liam had entered by led into what was called the kitchen courtyard, a small area between two massive stone walkways with arched openings either side to other larger courtyards. He made his way to the large kitchen in search of the Steward. He considered seeing if he could persuade the cooks there to let him have an early supper. He had quickly learnt that it paid to make friends in the kitchen. No... it would have to wait. He had duties to perform first.

He found the Steward at his desk under the stairs at the back of the kitchen and delivered his messages. The Lord was arriving later that evening; he was only about two hours behind Liam.

"And they'll be hungry," Liam finished. "Our Lord has been riding us hard."

"We'll be ready," the steward said. "Even though he wasn't expected for a day or two."

Liam had other messages to deliver so asked the steward where their Lady was to be found, gave a slight nod of the head and went up the stairs and on into the main body of the castle. He made his way by the backstairs towards the Lady's Chamber. He had messages for Sarah from her Lord.

Saul was walking the corridors on duty. He had his back to Liam and didn't see him.

"This is a good guard," Liam said. "Anyone could sneak up on you and why only one of you? Things have obviously become lax in my absence."
Saul stared at him, a look of horrified surprise on his face that puzzled Liam.

"It's all right," Liam said. "I'm sure there's no harm done," and he knocked on the Lady's door and waited for permission to enter. There was no reply and Liam wondered if the Steward had been wrong and Sarah was somewhere else in the castle. But if that was the case why was Saul on duty? He looked again at Saul, a growing suspicion gnawing away at his innards. He opened the door to the Lady's rooms and entered.

"Liam... don't," he heard Saul begin to say.

There was no one in the outer sitting room. But there was the sound of laughter coming from the inner bedroom and Liam smiled. His worries were unfounded.

Sarah was playing with her son. It was probably his bedtime.

He walked slowly towards the bedroom door. It was slightly open, he could hear Sarah's voice and he raised his hand to knock on the door. Then he stopped, his hand poised to in mid air.

There was a man's voice also.

It could not be that of Lord Menethes. Nor could it be the spymaster. And there was no one else that Sarah could innocently have taken into her inner chamber. No uncle, no brother, no one.

He pushed the door further open.

Sarah was lying naked on the bed, her back to Liam. Leaning over her, kissing her shoulder was one of Sarah's guards.

One of his men.

One of his men was...

Liam rushed round the bed in a blind fury.

So angry was he that he couldn't remember the man's name.

Couldn't speak.

Sarah saw him first and gave a scream. The man half turned but had no time to do anything before Liam had dragged him from the bed and pushed him up against the wall.

He wanted to kill.

Were all women whores?

"Get out," he said. "Get out before I kill you."

"You'll have to let go of him first," Sarah said. Now she had realised who had discovered them, she was no longer afraid.

He dropped the naked warrior and turned to face her. Something in his face must have worried her for she quickly pulled the sheet up to cover her nakedness. Liam heard rather than saw her lover pick up his discarded clothes and hurry from the room. Sarah watched him leave calmly.

"There's really no need for this," she told Liam. "It's not your concern."

"It's my job to protect you." He spat the words out, barely in control of himself. "If that means from yourself, then so be it."

She got up from the bed, pulling the sheet round herself.

"Are you going to leave?" she said coldly, "or just stand there and watch me get dressed?"

"Our Lord is a bare two hours behind me," he said. "He may be here very soon."

There was a flash of something in her eyes.

Fear?

"Galen doesn't care," she said bitterly.

"He's your Lord!" He couldn't keep the disgust from his voice and she flushed at his obvious loathing of her.

"Liam, I..."

"Just get dressed," he said walking out of the door.

Saul was still standing outside of the main door, but the look on Liam's face was enough. He wisely said nothing and continued his watch.

Liam was sober.

Stone cold sober.

He shouldn't have been.

Not the amount he had drunk.

Not on an empty stomach.

But he was.

"Where are you when I need you?" he said aloud in the sanctuary of his small room above the stables, thinking of Finn.

He needed to talk to someone.

About Emma.

About Sarah.

He gave a wry smile.

Perhaps he should talk to the Lord Menethes.

They could compare notes.

He heard voices on the stairs and in the corridor outside. It was time to change the watch and the watch captains were getting ready. There was a soft tap on his door and someone opened it without waiting for him to respond. Liam glanced up, a woman with a plate of food. She put the plate on the table in front of him and then sat down on his bed. There was only one chair in the room and Liam was sitting on that.

"Should you be in here?" he asked his voice sounding harsh in his ears. "This must be a first. You betraying a husband with me."

"You're drunk," Judith said in disgust.

"I wish."

"You have to understand…"

"Understand what? She was lonely, he was away a lot." Liam leant back in his chair and stared straight at Judith. "I seem to have heard that somewhere before."

"You have no idea what is going on here," she said angrily but Liam was in no mood to listen to any excuses she might dream up. He had heard them all before.

"I know exactly what is going on," he snapped. He suddenly felt very old and very tired. Life was hard enough without complications like this.

Dangerous complications that could cost a man his life.

And a Lady hers if the Lord so chose.

"She's a *bloody* fool," he said, but he was too tired to put much venom in his voice.

"No, you are," Judith snapped. "It would be best if you said nothing to anyone though. You really don't understand what is going on and Sarah hates upsetting you, she's very fond of you. Don't be too angry with her."

He buried his face in his hands, pushing his long hair back with his fingers as he looked up at her.

"I found Emma," he said simply.

"Emma?" Judith frowned. "Oh, the girl on Urth."

"She's here. She's mistress to the Toth."

"I'm sorry." She didn't sound particularly sorry. Liam raised his head from his hands. He wanted Judith to go so he could finish the task that he had set himself for that evening.

Getting drunk... Forgetting women.

But there was something that was puzzling him and now was probably the only opportunity he would have to get some answers.

"Tell me something. How long have you been married to the Spymaster?"

Judith looked puzzled for a moment then she realised the purpose of his question.

"Liam…"

"How long?"

"About twenty five tarns."

Twenty five tarns… that was about seventy five *years*.

And he could only remember three or four at best.

Judith was becoming impatient. "I came here to talk about Sarah," she said. "She's very upset that you're angry with her."

"What does she expect?" He was becoming angry again.

She opened the door to his room, stopping on the threshold to look back in at him.

"It would be better for all concerned if you said nothing about what you saw. You have no idea what is going on and could make things worse. Make that clear to your guard also."

She left, gently shutting the door behind her leaving Liam to stare at the rough wood.

He really didn't care just then what Sarah did. If she wanted to make a mess of her life then good luck to her.

"I'm sorry," he whispered. "I'm so sorry. I promised to protect you and I couldn't."

He pushed away the plate of food in front of him and stretched out on the bed. Images of Emma kept floating into his mind. Images from Urth. When he finally fell asleep he dreamt of Emma.

But she wasn't on the strange bed with him.

The man with her was an old Lord.

And she wasn't smiling as she had been in his earlier dreams.

She was afraid, ashamed, in pain.

He woke up, again calling her name.

Liam watched Sarah like a hawk. It soon became obvious to him from the rumours circulating that Pol hadn't been the first, in spite of Sarah's protestations, but as far as Liam was concerned he was going to be the last. It didn't take the rest of the Lady's guard long to find out how best to please their Captain and so every time Sarah turned round there was Liam or one of his men watching her. They would interrupt her if Liam thought a conversation with anyone unsuitable had gone on for too long, they would accompany her on her walks round the castle walls and they would be there when she played with her son in the walled garden.

"I don't like them," Sarah complained to her father. "Get rid of them, all of them."

"But you wanted the gladiator promoted," Gerran pointed out. "He's proved good at his job, he is happy with the men. They stay."

And the Spymaster went back to his duties with a broad smile on his face. In keeping his nose on one problem he had inadvertently solved another. He was very pleased.

The last of summer faded in the memory and winter set in. The castle shivered for a few decans and then the Lord decided to move to Menethes Secund. Being so much further south it should be warmer. It also put more distance between the High Lord and Pharaoh. Once the snows arrived most of the north roads would be virtually impassable and no one in their right mind would think of crossing even a narrow seaway like that between Menethes and Kush during the winter. The storms were too fierce and unpredictable for it to be a viable option.

The Lord had left his decision until it was almost too late for his party to use the Highway. Liam discovered that for some reason during the winter months the Highways did not work. It meant that once the season was underway and the snows came they would be virtually cut off. But it also meant that any decision Lord Menethes had to make about Tribute could be pondered and discussed at length during the long winter season before a decision had to be finally arrived at and Pharaoh informed.

Liam shivered his way through the season. Secund was only marginally warmer than Prime had been. Originally built when the climate was much warmer, the long open verandas of the palace at Secund channelled the wind into a howling gale that penetrated every crack in the wooden shutters. Even the heavy woollen tapestries couldn't keep it out.

"It would be impossible to defend this place," Liam observed to Saul. "The walls aren't high enough or strong enough. There is nowhere to make a stand."
He looked around the open plan design of the palace with a critical eye.

"It was built in more peaceful times," Saul said. "I shall be glad when we're back in Prime."

Although the snows had arrived in the north making Prime a great deal colder than when they had left, Liam had to agree with him. The times were too unsettled for Liam to feel safe at Secund, even in the depths of an impassable winter. There were problems with Nye too. The young lad had formed a strong attachment to a maid in the castle and was loafing around in a fit of despair because she had stayed at Prime whilst he had had to come south.

"If she's the one for you," Liam told him, "she'll be waiting for you when you get back."
Not that that had cheered Nye up much and a lot of his duties had to be done by the rest of the guard with an increase in the amount of grumbling as a result.
It was going to be a long winter.
There were, however, two bright spots to look forward to.

Being so much further south meant that the sowing season started so much earlier and everyone at the palace would be able to enjoy a few pleasant days of sunshine before they headed back north. The second event was more personal to Liam. Lord Menethes announced when they would be going back to Prime and mentioned that he had arranged to meet the Toth four decans into the start of the new season. This meant Liam might be able to catch up with Finn who had been employed by the Toth as an attendant to the bedchamber. Lord Toth would therefore be sure to bring Finn with him or so Liam hoped.

But more importantly the Lord must surely have Emma with him too. The visit was supposed to last three or four decans. With travelling time of at least six days the Toth surely wouldn't want to be parted from his mistress for so long and the meeting could last longer if things went well. Liam was sure he would be able to meet with Emma again.

And this time no dour old Lord was going to stop him.

"Gerran is very pleased with you," Judith said. Their paths had crossed as Liam had stood on the walls of Secund Palace looking out over the town. He had a beaker of hot spiced ale cupped in his hand that someone had brought all the sentries on duty. Liam often thought it was the only thing that stopped him from freezing.

He looked at Judith and shivered. She seemed impervious to the cold but then it was her choice to be out in it. She didn't have several more hours on duty, checking on the guard.

"You look well," he said at last. Life with the Spymaster seemed to have agreed with her. There was certainly no hint of scandal about the Spymaster's wife. She seemed perfectly faithful to him. Liam felt vaguely annoyed by this. She hadn't been that faithful when she had been married to Liam.

"Thank you," she said, a satisfied smile on her face. She pulled her expensive fur lined cloak a little tighter around her and stamped elegantly booted feet. "Why are you out here? This isn't your job."

"I'm filling in for a friend," Liam told her. "A lot of our Lord's guard have gone down with this cold that's doing the rounds. Why are you out here? I thought you'd stay snug inside on a day like this."

"I like to walk on a crisp day like this. It reminds me of home." She smiled at him. "And I saw you from the doorway. I thought you might like to know how pleased Gerran is with you. About Sarah I mean."

"He should be," Liam chuckled. "Sarah is luckier than most. It should be a Spymaster's job to inform his Lord of such things." He couldn't help the touch of bitterness that had crept into his voice. Who had Emma had to protect her?

Judith gave a sigh of exasperation. She picked up the folds of her cloak in one hand and began to walk back towards the steps down to the courtyard. After a few feet she turned round and stared back at him.

"Believe it or not," she said defensively. "I did try to warn her, stop her. But she wouldn't listen… and there are other things going on…"

"So you keep saying," Liam snapped and he turned away to look out over the town. But he turned back to watch her walk back across the courtyard and into the palace. She posed an elegant picture in her expensive clothes. But he felt nothing for her. He had great difficulty in remembering ever feeling anything for her. But then she had been his 'other self's' choice really. Emma had been his. He started to walk back towards the palace himself. He needed another beaker of something hot to keep his mind from freezing up. A sudden thought occurred to him and he hurried after Judith and caught up with her just inside the palace.

"Judith," he said catching hold of her arm to stop her. "Who is Sean?"

"Sean! What made you think of him after all this time?" A soft look came over her face as she remembered. "That was a long time ago. He was your brother."

"My brother!" Liam couldn't remember having a brother at all. "Was? You said was."

"He died... about four tarns before we were brought here. Sarah was about three. You and I had just started going out together." She paused, frowning as she concentrated on bringing long forgotten memories to the surface. "He was killed somewhere in the... um... *Middle east... a car bomb...*" She paused again, making sure he had understood the Urth words. "Do you remember his funeral and ..."

"Cassie."

Judith nodded. "She was his betrothed but he had broken it off when he joined up. She came to the funeral very upset and ..."

"Blamed me for Sean's death."

Judith laid a hand on his arm. "It wasn't your fault. He was very determined to become... a warrior... like his older brother."

"What happened to Cassie?" Liam asked although he was beginning to remember.

"It was very sad..." Judith said. "She threw herself in the river that night. No one realised how upset she was... well she had lost her parents only a short time before and..."

"Does *Truth and dare* mean anything to you?"

Judith shook her head. "It's a party game... a silly children's game." She looked round impatiently. "I have to go," and she hurried away towards her rooms before Liam could ask any more questions, leaving him deep in thought. At least now most of his dreams were beginning to make sense.

After downing another beaker of spiced ale, a captain's privilege that Liam whole-heartedly agreed with, he went to report to the Lord's captain, who was sharing a room with two other elite. All three of them were laid up with a bad cold. Liam didn't stay too long; he didn't want to catch anything. His gladiator training had given him a healthy respect for illness. Survival seemed more a matter of not getting sick than any consequence of Anant medicine.

After giving a brief report and promising to do another check before the next change of guard he headed towards the dormitory where most of the guard slept. Liam had a small curtained off section at the far end, another privilege of rank. There were other similar cubicles for other officers and there was also a small sitting area with a table where Liam and the others could eat their meals, away from the common warriors, with its own crystal fire. He needed to think and it was easier to do this where it was warm. Besides it was nearly midday so there would be food waiting. He grinned to himself in expectation.

Liam entered the dormitory and made his way past his bed. There was some food keeping warm by the fire and he helped himself to a plateful of a grey coloured stew.

At least it was hot and filled the stomach.

"Our Lord should have kept Emma," Liam thought. "She could have transformed our kitchens instead."

He stretched out on his bed to eat and began to think of Emma. He had done a lot of that lately. It helped him to get through the long days.

But now he had other memories to think about too.

XVII

The day before they left Secund Lord Menethes visited the local temple, sacred to Ammon, to offer gifts for a safe journey. Liam accompanied Lady Sarah and her mother and watched them as they made their devotions. Both Sarah and her mother put a gold coin on the platter on the stone alter in the middle of the large vestibule.

To his surprise he saw Saul enter and drop a few coins onto the plate. Saul noticed Liam waiting patiently at the back for the ladies and came over.

"You are not making an offering?" he asked.

Liam shook his head.

"This is not my God," he said.

Saul nodded. He understood.

"You still worship the Pirate God," he said. "Senu is my personal God but I always think it is wise to keep on the side of the powerful ones. Don't you?"

Liam grunted. He hadn't been particularly religious on Earth and had considered the whole idea of it a little archaic and embarrassing. This was only the third time he had been inside a temple since arriving over a tarn before. Saul inclined his head and left Liam to his thoughts.

As he waited for the Priest to finish his mutterings, Liam looked round the temple with indifference. This was not a temple such as that found at Prime. It was much smaller and the central altar was roughly hewn out of grey stone. The door in the far wall behind the altar was a light colour, not darkened with age as it was at Prime but it too was studded with metal discs stamped with the figure of the Horse.

He sighed quietly with boredom. He doubted the Gods ever saw any of the offerings. They probably went straight into the priests' pockets. But then he began to wonder about Osiris, if that was his name.

Could the Gods actually exist?

Be some form of life form that existed purely as energy?

It was an intriguing thought.

It was a chilling thought.

Once back in Prime, Liam quickly settled into his old routine. It was, he often thought, extremely boring.

"I would be doing more exciting work on Earth," he thought, walking the castle battlements. It was something he had started doing quite recently for exercise, much to the amusement of the other warriors. But there was only so much training one could do, only so much checking on the watches and guards on duty. He even did duty for other captains on occasion to try and relieve his boredom.

The festival of Tiamat came and went. Liam accompanied Elon and the other captains with whom he had become friendly but none were lucky. No one received the Gift. Some of the more superstitious warriors took this as a bad omen particularly when they coupled it with their Lord's fall in the previous season and his resultant broken nose. But since Tiamat was only a minor deity, most didn't worry too much about it.

When the time came for the Toth's visit Liam was surprised to see the Lord Menethes rode out to meet him at the Gate.

"Relations have certainly improved." Liam remarked to Saul as they watched the guard ride out, from the battlements high above the main gate.

"Does this mean we have to be polite," Saul asked him. "No more remarks about pretty young women and old men?"

Liam glared at him and Saul retreated into silence, puzzled by his captain's attitude. But then, he had been in a strange mood since the Gathering over a season before.

Saul went in search of food for a mid-day break expecting Liam to do the same. But for once Liam was in no mood for food. He wanted to see who came with Lord Toth. He didn't want to miss anything.... Or anyone.

By the time Lord Menethes arrived back at the castle some hours later, Liam was tired and irritable. His mood wasn't improved when he saw that, in spite of the large party that had accompanied the Toth, Emma wasn't with him. He was luckier with Finn, who saw him and raised a hand in greeting as he passed through the gate below.

Liam watched as the Lords dismounted and went inside followed closely by their Spymasters. Several Toth Elite followed their Lord in. Liam had the strong impression that they were ill at ease.

"They're still not sure we can be trusted." Liam thought. "Or at least that our Lord and his Anarian guard can."

No Anant ever kills another. He remembered Finn telling him that… or had it been Paul. He couldn't remember.

He watched for a little while longer as the remaining Toth warriors were shown to their quarters. Finn and several of the castle servants were busy unloading the packhorses. His Lord travelled light, it seemed. Two small boxes and several bags seemed to be all the Lord had brought with him. Liam smiled when he remembered the amount of boxes and bags that had been sent down to Secund for the winter. But then there had been Ladies going… that always made a big difference.

Thinking of Ladies reminded him of Emma and he picked up a bag, throwing it over his shoulder by one of its straps, and followed the other servants into the castle and up to the rooms that had been cleaned and aired for the visiting Lord. There were two Toth Elite already on guard and they would have stopped Liam entering if Finn hadn't spoken up for him.

Watching Finn busily unpacking the luggage and directing the servants where to put everything, Liam came swiftly to the conclusion that he had never seen Finn more happy or content.

"Working for the Toth seems to agree with you," Liam remarked.

Finn just smiled.

"No, not those," he said quickly, as a servant picked up two heavy bags. "Leave those there. Our Spymaster will deal with those himself."

Quite quickly there was only one bag left.

"And that's mine," Finn said. "Where am I to sleep?" Liam was able to answer that. He had found out earlier where the Toth's manservant was to sleep and he showed Finn the nearby backstairs that led up to the attics and Finns room.

"Handy for My Lord's room." Finn said, throwing his bag onto the little bed that took up most of the floor space. "I've been in the saddle for days, I could do with stretching my legs."

Liam led the way down the backstairs and along the corridors to the kitchen and beyond to the courtyard.

"Long walk or short walk." Liam said jokingly.

"Let's find some decent food." Finn said. "I have a lot to tell you and I won't be wanted until my

Lord needs to change for supper." He sounded almost cheerful… almost like his old self.

They left the castle by a side gate and walked towards the centre of town. After a few minutes they found a small inn that had started serving food and sat down outside in the small square. Liam ordered ale and after a moments hesitation Finn ordered a small wine. As they waited he looked around the square, which was busy with people buying and selling at the little shops lining the sides. Tags jostled among the crowds begging for food or money.

"So… how have things been?" Liam asked once their drinks had been served. "You certainly seem a lot happier."

"Mmm," Finn agreed. "I've enjoyed working at Toth castle. Finding Emma has helped a lot… and Timon." He waited as a servant brought plates of bread and meat and placed them on the table. Liam paid him and ordered more drinks.

"How is Emma?" he asked able to contain his curiosity no longer.

Finn frowned.

"When we left, she had plague. But don't worry," he added quickly. "It wasn't serious and we managed to contain it before it spread too far."

"And he left her to come here?"

"She insisted. My Lord didn't want to, but you know Emma…" He started to eat his food and Liam had the feeling he had something important to say but was waiting for the right moment. "We think we know where the spaceship must be."

"What!" Liam had to wait with growing impatience for Finn to finish a mouthful of food.

"Eat up." Finn said grinning and then he relented. "Alright…. It's probably best if I start at the beginning." He thought for a moment. "I was all set to return to Menethes Prime with you when the Spymaster told me I was to stay. Well, I didn't need telling twice, I wanted to stay... with Emma. Then the castle Steward came to me, told me I am going to be looking after the Lord and introduced me to an old man called Axel who's about to retire. It's his job I've taken over. So, Axel showed me where everything was, started telling me how the Lord liked things done, took me to the kitchens for supper and showed me where I was to sleep. I had to be up early in the morning. The Lord likes to rise early."

Finn was silent for a while as he took another bite of his bread. Liam had a good idea what was coming. He glanced across at Finn and found he was being scrutinised by a pair of mocking blue eyes.

"You could have warned me." Finn said, although he didn't sound angry. "We took in an early morning drink to wake the Lord. Axel pulled back the window tapestries and there she was... in bed with him."

"You were shocked?" Liam would have been... and angry.

"No... I was half expecting something like that. In the gardens... there was a lot she didn't say, avoided talking about. I had my suspicions. She'd actually said she'd transformed his kitchens.... Lord Toth's mistress was famous for doing just that. I should have realised earlier.   And for someone who was supposed to be working in the kitchens, she hadn't been in them whenever I'd been there."

They finished the food and Liam drained his second tankard of ale.

"How did you discover where the ship was?"

"Oh that was Emma's doing too. I quickly discovered Timon's whereabouts and used to spend evenings with him, duties permitting. It seems Emma has some strange idea that there are black crystals hidden somewhere that can solve the problem of the red Sun."

"Where did she get this idea from?" Liam was trying to keep the excitement out of his voice. There might be a way of staying here after all. If the planet was saved... Liam could leave the service of the Lord and travel round, explore. It was only the fear of the others escaping and leaving him to die that kept him at Castle Menethes. But now...

"Only the Gods know that one. She won't say. But she's very determined." Finn sipped at his drink. He was still on the first glass. Liam signalled to the inn servant and ordered another ale for himself. "But she did let slip that the ship that brought us here was on the Blessed Isles and that the Lord and his men travelled there on Pirate ships." Finn shook his head. "I don't know why she's got this idea fixed in her head but..."

"Osiris, perhaps?" wondered Liam.
Could it be?
He would certainly know if such things had once existed on Anaria and how to use them if Emma could find them.
Finn shrugged, such things were unimportant.

"My point is," he went on, "the Blessed Isles are decans sailing time away and yet the Spymaster was never gone for all that long, his journals say so."

"You read his journals?"

"Of course. He never found out," Finn said. "I was very careful. If the ship is only a decan or two away by boat, I reckon it must be on the Pirate Islands. It would make sense. If the pirates take them, then where better to keep it than on one of their islands?"

Liam considered this. Finn was probably right, it did make sense. Although he had no recollection of a spaceship on the islands, as a supposed captured pirate he knew all about the islands and where to find them. He wondered whether he should admit this to Finn.

"So what are you going to do now?" he asked.

"That's the difficult bit." Finn admitted. "Of the ten slaves sold to Darg, eight are in or around Toth Prime and two are at Secund... plus you and me. That leaves another ten still at the Gladiator school... if we're lucky and they haven't been sold on. Then there's Emma and...." Finn looked carefully at Liam. "What about Sarah and Judith?"

"Judith wouldn't leave Gerran, I'm certain of that," he said. "And Sarah wouldn't leave without Dom. I can't see our Lord allowing us to take him.... So should we consider taking him too...? And his guard and their families and servants...Where do you stop?"

Finn shook his head. He finished his glass of watered wine and stood up. A timekeeper was calling the hour from the town walls. It was getting late; the Lords would be getting ready for supper soon. Liam stood up slowly and joined his friend on the walk back to the castle. For a while they walked in silence, each deep in his own thoughts on the problem.

At last, as they neared the side door to the castle Liam broke the silence.

"Perhaps you should help Emma to find these crystals. Then you can leave anyone who wants to stay with a clear conscience."

Finn grimaced. He clearly thought Emma's search was a waste of time.

"If it looks like she can't find them, then we can think again." Liam continued.

They walked across the kitchen courtyard and came to halt outside one of the kitchen doors. Finn was obviously considering Liam's suggestion.

"All right." he said at last. "Emma has spent the winter teaching me to read. It would be a shame to let her hard work go to waste. I'll give it a season or two, but that's all."

They parted company at the door. Finn to prepare his Lord's clothes for supper and Liam to check on the guard on duty for Elon who still hadn't shaken off the cold he had caught in Secund.

Liam was excited as he began his tour of the castle walls. Life might be becoming more interesting after all.

Crystals.

Huge green and blue crystals.

Chasing him, trying to crush him.

"Do crystals have legs?" he thought, which was when he realised he was dreaming. "Come on, get up. Before one of these things gets you."

Liam struggled to wake up. It had been a long time since he had had such vivid dream. "Too much ale last night." he thought. But their Lord had done himself proud for the first decan of the Toth's visit. The cooks had excelled themselves, the entertainment had been both lively and varied and the Lady Sarah....

Liam smiled. He couldn't help feeling a touch proud at the memory. She had never looked prettier, dancing in the crystal light with her Lord. Even Lord Toth had been persuaded up to dance with her.

Thoughts of the Toth made Liam wake up fully and throw back his covers angrily. He had seen another side of the old Lord last night and he had been forced to admit, to himself if to no one else, that the man seemed a decent enough Lord. If it hadn't been for Emma, Liam might even have admitted he liked the Lord.

But no matter how often Finn told him how happy she was with her Lord, Liam refused to believe him.

What made matters worse was the fact that every time Lord Toth had caught sight of Liam he would smile a sardonic smile as if he knew exactly what Liam was thinking.

She's mine, that smile said.

And she's staying mine.

No... Liam couldn't bring himself to like Lord Toth.... No matter how many times Finn extolled his virtues.

"Not that they don't argue." Finn said. "They're both very determined people." And he looked as if he could say a lot more, but discretion prevailed and Finn just smiled at some secret memory.

No... Liam was never going to like the Lord.

Maybe after he had taken Emma away from him.

Maybe then.

There was a commotion in the courtyard and Liam heard someone calling to be taken to Lord Toth immediately. A messenger had arrived from Toth Prime with news. For some reason Liam felt disturbed by this and got dressed quickly. He went in search of Finn. He doubted the Lord would be up and about early that morning. He eventually found Finn in the kitchens organising first meal to be taken up to the Lord.

"I didn't think he'd be up yet," Liam said and Finn looked at him grey faced and unsmiling.

"It's Emma," he said simply. "She has started to cough up blood. The plague has become the virulent kind." He turned away quickly but Liam could see how close to tears Finn was. To have found Emma after so long and for this to happen... Liam put his hand on his friend's shoulder. There was nothing he could say.

Thoughts of how he could meet Emma again and how he could persuade her that life as a warrior's wife was better than life as a Lord's mistress had filled Liam's waking hours, making the boredom bearable. It had given him a reason to carry on when things were particularly bad. If anything happened to Emma... it wouldn't only be Finn who would find it difficult to carry on.

Finn picked up the tray and turned to Liam.

"We must pray for a miracle," he said.

Over the next decan Liam lost himself in his duties. He took on any work he could find even a stint at unloading barrels of ale from the continual line of supply wagons that came to the castle. That caused some comment from the Lord's Elite but Liam ignored them. He had to keep busy.

He was walking the walls of the castle in the late evening on the twentieth day of the Toth's visit when another messenger arrived. From his livery he was Toth and had obviously come from Prime.

"News of Emma," Liam thought sadly. It could mean only thing.

A few minutes later he observed Finn enter the kitchen courtyard and he called down to him. Finn hurried up to battlements. Liam stared at him as he approached. It couldn't be...he was smiling.

"Emma has recovered," he said out of breath. "We lost eight but Emma is going to be all right." The two men hugged each other.

"How?" Liam asked but Finn could only shake his head. It was a miracle.

"I must go," Finn said. "I was given permission to tell you the news but only if I was quick." He started to hurry down. "As soon as I know more I will let you know," he called over his shoulder as he disappeared back into the castle.

Lord Toth cut short his visit to Menethes Prime and no one felt insulted by this, which was a measure of the better relations between the two tribes. Even Liam approved of such an action. Maybe the Lord had some decent feelings after all.

On that last day Liam got dressed quickly, fastening his torc with practised ease. Lord Toth was planning on leaving soon after first meal and Finn would be busy before then packing and loading the horses ready for the trip to Prime Gate. Liam wanted to share a last meal with Finn and say goodbye properly this time. He also wanted to make sure Finn still agreed to help Emma find the crystals.

"He mustn't change his mind," Liam thought as he made his to the Castle refectory where most of the warriors had their meals.

To Liam's surprise, Finn was already there. Liam helped himself to porridge and rough bread with a helping of preserve... one of the first fruits of a better understanding with the Toth had been the recipe for Emma's preserve that Lord Menethes had so enjoyed at the Gathering.

"I thought you'd still be busy packing," Liam said, sitting down across the long table from Finn.

"I did most of it last night," Finn said.

Liam looked at him sharply. He sounded upset, angry even.

"What's wrong?" he asked.

Finn stared at him for so long before answering that Liam began to wonder if Finn had finally lost his wits.

Had the pull of Earth finally become too much? It had happened to others.

"Your Spymaster has just informed me that I must return to Toth Prime," Finn said slowly as if each word had to be dragged from his memory, kicking and screaming, to his mouth, "and tell Emma that our Lord has sold her contract to your Lord."

"What!" Excitement poured through Liam's veins.

Emma was coming back.

Emma was coming back to him.

Finn lowered his voice to a bare whisper.

"Your Lord asked if Emma could accompany him to Kush Prime for the Sed Festival at the beginning of summer. He seems to think her... abilities as an empath will be of use to him. She is to go as his mistress." Finn shook his head. "I can't see her liking that. What was he thinking...? I thought.... She'll never agree."

"And you said your Lord really cared for her," Liam cried exultant. "Now will you listen to me?" A sudden thought flashed through his mind and he gripped Finn's arm.

"You will have to continue the search for the crystals," he said. Finn began to shake his head. "You must, you said you would give it a season or two. At least try until Emma returns from Kush Prime. If she returns to you at Toth Prime, then the decision is yours. If she returns here with me, then I will persuade her to give up the search." Liam thought for a moment. It was time to make a decision. "I can contact the gladiator school from here. If Emma returns here take that as a signal to escape. Make your way to Menethes Port and the rest of us will meet you there. We can steal a boat and I will take us to the Pirate Islands. Agreed?"

Finn held out his hand in an Earth handshake.

"Agreed." He stood up. "I'll see you then." He hesitated, "and Sarah?"

"That will be my decision." Liam said. "I'll see how things are, if and when the time comes."

Finn nodded his head once and turned away. Liam watched him making his way between the refectory tables and out into the kitchen yard beyond. Then he went back to his meal, deep in thought.

"No doubt your friend told you about the Toth's mistress joining us." The Spymaster was sitting behind his desk, his eyes never leaving Liam's face for a moment.

"He mentioned something." Liam stared back. He wasn't a slave to be intimidated by the likes of a spymaster. He was a warrior. He had earned the right.

The Spymaster chuckled and indicated a seat in front of his desk. As Liam sat down warily, the Spymaster poured two glasses of wine from a crystal jug on his desk and passed one to Liam. Liam sipped at his drink. It was a very pleasant smooth red, as good as some of the wine Liam had enjoyed on Earth.

He took the opportunity to cast a surreptitious glance round the Spymaster's room. He had never been in there before and he wasn't sure what he had expected. Certainly nothing as tidy as this.

"Judith keeps it tidy for me," the Spymaster explained.

"Are you reading my mind?" Liam asked. He had thought himself better shielded.

"With difficulty." the Spymaster admitted. "You are not weak exactly... more on a different level than the rest of us... Strange." The Spymaster leant forward and poured them both more wine. "No matter. However strange you are, she seems to like it. And I don't think she likes our Lord that much."

Liam wondered if he had momentarily fallen asleep and missed some vital statement. Who were they talking about? Not the Lady Sarah surely?

"Mistress Emma." the Spymaster said. "Our Lord is anxious that she stay with us if at all possible."

"I'm not sure I understand?"

"At their meeting at the beginning of the season, it was agreed that Mistress Emma would accompany our Lord to Kush Prime. I surely don't have to explain why." Liam shook his head. Emma's empathy, and the fact that female telepaths were unheard of on Anaria, made her the ideal spy.

"However it would seem that the girl is somewhat reluctant to undertake the mission. Rumour has it…"

"You have an informant in Toth Castle." Liam interrupted.

The Spymaster grunted.

Neither yes nor no.

"Rumour has it," he continued, as if there had been no interruption, "that the girl became angry and refused to speak to Toth for several hours."

The Spymaster raised the wine jug and would have poured Liam a third glass, but Liam declined with a wave of his hand. He wanted to keep a clear head.

"I should explain that the Toth only agreed to her coming with us because he believed her to be dying. The story of the sale of her contract to our Lord, when it is released, will only be a blind to avert suspicion." The Spymaster looked at the jug, as if contemplating another glass himself, then put it back on the tray.

"It could not have been sold anyway, without her consent," Liam pointed out. He had investigated contracts and the law in great detail since returning from the Gathering.

"True.... She did eventually talk to the Toth. But only to point out that if he insisted she come to our Lord, he would have broken the terms of their contract."

"That is her right. Did he ... insist?"

"Our Lord did. Mistress Emma should be arriving at the Prime Gate sometime this afternoon."

Liam fought hard to hide his feelings at this news. He kept his face as unemotional as a Spymaster's.

It was not easy.

"And what exactly do you want me to do?" he asked.

"Meet her. The girl is now a free agent. She cannot lawfully be enslaved again. She can choose whom she serves." The Spymaster looked at Liam without blinking. It reminded Liam of a cobra, poised to strike. He shivered. "Persuade her to stay with us. Our Lord would try, but I don't think she likes him, not in ... that way." The Spymaster seemed embarrassed. "She seems to like you though."

"You want me to seduce her." Liam said and he felt suddenly cold at the prospect. He didn't want it to be like this.

"Do whatever is necessary." The Spymaster smiled at him. "I don't think you will find the task... too unpleasant."

"And if she wants to return to the Toth, or go elsewhere?"

"Then, of course, she is free to do so. But in such circumstances it would be better for her if she were to return to the Toth."

Liam wondered if that was a threat.

Was Emma too dangerous to be allowed to roam free?

She could be used against the Anant. Or, worse still, cause awkward questions to be asked, if she fell into the wrong hands. Dangerous questions for all concerned.

"I'll do my best," he said, bowing his head as he took his leave.

He walked towards the stable yard, thinking of all the Spymaster had said, in search of some of his guard not on duty. They were not pleased when he told them the Lord had ordered them to escort someone back from the gate.

"Your wife will have your supper ready by the time we get back." Liam said to Nye. He wasn't sure which was worse, the lovestruck Nye pining for his Eyleen, or the married Nye, sneaking off at all hours to be with his new wife. But thinking of Nye made Liam think of Emma and what the spymaster had asked him to do. He couldn't blame the young man, if he had Emma waiting for him he'd want to spend as much time as he could with her. Which was probably why Elite generally didn't get married until they were close to retirement.

"Come on," he said, a little more lenient than he should have been. "We won't be gone long."

By riding fast they were at Prime Gate a little after the mid-day. Liam was relieved to see that no one was waiting for them outside. The usual guard of two was inside, sheltering from a cold breeze that had sprung up. Ordering the others to wait outside Liam entered the now familiar grey building.

"Are you the escort?" one of the guards asked. "They've been waiting at the Port Gate for over an hour.

Even as he spoke the air between the two yellow pillars sparkled and Finn appeared.

"Liam?" he said, obviously puzzled as to why Liam had been sent as escort. But Liam had no time to respond. The Gate flashed again and Emma quickly followed her brother through the Gate. She looked around blinking as if dazed by the suddenness of the journey. Liam hurried forward and took her hand.

"You are well come," he said, raising her hand to his lips. She gave him a hesitant smile as he led her away from the Gate towards the doorway. The two guards were staring, almost open-mouthed in amazement, but she didn't seem to notice them. Finn followed them out, carrying a large bag over his shoulder.

"We've only just arrived," Liam apologised. "Nothing is ready. I'll send for a horse from the stables."

"I would prefer to ride behind someone," Emma said quietly, "if they wouldn't mind."

"You can ride behind me," Liam said immediately, not that any of the escort had enough wits to volunteer quickly enough anyway. They were as bemused as the Gate guards at the identity of the visitor. There were enough tales spread by the Elite about the beauty of the Toth's mistress for no one to be in any doubt that this was she.

Finn handed the bag to Neri and then jerked his head back towards the building.

"A word," he said to Liam. They walked towards the doorway until Finn stopped suddenly. He had obviously decided that they couldn't be overheard. "Emma is... very upset and angry," he told Liam. "She won't tell me what was said, but something has really upset her."

Liam frowned. "So?"

"I'm asking you, as a friend, not to take advantage when she's so vulnerable."

"Finn!" Liam laughed, but his friend was close to the truth.

"I mean it, Liam." Finn was talking quietly but his tone was fierce and angry. "Why else would they have sent you?"

Liam rubbed the back of his neck. He was getting another bad headache.

"They're not going to let her run loose," he said at last. "It would be too dangerous."

"When she calms down, she'll want to return home," Finn said. "The Toth is a proud man. I am just asking that you don't do anything that will make it impossible for her to return." He turned away and walked into the building. As he neared the Gate he turned and looked back. Liam had followed him in. "For once think of someone else, not just yourself." Finn said.

This stung Liam but before he could think of a reply Finn had walked through the Gate and was gone. Annoyed Liam returned to his men and mounted his horse. Neri helped Emma up behind him and she slipped her arms round his waist, her head resting against his back.

It felt good.

Too good.

Who was he to obey?

His friend or his Lord.

XVIII

"Worried?"

"A little." she admitted, staring across out across the bay at the small ships. "I don't seem to like boats anymore than I like horses."

"You'll be fine." Liam reassured her. "Six days sailing and we should be at Kush Port."

He turned his head away from the ships and looked instead at Emma. He could smell the faint trace of her lavender perfume on the breeze.

"She has a lovely profile," he thought to himself. "Very delicate." It brought out the protective in a warrior. That must be why Anarian whores fetched such a higher price than Anant. He suddenly found himself being scrutinised by a pair of cold blue eyes but she said nothing and merely turned away and walked back up the beach towards the small fishing village.

With one last look at the ships that would shortly be taking them to the Sed Festival, Liam started after her. With his long stride he soon caught up and found himself having to shorten his pace to walk beside her.

"There is a lot of building work going on." she remarked. They turned down onto the narrow mud street that ran through the village and began a slow walk towards the camp. Liam glanced back at the wall that was being built behind the tiny hamlet.

"I think our Lord has plans to turn this into a second Port." he said.

"And use Secund as his main city?" She laughed at the look on Liam's face. "You obviously don't like the place as much as he does."

Liam grunted.

"Too difficult to defend, too draughty to be comfortable in winter and…"

"You should try Toth Prime in winter." She laughed again.

Liam said nothing. He had deliberately refrained from mentioning the Toth in the decans since Emma's arrival and she had said nothing either. This was the first time she had mentioned the Toth in any of their long walks together. And there had been plenty of those.

"Eight feet of snow… the warriors had to dig out the courtyards before they could reach the kitchens and be fed." She smiled at the memory.

"That must have made them work all the harder!" Liam remarked dryly. "Deprive a warrior of his food and he'll do almost anything."

"The snow fights were fun," she said quietly, more to herself than to him, as they reached the outskirts of the camp.

A large tent in the very middle was the Lord's and Emma made her way towards it, carefully walking between the warriors' tents. These were little more than waterproof canvas pegged out between uprights. Only the Lord's tent was of any size, boasting four rooms or partitioned sections. One of these was Emma's. He couldn't help wondering if she really was the Lord's mistress, in spite of what the Spymaster had said. With Sarah away at one of the Spymaster's estates outside Prime recovering from another miscarriage, their Lord might have been tempted…

No… it didn't help him to think like that. Everyone else thought she was his mistress, but the Spymaster had said that was merely a ruse and no one had told him to stay away from Emma. He was still to…

"You all think like that, don't you?" Her voice cut into his thoughts like a knife. She had stopped short of the tent and was looking at him sadly. He was dismayed to see there were tears in her eyes.

"Isn't that what we're supposed to think?" he said, confused.

"Not that." she said shaking her head angrily. "Whore.... no matter how it starts, no matter what promises are made... it always comes back to .... that word, in the end."

"I never...." he began, but she stamped her foot angrily and glared at him.

"Yes you do. You're all the same." She brushed her eyes with her fingertips. "That's what he thought.... just a whore and they're as common as white crystals." She would have left him and entered the tent but Liam caught hold of her arm and pulled her towards him.

"Is that why you agreed to come?" he asked. So much was beginning to make sense.
A tear ran down her cheek and he reached out and tenderly caught it with a finger.

"Do you want to talk.... properly." He nodded towards the tent. "We could..."

"And have them all think I entertain you too." she snapped, pulling her arm free of his grasp. "Go to *hell*, Liam." and without looking back at him she pulled aside the entrance flap and entered the Lord's tent.

"Damn." he thought. Things had been going so well.

But as he reflected on the little he had learnt, he found new hope. It looked as if Finn might be wrong. Emma might not want to return to a Lord who had so deeply hurt her.
Things might not be as bad as he thought.
In fact things might be looking up.

For a moment he considered going after her but decided against it. It might be better to give her time to calm down and there would be plenty of opportunities to talk on the ship. Satisfied with this, Liam walked towards his own bed. With no lady to guard and no castle walls to patrol there was little for him to do. He would be glad when the voyage began. The visit to an Anari city promised to be interesting and away from so much that reminded her of the Anant, Emma might be more easily persuaded to forget Lord Toth and remember him instead.

The harbour and walls of Port Kush were built of a white stone that sparkled in the mid-day sun. The walls of the city rose sheer out of the sand. Two L-shaped piers created the harbour out into the bay with a paved road between it and the wall. There were no buildings to be seen. Either side of the harbour the beach stretched straight as far as the eye could see. Sand dunes and sparse grass huddled against the towering white walls.

Kush Port was built in the desert.

"It was originally a fertile plain," the Spymaster told Liam as they stood at the guardrail and looked over the side of the ship towards the port. "But over a thousand tarns ago it began to dry and now there is only a narrow strip of land, either side of the canal from the Great Lake, where crops can be grown. The rest is desert." The Spymaster looked thoughtfully at Liam for a moment. "And how goes it with Mistress Emma?"

Liam had the feeling that the Spymaster already knew the answer to his question.

"I think we were getting somewhere," he said. " But then we came on board and…" He shrugged. Emma had almost immediately been taken ill and retired to her cabin where she had stayed for the entire six days of the voyage. Only the Lord had been allowed in to see her. Liam had had to be content with reports from Lena who was Emma's new maid. He sighed. He had hoped for so much from the voyage and been sadly disappointed.

The Spymaster suddenly left his side and walked towards the door leading down to the cabins below. As he approached the door opened and Emma emerged closely followed by her maid. The Spymaster smiled and held out his hand, which Emma took gracefully.

"You look a little better," he said, leading her across the deck towards Liam.

"Thank you." She smiled back at the Spymaster who gave her hand to Liam. Liam raised it to his lips.

"You do look better," he agreed.

"I could hardly look worse," she laughed.

The Spymaster left them, signalling to Lena as he did so to leave them alone too. Lena hesitated, her mouth a thin line of disapproval as she stared at Liam. Then she obeyed the Spymaster's silent command and went back below deck.

Liam wondered briefly what that had been about. Lena had been told the truth about Emma's visit. She was supposed to be the Spymaster's second front of attack. Was she forgetting?

Becoming protective of her charge.

Liam brought his attention back to Emma.

"You seem happier than when we met on the beach" she asked, surprising him.

"It's just..." he said, not wanting to admit to her the reason for his renewed optimism

"I'm not lying with the lord, if that's what you're worried about." He was somewhat taken aback by her blunt honesty. He found himself becoming uncomfortable; it didn't seem polite to discuss such things.

"But I'm not a Lady." she pointed out.

"I wish people would stop reading my thoughts so easily." he grumbled. "I try very hard to shield them."

"Most Anant wouldn't find you easy to read." she said. "Gerran is almost a Master and I find you easier to read than I do the Anant. I don't know why." She suddenly tapped him on the arm playfully. "You are changing the subject."

He was still holding her hand in his and he now brought his other hand up and clasped hers firmly between his two.

"Emma..." he began and he felt her trying to pull free. He grasped her hand more firmly and refused to let go.

"Don't spoil it," she said. "You are doing so well." He shook his head and frowned as if unsure of her meaning. "Oh, come." she said. "Gerran has told you to ... persuade me to stay with the Menethes, hasn't he? And you have been trying very hard to make me fall in love with you."

He considered denying it, but it was obvious that only honesty would work with her. He nodded.

"They won't let you go free," he told her. "It's stay with us or the Toth... or...."

"I know," she said quickly. "My Lord made it clear over a tarn ago. I will be dealt with."

"I'm sorry." He shook his head. He didn't like it at all.

She patted his arm with her free hand.

"I understand." and she turned away to look over the side of the ship at the rapidly approaching Port. "I won't return to the Toth," she said quietly. "Perhaps Gerran and your Lord will give me better terms than our Spymaster... and Lord."

There was something in the way she said this last word that made Liam realise that it wasn't going to so easy to persuade her after all.

"You still care for him," he said. Perhaps if she talked about him…

She shook her head, glancing round the ship and catching sight of the Spymaster trying hard to look as if he wasn't watching them.

"Not here. Perhaps at Kush Prime. We could continue with our walks and I will explain what happened… what you want to know." She regarded him thoughtfully. "If I do, will you tell the Spymaster?"

"Not if you don't want me to." Liam promised. He felt her hand squeeze his and he quickly kissed it again. "Let the Spymaster make what he will of that," he said and she laughed.

"Let the Spymaster make what he will of this then," and she stretched up and kissed him lightly on the cheek. "Friends," she whispered, but before he could answer she hurried away towards her cabin.

Liam leant heavily on the rail. "I don't want to be friends," he thought, but he knew he would agree because he was beginning to care about Emma and wanted her to be happy.

He couldn't help smiling at his situation though. If he couldn't persuade her to stay with him it looked as if he might have to persuade her to go back to her old Lord after all.

What an irony.

What a mess.

Lord Menethes escorted Emma from the boat surrounded by his elite. A high-ranking Kush official met him on the quayside and they were shown to an open carriage with a green canopy. Liam was pleased to see the Lord help Emma in first before climbing in himself.

It was very warm.

Liam picked up his bag and waited patiently for his turn to walk down the plank to the quayside. The Spymaster hurried past, supervising the unloading of the luggage. Puzzled, Liam watched him. It was a strange duty for a spymaster.

Seemingly satisfied that all was running smoothly the Spymaster stood back as the servants lifted a heavy box over the side. Looking round the Spymaster seemed to catch sight of Liam and walked over.

"How casual is this?" Liam wondered. He was beginning to realise that the Spymaster did and said nothing without an ulterior motive.

"After I spoke to you," the Spymaster said." about being the Mistress's guard, I thought it might be too much for one man so I ordered Saul and Neri from Sarah's guard to join you. They are on one of the other boats. But don't worry; they won't get in your way. You'll hardly know they are there."

Liam couldn't help raising one eyebrow at this or uttering a dry "Indeed." as the Spymaster walked away. He knew for a fact that Neri had taken advantage of Lady Sarah retiring to the country for a rest, with a reduced need for a large guard, to visit his mother, several days journey from Prime. Liam had seen him leave just before the Lord left Prime himself for the boats. There was no time for Neri to have been recalled and for him to have joined them before the boats left. In any case the Spymaster had spoken to Liam well before then. Why leave it to the last minute to change the arrangements.

It didn't make sense.

Liam smiled grimly. He would be very interested to see what this Neri and Saul looked like.

The port Gate was situated outside the city walls on the far side from the harbour. The luggage was put onto two carts and Liam found himself walking behind these with the rest of the party. They didn't enter the port but skirted its walls on the narrow paved road. At least this meant that for a large part of the walk they were shaded from the hot sun by the port walls.

As the party neared the gate Liam saw that several canopies had been erected outside the white building and that the Lord Menethes was being served refreshments while he waited for the rest of his party.

"Do you think we'll be offered something?" one of the warriors behind Liam muttered.

"Only if we're in favour with old Kush," another said.

It seemed they were in favour, at least for now. Liam was given a large beaker of cold water and a bowl of highly spiced rice, nuts and vegetables. A large flat bread served as a spoon and Liam found himself breaking off a piece of bread, scooping up rice and eating it with relish. It was very good. He hadn't realised how hungry he was.

Some of the other warriors were looking at their bowls with suspicion. Seeing Liam eat it without coming to any obvious harm two of the warriors closest to Liam tried it also.

"Our captain will eat anything," one of them said." But... this isn't too bad."

Liam continued to eat while carefully scrutinising the warrior. This must be Saul... or Neri. He decided the man looked most like Saul, the one behind him was younger, he could be Neri.

"You should always keep your mind open to new things, Saul." Liam said and the man inclined his head. He understood. "Damn him." Liam thought. The Spymaster had given him two of his spies. It was a complication he could have done without.

They had barely enough time to finish their meal before the command was given to enter the Gate. Liam saw Lord Menethes rise and thank the Kush for their hospitality. He held out his hand to Emma who had been sitting some feet away, under a canopy of her own with her maid and together they entered the building out of the hot sun. Warriors went through first, followed by some of the Elite, then Emma and the Lord together. More Elite followed them and it was quickly Liam's turn to enter. He remembered to close his eyes tightly.

The Gate at Kush Prime, like all Gates, was situated outside the city. Once it had been some distance from the city but as the town had grown and spread its walls, the Gate had crept nearer until it was now only a ten-minute walk to a main city gate. Liam paused before beginning the walk down to get a good look at his first Anarian city.

Like the Port the walls were built of white stone and most of the buildings in the centre and north of the city seemed to be of the same material. Only the newer buildings were a different colour, being built of red clay or brick. Some of the new buildings were having a white plaster applied to their outside so that they would match. At a distance it was impossible to tell which buildings were stone and which had been plastered. In what must once have been the centre of the city there was a huge temple, its pyramid-shaped roof, supported by colonnades of white pillars, dominating the encircling town. Surrounding the temple were the various religious buildings, minor temples, workshops, living areas and slaves quarters that invariably grew up around a major temple. Avenues of trees and a formal garden of fountains and raised beds of shrubs surrounded the entire complex on all sides.

To the right, as Liam looked, was another collection of buildings surrounded by an equally extensive garden of trees and fountains and a large ornamental lake. As he looked Liam realised it wasn't a complex of buildings as such but one building built around a pattern of courtyards. He guessed there were sixteen in all, although the central dome that rose out of the centre obscured those at the far side, covering what should have been the centre four courtyards of a four by four design. Built of the same white stone as the surrounding town the dome covered a three or four storey building underneath. The visible walls of this structure and the dome were decorated with metal that shone yellow in the sunlight. Liam realised it was probably gold.

"That is Kush palace," someone whispered over Liam's shoulder. Half turning he saw it was Saul, the new Saul. "And that is Ammon's great temple," Saul continued. "Ammon is principle god to the Kush."

"And to the Menethes." Liam pointed out.

"Now, yes. But before our Lord came and changed it we worshipped Ptah as principle, as do all the Anant."

"And what did Ptah have to say about that?" Liam asked. For once he was being serious.
Saul looked at him, his eyes narrowing as he searched for a hint of disrespect. Finally deciding that none was intended he gave the question serious thought.

"If he objected, he gave no sign of it," he said. "The Toth enlarged the temple outside Toth Prime and Ptah now lives there."

With one last glance at the city Liam began the descent towards the road leading in. Saul closely followed him; Neri was a few warriors behind. Liam hoped whatever those two had come to Kush Prime for they would soon go and do it and leave him in peace. He felt uncomfortable and vaguely threatened by their presence.

To his dismay, when he was shown to the tiny room that was to be his for the duration of the stay, he found he was expected to share with them. There was barely enough room for one, never mind three. It was just as well that he didn't have to spend much time there.

"Privilege of being a High Lord." Saul remarked. "Otherwise we'd be housed in the town and things look even more crowded down there."

Liam threw his bag onto a small bed under the window. At least there was a slight breeze there and it had a good view over the courtyard, even if it was of the kitchens.

"Privilege of being captain." he said before anyone could complain. He contemplated asking about the Sed Festival but then decided against revealing his ignorance. He would just have to ask Emma next time he saw her.

Which reminded him....

"Where is Mistress Emma's room," he said. "We're supposed to be guarding her aren't we?"

Saul pointed out of the door.

"Our Lord is in the next courtyard. I think he is sharing it with the Lord Thamad. He'll be in this half. In fact his room is probably directly opposite ours."

But there was only a wall outside Liam's room and stairs leading down to the courtyard. He followed these and found himself in the kitchen area. The rooms above jutted out over the courtyard and were supported by pillars forming an open passageway underneath. He walked along this to an arch that led into the next courtyard. Somewhat regretfully he walked under the arch ignoring the stairs that led up. Making friends in the kitchen would have to wait. First he had to find Emma. But even that could wait a little while.

Liam walked into the courtyard and decided to have a look at the fountain and small pool in the middle. He could feel the spray on his face as he neared and he sat on the low wall surrounding the pool and enjoyed the refreshing breeze that was playing with the water. He dipped his hand in the water and startled a large pink fish that was hiding under the floating leaf of some kind of water lily. Tubs of flowers and small shrubs were carefully placed around, being watered by slaves. It was extremely relaxing.

"Captain."

Lena.

Liam sighed. But he had come in search of Emma so he stood up quickly and followed the maid.

As in the first courtyard pillars supported the rooms above but underneath this time there was no passageway or blank wall. A series of rooms had been created, with their own little patio, railed off and decorated with screening shrubs and climbing plants. Lena led him to a centre doorway. Two hinged shutters formed the door and these had been folded back. Curtains of sheer cotton hung down to give some privacy. Lena pushed one of these back and entered. Liam hesitated on the threshold and looked around at the room.

It was quite large, at least compared to his, and obviously backed on to the courtyard behind. It was sparsely furnished but the three chairs and small table to one side were delicately carved and expensively decorated with gold leaf. A large settee against the back wall was covered in embroidered cushions and a highly coloured throw rug.

Simple but elegant.

"Do you like it?" Emma asked. She had emerged from the room next to this one. Through the open door Liam could see a low bed surrounded by curtains of the same sheer fabric. "I have my own bathroom too," she told him. "I shall become spoilt."

"I'm jealous," he said, matching her own playful tone. Although, if he were honest, that was the one thing he missed most. Communal baths were all very well but they tended to be noisy places. One couldn't really relax. He had a flash of half remembered memories.

A glass of red wine.

Emma sitting on the floor, resting her head...

Then it was gone.

"Our Lord is above us," she continued, holding her hands wide at the side of her head to indicate the breadth of his suite of rooms. "The spymaster is next door to me, Elite beyond that and down part of the sides. There is another Lord over the other side but the courtyard is so big, I doubt we need ever meet them."

"Thamad, I think." Liam said, pleased at being able to show he knew something.

"Really?" She seemed quite pleased by this.

"Do you know him, Mistress?" Lena asked, folding up a discarded overmantle

"No..." Emma spoke slowly. "But I did meet his daughter." She looked at Liam suddenly and clasped her hands together. "So... what are we going to do?" she said excitedly. "Mistresses are not supposed to be around during the day. My Lord has given me a great deal of money and told me to buy myself some clothes suitable to this climate. Shall we go shopping?" and she laughed with childlike delight at Liam's face. "You don't have to come."

XIX

Liam accompanied the two women on their shopping trip and on subsequent trips too. Saul and Neri had disappeared so there was no one else to go with them and they couldn't be allowed to go on their own. Not into a large city like Kush Prime teeming with visiting Lords and their warriors and servants. Such a large gathering attracted all manner of low-lives, professional pickpockets and thieves as well as the opportunist tag. It would be asking for trouble if Emma went out into the crowds with a large purse.

"Did you go shopping with Emma on Urth?" she teased him. The look on his face was enough to send her into peals of laughter. "Poor Liam" she said to Lena. "He is missing his perfect Mistress, always ready for him in the evening."

He found himself becoming annoyed with her. Why was she being like this?

As they emerged from the main palace gate she stopped and looked around.

"Which way shall we go today?" Like most of the major cities on Anaria, Kush Prime was laid out in a geometrical pattern of straight roads, north to south, east to west. It should be easy to find the main square where all the best shops would be, Liam told them. It was always a short distance south from the Temple or Castle.

Emma was in luck. To make way for the Sed Festival and all the celebrations and entertainment that went with it, the usual market had been brought forward and the main square was busy with stalls and traders engaged in selling their wares.

It was already past mid-day and the market was crowded with buyers.... and tags.

Liam spotted several beggars who seemed to be eyeing up the unwary customers and he kept a close eye on Emma as she walked amongst the jostling crowds, seemingly impervious to the noise and heat. It was giving him a headache and his feet were becoming sore.

"I've been talking to one of the stall holders." Emma said after an hour of fruitless searching at one stall after another. "There's a merchant's shop not far from here which might have what I want. We have to find a side street off the main square with an inn at the bottom called Ra's Crown."

"Then we would do better to go down a block and find the inn first." Liam said and the women agreed. Before they finally left the market, Emma made her first purchase. A small packet of herbs.

As they walked down the first side street they had come to Lena hurried ahead leaving the two of them momentarily alone. They walked in silence; Liam was still feeling a little annoyed at her teasing and his headache wasn't helping things.

"I didn't mean to annoy you" Emma apologised. "It's just that sometimes I get fed up with you thinking of me as your Emma. I'm not your Emma."
Liam stopped walking suddenly and she passed him before she realised and stopped herself. She turned round to face him.

"I may have been once, I don't remember. But I'm not now. I can't be her, I don't know her." She was shaking her head. "You have to accept me as I am now.... or not at all." She gave an audible sigh. "I'm tired of trying to be what everyone else wants me to be. I want to be me...even if I'm not sure who me is."
She looked as if she wanted to explain further but at that moment Lena came hurrying back. She had found the

inn and a shop selling cloth and second-hand clothes was next door.

With only the briefest of glances to him Emma followed Lena to the right street. When they at last found the inn Liam was grateful when Emma suggested he sit outside the inn in the shade and wait for them. She disappeared into the inn for a few minutes. When she emerged it was too announce that she had ordered and paid for some food and it would be served when they had finished their business next door. With that she disappeared again into the shop accompanied by Lena.

Liam settled back in a seat against the wall of the inn. He didn't know where she got all her energy from. She was tiring him out. He closed his eyes for a moment and found himself drifting off to sleep.

He woke with a start but there was no sign of the two women. They were still busy next door.

"I'm getting too old for this," he muttered. A small boy, probably the innkeeper's son, since he wore no slave collar, carefully placed a tankard of steaming liquid in front of him. Liam looked round. A woman, obviously his mother was keeping a watchful eye on him and Liam smiled at her reassuringly. He hadn't spilt any. "Is that for me?" he asked puzzled.

The woman stepped forward to answer. The lady had ordered it for him. An infusion of herbs she had brought with her. It was for his headache.

Liam dug deep into his pouch and found a small coin to give to the boy who immediately ran to show his mother excited at his good fortune. Liam smiled. Such a small thing to him, yet such a big thing to the boy. He almost wished he were that young again himself.

Liam looked again at next door. There was still no sign of either woman. Resigned to a long wait he began to sip his drink. It wasn't too bad, it had a faint taste of lemon and honey had been added to make it sweeter.

As long as it got rid of his headache.

It was another twenty minutes before Emma appeared carrying three parcels tied together with leather strips. These had again been tied to form loops, which she had slipped over her wrist for ease of carrying. She sat down next to him taking a few moments to untangle the straps and free herself. Almost immediately the boy came out again followed by his mother. Both were carrying plates of food, which they placed on the table.

Cubes of meat on skewers.

Finger shaped patties of minced meat with a sauce of what Liam thought might be *yoghurt*.

A pitcher of water came next and then more plates of food. This time vegetables fried in a batter with more sauce for dipping, this one red in colour and more of the flat bread that Liam had enjoyed at the Port Gate. Finally a bowl of stew that smelt deliciously spiced. He began to feel better.

"You said he'd cheer up when food arrived" Lena said, joining them with two more parcels to add to the rapidly growing pile.

"The food seems to be heavily spiced here." Emma said. "I ordered a selection of mild snacks... to suit our delicate Anant stomachs. But that..." She pointed at the stew, "...is really for you, Liam. I thought you might like it." She broke off a small piece of bread and dipped it into the bowl. Liam couldn't help smiling as she gamely chewed and swallowed the mouthful with only a slight grimace. "I think I'll try the skewers," she said pouring herself a large glass of water.

Liam helped himself to the stew. It was delicious.

Lena was still dubious about the food and Emma had to coax her into trying the patties dipped in the sauce. But she must have liked it for she had a second and then helped herself to the vegetables.

Emma, Liam noted, ate very little.

When they had finished eating Liam suggested they return to the palace and he offered to carry the parcels. Emma handed him one, the smallest.

"That one's for you," she said. He began to protest but she silenced him with a raise of her hand. "It's too hot for our Anant clothes," she explained. "Of course if you'd rather have an Anari man's gown…"

That quickly silenced him. It seemed she had bought clothes for Lena too and Liam was amused by the conflict of emotions he could see in the woman's face.

Horror, that Emma should have spent the Lord's money on a mere maid.

Delight at the prospect of cooler clothes.

Liam did however refuse to let Emma carry the heaviest two parcels.

"But I don't want to go straight back" Emma said. "It's not right you should carry it all, when I intend to stay out longer."

Liam groaned. Not more shopping.

But Emma, it seemed, had a desire to see the Great Lake on whose southern shore Kush Prime was built.

"If we go this way," she said, pointing away from the way they had come. "We shall eventually reach the West Wall. We can walk along the top of it and see the lake. If isn't too far we could walk to the North Gate along the walls and then down, back to the Temple."

Liam considered the idea for a moment. It would mean walking nearly all the sides of a large rectangle and his feet were aching. Instead he suggested that they leave the parcels at the Palace and walk straight to the North wall from there. It would be less distance. He could see Emma was disappointed with his idea and he was surprised when she agreed.

"It won't be as interesting a walk, but it'll do," she said.

It was agreed.

A little over an hour and a half later Liam found himself following Emma up the circular steps of a Gate tower onto the walls of the city. She had changed into one of the dresses she had bought. Made of a soft lightweight material, it had a low neckline and no sleeves. Gathered under the breast, its full skirt swirled lightly round her legs as she climbed. Propriety was observed in the form of the overmantle. Not a waistcoat but a jacket of a diaphanous material the same colour as the dress. The jacket had embroidered cuffs and small stand up collar. It made her look incredibly young and very lovely. Liam rather enjoyed the envious looks he got which Emma didn't seem to notice.

He emerged from the steps into the late afternoon sunshine. The worst of the heat was over and in a few hours it would be sunset. Emma was already at the outer wall looking down at the lake and small boats sailing across the lake.

"Isn't it beautiful" Emma cried and a nearby city guard smiled at her enthusiasm. She leaned over the edge of the wall and Liam quickly caught hold of her arm and pulled her back. "Not afraid are you?" she laughed. Then she pointed out across the lake. "Those ships," she said to the guard. "They're so big."

He nodded.

"Those are the Tribute ships," he told her. "The larger two will hold about seven thousand, the smaller, one or two."

"So many" gasped Emma. "How...."

Liam looked out at the huge ships. They had masts and presumably therefore sails but they also had enormous paddlewheels at the side. He wondered what powered them. Crystals or slaves. He began to look along the shoreline as Emma continued her chatter. Kush Prime clearly had a thriving fishing industry for there were several small boats pulled up on the foreshore and nets spread out to dry. Liam could smell the faint odour of fish on the light breeze blowing in from the lake. He hadn't eaten fresh fish in a long time.

"Liam." Emma lightly touched his arm and he bought his full attention back to her. "It's time we started back," she said.

He offered her his arm, which she accepted and they made their way down the stairs and along the avenue leading from Gate to Temple. Emma was deep in thought as they walked slowly, arm in arm.

"Are you going to talk to me then?" he said after several minutes of silence.

"What would you like to talk about?" She sounded tired. "Like Lord Toth you seem to think my chatter annoying and don't listen."

He was a little embarrassed at this. He had turned to his own thoughts, and let her talk away to the guard, it was true. He apologised and she gave him a sad smile.

"I will satisfy your curiosity" she said "and tell you why I agreed to come."

They sat down on the low edge of a wall surrounding one of the pools near the Temple and Emma ran her fingers through the water. He waited patiently for her to begin. Like her brother she would not be rushed.

"I had no choice. I did something which would have made my Lord very angry and the spymaster found out and threatened to tell."

"What?"

"I employed someone I should not have done, but there were reasons. I would do the same again," she said. "But by then I had decided to come anyway."

"Why?"

She shrugged. It was obviously something she did not want to discuss.

"Let's just say I learnt my lesson. It is not a mistake I intend to make again."

"You fell in love," he said. "But he...."

"I told you what he thought," she said firmly. "I forgot this is a business. I won't forget again."

He reached out and stroked the side of her face.

"Don't become hard and cynical in the process," he said. "That would be a shame."

He was vaguely disturbed by the sadness he could see and hear in her. The Toth seemed intent on destroying all that was beautiful in Emma. Perhaps Finn was right. The sooner they escaped back to Earth the better.

Emma gave him a puzzled glance, her eyes narrowing as she concentrated.

"You're planning on leaving," she cried. "That is why Finn has been so co-operative. He was lying to me." She looked at Liam suspiciously. "You told him to" she accused. "How could you? I have no intention of leaving everyone to die. I'm ashamed of you for thinking so." She stood up and began to walk quickly towards the palace.

"She really is the most infuriating girl," he thought, unwittingly echoing the words of a distant Lord. But he also felt proud at her bravery and determination. "I must ask where this idea of crystals came from."

He eventually caught up with her at the palace gate but she refused to talk further and went straight to her room. Liam would have followed and tried to explain but his entry was blocked by Lena. Her mistress was to accompany Lord Menethes into supper with Pharaoh. There wasn't time to talk, Emma had to get ready and Lena closed the door shutters firmly on him. Somewhat downcast by the turn of events, Liam went in search of his supper.

"And... what do you think to our Pharaoh?" Lord Menethes handed Emma a large crystal goblet, decorated with gold inlay. He poured her wine himself from a similarly decorated decanter. "You have had plenty of opportunity to form an opinion."

"The palace is very beautiful," she said slowly, choosing her words with care.

That was certainly true. She had been amazed at the opulence of Kush Palace, its high ceilings decorated with gold and crystals, its intricate mosaic floors and the delicate finery of the wall hangings and curtains, so unlike the heavy functional tapestries of Toth Prime.

The furnishing of the two castles was so different too. Kush palace was sparsely furnished, most of the furniture delicately carved fine-legged tables and chairs that Emma was almost afraid to use in case she broke them. Not for Kush the heavy carved, thick padded chairs of the Toth. Rugged and sturdy like the Toth themselves.

"And Pharaoh?" the Spymaster prompted.
Emma frowned. For all that the Menethes were Anant, their Lord was Anarian. It was very difficult to know the right thing to say.

"Forgive me, Lord," she said. "But there is something very strange going on here." She looked from Lord to Spymaster and back, uncertain whether to continue.

"When you announced that the Anant would not help with Tribute at our first supper with Pharaoh," she said, deciding he should hear the truth. "They were not surprised."

"That was to be expected" Gerran pointed out. "We have never…"

"True," she interrupted "but I would have expected them to be worried at the very least. I would be, if I were them."

The Spymaster nodded in agreement.

"The Tribute ships are moored out there on the lake, not half full and yet they must sail before the end of summer if they are to avoid the winter storms" he said. "Where does he plan to fill them from?"

Emma shrugged. She couldn't answer that.

"I have been shopping in the market," she said with a grateful smile to the Lord who had been so generous with money. "And the people are not disturbed by the sight of these ships."

"Why not?" Lord Menethes was anxious to know.

"I asked. Pharaoh has told the people that the Anant will provide the Tribute and that they will not have to."

Lord Menethes shook his head, puzzled by this change in attitude.

"When the subject was first broached over a tarn ago, he was desperate to find tribute. What has changed?"

She could not answer that either. Pharaoh was not Anant; she could not read his thoughts, only his feelings but he was not worried at all.

"You have done well". Lord Menethes dismissed her and she curtseyed and prepared to leave.

"My Lord…" she said hesitantly.

The Lord looked annoyed, she had been dismissed but a look from his Spymaster stilled the angry command that he would have given. The Spymaster nodded at her. She was to continue.

"I do not like your Pharaoh" she said again unsure he would listen. Lord Toth had always thought her opinions of no account. "There is a darkness in him that colours all around. There are many feelings in him that I do not fully understand, have no experience of. I do not feel comfortable with the feelings I get from him."

"In what way" the Spymaster asked.

"When he looks at certain women.... including myself," She quickly shook her head. "No no... it is not like that. There is no desire, more.... a dark feeling of hatred and ... a desire to inflict pain." She could feel her cheeks going red with embarrassment and she stared down at the floor, not wanting to meet the eye of either man in the room. "He feels the same when he looks at you and the warriors. He is.... gloating." She shook her head with frustration at her inability to explain clearly the fear Pharaoh invoked in her. "He is very dangerous, Lord. You should take great care."

She curtseyed again and left the two of them to their thoughts. She rubbed her temple as she walked back to her room. Ever since the boat she had had a bad headache and the herbs she had bought for Liam didn't seem to be helping.

"They helped Liam," she thought. "Why won't they help me?"

She shivered as she walked into the courtyard. The days might be very warm, but the nights could be equally as cold. She picked up a woollen shawl from a chair in her room and slipped it round her shoulders.

More fruits from her forays into the markets of Kush Prime.

"You're not going out?" Lena was busy folding newly washed clothes. They could be washed and dried very quickly in the heat.

"I'm going for a walk... alone." Emma said firmly. "I'll be fine, don't fuss."

Lena knew better than to argue with her mistress when she was in such a frame of mind.

"Shall I prepare an infusion for when you get back?" she asked.

"No. It's not working. I'll see if I can get something stronger from the apothecary tomorrow." With that Emma left the room and walked through the kitchen courtyard towards a side door.

XX

Liam leant against the wall by the stairs up to where the Lord's rooms were. He had watched Emma come down and head in the direction of her rooms. He wasn't sure why he stood there after Emma had gone. Perhaps it was to enjoy the quiet. Castles were noisy places and palaces were even more so. But there were times when they became quiet and Liam enjoyed those moments to the full when he found one.

He had observed all the Lords and Ladies arriving in their finery and watched them entering the main hall under the great dome and he had sat for some time listening to the music that had floated out from the hall. Then he had gone out into the town in search of supper with some the Lord's Elite that were not on duty. As usual there had been no sign of Saul or Neri and he wondered what was keeping them so occupied.

So lost in his thoughts was he that he almost missed Emma slipping out of the palace through the courtyard door. He hurried after her wondering which way she had gone. Then he caught sight of a pale figure just ahead of him. Praying it was her he cautiously followed. He had the feeling she wanted to be alone but he couldn't allow that. It was too dangerous but he could allow her the illusion of solitude.

Soon after leaving the palace she turned right and began to walk through the gardens at the side of the Temple. After a little while she stopped and waited. He slowed down too and waited. Was she meeting someone? Then she turned round and looked back the way she had come.

"Liam." she said and he sensed she was annoyed at her failure to slip out unseen. He emerged from the gloom of a large tree and grinned sheepishly.

"I thought you might not notice me," he said. She didn't bother replying to that but turned and began walking briskly away from the palace towards the North Gate. Liam followed behind easily keeping up with her.

It took them nearly an hour to reach the gate. The gatekeeper let them out through a small door inset into the larger iron gate. They had not spoken since the Temple. He followed her down to the shoreline and she turned west and began to walk along the water's edge, parallel to the city walls. After a little while, she raised her skirt above her ankles and stepped into the lake until the water covered her feet.

"It's not that cold," she said. "Do you think we could go for a swim?"

"Not here." Liam was horrified at the suggestion. Not only were they in full sight of the guards on the city walls but both moons were full, it was almost as bright as day.

She shook her head, amused by his reaction.

"We'll have to go further along then" she said with a mischievous grin on her face and began to run along the shoreline. Liam could hear her laughing as she ran.

It took a further half an hour to reach the end of the city walls. There were still boats beached on the shore and back beyond the shoreline, among an outcrop of rocks and tall bushes, Liam could make out the outline of makeshifts tents and ramshackle dwellings of scraps of wood and leather.

A tag encampment.

He hurried to catch up with Emma. This was no place for her.

"You have the typical warrior's reaction to those less fortunate," she said as he approached. She had stopped walking and was gazing unsmiling at the squalid slum that was home to so many tags. "That could be any of us if the gods turn away."

He took hold of her arm above the elbow.

"Let's go back."

"No" she said firmly. "I can't sleep.... this headache. I want to walk a little further, until I'm too tired for it to keep me awake." and she began to walk along the shoreline again away from the city, passed the tags, passed the boats, to the countryside beyond.

Ten more minutes of walking brought them to an outcrop of rocks, which Emma easily climbed over. It might have been the remains of a stone jetty but if it was, it had fallen down so long ago that it now formed a natural part of the shore. About fifteen feet further on the bank had collapsed into the water causing a large tree to overhang the water at an angle. Between was a perfectly secluded beach.

"If you really want to swim," Liam said, "here would be the ideal place."

The area inshore was heavily wooded and he went off in search of fallen branches and twigs to make a fire with, there would be plenty lying around. It was a lovely warm evening but a fire would be nice if she did decide to swim.

By the time he had found enough to start a fire with and to keep it going for some time Emma was already in the water, her clothes neatly folded and resting on the trunk of the falling tree. Her shawl was draped over one of its branches creating a screened off area. Liam smiled at this unexpected display of modesty; after all she had been the one to suggest a swim. Clearly a creature of contradictions. Was this what made her so exciting?

"Are you coming in?" she called from out in the lake. "Or are you going to stand there all night?"

He quickly stacked some of the wood and packed the spaces with handfuls of dry grass. Opening his pouch he searched for a few moments and then found what he was looking for. A red crystal. He could hear her calling from the lake and he raised his hand in acknowledgement. He put the red crystal on a flat stone near the dry grass and struck it with his empowered sword. He was rewarded with a spark, which quickly took hold and the grass flared into yellow flame. He quickly put on more until the flames began to catch on the twigs. Soon he had a decent fire. Once he was satisfied that it wouldn't go out he began to strip off.

Standing at the edge of the lake, its water lapping at his toes, he searched for Emma. She was some way out; he could only just make out her head. Worried by how far out she was he gritted his teeth and strode out, throwing himself in as the lake floor shelved quickly and there was enough depth to swim. To his surprise the water was warm. With a powerful over arm motion he began to swim towards the distant girl. As he neared he saw she was waiting for him, treading water and he began to do the same.

"Not too cold!" he joked. "The water's lovely and warm."

He heard her cough as she swallowed some water.

"Is it?" she gasped. "Well I'm cold."

"You're too pampered," he laughed and she cupped her hand and threw water over him. He went to do the same but she slipped underneath the water and surfaced some feet behind him. He swam towards her but before he could catch her she had disappeared again.

He could hear her laughing some distance to his right and he spun round.

"You're too slow," she taunted.

He tried to catch her again but each time she eluded him. Eventually, in frustration, he tried her own tactics against her and diving under the surface himself he managed to grasp hold of her ankles and momentarily pull her under. He felt her struggling and kicking and he quickly let go and surfaced just behind her. He slipped his arms round her waist and held her close. He kissed her neck, keeping both of them afloat as he did so.

"What's this?" he asked, fingering the collar of a linen shirt she was wearing. "That's cheating."

"Well I'm not taking it off," she said over her shoulder. "It's the only thing keeping me warm."

He let go of her and touched her shoulder, then her neck.

"You really are cold," he said, suddenly concerned. "We're getting out now and you can get warm by the fire."

He half expected her to protest but she turned back to shore and began to swim slowly in. He followed close behind keeping a watchful eye in case she got into trouble but she made it to the shore without incident and quickly sat down near the fire. He put more wood on the fire but he could see she was still shivering.

"You shouldn't have let yourself get so cold," he admonished. "Here, dry yourself on my shirt, it'll soon dry out."

She disappeared behind her shawl and he sat down and let the warm night air dry him. After a few minutes she reappeared and sat down on the other side of the fire. She had been drying her loose hair on his shirt, now she spread it out with her fingers in the warmth of the fire. He picked up his shirt and laid it on the warm rocks then began to get dressed himself. After a few minutes Emma walked over and spread out the linen shirt she had swum in next to his.

"Are you still cold?" he asked and he slowly reached out and touched her cheek. His hand fell to her shoulder and he slipped it round her neck and pulled her to him. His lips brushed her hair, it was still slightly damp, then he kissed her ear.

"This isn't right" she said and pulled away from him. Her hands were against his chest as if to keep him away.

"It feels fine to me," he said. "Emma…"
She did not move but continued to stare up at him, unblinking. Suddenly she sat back down on the ground pulling him with her. He slipped one arm under her head to support it. With his other hand he began to undo her dress and slip it over her shoulders and down. He began to kiss her face.
He pinned her arms above her head.

"What were you looking forward too?" he asked "This?" and he kissed her neck.
"Yes."

"Or this?" and he kissed her breasts, exciting her with his tongue.
"Yes."
He sat up, kneeling astride her, and looked down at her. She hadn't moved, her arms were still raised above her head. He could hear his heart pounding in his chest; his breath coming in short gasps. At that moment he believed her to be the most beautiful thing he would ever see. It was an image that would stay with him always. He leant over her and she put her arms around his neck and pulled him down to her. The smell of her perfume surrounded him and he lost himself in it as he kissed her again.
All his promises to Finn were forgotten.

Liam woke with a start. Emma was sitting on the other side of the fire staring out across the water.

"How long have I been asleep?" he asked, sitting up and stretching.

"Not long." She sounded strange, distant.

"Emma...."

"I made a terrible mistake," she said." I've just done something very stupid. It should never have happened but...."

He knelt before her and would have taken her hand but she wouldn't let him.

"No one will ever know." he assured her.

She shook her head violently.

"You don't understand..." She suddenly twisted and stared behind them, away from the lake. "There's someone there," she whispered. "In the bushes."

He followed her gaze but couldn't see anyone at first. As his eyes slowly adjusted to the gloom he thought he could make out a shape crouched by a tree. It was probably a bush but.... He stood up.

"We better start back," he said. "But first.... I won't be a moment." He walked slowly back into the bushes, his hands on his belt as if he intended to undo it. He was some distance to the left of where the figure might be and once hidden by the tree line he began to quietly edge his way around to approach from behind.

He heard Emma call out to him.

"Hurry up, your shirt is dry."

Painstakingly slowly he began to inch nearer to the tree. His approach was made all the more difficult by the dry twigs underfoot. He didn't want to announce his presence by snapping a twig with his foot. He began to feel foolish. There was no figure it was just a bush. Emma was probably feeling guilty and that had made her overanxious. He put his foot down without thinking and there was a loud crack as a dry twig broke beneath his weight. The bush stood up and turned round. Liam threw himself at the figure and the two momentarily grappled with each other until the force of Liam's assault overbalanced them and Liam found himself rolling down a slope towards the water. He had let go of the intruder as he fell but he was sure the man had fallen too.

As soon he stopped falling Liam leapt to his feet and launched himself onto the man who was lying winded a few feet away.

"Right, you..." he began, pinning his opponent to the ground. The man groaned, took a shuddering breath and turned his head towards Liam. "Neri!"

"Ralf!" Emma had run over and was standing over the pair of them. "By Ammon's breath, what are you doing here?"
Liam rolled off the young man and stood up, offering Neri a hand up.

"I take it you two know each other." he said.

"Ralf is one of Lord Toth's elite." Emma said. "But what he's doing here..."

"He's also Neri, part of your elusive guard." Liam told her.

The young man smiled sheepishly at Emma and Liam realised that he was in love with her.
Although besotted might be a better description.

"Saul and I were sent to investigate something not far from here." Ralf told them as Liam put his shirt on and began to kill the fire. "He wanted to know who lit this fire in case it meant trouble, so I was sent to find out. I'm not very good at this spying business but our Lord thought it might be good for me to get away from the castle for a bit."

"Ralf isn't very popular with our Lord at the moment." Emma explained.

"I wonder why?" Liam said dryly.

"He started a fight with his Captain." she said, as if that were all.

He wondered if she was really that naïve or whether she just chose not to see what was so obvious.

"Where is Saul now?" he asked.

"He's waiting for me in the woods." Ralf said. He seemed quite upset to have failed so easily in his mission.

"Then take us to him" Liam pointed the way with his hand. Ralf glanced hesitantly at Emma and she nodded.

He began to lead them through the wood.

XXI

"What exactly are we looking for?" Liam asked as he lay in a ditch looking at a white stone building in a clearing about fifty yards away. The ditch ran alongside the track that joined the main road from the lands to the west and south of Kush Prime. Several carts were lined up in front of the building and as Liam watched six of these were driven off down the track away from Prime. "Where does it lead to?" he asked.

Saul shook his head.

"Doesn't make sense," he whispered. "There's only an old mined out quarry at the end. Kush has built something ... I need to get a look inside."

They continued to watch for another few minutes as slaves carried large pots out of the building and loaded them onto the remaining three carts. Liam tapped Saul on the shoulder; they should rejoin the others. Saul nodded and, keeping low, the two men crawled back along the ditch and into the trees.

Ralf had quickly found Saul and after some initial reluctance Saul had explained their mission.

"Pharaoh has had a large building erected secretly in the middle of the woods," he had told them. "The spymaster only found out about it because some of the workmen got drunk one evening and said too much in the hearing of one of his rangers."

"And why is Spymaster Toth so interested?" Liam wanted to know.

"Because its existence is kept secret, because we don't know what happens there and because Pharaoh has visited here four times since it was completed about a tarn ago."

"Perhaps he keeps his mistress there," Liam said and he felt a sharp pain as Emma kicked his leg.

"I doubt that." Saul said taking the suggestion seriously. "It doesn't look like a dwelling; there are no windows and only one large door at the one end."

They speculated for several minutes over what it could be for and how best to get inside without being seen until Emma, somewhat impatiently, suggested the best way to find anything out would be to go and have a look.

"Can't," Ralf explained. "Since yesterday there have been twenty slaves and an overseer, plus about ten carts and drivers and the normal guard of two."

"It has become a hothouse of activity." Saul said.

Liam decided he wanted to see the place for himself and soon found himself crawling down the drainage ditch that ran alongside the track. But getting nearer the strange building did not reveal much that was of use. As Saul had said there was only one door at the one end and no windows. Liam peered through the gloom relieved only by one moon and saw that there were grills all along the length of the wall he could see. These were set in the wall at a height of about a foot. But apart from that Liam could see nothing that gave any clue to the building's purpose. As they began to crawl back there was a loud crash and the cursing of the overseer and the crack of his whip could be clearly heard in the still night air.

"We need some kind of diversion so that I can get inside" Saul said as they rejoined the others.

"You don't need to get inside" Emma pointed out after several minutes fruitless discussion between the three men and they all turned to look at her.

"Why not?" Ralf asked.

"All you really need to know is what is inside those jars," she said. "It should give you some idea of what is going on inside."

Liam nodded. That made sense.

"But how do you know they didn't take something in and are coming out empty?" Ralf asked.

"Because they're very heavy." Liam said. "Were they that heavy going in?"

Saul shook his head.

"But we still need some kind of diversion. The carts are in the open. Anyone trying to get near would be easily seen."

"I can do that," Emma said quietly. "With Saul's help. Liam, lend me your shirt, mine is still damp." She borrowed Ralf's cloak and then made them turn their backs whilst she got changed. When he turned back Liam was horrified.

"You look like a tag," he said dismayed at the transformation.

"Who else would be out here at night" she said and there was coldness in her voice. She had wrapped the cloak round her waist as a skirt and as she moved there was sight of a shapely leg in the moonlight. Liam shook his head, this didn't seem right. She handed him her neatly folded dress and overmantle and then took off her shoes and gave them to him. "Don't lose those," she said. "They won't let me back in the city dressed like this."

Saul looked at Liam and shrugged. He began to follow her through the trees back along the road.

"Why me?" Liam heard him say.

"Because you're the only one who could pass as Anarian." They were quickly swallowed up by the darkness. Liam felt uneasy. This was no job for a woman; they should have been able to sort it out without involving Emma. He felt Ralf touch his bare arm.

"We better be ready," he said.

They slipped deeper into the woods themselves and began to circle the building, crossing the track further along out of sight of the remaining carts. They eventually emerged at the back of the building and there was no one around. No guards had been posted. Pharaoh must have been very confident that no one knew about the place. Liam made his way along the back wall and cautiously peered round the corner. He could see the horse of the first cart but not the cart itself. He had some idea of entering this cart once Saul and Emma had begun their diversion. He began to edge his way down the side wall, stopping briefly to test another small door half way along but it was locked. He looked behind. Ralf was still at the corner of the building and Liam indicated that the door was locked and that Ralf should make his way to the other door. He might be able to see inside if the guards were distracted long enough. Ralf nodded and disappeared.

Silently Liam made his way to the bottom corner and looked round. The three carts were lined up along the building. Two must have been fully laden. Only the last one nearest the open door was still being filled. He couldn't see any drivers or guards but he could hear voices raised in argument coming from the other side of the carts.

Liam was about to edge his way to the nearest cart and climb in the back when he saw Ralf. The fool had walked into the open and was kneeling over a broken pot. As Liam watched he scooped something up in his cupped hands. Liam fingered his sword nervously. Ralf stood up and with a glance towards the other side of the carts he began to run along the side of the building towards Liam. Liam expected a shout to go up at any second, but it seemed the boy had the luck of the Gods with him and he made it safely to where Liam was waiting, his hands carefully cupped and held out in front of him.

"Watch out!" Ralf whispered as Liam dragged him round the safety of the end wall.

"You *bloody* idiot!" Liam said, trying to put as much anger as he could into his whisper. "You might have been seen."

"They were all looking the other way," Ralf said. "At Emma." There was a note of pride in his voice and Liam realised the young warrior had it bad. No wonder he had been sent away. Ralf looked down at his hands. "Where shall I put this?"

In the gloom Liam could see what looked like a fine powder in the boy's hands. He opened his pouch wide. It contained only a few coins and the fire crystal; Ralf could put it in there.

They made their way back into the wood, walking parallel to the track and towards Prime and the main road. They had agreed to meet Saul and Emma at the end of the track. Once they were well clear of the building and unlikely to be overheard, Liam asked Ralf what the others had done as a diversion. Ralf laughed.

"They pretended to be a tag whore and client, looking for a secluded place to go. The guards were quite taken with Emma. They wanted her to return when she had finished with Saul. They were haggling over price. Then Saul got impatient and demanded what he had already paid for... so I thought it best to get out of there."

He walked ahead trying to find the road again leaving Liam becoming angrier with Emma at every passing thought. It had been a stupid thing for her to do, anything could have happened.

Had she no self-respect, no pride?

He was going to have to have a serious talk with her. She couldn't continue with this behaviour.

It wasn't right.

It took them a while to find the track again but once they had they made good time. Saul and Emma were already waiting under the shelter of the trees. She quickly took her clothes from Liam and disappeared into the wood to change. Whilst she was doing this Saul took Liam to one side. He was concerned about her. Twice she had mentioned a bad headache and she was as cold as snow. Did she have a fever?

That decided Liam. He forgot his anger with Emma and told Saul they could examine what Ralf had found later in their room at the Palace. He gave his pouch to Saul, for now his priority was to get Emma back and safely tucked up in bed.

Liam and Emma headed towards the West gate of Prime first. Saul and Ralf would follow separately later, entering by a different gate. Fortunately, once he had explained that his wife had been taken ill which was why they were out so late, the Gatekeeper readily let them enter and even told them of a good Apothecary nearby.

It was dawn when they finally made it back to the palace. Lena had fallen asleep in a chair waiting for her mistress but she quickly awoke when Liam entered carrying Emma. He told the maid to get Emma to bed and to make her a warm drink. If that didn't help or Emma got worse she was to fetch the Apothecary immediately.

Liam left with Lena's promises ringing in his ears. He was very tired. He had no doubt that Saul and Ralf would have arrived back long before he had and would be anxiously waiting to examine the contents of the pouch. He was quite happy to leave it to them. It was their job after all.

As he neared the stairs leading up to the Lord's rooms the Spymaster emerged from the shadows and Liam was too tired to react in surprise.

"You are to go up to our Lord," the Spymaster told him tersely as he disappeared in the direction of Emma's room. Liam just wanted to sleep but he climbed the stairs slowly. At least he would find out what it was Ralf had scooped up.

It might be important.

XXII

By the time Liam had reached the door to the Lord's chamber the Spymaster and Emma had appeared and he waited for them to reach him before entering the outer chamber. Liam was concerned to see how tired Emma was looking, but she had been up all night so it was to be expected.

Ralf wasn't in the outer chamber but Saul was and he grinned at the girl as she entered. Liam saw her flush a deep red colour and briefly wondered what the Ranger was thinking to cause such a reaction. Then he promptly forgot the matter as Lord Menethes appeared from the bedroom.

"Have you shown them yet?" the Lord asked.

"I was about to," the Spymaster said. "This is what was found" and he pushed a small wooden box across the table towards Emma. Liam stared over her shoulder at what was on the table. Liam's empty pouch was lying there and Emma's hand brushed it as she reached across to the box. She jerked back her hand suddenly and let out a cry of pain.

"Something bit me," she said, rubbing the side of her hand. Liam examined the pouch and the table but there was nothing there and Gerran looked at her hand but could see nothing. She looked at the two items on the table suspiciously and seemed reluctant to touch either of them.

"What's inside?" she asked. The Spymaster didn't answer but impatiently opened the lid and showed her the contents. He pushed the box closer to her and watched her face carefully as she stretched out a finger and gently touched the wood.

"Grey powder?" she queried tentatively stretching out her finger to touch the surface.

"These were also in it," the spymaster said and he held out a small bundle of cloth towards her and began to unwrap it. Inside Liam saw the charred remains of small bones. "The Apothecary has identified these as human fingers, probably male from the size but he can't be sure." The Spymaster quickly looked at Emma to see her reaction but Liam realised she wasn't listening to him. She didn't appear to have heard him at all. Her attention was firmly fixed on the box and she was staring at the powder. As he continued to watch her closely he realised that she wasn't blinking, she appeared to be in some kind of trance.

"Emma?" He moved towards her slowly and reached out with his hand to touch her shoulder.

The Lord Menethes' chamber vanished and he found himself standing in a dim room amongst a crowd of people, very frightened people and he started to become afraid too. There were piles of straw on the floor but there was too much of it for it to be a rush covering. There was so much of it, it was covering his feet and lying against his shins. He looked around quickly. They were all men in the room with him, he sensed about fifty in all but it wasn't crowded, the room was quite long and it had a high ceiling.

As he looked up a crack appeared in the wall, about a foot up from the ground, and daylight streamed into the room about ten feet in front of where he was standing. For a few seconds nothing happened then the straw on the floor began to smoulder. A small curl of smoke slowly rose towards the light. Liam looked at it in horrified fascination, his mind refusing to believe what was happening. Then he dragged his eyes reluctantly from the smoke and looked at the walls of the room.

More grills were opening, more light was raining down and in that terrible light he saw the walls were studded with thousands of red fire crystals. He looked down at the floor and moved some of the straw with his foot. The floor too was covered with the deadly red crystals. He looked again for the wisp of smoke he had been watching only seconds earlier but it was impossible to see it any longer amongst the small yellow red flames licking at the straw.

The people in the room were beginning to crowd back against the walls but there was no escape. As all the grills on both sides were opened to their full extent all the crystals began to give out their lethal energy. He looked down at his feet. The straw against his leg was already on fire and he kicked it away stepping back as he did so. For a moment he didn't feel anything then there was a searing pain in his right calf as the smouldering straw behind him burst into flames and set fire to the hem of his trousers.

He could hear someone shouting in agony and realised it was himself. But his voice was lost in the screams from all those around him. His hand was out in front of him and he watched, horrified as the skin began to melt in the intense heat, one finger beginning to char and turn black. He jerked his hand back towards his face as he felt his coat flare up and set fire to his hair... and the room with the charred, pain-crazed figures vanished. He was once again in the Lord Menethes' rooms.

With a cry of pain he staggered back away from the box with its terrifying contents and leant against the wall. Lord Menethes and the ranger were looking at him, puzzled by his strange behaviour, but Gerran was looking shaken and frightened. He had obviously experienced something similar but neither of them was capable of putting into words what they had seen. Lord

Menethes turned round to Saul and ordered him to leave. The Ranger looked annoyed at being excluded but he obeyed.

Once Saul had gone and the door firmly shut behind him Lord Menethes poured Gerran a large glass of wine and handed it to him.

"What did you see?" he said and there was a sense of awe in his voice as he slowly turned and looked at the girl still standing by the table. Gerran couldn't answer. Like Liam he was staring at his right hand, slowly turning it back and forth. It looked normal and yet Liam had no doubt that, only seconds before, it was a hand that had been blackened and distorted with the heat and pain.

The Spymaster drained the glass and handed it back to his Lord.

"Well?" Lord Menethes said impatiently

"Men... he's burning men" the Spymaster managed to say before covering his face with his hands.

"We knew that," snapped Menethes puzzled by the Spymaster's behaviour.

"Earthmen," Emma said looking up from the contemplation of her own hand, "and it isn't very pleasant." she added.

The Spymaster was shaking his head in disbelief.

"I saw it... I could see it... I could feel it." He looked at Emma, still shaking his head. "What...How did you...?"

"I don't know," she admitted. "I've never done anything like that before." She stood up and walked slowly to the Lord. "He knows it is you who brought them here. That's what I could sense. He was ... gloating. If you don't deliver the Anant to him.... or at the very least the Toth he is going to use this information to destroy you." She seemed more certain now and Liam could see something in her assured manner and positive attitude had convinced the Lord.

The Spymaster gave a grim smile.

"That is why the Anari aren't worried about the tribute ships. The Anant, or more specifically the Toth, are to fill the ships."

"Did you know that was what he was planning?" Emma stared accusingly from Lord to Spymaster and back. "That the Toth are to fill the Tribute ships."

"No," the Lord said but she stepped back from the table not trusting him and bumped into Liam. He put his hands protectively on her shoulders. "No," Menethes said more firmly. "I was merely told to eliminate the troublesome Lord Toth. If possible to deliver him alive to Pharaoh…. If not ...to…" He left the rest unsaid. Then he raised both hands in front of him in a gesture of honesty. "Your Lord knows this. I told him at our meeting in the spring. That is why I suggested you come with me. To see if between us we could find out what Pharaoh planned." He smiled down at her. "It would seem you did as well as he expected."

"What do we do now?" Emma seemed to have recovered from her vision although she was still flexing her right hand as if not quite satisfied that she had full use of it.

"I am the Anant High Lord" Menethes said. "I will not deliver any of my people to Pharaoh. Spymaster, you must set our escape plan into operation. I want to be on my way home within two days."

Emma suddenly smiled.

"Pharaoh chose the wrong man when he made you High Lord," she said.

For a second the Lord frowned and Liam knew he was looking for the hidden insult. Then the Lord smiled as well as he realised what she meant.

"Yes he did," he agreed. "Go and get some rest," he added gently. "You have done very well".

Liam sensed Emma straighten her back at his words as if pleased by them. Didn't her old Lord ever praise her so?

Gerran stood up, leaning heavily on the table as he did so. Liam knew he wasn't entirely sure his legs were yet ready to support him... because he was feeling much the same himself. But the Spymaster recovered quickly and accompanied them to the outer door.

"You have a headache," he said as he held open the door. "Perhaps I can help," and he rested his hand briefly on her forehead. Liam heard her gasp with relief and she shyly smiled her thanks. "Go and rest now," the Spymaster told her and he looked at Liam silently ordering him to see that she did just that. "Your maid will have a cup of tea waiting."

As they walked down the corridor to the stairs Liam was conscious that the man was watching them.

Lord Menethes was holding the wooden box that had been on the table. The lid was shut but he didn't need to look inside to see its contents. The Spymaster closed the door behind the girl and came back to the table.

"Will she stay with us?" Menethes asked.

"The maid says she is determined not to return to Toth. What ever he said to her it seems to have upset her," the Spymaster said. "But the Captain has had little luck in his task. They are not yet lovers. I doubt it will happen."

"She is even better than I imagined when I first saw her on Urth." the Lord continued. "We must get her to stay." He thought for a moment then laughed aloud at the Spymaster's expression. "Do not worry, father-in-marriage, I do not intend to take another mistress.

234

Perhaps we should marry her to her Captain. Give her respectability."

The Spymaster nodded. That idea had been forming in his own mind for some time now.

"She was his long before she went to the Toth. I might be able to persuade her. I cannot see him being a problem"

Menethes put the box back on the table, his hand resting lightly on its lid.

"...and get us away from this terrible place as quickly as possible."

The Spymaster bowed. It was already in hand. Japhet had been instructed to put the necessary plans into effect. He wished his Lord a good night and retired to his own room and his thoughts.

XXIII

Liam slept until well past the start of second period. Ralf had been in the room, too excited to sleep but Liam had just wished him a good night and almost immediately fallen asleep. He would probably have slept the day around but he was violently awoken by someone slapping his face and shaking his shoulders.

"By Ammon's coat, you lazy good for nothing man, wake up."

Lena.

He turned over and buried his head in the pillow, ignoring the persistent maid. If he ignored her long enough perhaps she would go away.

"Wake up. It's my mistress. There is something wrong." Lena's insistent voice broke into his tired mind and he struggled to wake up properly. He forced himself to sit up and open his eyes. Blinking furiously in the bright light of day that was streaming in through the unshuttered window he stretched, yawned and stood up.

"I'll be with my mistress. Hurry up." and Lena quickly left. He could hear her footsteps hurrying down the corridor and a few moments later the swish of her skirts as she passed beneath his window. Liam glanced down and grinned. He was naked, no wonder she had left so quickly. Still chuckling to himself he splashed lukewarm water over his face and neck. It didn't make him feel a lot better.

He was getting too old to stay up all night.

But what a night! The revelation of what was happening in the woods.

The vision he had shared with Emma and the Spymaster.

But as he got dressed he only had memories of Emma lying in his arms, the feel of her, and the smell of her scent.

Tiredly he straightened the thin sheet on his bed and made his way to the courtyard next door. It was very quiet, there didn't seem to be anyone about. The shutters on the entrance window were pulled closed and he hesitated. Then he marched in and called the maid's name.

"You took your time," she snapped and she beckoned him into the next room.

Emma was lying on a low canopied bed, covered by a single sheet that hugged the contours of her body. One hand lay on top of the cover and Liam tentatively touched her wrist.

She was ice cold.

Liam looked at Lena. She had been crying and it was the sight of this that unnerved him more than anything. He saw the sheet rise very slightly then fall. Emma's breathing was so shallow it barely disturbed the cover at all.

"Have you sent for the Apothecary?"

Lena shook her head.

"He's gone. They've all gone to the opening ceremony." She sat down on the only chair in the room and a tear rolled down her face. "I kept looking in but she seemed to be sleeping. I thought it best to let her rest, but she was so quiet, I got frightened and I couldn't wake her...."

"Don't blame yourself," he said taking Emma's wrist and feeling for her pulse. It was racing, there seemed hardly a pause between beats and yet she was so calm, so quiet. What was wrong with her? "I'll find our elusive apothecary," he said. "You keep talking to her until I get back."

He started out of the door wondering where to start his search.

"Our Lord is in the temple," Lena called after him, "giving thanks for another fifty years of Pharaoh's rule."

As he walked through the kitchen yard to the side door he thought carefully. He wouldn't be allowed into the temple on such a day but, he reasoned, neither would a simple apothecary. He would be with the warriors outside the temple. Near enough to be called if needed but out of the way otherwise. But that still left a large area of Main Square to search and the man could be anywhere.

As he approached the Main Square his heart sank. It was crowded with thousands of people all coming to give thanks and show devotion to their Pharaoh. The Apothecary could be anywhere and the crowds didn't make it any easier. They seemed intent on getting in his way as he tried to move through them. At least he had decided where to start his search if he was ever allowed through and he began to elbow his way through the mass of people.

He made very slow progress and some way towards the middle of the square he came to a complete halt. The noise and the heat were beginning to hurt his head, the late night was finally catching up with him and he could feel his temper beginning to fray.

Someone touched his arm. A minor priest selling amulets.

"A prayer against early death or the plague perhaps?" The man held up his flat wicker tray and Liam saw dozens of tubes, some of a bronze coloured metal, others of simple clay. Some had both ends sealed either with wax or clay; others were still open at one end, ready for the buyer's own prayer.

"I have no money," Liam said shortly and the priest moved quickly away. Liam frowned. He should have asked if the man had seen any Anant warriors. They would surely stand out even in this crowd but as usual he had thought of it too late. He silently cursed and tried asking those standing near him, but no one had seen anything or seemed willing to help.

"If all you want is company for the festival, why not join us?"

Liam turned round. Behind him were two warriors whose torc he did not recognise but they were clearly Anari. "We share a courtyard," the second warrior said. "Why not company on this day also."
Thamad.
Liam groaned. He didn't want trouble but he had wasted enough time already.

"Thank you, I would be honoured," he said slowly. "But I am looking for someone. It is most urgent that I find them."

"Then let us help" the first warrior insisted. "Six eyes are always better than two."

Liam eyed the two men warily. He couldn't help being suspicious of their motives for helping him. There was little love lost between Anant and Anari in spite of Pharaoh's obvious intentions when he gave an Anant Lordship to an Anari Lordling. It was totally out of character for these warriors to offer help.
And yet they were.

"I need our Apothecary. Someone is … ill," he said.

"Lord Menethes' concubine?" The first warrior smiled at Liam's surprise. "You are her guard, are you not?" He turned to his companion. "Tomas can go in search of Menethes warriors. They should not be too difficult to find. The best inns are near this square."

Liam nodded at this. That had been his reasoning too.

Tomas inclined his head and marched away through the crowds with ease. Liam noticed how the crowds quickly made way for the warrior, something they had not done for him.

"Shouldn't we go too?" Liam said.

"You and I will return to the palace," the remaining warrior said. "Our apothecary is there, dosing his own bad head. We shall rouse him and he will be at your disposal for as long as is needed."

Remembering how readily the crowds had cleared a path for the other warrior, Liam indicated that the Thamad warrior should lead the way.

In much less time than it had taken him on the outward journey Liam found himself re-entering the Palace, this time by the main entrance. Within minutes the Thamad apothecary had been summoned and Liam ushered him in. He hesitated on the threshold and turned back to the warrior whose help had been so invaluable.

"Thank you," Liam said, a little embarrassed at being in debt to an Anari.

The warrior stared at him gravely.

"Our Lord owes a debt of gratitude to Mistress Emma. This goes a little way to repaying it."

Liam was surprised. He remembered Emma saying she had never met the Lord Thamad so how could she have put him under an obligation?

"Our Lord specifically asked to be in this courtyard in the hope of expressing his thanks personally, but he has not yet had the opportunity." the warrior said. Liam nodded at this. Emma had hardly stopped since they had arrived. She had walked for miles, seen everything there was to see and still had the energy to dance in the evenings at the great dinners given by Pharaoh. Just thinking about it made Liam feel old and tired.

"Perhaps she has done too much, exhausted herself," the warrior suggested and he gazed at Liam as if to see what reaction there would be to his words. Liam found himself becoming increasingly worried. The warrior seemed to know an awful lot about Emma's movements even if they were sharing a courtyard. Had someone been spying on her?

It was a simple step from there to wonder if they thought Emma was a spy. The High Lord to the Thamad was Kush himself. Had Pharaoh asked them to watch Emma?

"The Spymaster must be made aware of this" Liam thought. "Emma mustn't be put into danger because of the actions of Saul and Neri."

He thanked the warrior again for his help and entered Emma's sitting room. He could hear the voices of Lena and the Apothecary in the next room and he considered joining them but then decided against it. If the Apothecary was examining Emma she wouldn't want him present and he sat down on one of the chairs and waited for someone to come out and tell him what was wrong.

Nearly an hour passed before the Menethes apothecary appeared. The Spymaster and Ralf closely followed him. The apothecary and the Spymaster entered the bedroom leaving the two men staring at each other in helpless frustration. After another five minutes the first apothecary came out carrying his large bag over his shoulder closely followed by an angry Spymaster. He shook his head at the Spymaster's questions. He had no idea what was wrong but he had eliminated the possibility of snake or insect bite for there was no mark where poison could have entered. If it was a poison of some kind it must have been ingested in food or drink.

Liam raised his head suddenly. What about the lake water? Emma had been swimming the night before. The apothecary shook his head. If it was something from the lake then a lot more people would have it and the symptoms would be very different anyway.

The apothecary bowed and left.

Liam looked at the spymaster. Was poison suspected?

Gerran shrugged. It seemed likely. Unless Emma had some previously unknown disease poison was the obvious answer.

"Who would want to poison Emma?" Ralf asked and Liam remembered the Thamad warrior and his detailed knowledge of Emma's movements. He told Gerran about the warriors and their surprising offer of help and the spymaster thought about it for some time with a worried frown on his face.

"It could be genuine." For a moment neither man paid any attention then they both turned together to look at the quiet young warrior in the corner. "It could be genuine" Ralf repeated. "Emma persuaded our Lord to allow Lady Orin to stay at Toth Prime when she left her husband. He wanted to send her straight back but Emma convinced him to let her stay."

Liam couldn't understand the relevance of it but the Spymaster quickly explained that Lady Orin was Lord Thamad's daughter.

"So their help could be genuine after all," he concluded.

"Then who could have poisoned Emma and why?" Liam said.

The Menethes Apothecary pulled back the door curtain and entered the room. Through the opening Liam could see Emma still lying quietly on her bed. She looked so peaceful it was difficult to believe she might be dying. The apothecary shook his head.

"I know of no poison that would produce such symptoms," he said. "I have no idea what is wrong or what to do about it."

"She has been complaining of a bad headache and being cold for some days," Liam told him, "and she has been doing a lot. The Thamad warrior noticed how busy she's been. He thought she might just be exhausted."

"This is not simple exhaustion," the apothecary said. "I've never seen anything like it. I've done all I can, we'll just have to wait and see." With this he picked up his own bag of potions and started for the door.

"It's a pity she's not a man," Ralf said. "Then it would be obvious what was wrong."

"Why?" Liam said tiredly.

"If she were a man, it would be a bad becoming" Ralf said referring to the time that a warrior finally became a full telepath.
The Spymaster stared at him.

"The head ache, the nervous energy, the desire to keep moving... ahead of the pain... going within oneself." He looked through the open door at the figure on the bed. "Get the Apothecary back... now" and he hurried into the bedroom pulling the curtain back as he went.

"But she's a woman" Ralf said puzzled but Liam had already left the room.

XXIV

Somewhat reluctantly Liam handed Emma down to Ralf's care and dismounted himself. They were at the Gate at Kush Prime. Emma was being sent back to Lord Toth.

The Spymaster spent what seemed like hours coaxing Emma back from wherever her tortured mind had taken her. The Apothecary prepared the draught usually given in these cases but the problem had been how much to give her.

Too little, it would be ineffective and she might die.

Too much, it might propel her back into herself and she might die.

Ralf sat in the chair and stared into the distance. Pleased with himself because he had been the one to help her but frightened by the implications of the solution.

"How can it be?" he kept muttering, more to himself than in any expectation of an answer. In the end he suddenly stood up and turned to Liam. "What do I tell my Lord?" This thought seemed to frighten him more than anything. How was he to tell his Lord that his mistress was... What? "Perhaps that's why he sent her to your Lord," he said at last "to be rid of... Colm was right after all."

Liam realised that the young man had no inkling about Emma. Lord Toth, it seemed, had kept her secret well.

"He knew all along" Liam was forced to tell him. If Emma recovered he didn't want her being upset by some careless word from this foolish boy. "That is why he sent her to our Lord... as a spy, not as a mistress."

Ralf sat down again. He was clearly having trouble understanding it all.

Eventually the spymaster emerged and they were allowed in to see Emma. Whilst Ralf hovered nervously in the doorway Liam knelt by the bed and smiled down at her. She looked very tired, dark rings round her eyes and a slight twitch in her cheek the only indication of the pain she had suffered and was still suffering.

"How do you feel now?" he asked gently.

She glanced at the Spymaster standing just behind him.

"Up to travelling," she said.

Liam turned to Gerran for an explanation.

"Mistress Emma is to return to the Toth as soon as it can be arranged" he said. "I have done all I can, it would be better if she were near a Master…. in case anything happens."

"So, you were right, Liam" she said, giving him a weak smile. "You are to send me back to my Lord after all."

"And once you are sure she is safe you are to return to Menethes Prime." the Spymaster said. "We will not be far behind you." With this he had left to make the necessary arrangements for Emma's departure.

Within the hour they were on horse on their way to the Gate. Emma rode behind Liam, her head resting on his back.

"And how is your sudden departure to be explained?" he said as they rode to the West Gate of the city.

"My illness is due to an expectation," she said and Liam sensed sadness in her voice. "Since it is clearly a Toth problem I am to be returned to him. Your Lord is playing the outraged purchaser, demanding his money for my contract back. That is how it was always planned I would return…. if I returned."

"Don't you mind?" he said.

The indignity of it, the shame.

"Of course I mind," she hissed and they rode on in angry silence.

Once at the Gate Ralf helped Emma down but then Lena put her arm round Emma's shoulders and helped her into the building. Liam and Ralf divided the few bags between them and followed. Within seconds they were standing in the Gate building at Toth Secund. The guard pointed to another pair of crystal pillars pointing in a different direction.

"Go through." he said. "You are expected."

Liam stepped through first and was quickly followed by Lena and her mistress. As Emma stepped out the other end she gave a cry and clutched at her head with her hands. Liam hurried back and picked her up in his arms. For once Lena did not frown, she was too worried.

"Has Lord Toth been informed?" Ralf asked anxiously.

"He's already on his way," the gate attendant said. He looked curiously at Emma. "Is it true then?"

Liam wondered what the man had heard. Then he saw the grins on the guards' faces.

"Who'd have thought the old man had it in him?" one of them said.

"Put me down". Emma struggled to her feet and ran outside, her face as pink as the sky.

"Perhaps we should ride and meet him," Liam suggested to Ralf and the young man nodded.

There were horses waiting for them outside and Emma, her sudden activity appearing to have drained her of what little energy she had left, was sitting on a low wall near them. Ralf tied the bags onto one of the horses and then waited to help Emma up behind Liam. Lena was to ride behind him.

"It will be dark before we reach Prime," he said and Liam heard Emma mutter a short "Good" under her breath. He twisted round to speak to her. Would she like to sit in front, she could rest then, even sleep. But she quickly shook her head. The Spymaster had told her to stay awake, no matter how bad things got.

Liam urged his horse forward into a gentle trot but after a few seconds she begged him to stop. They would have to proceed at a slow walk.

"My Lord will be with us in about an hour and a half." Ralf said. Liam nodded. He had heard nothing but he had no reason to disbelieve the boy. He led the silent group forward.

True to his word the Lord duly appeared on the horizon an hour and half later. Liam stopped his horse and watched at the Lord's furious approach. This was the man who haunted his dreams. Lord Toth reined in his horse from a full gallop and came to a stop only feet away. With surprising agility he leapt from his horse and hurried over. Emma slipped readily from the horse into his arms. He kissed her, but that was to be expected, Liam thought. He was, after all, a Lord whose mistress was being returned to him *pregnant.* How else was he to behave?

Lord Toth led Emma away from the milling warriors that had accompanied him and spread his cloak on the ground some distance away for her to sit on. She looked up at him and he smiled and gently touched her face. An intimate gesture, one a man might make to his expectant mistress.

Except Liam had seen the Spymaster make exactly the same gesture only hours before. It had something to do with how he helped her. Liam had to admit though, the old Lord was very good. If he hadn't known better he might have been fooled into thinking Toth actually cared.

They talked for a while and then Lord Toth stared in Liam's direction for some time but whether at him or Ralf Liam couldn't be sure. He seemed to be thinking, then he nodded and helped Emma to her feet. There was a flurry of activity from the mounted riders and some rode off in the direction of the Gate. The majority remained and grouped themselves once more around the Lord as he remounted. For a moment Liam thought Emma would ride with him again but the Lord leant over and held out his hand to her. She sat in front of him facing forward and they began the journey back to Toth Prime.

Liam rode beside Ralf but he had no opportunity to question the young man for the Lord rode swiftly and Liam needed all his concentration to control his horse. He was glad when the city at last came into sight and the pace eased as they dropped onto the main road and prepared to enter the city by the West gate.

Emma was carried into the castle and disappeared. Ralf had also vanished quickly once they had entered the Castle; Liam wondered what he was supposed to do. A stable lad had taken his horse from him and he was left standing in the main courtyard of the castle.

One Menethes among so many Toth.

A man approached, by his dress the castle steward although he had the hair of a warrior. His forelock was unusually plaited and tied back into the ponytail. Probably a retired warrior, Liam thought. The steward indicated that Liam was to follow him into the castle. Liam was showed to a room on the first floor, probably quite small by a Lord's standards but it was the most luxurious accommodation Liam had yet experienced. He wondered why he had been so honoured.

"Our Lord has ordered some supper be served to you in your room" the steward told him and he left.

Liam frowned. He was obviously being kept away from the rest of the castle and it explained why Ralf had vanished so quickly. He knew too much. The Lord would obviously want Emma's secret to remain just that so Ralf would have to be talked to and Liam was to be kept away from inquisitive warriors in case he let something slip. That was fine by him; the last few days had tired him, he was quite happy to be left alone. He yawned and stretched out on the bed. It was extremely comfortable, he could get used to this he decided and closing his eyes he quickly fell asleep.

When he awoke it was to find someone had laid out clean clothes for him. The crystal fire in the hearth was alight and someone had pulled across a side grate and put water on to boil. Presumably to wash in, for on the table were a selection of cold dishes and a jug of ale.

What to do first, eat then wash or wash then eat. Liam smiled at the luxury of such choice. Within half an hour he was sitting down to eat. He had had a good wash and changed into the clean clothes. Feeling refreshed by this and his sleep he was looking forward to the food.

Once he had finished eating, he began to wonder what he was expected to do now. He refilled his tankard with the last of the ale and walked over to the window to look out whilst he drank it. His room overlooked the main courtyard, the middle of three that made up the castle. Toth Castle was rather like Kush Palace he decided but consisting of only three courtyards instead of sixteen. Of course the buildings themselves were very different, no elegant colonnades and fountains in these courtyards, everything was solid and functional like the Toth themselves. But the basic design was the same.

The main courtyard was much larger than the other two, more rectangular than square; the main accommodation for the Lord was in the side where Liam was. Opposite was the huge archway and studded gate of the gatehouse. As in the castle at Menethes Prime the rooms down either side and by the gatehouse would probably house the Spymaster's rooms, quarters for the Elite and probably smaller rooms for less favoured members of a visiting Lord's entourage.
Liam had been honoured.

He was in the main residence, on the top floor and had a good view over to the outer walls of the castle. He would have liked to go exploring, to see how this castle differed from the Menethes. His mind was already appreciating the ease with which it could be defended, assuming an attacker managed to scale the outer walls in the first place. After those he would have to cross the open ground to the castle walls proper.
Yes, he liked this place…Although the formal gardens at the back were a weak spot, offering cover to any would be attacker.

Liam smiled. He had no doubt that in the event of war Lord Toth would have the hedge immediately cut down, without a second thought. He had his priorities firmly centred, as a Lord should.
No! Liam was angry with himself. The Toth wasn't a good Lord.
He needed to be less rigid, less set in his ways.
At least where people were concerned.
Where Emma was concerned.

He drained his tankard and put it tidily on the table. Then he made the bed and folded his discarded clothes into a neat pile. As he critically surveyed his efforts to tidy up there was a knock on the door.

"I thought you might still be asleep," Finn said and he stood aside to admit a maid to clear the table of Liam's dishes. "Have you had enough to eat?"

Liam nodded.

"I would have had those cleaned," Finn said, nodding at the pile of clothes, "but there isn't time. I expect you're anxious to be on your way," and he watched the maid closely until she had finished loading her tray. Only once she had left the room did Finn relax, He closed the door behind her and turning back to Liam gave a warm smile. "You're looking well," he said. "The Kush sun must agree with you, at least."

Liam was impatient for news of Emma. Was she recovering?

"My Lord has been up all night with her," Finn told him. "She had another attack soon after you arrived, but she seems stable now. I think the worst is over." He picked up Liam's clothes. "I'll have these put in a bag with some food for your journey."

"When am I to leave?" Liam would have liked the opportunity to say goodbye to Emma.

There was something that he wanted to ask her.

"My Lord wants to see you before you leave. He's having firstmeal at the moment. I can take you to him when he's finished."

"Can't I see Emma while I'm waiting?"

Finn stared into space for a moment, concentrating then he nodded.

"I'll take you to her" he said.

To Liam's surprise Finn didn't take him to the room on the ground floor that Emma had said was hers when they had met at the Gathering, but walked along a first floor corridor to a large wooden door with two Elite on duty outside.

Finn knocked and a tall battle scarred warrior with the longest braids Liam had ever seen on a warrior opened the door for him. He was clearly a veteran.

"Explain to your son that some things are best kept to himself." Lord Toth was at firstmeal in the room they had entered. It was part of his private chambers.

The tall warrior bowed and left, closing the door firmly behind him.

For a moment Liam stopped and watched the lord as he wiped his lips on a huge napkin and took two Tanis leaves. He said nothing as he chewed but Liam was conscious of the Lord's eyes following him as he crossed the room behind Finn towards a door on the right.

Finn opened the door but did not enter. He stood by it as Liam entered and then left pulling it to but not closing it. Lena was in the room just taking a glass of tea from Emma who was lying on an enormous tapestried four-poster bed. The room was at least twice the size of her old one and Liam realised it was the Lady's Room.

"You have come up in the world" he remarked as he took her outstretched hand. She was looking so much better.

He sat on the edge of the bed whilst Lena hovered, obviously keeping an eye on him. Then she suddenly left. Liam twisted round and looked at Lord Toth who was regarding him. The man was so closed. It was impossible to tell what he was thinking.

Abruptly the Lord turned away and walked over to the window, which he began to stare out of, his back to them.

"Well?" Toth said, shortly.

"I haven't...." Emma said. She squeezed Liam's hand and he turned his attention back to her. *"My Lord wants me to tell you something."*

Liam gasped in surprise.

"I can hear you!" he thought and he let go of her hand as she pulled it away from him.

"Can you hear me now?"

"Clearly."

"Good, for there is something I must say...I'm really sorry..."

"For what?" he interrupted and she gave an audible sigh of exasperation.

"Will you hear me out?" she said aloud and she glanced across at the Lord who was still finding something of great interest outside in the gardens.

"I shouldn't have led you on... given you reason to believe... I'm sorry Liam but there can never be anything between us." She laid her hand on his bare arm. "I'm not the girl in your dreams, Liam. I don't know who she is, perhaps a mix of all the women you have known... but it isn't me."

Before he had chance to argue with her or begin to persuade that it didn't have to be this way Lord Toth left the window and walked over to the bed.

"Emma needs to rest," he said firmly and Liam followed him out of the bedroom and back into the sitting room. He closed the door behind him, catching one last glimpse of Emma as he did so. He wondered if she had the strength to walk to the door and eavesdrop.

He rather thought she had.

Lord Toth indicated a chair by the table and Liam sat down. Lord Toth poured him a tankard of ale and then sat down in a chair opposite.

"What you found at Kush Prime," he said as Liam sipped at his ale. "Kush is burning people he believes are from Urth." The Lord looked at Liam carefully. "Emma may be in danger, you almost certainly are."

Liam went cold inside.

"It could be people who have died naturally… plague…." He knew he was clutching at straws and his voice died away as the Toth shook his head.

"The Anari believe for the soul to be released the body must rot naturally. Therefore they expose the dead to the elements and bury the bones when they have been picked clean. It is the Anant who cremate their dead, believing the spirit is released as the flesh is destroyed by fire. The spirit is quickly released and can begin its journey to whatever awaits it." Toth smiled. "Do men on Urth believe in an afterlife?"

Liam nodded.

"We have many different beliefs but I think an afterlife of some description features in most."

"Interesting." The Lord fell silent for a moment and Liam began to feel uncomfortable again.

If Emma was in danger then the sooner they escaped to Earth the better.

Lord Toth poured himself another ale then passed the jug to Liam. "Since I bought ten slaves from Lord Darg… including your blacksmith friend… I have had my rangers listening for rumours of daemons. Hence my interest in the building outside Kush Prime."

"Where Kush burns those he believes are from Urth," Liam agreed. There was no other logical explanation, as much as he might hope. He stood up quickly. "My Lord is in great danger."

And Sarah. He still cared deeply for Sarah in spite of everything. She had been his stepdaughter for a long time; he had to protect her still. "I have to get back to Kush Prime and warn him."

"He already knows the implications, Emma was able to warn him of Kush's strange mood, even if she didn't fully understand the reasons for it," Toth reassured him. "Besides your Lord has already left for Menethes Prime. Pharaoh cancelled the festival when he heard his heir had been seriously injured... He's not expected to live. Your Lord will be back in Menthes Prime before you."

Liam sat back down heavily in his chair. That at least was some comfort. "What will Kush do now?"

"I do not know," Toth admitted standing up abruptly.

Liam realised that that was his dismissal, he had been told enough. But there was something he had to say to Emma before he left. As he wondered if he would be allowed to see her again the door to her chamber opened and she peered round the door.

"Have you finished yet?" she asked.

"You know we have" Lord Toth said although he didn't sound annoyed, more amused. "You have been listening at the door."

"It's a very thick door," she complained entering the room and walking slowly towards them. "I couldn't hear anything."

Liam stood up quickly and offered her his chair. She took it gratefully; even that short walk seemed to have tired her. He raised her hand to his lips.

"Farewell," he said but the Lord had not quite finished.

"You may take a message to your Lord that whatever Kush does the Menethes will have my full support."

Liam was taken aback by Toth's words. The man was full of surprises. It was almost impossible to continue disliking him. But... the sooner they left the better and he realised that he was going to leave with the others now and take Emma with him whether she wanted to go or not.

"Will you contact me from the Gate?" she asked. *"I would like to know if I can hear you at that distance."* She smiled up at him. *"Until now distance has been my enemy."*

He nodded, bowed to the Lord and made for the door. Turning to close it behind him he saw Lord Toth pick Emma up in his arms and carry her towards her bedchamber.

He was so gentle when he thought no one watching.

Did he care for her after all?

Liam shrugged. It made no difference. When the time came Emma would leave with him.

Finn was waiting in the main entrance hall, Liam's clothes and food in a warrior's small pack. They walked out to where Liam's horse was waiting. Liam glanced round; there was no one near.

"You were right, it's time to start thinking of leaving," he whispered. The only show of surprise was a sudden widening of Finn's eyes. He continued to tie the pack onto the saddle. "Kush is burning anyone from Urth," Liam continued, under his breath as he checked the horse's girth was tight enough and adjusted the stirrups slightly. Finn gave a slight nod.

"Thank you for taking such good care of Emma," he said loudly.

Liam smiled.

"Start gathering everyone you can find. I'll try and contact Gwydyr at the gladiator camp," he muttered as he mounted his horse.

Within minutes he was through the gatehouse and trotting towards the outer walls, across the grass in front of the castle. A herd of long horned cattle were grazing, fresh milk for the kitchens. It looked so peaceful in the clear pink sky of the late spring day. Liam slowed his horse to a walk as he looked at the sky.

"I don't want to leave," he said to no one in particular. "But I no longer have any choice," and he urged his horse into a fast trot and made for the outer gate.

XXV

Liam reached Menethes Prime in five days. He immediately reported to the Spymaster that Emma seemed to have recovered well but was tired. The Spymaster was obviously relieved to hear this and Liam wondered if he felt guilty about her. Nothing was said and Liam was left to his own thoughts.

He inspected the Lady's guard and found Saul had done his usual excellent job as deputy. Liam felt strangely unwanted... unneeded. There was a tension in the air, uneasiness, partly prompted by the sudden departure from Kush Prime and, for those that knew and realised what it meant, by the grey dust currently residing in a small wooden box in the Spymaster's office.

Spring was announced as officially over by the priests and summer begun, but Liam could see little difference in the days. The air of gloom that hung over Prime was reflected in the sky and its light brown cloud cover. Liam found himself longing for the blue sky and white clouds of Earth. Even a grey sky would be preferable to the depressing brown of those early summer days at Menethes Prime.

About a decan into summer Liam was walking the castle walls looking over at the town. He greeted Japhet who was checking on the cohort on duty and they walked together for a while. The air of expectancy that had hung over the place in the previous days had slowly faded and been replaced by a lethargy that was worrying Liam just as much. He had the strangest feeling that he was being watched but when he turned round suddenly there was no one there.
It was eerie feeling.

He and Japhet talked about inconsequential matters; a replacement for one of Japhet's men who was retiring, Liam thought Neri might suit; the news of pharaoh's grandson who had been badly burnt in a fire but who, it seemed, was stronger than any had believed and now looked set to survive; the delayed Anari games which had been put back until later in the summer... and who to bet on. Liam was considered knowledgeable in such matters if he could be got to reveal his thoughts. But Liam was wary about recommending gladiators. The ring was too uncertain a place for safe bets and he didn't want to be the cause of anyone losing money. So he agreed with Japhet that Haldar looked good, added that Gwydyr the lesser was also promising and with a parting "Of course, one should never write off the veterans," left the perplexed Captain of the Watch and started to make his way to the warriors' refectory. He tried to avoid meals in the Great Hall; they were too noisy and frantic. The small refectory, little more than a large room off the kitchen courtyard, was much quieter because warriors tended to come in at differing times and then take their food out into the sun to eat. It was a habit that Liam had come to enjoy and the others soon learnt that he preferred to be left alone when he was eating. He quickly got the reputation as a warrior who took his food seriously.

He enjoyed the reputation. There were far worse ones to have.

On that particular day he took his food and sat on the steps leading up to the walls by the archway into the stables. It got the sun for most of the afternoon and, by the time Liam was ready to eat, was warm. There was also an amount of shade by the wall that Liam could rest in.

A most pleasant spot.

And one in which Liam could relax for a few minutes and enjoy life.

Or try to.

But on this day he found himself unable to get comfortable, the food seemed worse than ever and he had the feeling that someone was watching him again.

He looked round but there was still no one there. Annoyed he quickly finished his food, drank the tankard of water that he had decided to start having with his meals instead of ale and contemplated how best to contact the others at the gladiator school. With the delayed Anari games due soon, even reduced in size as they were to be, there would be fights ...and gladiators to bet on. When he next had any time free he would make a special trip to the school, ostensibly to see old friends still there. The other warriors would accept such an excuse and see no cause for suspicion.

The feeling of unease that he had been experiencing all day had not left by the time he decided to turn in but, he reflected as he undressed and lay down, a good nights sleep might be all that he needed.

He was awoken violently, the covers dragged from his body and thrown down.

"Get up now if you still want to be alive in the morning," someone growled at him in the dark. He reached across to open the crystal on the wall by his head but someone was there before him and light flooded onto the bed momentarily blinding him. His clothes were thrown at him and he clutched at them blinking furiously. He sat up on the edge of the bed and pulled his trousers on. Quickly lacing his shirt at the neck he rubbed his eyes and finally looked at his visitor. Perhaps if he had known who or what he would see he would have quicker about it but he had assumed whoever had woken him was another warrior or a servant. Somewhere low on the list of possible people was Judith but even she was more likely than the sight that greeted his eyes.

Six and a half feet of ...fur?

Liam blinked.

Smooth fur, like a *Labrador's*. But fur nonetheless.

A flattened muzzle, not as sharp a one as on the statues he had seen. But a muzzle nonetheless.

Golden cats eyes and a mane of hair the same colour.

A thumb and three fingers to each hand.

Fingers with wickedly sharp black claws at the end.

A Nestor!

"Oh my God," Liam said.

"Hardly," the creature growled. "But a nice way to greet an old friend, all the same." ... Osiris? ... The Nestor bowed. "But unfortunately there is little time for us to reminisce. The Kush are about to attack. With the help of Ammon they will breach the outer city walls and rapidly make their way here. I suggest you sound an alarm or something." With that he vanished.

Liam stood up slowly. Was he dreaming?

If he was it was the most vivid dream he had ever had.

Then he realised exactly what Osiris had told him and he threw open the door to his room and ran madly for the alarm bell situated in the main courtyard.

If it had been a dream he was going to look a complete idiot, probably be demoted to guarding the mines near Secund or worse... actually digging in the mines near Secund.

If it had been a dream...

"My son, where is my son?" The Lady was distraught and would not be comforted by her maid.

"There is no news yet," Liam said. "But he was with Dolan and his guard. If anyone can get him out of the city it will be them."

He took off his cloak and put it round Sarah's shoulders. It was a cold night but they couldn't risk lighting a fire.

"Someone's coming." The sentry came running up, his sword empowered, ready.

"It's Japhet," Saul said and they all looked with horror as five riders pulled up. They were covered in blood, their faces grey with tiredness.

"Is this all of you?" Liam asked. Surely more must have escaped.

"There's about twenty more on foot, a mile or so back... but..."

He took Liam by the arm and pulled him away from the group of women sitting on the ground. With an anxious glance at the Lady he began to tell Liam and the others of the Lady's guard who had clustered round what he had seen.

"My Lord and a two or three hundred strong band were seen cutting a path to the South Gate. They may have escaped but... the Kush are slaughtering everyone, women, children..."

"Not all." One of the men who had ridden in with Japhet interrupted him. "They're killing the very young, the old, expectant women and any warrior who doesn't immediately surrender."

"The streets were running with blood," Japhet continued. "The dead were just left where they fell."

"And the rest?" Nye asked. "What was happening to the rest?" His wife may have survived after all.

"They were being herded to the east gate. But the Kush weren't being that fussy who they killed. If you've someone in the castle then they're gone. Everyone in the castle was being slaughtered."

"You don't know that for sure," Liam snapped. He had to keep up their morale. "Eyleen may have escaped." He took the young man by the shoulders and stared down at him. "Keep that thought in your head. We were in the castle, we got out and so could she. Eyleen is a clever girl. I'm sure she'll be alright."
Nye nodded.

"There was time, wasn't there. Thanks to the warning... there was time."
Liam could see he was close to breaking down completely. The last thing he needed right now was for the warriors to start to come apart.

"We have a job to do," he said. "We must protect the Lady." He thought for a moment. "The women can ride the horses, we'll have to walk." He looked at Japhet and his men. They looked tired, drained but then he probably did too. "Two of you go back and find these stragglers. Bring them here as quickly as possible."
He was obeyed without question.

"Japhet, Saul. Yours is the most dangerous task. I want you to stay here as long as possible and gather together any survivors you can find. Send them on after us."

"Where will you go?" Saul asked.

"We'll head north. I'll keep off the roads though, go across country. The Kush seem intent on our...Oh No....Of course!"
The gathered warriors stared at Liam concerned. He was the only one who seemed to know what to do. He couldn't start to fail them now. His own men had faith in him though, they waited patiently.

"That's why he doesn't want the old, the young or any of the others," Liam explained. It was so obvious. "He's gathering Tribute."

"Then we must take everyone we find still alive," Saul said. "He will empty this land for Tribute and have no need to find any himself."
Liam nodded.

"We best make a move now. I don't want to be found so near to Prime when the sun rises."

Liam selected the fittest horse for Sarah and helped her to mount.

"My son?" she asked.

"We will find him," Liam assured her as he gave the rein to Nye. He watched as the forlorn group began its journey north. He would bring up its rear.

"Which way will you go?" Saul asked.

"I'll take the old mining road into the hills," he said after carefully considering all the options. "Maybe cross the North road after dark and travel across country towards the Great Forest. We can disappear into there for days."

"You're going to the Toth?"

"Where else can we go? There aren't enough warriors left to mount an attack on the Kush and we have no one to lead it anyway. I don't have to decide finally for a few days."

"But if our Lord survived..."
Liam shook his head sadly. He was trying to keep hopeful for Sarah's sake but he didn't think Lord Menethes had survived.

"It would be quicker to go straight to Menethes Port," Saul pointed out as Liam prepared to follow the rest of the Lady's guard.

But that was what the Kush would expect any survivors to think and Liam wasn't going to do what was expected of him. He intended to survive.

They travelled slowly north for nine days following the old road. Occasionally they would find a burnt out shell of a farmhouse or a small village. Always deserted except for the bodies of the old or the young. Twice they found some overlooked stores and the food was divided out equally. On the tenth night as Liam carefully scanned the North Road, checking and rechecking that it was safe before risking a crossing, Saul and Japhet caught up with them and the small band of travellers doubled in size.

Sarah was overjoyed. Dom was safe.

"Don't know what all the fuss is about," Dolan said as Sarah thanked him yet again. But Liam could see how proud the old man was.

Nye too had found his smile again. Eyleen had escaped from the castle with Dolan and the young Lord. Liam sighed as he watched the two young lovers together. He wasn't going to get much sense out of Nye for a while. Still, it was a good boost to the group's flagging morale.

They crossed the road without incident and rested for what little remained of the night under the comparative safety of the forest. As the sun rose Liam wandered down to the edge of the trees. In the far distance he saw a massive army of warriors gathering.

"Kush?" Saul had joined him and was watching the distant warriors beginning to march south.

"Who else," Liam muttered. "They must already have attacked Menethes Port." It had been one of the places he had considered going to and he was glad now that he had rejected the idea. "Come on, we must get back before the Lady starts to worry," he said. "It might be best not to mention what we saw."

They continued their trek through the forest, Liam becoming increasingly worried by how long it was taking them to get through. They were beginning to run dangerously short of food. On the sixteenth day they finally cleared the forest and walked down a gentle slope to rugged moorland. The last of their food had been eaten at daybreak and Liam had hoped they would find a farm or even a village where they could have got more. But there was nothing ahead of them but more grass and boulders as far as the eye could see.

It was now that he came closest to despair.

He had failed.

The group, even the strongest warriors, was becoming too exhausted to go on. He knew it wasn't just the food problem that was causing it. They were giving up hope and he couldn't think of any way to help them. He was becoming too tired himself.

They took shelter in a hollow in the ground, surrounded by a group of large boulders. At least it was dry and out of the wind.

"You haven't posted a guard," Nye pointed out.

Liam looked at him wearily.

"If you have the energy," he said, "you can take first watch. But if the Kush come upon us now... we couldn't do anything to stop them." The other warriors looked at him. They knew he was right, but it didn't seem right somehow. Liam saw the looks and rubbed his stiff neck. "Get some rest," he ordered Nye. "I'll take the first watch."

"No," Japhet said. "You've done more than your fair share. Neri and I will take the first watch. Elon and Nye can relieve us in a couple of hours."

Liam didn't have the strength to argue. He stretched out on the grass beneath one of the larger boulders and almost immediately fell asleep.

Liam groaned as someone started to shake him roughly. He hadn't been asleep that long surely.

"Riders," Saul hissed and Liam was instantly alert and on his feet. "From the south." Saul pointed and Liam followed the direction of his hand. The riders were still some distance away but there was no mistake. They were heading straight for Liam's group.

"Get everyone together," he ordered and turned back to watch the approaching horsemen.

"Kush?" Japhet asked from behind Liam's right shoulder.

Liam was staring intently at the group. He wasn't sure yet.

"I think they're Toth," he said at last and he sensed rather than saw everyone relax a little.

"Will they help us?" Lady Sarah had left the women huddled against the boulders and joined Liam with the warriors.

"Perhaps," he said shortly. "You should get back with the others. How can we protect you...?"

"No Anant kills another," she interrupted. "They must help us."

"They probably consider the Menethes to be Anarian," Liam reminded her. "Besides Pharaoh seems to be changing all the rules... like the other night. Maybe the Toth will too" Sarah frowned at him but then she nodded and went back to the other women. Liam watched as she took Dom in her arms and held him close. He had been shorter with her than he had intended but she didn't seem to realise the danger they were in. No one seemed to be playing by the rules anymore. It was a frightening time.

"I think that's Lord Toth," Dolan said in amazement as the riders came closer. Liam turned and scanned the group.

It was Lord Toth.

The man who had haunted his dreams and filled his waking thoughts was riding towards them.

With food and blankets.

"My watchers tell me you have Lady Menethes and her boy with you," Lord Toth said from his horse. "You are well come. We have brought food, when you have eaten Toth Secund is only five hours walk from here. You can rest there then continue the journey to Prime when you are more able."

His warriors unloaded packhorses laden with the food they had brought. It was the simplest fare but it was one of the best meals Liam could remember. But before he could eat himself he made sure that the Lady and her son were fed and that the warriors and the other survivors were seen to. Only once this had been done and Dom was wrapped in a rough woollen blanket and had fallen asleep near to the fire under the watchful eye of Dolan did he seek out food for himself.

As tired as he was Liam kept a watchful eye himself on the Toth warriors and on their Lord. He did not entirely trust them, in spite of all the Lord's fine words.

When it was time to move again Sarah allowed Lord Toth to carry Dom on his horse, much to Liam's consternation.

Lord Toth saw his disquiet and smiled.

"Do not worry, Gladiator," he said. Liam frowned at this, which seemed to amuse the Lord even more. "I intend no harm. Our... mutual friend would never forgive me if I allowed anything to happen to the Lady or her son." He looked around from his horse at the

remains of the meal and the dying fire round which most of Liam's group were still gathered. "You have her to thank for all of this." He stared down at Liam, his face set and emotionless. "She persuaded me to help you. She is so very good at ... persuasion."
Liam flushed with anger. This was no way to talk of Emma.

The Lord urged his horse forward and began to lead them at a walking pace towards Toth Secund. Liam watched until the entire group had passed by and he could bring up the rear.

"You may be a Lord," he vowed, "but I will take her away from you... back to Earth." He pulled a blanket round his shoulders and smiled. He was very tired but every step was taking him closer to Emma and to escape.

After a half-hour of steady walking Lord Toth sent a warrior back to invite Liam to join him. He had many questions that needed answers but he was to be disappointed, Liam had only seen Kush warriors fighting, the rumours that Nestor had helped in the fight remained just rumours. But he was able to confirm that one of the Lady Sarah's women had been killed and that the Lady herself had been in mortal danger.

"Japhet was in the castle and city longer than I," Liam said. "He may be able to tell you more."
Japhet was duly sent for and he was able to shed some light on the rumour.

"It was the cry that went up from the walls as the attack began," he told them. "Kush were inside the city and there were Nestor with them. Then everything went quiet." He looked puzzled. "It was strange but we could not hear each other." He looked at Liam for confirmation but Liam could only shake his head. He was so used to not hearing the warriors that he hadn't noticed anything was amiss.

"That is why we heard no request for help," Toth said.

"After a few hours it was possible to hear each other once again, but it felt strange for a while." Japhet continued.

"Strange how?"

Japhet frowned with concentration as he tried to remember and put the feeling into clear words.

"Like trying to see in a thick mist," he said eventually and nodded with satisfaction. It had been exactly like that.

The two men dropped back to their positions at the rear leaving the Toth deep in thought.

They approached Toth Secund from the south. The city was built on a vast plain and all that could be seen was a tall wooden palisade atop an enormous stone and soil earthwork. Two round stone towers higher than the palisade guarded the only entrance. An iron gate studded with the Toth emblem of twisted snakes was between the two towers and it slowly swung open as the Lord approached. The Menethes walked in slowly unsure that they could trust the Lord. But Lady Sarah showed no such hesitation and they reluctantly followed her in. Liam brought up the rear as he had done for most of the journey. Once they are all inside the gate swung shut again with a dull thud that sounds ominous to Liam's ears. The column turned right, then left, then left again after a little while. There were walls all around with warriors atop them. It was a maze.

After a while they entered Secund proper. Not really a city, more a garrison.
But at least there was a castle where the Lady and her son could rest. Liam saw that every one was taken care

of before he began to think of his own needs. He was conscious of the Lord's eye on him as he walked back and forth across the courtyard seeing to his charges. Eventually all were found food, dry clothes, somewhere to sleep.

"I thought you might want some dry clothes yourself." Finn said and showed him to his own room. "You can share with me," he said. "Things are a little crowded at the moment."

"How is Emma?" Liam was anxious to know. Now they were all together it was time to think of escaping. Sarah was now free to come with them.
Finn looked at him, an angry frown on his face.

"Emma is gone," he said. "They say she has run off with a young warrior... Ralf...but it's not true. It can't be true."

"Does the Toth believe it?" Liam asked. He tried to remember if there had been any hint of an affair at the Sed Festival. He remembered Ralf and how besotted he was. But Emma hardly noticed him.

"My Lord has ordered them found," Finn said, "and brought back to face him."

"The warriors will find them," Liam said but Finn didn't seem so sure.

"They are looking for two people, running away together," he said, "But if something else has happened..." He shook his head. "I'm going to have to look for her."

Liam sighed. They would have to delay their escape a little while longer.

XXVI

"How long have they been gone?" the First Captain asked, his anger barely concealed. His long thin side plaits quivered an outward sign of his suppressed rage.

"About five hours," the Steward said. "Most of the Lady's guard were ill; half the Castle are down with it... the meat looked all right but...." He shrugged.

"Never mind the meat," the warrior snapped. "What happened?"

"The Lady insisted she had to go out and would have gone by herself but this young warrior came along as she was arguing with the Watch Captain and he said he would accompany her and off they went... together."

Liam heard the Captain growl deep in his throat but Liam couldn't blame him. It was his son they were talking of.

"She had a small bag of gold coin with her. Our Lord's man... her brother? ... left it for her before he rode off. I had just remembered to give it to her."
This seemed to settle things for the Steward. What more proof was needed?

Liam leant back against a pillar and surveyed the assembled warriors. Lord Toth was standing in the middle of the hall, in the ring formed by the massive stone pillars that supported the high roof. Several of his Elite surrounded him. Emma's two maids were also there, the younger one crying and being comforted by Lena. Finn was standing in front of Lord Toth arguing angrily with the Spymaster.

"They have only five hours start on us, I will quickly find them and bring them back," the Spymaster said.

"And you won't find them because your men will be looking for two people travelling together," interrupted Finn. "Emma would never have run away with that young man, she just wouldn't."

Lena was nodding vigorously and Liam found himself agreeing with them. Nothing he had heard yet convinced him that Emma had run away.

"She said she was going to get clothes repaired by a tailor in the town and had something in a basket that was supposed to be her dress as well as a small bag of gold," the Steward said.

Finn jerked his head up at this and Lord Toth regarded him thoughtfully before turning to the maids.

"You would normally be expected to repair any clothes?"

Lena nodded and the other maid began to cry afresh.

"My mistress wouldn't have run off with a mere boy. Why would she?" Lena said and the other maid nodded. Liam realised that they were probably the people who knew Emma best and that they were right. Why would Emma run away with a third son of a minor landowner, even an Elite one, when she already had a Lord? It didn't make sense.

"Ralf wouldn't forget his oath," his father said, his deep voice echoing across the hall.

"Then where are they? The city has been searched," asked the Spymaster.

Lord Toth raised his hand for silence as the warrior glared across at the Spymaster.

"Go, conduct your search and keep me informed," Toth said to him and then he looked speculatively at Finn. "And you go conduct your search," he added to Finn as the Spymaster turned to leave. "Between you, you should find them."

Liam hid a smile as the Spymaster began to protest at what he saw as a usurpation of his duties but the Lord was in no mood for more discussion.

"Finn has methods and sources that you have not thought of," Toth said shortly in a tone that refused further argument. "Am I correct?" and Finn admitted that he might know where Emma had been going.

"But my sources might be reluctant to tell me anything for fear of what might happen to them," he said. "They are not exactly respectable."

"Tags!" The Spymaster's contempt was obvious. He looked at the Lord expecting a similar reaction but the Toth seemed to be considering things carefully and said nothing for a while.

"Your sources have my word," Lord Toth said slowly, "that no harm will come to them. Anyone who gives me any information on Emma's whereabouts can expect to be rewarded." He looked at Finn. "Is that good enough for you?" and Finn nodded as the Spymaster snorted in anger.

"Knowing Emma," Liam said standing up from his pillar, "she has probably gone for a long walk and just forgotten the time." Finn turned and smiled as Liam walked forward and inclined his head respectfully at the Lord. "But if it is permitted I will help you look."

"Like old times," Finn said.

"Go," Lord Toth said, dismissing them all. "Bring me news of my Lady." And Liam raised an eyebrow at Finn. *"Lady?"*

Finn nodded and then indicated they should go outside. They could talk more privately there. The Spymaster hurried away as Liam and Finn walked slowly to the door. Liam was conscious that Ralf's father was following them and that he was hanging back as they stopped just outside the door.

"Do you honestly think she has just gone for a walk?" Finn asked.

"No. I think the boy is dead and Emma probably is too or soon will be." Liam said. "Pharaoh wanted to strike at your Lord and he did so in the best possible way."

"How?" Finn asked clearly puzzled. "Wouldn't it have been better to kill the Toth? Without him we have no real leader."

Ralf's father stepped forward and the two men stopped talking and stared at him.

"By taking his Lady, Pharaoh has shown himself to be stronger than our Lord and it has brought shame on the Toth Elite who were supposed to protect her."

"Which is why they were all so ready to believe she had run off with Ralf," Liam continued. "You must be his father. He talked of you when we were at Kush Prime together," and he laughed at the look of surprise on the warrior's face. "I'll tell you all about it whilst we find out if Emma is still in the city."

"And how do we do that?"

Liam considered for a moment.

"Emma is now telepathic. I should be able to hear her. I don't know what range we have but I should be able to reach her from the street if she is in a building."

"The Kush prevented thoughts from being heard." The seasoned warrior had remembered the conversation on the way back to Secund. "Perhaps they have done so again. Ralf was a good telepath; he would have summoned help if they were in trouble."

Liam looked at him approvingly.

"We'll make a spymaster of you yet," he grinned. "Japhet said there was a residual effect for some time after. It may have been in the mind or it could have

been a local effect. If it was you may be able to feel it."
He looked at Ralf's father. "Are you willing to help us?"
The Elite Captain drew himself up to his full height.

"Ralf is my son. I must clear his name of any shame."

"I have another line of enquiry to follow," Finn said. "If I can persuade Lord Toth that Emma had a very good reason for what she did and the money she had was for something else then the Spymaster's resources can be put to better effect in helping us, not wasting time chasing non existent lovers." He started to walk across one of the covered walkways that led to the outer ring building and an exit. Half way across he turned back. "Search for your anomaly but I don't think Emma is in Secund anymore but I don't think she is dead either. I think Pharaoh would want to gloat a little over her before he does anything so perhaps you should concentrate on how they got her out of the city without being spotted. They've only been gone six hours; you might be able to catch them."

With that he turned and marched away. The Toth warrior tugged thoughtfully on his braids.

"Captain, I think it is your friend who would make a Spymaster," he said. "He thinks and then gets others to do."

"Then we better do as he suggests. The guards on duty at the gates will be changing soon; perhaps we should start there and see what has left the city in the last few hours… and one more thing…"

"Yes?"

"Call me Liam."
The warrior thought about it for a moment.

"Ragnar," he said and Liam inclined his head and held out his hand. Ragnar held his own out, hesitantly and Liam laughed and grasped it.

"That is how we do it where I come from," he said.

"Urth?" Ragnar said and Liam stopped walking and turned to face him, a slight frown on his face.

"Does that worry you?" he said.

Ragnar considered the question carefully.

"No," he said firmly, some minutes later and they resumed their walk to the nearest Gate in silence once more. "But...." he said, after several more minutes of deep concentration. "I was brought up on tales of Urth and how it was ruled by daemons who would eat naughty children if they weren't obedient and respectful to their parents. So... I was wondering... what is Urth really like?"

His question surprised Liam.

"Well, it sure as *hell* isn't ruled by daemons," and Liam began to chuckle at his little joke. "It has blue skies, a bright blue on a good day, and only one moon..." and for a second both of them gazed up at the two Anarian moons that were high in the darkening sky, "and we have only one sun," Liam continued.

"It must be a very small place then?" Ragnar said, unable to fully imagine what such a place could be like.

"I don't know if the world is bigger or smaller than yours but we do have a lot more people than you do."

"How many more?"

"At the last count, six billion and still climbing." It seemed to take a while for the warrior to come to terms with this.

"Our world must be much smaller then," Ragnar said. "The priests tell us there are about a hundred million souls in our world and this number does not increase with the years... rather it declines."

"We live a lot closer together," Liam remarked dryly and he continued to describe his Urth until they were near to a main gate.

Nothing of any size that could have hidden the pair had left by this gate and no one answering to the description of either Emma or Ralf had been seen.

"They took no horses," Ragnar remarked as they walked quickly to the second of the gates that were open that day.

"You still think they have run away together?" Liam asked.

Ragnar had to admit he wasn't sure what he believed. Ralf had been very fond of his Lord's mistress and Ragnar believed she had been friendly with him.

"But I never saw anything to make me suppose it was anything more than that," he hurriedly added. "They were both young and he never... voiced any criticism as some of us did."

"Criticism?"

"She was not what we expected of a mistress," Ragnar explained. "Colm was always saying our Lord treated her more as his wife than his mistress. He certainly gave her more freedom than we expected. We were showing our disapproval. Perhaps we were too hard on her. She was very young." His voice died away as he realised what he had said.

"You think they are both dead?" Liam asked and Ragnar nodded. He began to tell Liam about Laro, a former mistress of Lord Toth's.

"It was well before my time," Ragnar finished. "But there were some still in service who had been with our Lord then. They said it was not... pleasant... what had been done to her."

"If he harms Emma in any way I have no doubt that Osiris will make sure that Pharaoh pays for it."

Ragnar smiled at this.

"I thought you said Osiris didn't rule Urth."

"He doesn't," Liam said and he kept his face emotionless. He was beginning to think that Emma knew Osiris very well, that she had been working for him all along. Who else could have told Emma about the black crystals? Who else but Osiris would have known about them? "Osiris may be nearer than you think," he added cryptically and Ragnar made the sign of Ra.

"Don't joke about such things," he said and he marched ahead towards the gate.

They had more luck there. Several large wagons had left in a caravan only four hours before. Mostly merchants taking their unsold wares east but there had been a funeral wagon.

"Taking Anarian dead back to their land for burial." Ragnar explained. He shrugged. "They do things differently." But he began to take an interest when Liam pointed out that there wasn't much difference between a dead body and an unconscious one.

"But all the coffins would have to be accounted for," he said. "There would have to be papers for each one."

"What would stop someone putting two bodies in one coffin?" Liam said and Ragnar shuddered. He hoped Emma had been unconscious when it had happened.

"What kind of men would defile the dead so?" he muttered as they made their way back towards the Castle.

The bells were already tolling the second hour of third period when they arrived back at the main Hall. Lord Toth hadn't retired. He was still sitting in the same chair that he had occupied when they had left. A few crystal lamps were lit and they cast long shadows across the silent hall. Several Elite were standing around and Ragnar pointed out the most important. Colm, the most senior, next to Ragnar, of the Lord's guard, was standing to the right of the Toth's chair. Dec, who had only recently been put in charge of a new guard for the Lady, was pacing from pillar to pillar in front. He looked pale and drawn, not yet recovered from the illness that had struck down most of the guard. At the sound of new footsteps on the stone floor Lord Toth raised his head.

"Well?"

"There is no echo of Emma in the city," Liam said.

"It has taken you this long to find that out," Colm said sarcastically. "I could have told you that hours ago."

"Have you found any trace of them then?" Ragnar snapped, losing patience with him. Ralf was probably dead and all they could think to do was blacken his name.

"Enough," Toth said but he sounded more tired than angry.

"We have found a way that Emma could have been smuggled out of the city," Liam said as Ragnar continued to glare at Colm and he explained his theory.

"By Ra's beard, I pray it was not done so." Dec looked even paler, if that were possible, but at least, thought Liam, he was no longer thinking they had run away together.

Silence fell once more on the sombre group as they all slipped into their own dark thoughts. No man wanting to put into words the horror he was feeling at such a possibility. Liam started as a door banged shut but it was only the Spymaster returning. Toth briefly enlightened him about Liam's idea and to their surprise the Spymaster readily agreed.

"That is why I have sent men after the wagon, it can't have gone far in the time." the Spymaster said and Liam got the distinct impression the man was pleased with himself although he showed no emotion. They had been unable to find anything out that he had not discovered already and done something about. Honour was preserved.

"Do you still think Ralf is with her?" Lord Toth asked. He sat back in the chair and Liam saw how tired he was. If Pharaoh had taken Emma, as Liam believed, he could have found no better way to unnerve the Lord.

"No," the Spymaster answered. "You asked to investigate the possibility and I have done so. They took no horses from the Castle stables nor did they hire any from the town. They were not seen walking through any gate…" He paused and gave a slight smile. "The lady is not one who could walk far without attracting attention. Even a man who did not know who she was would spare a glance or two at such as she. And the guards on the gates have been told to be vigilant. Anyone trying to pass unnoticed would attract attention. Even if Ralf removed his torc, his bearing and manner would betray him. He is not one to whom subterfuge comes easily. Kush Prime proved that."

The Spymaster stared across the group of assembled warriors at Ragnar who reluctantly bowed his head in thanks and acknowledgement of the man's support. It took a lot of willpower but somehow he managed it.

"Of course, I could be wrong," the Spymaster continued. "But if so, would you want her back? What punishment could you inflict that would be worse than their own consciences and the constant need to hide. They would have very little money with them…."

"They have no money." Finn had entered silently, unobserved by anyone.

He stood some feet from the ring of pillars at the very edge of the light. Liam slowly became aware that someone was standing behind him, hidden by the shadows and by Finn's body. Finn walked a little way forward and then motioned to his companion to follow.

"Ilone!" The Spymaster was clearly surprised. "I thought you dead with the Menethes."

"You know this woman?" Lord Toth asked and several of the assembled warriors identified her as one of the needlework women employed at Prime by Emma.

"She is also the wife of one of the assassins," the Spymaster said and there were gasps of astonishment from nearly all present. Liam raised a questioning eyebrow at Finn... what assassins? But Finn was in no position to answer. Several of the Elite were taking steps toward the woman and Finn backed away until he was standing directly in front of her. He had no sword but Liam could see he had every intention of defending her, with his life if necessary. Liam moved to just behind the small group. He at least had a sword but it would be an unequal fight even so.

Then Ragnar stepped forward and drew his own sword. Facing his fellow Elite gathered round the Lord, he empowered it.

"Have you forgotten? Our Lord gave his word," he bellowed and Liam was relieved to see flickers of doubt cross most of their faces.

Lord Toth indicated with his hand that they should come forward. Ragnar stepped to one side and Finn took the woman's arm and smiled reassuringly. She looked terrified. For the first time Liam saw the boy standing beside his mother. The boy looked up at Ragnar and smiled. He had obviously remembered Ragnar.

"Happier times," Liam heard Ragnar whisper to him and the boy nodded, then scurried after his mother who was now standing in front of the Lord.

"So the money was intended for you," Liam heard the Lord say.

"To travel south with," Ilone confirmed. "She said it was too dangerous to stay in Secund." She glanced nervously at the Spymaster. "She didn't trust you to keep your word."

All eyes turned on the Spymaster who continued to look unconcerned.

"I had my nose on the pair…. Until they went to Menethes Prime with Emma, or so I thought."

Lord Toth threw back his head and roared with laughter. The warriors looked at each other uneasily. Had the Lord gone mad, broken by the loss of his Lady?

"How like Emma," he chortled. "To hide them under your very nose." He looked at Ilone thoughtfully. "I promised a reward to any bringing me news," he said. "Go back to Prime; your reward awaits you there. I will give you a letter for the Steward. Colm, you will accompany them. You have my permission to use the Highway." And he dismissed them with a wave of his hand. Ilone backed away but the boy stood his ground before the Lord. Toth looked at him with some surprise, then he smiled. "You have something you want to say?" he said gently and the boy nodded. He glanced first at the Spymaster then back to the Lord.

"Speak," Toth said. "You have my word…"

"When my father… when he…. My mother sent me to follow him," the boy said.

Toth leaned forward in his chair, resting his elbows on his knees.

"You saw the man who paid your father to attack me?" and the boy began nodding again. Liam looked across at Finn. Emma betrothed to the Toth and now talk of an attempt on the Toth's life. How much more had Finn kept from him?

"He was very big, a warrior," the boy said and the Spymaster gave a loud sigh.

"We know this already," he pointed out.

"But I followed him," the boy said quickly and grinned at the looks on their faces. "I saw whom he reported back to," he added triumphantly. "It was a Lady."

It was so quiet in the chamber that it was possible to hear a neighbour's breathing.

"Are you certain?" Toth asked him gently. "Did you see her face?"

To everyone's disappointment the boy hadn't seen the Lady's face clearly, only the elegant carriage with an unidentified crest on the side.

"It was dark," the boy said, "but I did hear her voice." Lord Toth questioned him for several more minutes but there was nothing further to be learnt. After asking the boy his name, he ordered Colm to take them to kitchens for supper. By the time they had eaten the letter for the Steward should be ready and they could leave.

"Little boys are always hungry," Lord Toth said. "You have done well, Bryn." And the little boy gasped with pleasure at the praise. He gave an awkward bow that made the Lord smile and then ran to his mother waiting by the door.

"And you would have had me kill them," Lord Toth said watching until the boy was through the door. "Perhaps Emma was right about more things than we gave credit for." He stood up suddenly. "Go after this wagon," he said to Finn and Ragnar. "The Spymaster will give you any assistance you need"

284

Liam stepped forward.

"If my Lady gives permission, I would like to go to," he said and the Toth nodded.

"Whatever has happened, bring her home," he said and all present heard the anguish in his voice.

They bowed and left silently.

XXVII

Ten warriors breasted the hill and reined in their tired mounts. They had been riding all day and now as the sun was starting its descent into the east, leaving trails of purple in its wake, their quarry was finally in sight. At a signal from one man the group split into two, five riding to the right and five waiting patiently atop the hill. This waiting group watched as the others crossed the open countryside, skirting the road to the west, giving the lone occupant of the road a wide berth, and then cut in to rejoin the road some distance ahead.

"We can go now," the Toth Spymaster said. "If they try to run for it Dec will stop them." And he kicked his horse into motion and headed for the track.

Their quarry seemed oblivious to their presence although the waiting group ahead must have been clearly visible as the Spymaster drew abreast of the wagon and shouted for them to stop.

"What's to do?" shouted the waggoner as he reined in the team of four horses.

"We need to examine your cargo and your papers," the Spymaster informed him and he held out his hand for the documents. The waggoner reached under his seat for a leather pouch.

"It's all in order," he said. "You'll find nowt wrong with them... Hey what're you doing?" He looked round with some concern as two of the warriors climbed on board and began to push out the wooden boxes in the back. "You're not opening them," he protested as a warrior hammered a metal stake under the lid of the first coffin and began to lever it off.

"Perhaps you would care to give them a hand," the Spymaster suggested but the two men declined.

"Shouldn't interfere with the dead," the waggoner muttered darkly and his helpmate agreed.

The Spymaster was watching the pair closely, seemingly uninterested in what was happening at the back of the wagon.

"You look nervous," he suddenly said to the second waggoner as a third box was opened. Beads of sweat were running down the sides of his face.

"Like Mohan says, shouldn't interfere with the dead," the man said. "No good'll come of it."

"Sir." Dec held up his hand but the Spymaster waited until Ragnar had taken his place watching the two men before walking towards the fourth box. Dec handed him what had been found. "It had slipped down between the side of the box and the corpse." Dec said. "Finn has sharp eyes," he added, giving credit where it was due.

"He knows his sister," the Spymaster said examining the find closely. "Search the rest of the boxes. Open the shrouds and make sure who is supposed to be there really is."

"Some are wrapped in lead," Dec pointed out.

"Then unwrap them," was the short reply.

The Spymaster walked back to the front of the wagon. With a glance at Finn, Liam followed and stared up at the two men. Both looked visibly ill at ease.

"What is this," the Spymaster said holding aloft a small gold bracelet that sparkled in the last rays of the setting sun.

"A burial gift?" the waggoner Mohan said. He seemed to be having trouble swallowing and Liam watched his bobbing Adam's apple with some fascination.

"This looks like two snakes twisting round each other." the Spymaster said to Liam. "An Anant symbol, a Toth symbol indeed. A strange gift for an Anarian."

"Very strange," Liam agreed.

Dec hurried up and stood close to the Spymaster. With an ill-concealed glance at Ragnar he whispered to the Spymaster.

"We have found Ralf," he said simply.

"Wait here," the Spymaster ordered but Liam had no intention of moving. He preferred to remember the young man as he had been in Kush Prime, young, eager, and full of life... and love. A love that had cost him dear.

He turned his head to watch Ragnar walk slowly to the open coffin. The warrior stared down for a moment, his shoulders sagged briefly then he stooped and reached into the box to cut the torc loose.

"He has cut the torc from its fastening," Liam told the waggoners, "because it is his son and he wants revenge. Once he is satisfied that those who have murdered his son have been punished the torc will be buried with Ralf's ashes in his family tomb." And he had the satisfaction of seeing both men pale.

The warriors began to reseal the coffin with Ralf in it and the Spymaster returned again to the two Anarians. Ragnar followed close behind, his face set into a grim smile that unnerved Liam and he wondered what effect it would have on the two men.

"Mohan? Mohan... that wouldn't be Mohan of Arak, who has the concession for transporting the Anarian dead from Anant lands, would it? No, surely not. Such a rich man would have underlings to do such mundane tasks as taking a wagon from Toth Secund." The Spymaster looked around at the two warriors standing at his side as if he were asking them a serious question. "Now," he continued looking at the sheaf of papers in his hand, "According to these, that coffin should have contained the body of a six tarn old Henek girl, cause of death..." He consulted the papers again, peering at them as if suddenly shortsighted, "... a fall from a window. Now why then..."

The other waggoner suddenly leapt down from his seat on the far side of the wagon and began to run towards the safety of some distant trees.

"Where does he think he's going," Ragnar growled and, turning his head, ordered Arin to go after him. A seasoned warrior standing close to the tethered horses immediately mounted and took chase, his empowered sword glowing in the twilight. There was a faint cry and then Arin appeared, dragging the man by his arm. He reined in his horse some feet from the Spymaster and dropped his captive onto the floor.

"He appears to be dead," Arin said and Liam saw the spreading red stain across the man's back where the sword had severed his spine.

"Pity," the Spymaster said looking at Mohan. "Now there is only you to accuse with this crime."

"No...no." The man was in a state of near terror but Liam felt little sympathy for him. What terrors must Emma have felt shut in a small box with a corpse?

The man began to babble, explaining how he had been approached, threatened; his family threatened; and finally promised a large sum of money, to transport a live person out of Toth Secund.

"Only out of the city, I wasn't told who," he raved. "I thought young lovers... until they came with the body of the warrior." The Spymaster allowed him to ramble on for several more minutes, only occasionally interrupting with a question. By the time the man had finished they had learnt everything, including the direction the three horsemen had ridden off in.

The Spymaster had listened patiently, barely moving. Now he was suddenly active. He ordered all but one of the coffins to be taken from the cart, ignoring the protests of its owner. The warriors set about gathering fallen wood and dry grass from the surrounding countryside and stacked it around the coffins. Then it was set alight; the body of the dead waggoner being thrown on once it was well ablaze. The Anarian, Mohan, stood watching, visibly trembling. Ragnar stood behind, silently watching him in turn. Liam could see something was troubling Finn and he wondered what conversation was passing in the heads of the taciturn Spymaster and the grim faced Ragnar.

Finn moved closer to the Spymaster.

"What do we do with him," he said indicating the Anarian with a nod of his head. "If his family was threatened…"

"Don't waste your sympathy on him." The Spymaster's contempt for the man was evident in his voice. "He has long been known to me as a spy for the Kush Spymaster. It wasn't threats but money that drove him."

Liam saw Ragnar bend forward silently and something flashed silver in the moonslight. The waggoner jerked forward, his hands clutching at his throat. Then he fell to his knees. Ragnar gave him a contemptuous shove and he fell onto his face and didn't rise. After a few minutes Ragnar stooped down and wiped the blade of his knife on the man's jacket. Then he and Dec took hold of the arms and dragged the body towards the fire.

The Spymaster caught the look on Finn's face.

"A more merciful death than the one your sister faces… or faced," he said. He ordered the warriors to mount. Two would go with the cart and Ralf back to Secund. Ragnar refused to accompany his son's body. He intended to ride down the three riders who had been responsible for Ralf's murder and no one suggested otherwise.

They rode swiftly south, following the road the three were supposed to be on. After an hour the Spymaster ordered the party to halt and rest. It was too dark to continue and the horses were tired.

"Will they rest?" wondered Liam, thinking about the men they were pursuing but he kept that thought to himself as he ate the meagre rations they had brought with them and prepared to settle for the night. He watched with interest the Spymaster and Finn sitting close together, pouring over the maps the Spymaster had brought from Secund. They were discussing possible routes the three murderers might have taken and snatches of their conversation kept drifting across to Liam keeping him awake. Liam smiled to himself. Finn seemed to have finally found his niche in this new world. A place where he fitted perfectly…would he really want to leave and return to Earth? He sighed, that decision had been postponed for a time. He had a feeling that the answer would depend on the outcome of this task.

Finn walked over and settled himself down beside Liam. He warmed his hands in front of the wood fire.

"Spymaster Toth thinks they must have cut across country to join the main road south," he said. "The road they're otherwise on only leads to Darg and Orin land, then there's only extremely rugged and uninhabited country until Khaled territory."

"You're not sure though?" Liam was guessing but there was something in Finn's manner that suggested a doubt that did not match the certainty with which he spoke.

"I can't help feeling it's been too easy," Finn said. "We were bound to find out about the wagon…

there was no attempt to provide anything else for us to follow. And now we are sent chasing after three riders, who again seem to have made no attempt to hide their tracks."

Liam nodded. It had been very easy.

Finn stared across at the Spymaster, still pouring over his maps.

"I think I have put an element of doubt into his mind," he said and he pulled a blanket round him and lay back on the ground staring up at the night sky. He was silent for so long that Liam thought he must have fallen asleep and he started to think about sleep himself. "Do you think she is still alive?"

"Yes, they wouldn't have gone to all this trouble..." Liam was thinking about Ralf and the effect Emma had had on him at Kush Prime. He smiled. She had had that affect on them all, even him. He remembered the look in Saul's eyes when she had appeared dressed as a tag whore...in the woods. He sat up, excited by a sudden thought. "Pharaoh hasn't taken her to upset your Lord," he said, loud enough for the Spymaster to stop what he was doing and look up. "He thinks she is a daemon. He's going to burn her alive with the others he thinks are from Urth. We have to get to that building... in the woods." He didn't know where that thought had come from but he knew he was right.

The Spymaster was nodding.

"I too am coming to a similar unpleasant conclusion," he said and those warriors who hadn't already fallen asleep nudged the others awake and began to listen, drawing away from the fires and nearer to the Spymaster. "If this were the usual power game Emma would been left somewhere for us to find. Perhaps used but otherwise unharmed and our Lord would have been suitably humiliated." He spread out a map for them all to see. "We are being led away from where Emma is or was." He pointed to a wavering blue line on his map. "This area used to be good for sheep and there were many boats that would come up this river for the fleeces. Plague has largely depopulated the area but there are still a few remote farms that produce wool... and there are still a few boats that ply their trade along this river. Our quarry could easily have met with such a boat and then doubled back to lead us away."

"What then do we do?" Ragnar's deep voice rumbled across the fire. "I want those riders," he added in case anyone was in any doubt.

"A group of Toth warriors couldn't enter Kush lands without being spotted," Finn said. "Two might though... suitably disguised."

"You and me?" Liam said.

"If you are willing to give up your hard earned torc and become what you were," Finn said and Liam frowned. "A ex-gladiator who has earned the right to a torc and is now Lordless because the Menethes are destroyed."

The Spymaster smiled.

"A mercenary looking for a Lord. And you...?"

"Will be a slave freed because his Menethes master was slaughtered along with his family," said Finn.

"Best be Nedjha then" the Spymaster told him. "It is as cold as in Toth. Your fair colouring will fit well there." He turned to the assembled warriors. "Get rest," he ordered. "We will start at first light." He looked at Ragnar. "We still have a Toth warrior to avenge."

It took them over three decans to reach the plain and their first sight of the Great Lake. Taking the oldest, most tired looking, horses in the group they had bid farewell to the Spymaster and the warriors before dawn and set out on their own across open country to the river on the map. Liam had little hope of actually finding a boat with Emma on it, it would be well ahead of them by now but it was the shortest route to Kush Prime if one went as the *crow* flies and didn't follow the meandering roads south. Liam was anxious to reach Prime. Once Pharaoh had Emma there, how long would it be before he tired of gloating over Lord Toth's humiliation and just sent her to her death?

They made good time, the weather was good and the horses, in spite of their ragged appearance, were bred for endurance. It was surprising the number of fellow travellers they met on the paths and tracks they travelled. All heading south, away from lands that bordered with the Anant. No one was in any doubt... war was coming. The feared Lord Toth would soon be riding down from his castle to slaughter them all.

"The must have heard what happened at Menethes Prime and fear the same," Liam said one day as they passed yet another group of heavily laden carts and trailing cattle. "Why are they so worried?"

"The Lords aren't beyond slaughtering the odd village or two... to make a point. And they're not beyond making extra money by a bit of slavery... or fun," Finn explained. "And after what happened to the Menethes..." Finn frowned. "Someone has done a very good job of spreading rumours." And he continued to think deeply about the problem for several hours making him a most unsatisfactory travelling companion.

However the presence of so many on the road did make it easier for them to travel together without arousing suspicion. Fear of robbers made allies of the most unlikely people and everyone accepted their stories without question. Liam dropped any idea of being a warrior and became a former gladiator looking for a position as bodyguard.

Everyone they met suggested that Kush Prime, with its huge market and consequently large number of merchants travelling to and from the place, would be his best hope of finding work. Finn attached himself to the back of a group of refugees that Liam had somehow been persuaded to guard until they well away from the danger of robbers, and became just another fleeing the threat of the Anant. Once the group had reached the comparative safety of a large village with an attendant Lordling with whom they could appeal for shelter, Liam said goodbye and continued on his way. Finn had slipped away well beforehand and was waiting for him further along the road. He was unable to resist making fun of Liam and his difficulty in leaving the group.

"She obviously thought you were very good husband material," laughed Finn and Liam growled at him and glowered until sunset.

They made better time after that, avoiding becoming involved with any more refugees and exactly thirty days after leaving the Spymaster caught their first sight of Kush Prime with its sparkling white walls.

"What now?" Finn asked as they trotted across the grassy plain towards the lake.

"We can ride some hours east and cross the river by bridge," Liam said practically, "or we can pay and cross the lake by ferry."

"That wasn't what I meant," Finn muttered as they rode towards the lake and its boats. Here they hit their first difficulty. They had to stable the horses on this side of the lake and go across on foot. Liam was reluctant to leave the horses. They might be needed if they had to leave in a hurry and he would have liked them close at hand.

"We'll have to hire horses to go to this building you spoke of," Finn pointed out. "We can just take those."

Liam stared around him. He was standing at the prow of a small flat-bottomed ferry half way across the lake. The ferryman was at the stern wielding his one oar with skill. His six other passengers were sitting on the rough sacks provided for their comfort. He had deliberately chosen this boat because it travelled the lake at the westernmost point of the city. Liam nodded gently over to the right.

"Those are the woods we have to get to," he said indicating the start of an expanse of trees to the west of the city.

"So close?" Finn queried. "I expected them to be much further away and yet..." Liam waited patiently but Finn remained quiet.

"And yet?" Liam prompted.

"Emma was always saying how no one ever asks questions. A very *uncurious* lot, Anarians. They don't even really have a word to describe it. That's why Spymasters are so valued. They have the capacity to ask questions." Finn stared out across the water. "Yes, why not close. Less far to transport the victims and less chance to escape." He lapsed into a thoughtful silence and continued to stare at the approaching shore.

Liam left him to his thoughts and looked over to the left side of the boat. Two of the three huge Tribute ships that had been there the last time he had looked at the harbour were gone. Only the smaller one was still moored at the dock and there was a lot of activity round it. He wondered if it was ready to sail and how many of those on board were Menethes. One of his fellow passengers noticed his interest and came to stand next to him.

"Should have sailed a decan ago with the others but there was some problem. Pharaoh has ordered a lot of metal beams cast. I've seen them being delivered," the man said and Liam backed away slightly. The man stank of rotting fish. Noticing Liam's disgust the man let out a bark like laugh. "You don't smell so sweet yourself," he remarked. "Hard journey?"

Liam became aware that Finn was listening intently to their conversation although he had continued to keep his back to them as if unconcerned.

"He is showing too much interest in us," came faintly into Liam's mind. *"He could be a Kush spy...we may have to deal with him... be careful."*

"Now that's not very friendly, is it?" the man muttered as he turned away. "No way to treat an old friend…"

Liam stared after him. He was sure he had never seen the man before and yet he seemed vaguely familiar.

For the next half-hour, until the ferry reached the far shore, he thought about the man, his ragged dirty clothes and unkempt hair but couldn't think where he might have met him. Certainly not on his visit to Kush Prime in the spring. He was still trying to puzzle it out as the boatman threw down a plank for them to walk down. It fell some feet short of the sand but the water was shallow and Liam splashed through the water, rather enjoying the childish feelings he was experiencing.

"Emma would like this," he thought and then he remembered.

Finn had already disembarked and was waiting further up the beach.

"Where now?" he said as Liam joined him.

"I think we should follow our friend," Liam said and Finn grinned at him.

"You've remembered him," he said but Liam had to shake his head. "His name is Saul, well one of them is," Finn told him as they headed for the city gates. "He is a telepath. I've had quite an interesting conversation with him. A...mutual friend told him we were coming. He's been waiting for us to arrive."

"Saul?" Liam muttered to himself, trying hard to reconcile the sight of the dishevelled extremely smelly labourer with the clean warrior that had accompanied him to the Sed Festival.

Saul led them into the city, through narrow streets that were oppressive with the heat. There was no breeze to move the heavy air and Liam found it hard going. By the time Saul stopped and went under an old archway into a small courtyard Liam was dripping with sweat.

"I had forgotten how hot it gets here," he said as Saul unlocked an old wooden door that had seen better days. It hung lopsidedly from its hinges and Liam wondered why he bothered to lock it. One good kick would send it flying.

The room they entered was quite small, divided in two by a curtain hung from a rope stretched across between the side walls. Saul disappeared behind this and Liam saw briefly the small bed as the curtain moved. Then he reappeared carrying clothes, all as threadbare as each other, but clean....which had suddenly become important to Liam.

"One of the beauties of this place," Saul told them as they followed him into the courtyard and he relocked the door, "is that there are few neighbours and those that I have are too worn down merely surviving to show any interest in what I do." He smiled at them both.

"Another beauty is there is a public baths next door and since it has few patrons is relatively inexpensive and quiet."

He led them down the street and through another archway. Liam immediately smelt the overpowering smell of soap.

"The owners of this place supplement their meagre income by manufacturing soap and selling to other baths in the city," Saul explained as he ordered three cool baths from the waiting slave, handing over a few coins and receiving towels and small jars of liquid soap in return.

Liam sank into the first of three tubs filled with water and watched with interest as the clear water turned a grey colour almost immediately. The cool water made a pleasant change from the heat outside and he sank down and submerged himself completely in it. He held his breath as long as he could, enjoying the cooling sensation on his skin. Then he came up for air and began to lather some of the soap and wash himself.

"This is *heaven*," he said and Saul looked enquiringly at Finn.

"The Halls of Ra," explained Finn.

"Nej'van," Saul suddenly exclaimed. "In the dialect of one of the southern tribes, the Halls of Ra are known as Nej'van... the Fields of Rapture....interesting." He looked at Liam with a speculative gleam in his eye but he said nothing more and they finished their bathing and got dressed.

Saul took them back to his room and prepared them a simple supper of bread, cold fish, cheese and fruit. There was only water to drink but Liam was glad of that. They would need all their wits clear for what lay ahead. Saul drew back the curtain and sat on his small bed whilst Liam and Finn sat on two stools. It was cool in the room, but Saul kept the door open and Liam realised, from his advantage point on the bed, he could look through it and keep an eye out for anyone coming into the courtyard. At last they were able to talk freely.

"There's something I don't understand," Liam said as they began their meal. "You look Anarian and yet you are a telepath. How come?"

"I am Anarian. But the Mersin attacked my great grandmother's village in some argument with the Arak over land and although the village was left almost unharmed the Mersin had enjoyed themselves enough to leave several bastards behind them when they left," he said and there was a defiant look in his eye that dared them to make something of it. "My grandfather was one. However he was the only one who found he was telepathic. Not that he made much use of it. For some reason the ability has stayed in our family in spite of marrying non-telepathic women for the last two generations." He shrugged. "I merely decided to make use of it and so offered my services to the Toth Spymaster." His face suddenly broke into a wide grin. "Of course he wasn't allied with the Toth then."

Finn put down his empty plate.

"What can you tell us about this place in the woods?" he said impatiently. "Have you seen anything of Emma?"

"Emma?" Saul seemed genuinely surprised. "Rojan said Lady Toth had been taken."

"Same thing," Liam told him. "I was surprised too," he added. "Apparently a betrothal is as good as a marriage to the Anant."

Saul considered for a moment.

"My job on the shore keeps me busy but it does offer me a good view of the road through the woods. I've been able to watch the transport of prisoners to that building. Always in small groups of about twenty. About one every three or four days but there's no attempt to hide them. No one is that bothered." He took a deep breath and continued. "There must be a holding pen somewhere because the wagons only go to the quarry with the ashes once for every seven or eight wagons of prisoners. Things have been a bit slow lately. I reckon there is only about ten waiting to die and there haven't been any more wagons for nearly a decan." He stood up and refilled their cups with more water. "The last wagon did contain a woman. It was difficult to see clearly. I wasn't that close but I am certain it wasn't Emma."

"Why?" Finn asked quickly. Liam could sense the feeling of hope that was growing inside him.

"Mmm... Too tall... heavier build."

"Then if she isn't in this holding pen, where could she be?" Liam asked.

"She could be there," Saul was quick to point out. "I could easily have missed a wagon, if I was delivering baskets of fertiliser across the lake or if it was late at night."

"But if she isn't?"

"Then she might be in the dungeons underneath the Palace." Saul saw the look on Liam's face and began to shake his head. "There is no way we could break in there," he said firmly.

"We must find this holding pen and go in there," Finn said. "If the prisoners there came from the Palace then they might have news of Emma."

"If we did manage to find these prisoners," Liam said slowly, "then I don't see how we can leave them behind. But if we have to take them with us then we would have to leave the same night. The guards will be alerted to our presence and any hope of finding Emma will be gone."

"Then you and Saul must go there and devise some means of escape whilst I stay near the palace." Finn said. "Saul can contact me, the distance isn't far. If you learn that Emma is still in the palace then I will have to try and rescue her whilst you make your escape. Who knows, you might create just the diversion I need."

"It might work," agreed Saul. "But it would be better if I were the one at the palace. I have a reason to be here. If she isn't there, then you would be stranded here. I could just go about my normal business and continue keeping my nose on things." He looked from one man to the other and they both slowly nodded.

It was agreed.

XXVIII

The Gods were against them.

The very next day Saul reported seeing empty wagons going towards the woods as he went to his job in the gutting sheds. "The last set of prisoners must have been killed," he said as soon as he returned at the end of his shift.

It threw them all into a melancholy mood. Finn sat with his chin resting in his cupped hands and stared into space. In the end Liam suggested they go out and find an inn for supper, they could all do with a decent meal. To his surprise Finn agreed.

"The best inns are in the main square, aren't they?" he said as they walked through the narrow streets.

"And the most expensive," objected Saul but at Finn's insistence he led the way and they soon found themselves sitting outside one of the smaller establishments ordering food. Liam was soon enjoying a similar spicy stew to the one Emma had bought him and he remembered with sadness how excited she had been with her new clothes and how she had teased him when she had given him his shirt. The shirt was long gone, probably burnt during the sack of Menethes Prime or taken as plunder by a Kush warrior.

Finn had ordered a simple sallet of tomato and goat's cheese, drizzled with olive oil, mopped up with bread, and Liam found his thoughts going even further back to a meal at Menethes Port with Paul.

It was a night for remembering the dead.

Finn was picking at the food staring ahead of him across the main square at the Palace with a thoughtful look on his face. It was a look that Liam recognised.

"Please tell me you're not thinking what I think you're thinking," he said and Saul looked at both them and then at the Palace and let out a loud sigh.

"You must be mad," he said. "It's impossible."

"Nothing is impossible," Finn said quietly. "The impossible just takes a little longer." And he proceeded to finish his meal in meditative silence as Liam and Saul grew increasingly worried.

Once he had finished he stood up and told them he needed to stretch his legs before going to bed. They could accompany him if they liked. Liam sighed.

"Someone has to keep you from doing something stupid," he muttered and leaving a rather large pile of coins to settle the bill, he followed Finn in a slow amble across the square towards the main north south avenue.

"I wonder why the Palace is built facing west," Finn remarked as they began to walk along the road outside the Palace. "You'd think it would face south towards the traditional Kush territory." They walked to the end of the Palace wall and Liam laid a hand on Finn's arm.

"We are being watched from the roof," he said. "Let's continue to walk along the road as if on our way home. We need to come back in daylight anyway."

Finn nodded and they continued their slow, now slightly unsteady, walk. They went passed another white stone building that Liam remembered was the barracks for the Palace guard. "If there is a prison anywhere," he said, "it might well be there." And Finn studied it carefully in the fading light as they walked on. Some minutes later Liam heard the sound of running feet coming from behind them and he fingered the barrel of his sword in his pocket. It was with a great deal of relief that he saw Saul emerge from the gloom and push them both into the shelter of a nearby doorway.

"Quick," he said and Liam had the strangest feeling he was grinning at them. "Something is coming." Now Liam was sure he was smiling. He could hear it in the man's voice. "From the barracks."

They waited patiently and slowly Liam began to hear the creaking of wheels and the steady clop of horses' hooves.

"A wagon?" Finn asked excitedly and Liam could feel his own excitement growing. Perhaps Emma would be in it.

The cart appeared followed by two warriors on horseback and it was immediately obvious that she wasn't there. The open topped wagon contained only men.

"Five... no six," Finn counted. One of the prisoners was lying down and only his head, supported in the lap of another man, could be dimly seen. "Perhaps my Lord is right," he muttered. "The Gods are at war with each other. One side knocks us back; the other gives us this gift." Liam looked at Finn but he was staring straight at the cart. Liam turned back, puzzled. Then he saw what Finn and Saul had already seen.
The Menethes Spymaster was in the cart.

"We have to rescue them," Liam said but Saul laid a restraining hand on his arm.

"Not here," he hissed. "Too near to the barracks. Out in the woods, away from prying eyes on the walls." Finn nodded and the three men slipped away down a side street.

"If we hurry," Finn said," we could do this tonight."

"You would need horses," Saul pointed out. "Can't hire those until the morning... too late now."

"There are four horses with the wagon," Finn said. "Two pulling and two guards'. We can take those. Two to each horse… more than enough."

Saul looked at him and his face broke into an excited grin.

"Let's do it," he said.

They almost flew through the narrow streets towards the West Gate.

"Why are they going to the South Gate?" Liam asked. If the prisoners weren't going into the woods, the opportunity to rescue them would be lost.

"It's the only one open to large traffic at this time of night," Saul told him. "The West Gate is still open to foot traffic and if we hurry we should be able to get ahead of them."

They slowed down as they approached the gate and went through separately. Liam found himself waiting outside impatiently as Saul and then Finn took an age to appear.

"You were going to stay close to the Palace," Liam remembered as they drew near to the edge of the wood.

"There are two guards and two waggoners; you're going to need me." Saul said. "I'll be able to get back in the city without any questions being asked. I have cultivated a reputation for visiting the Tag whores. That's where I've been… if any one asks."

"Then we can't leave any witnesses," Liam said grimly and for once Finn didn't argue.

Once they had entered the trees Liam looked round and began to think of strategies for the fight.

"What are we going to do?" Finn asked and Saul too looked to Liam. He realised that Finn might be the Spymaster of the group but it was to him they looked for leadership in battle.

"The warriors are armed, we must take those first," Liam told them. "That will be up to me and Saul," he decided. "Finn, you must stop the wagon to begin with and once we have started our attack, it will be up to you to see the driver doesn't go off for help." Liam looked back along the track. The wagon had just come into sight, turning off the main road south and starting towards them. He signalled Saul to hide at one side of the road and he went into the trees on the other.

"Good luck," he heard Finn say and when he looked back from his hiding place he saw Finn lying on the middle of the road some distance further along. With luck the wagon would stop close to him, allowing Liam and Saul to approach unseen from behind.

This time the Gods were with them and the cart stopped some yards ahead of where they lay in wait. The driver got down from the cart and went over to where Finn was lying. Finn allowed himself to be helped into a sitting position, holding his head and groaning loudly. Liam went straight for the warrior on his side, pulling him from his horse with surprising ease. Before the man had a chance to draw his own sword Liam had run him through. As the man collapsed, Liam caught his horse and swiftly tied it to an overhanging branch. Then he ran to the front of the cart to deal with the other driver and to help Saul or Finn if they needed it. Saul was already wiping the blade of his knife on a clump of grass and Finn, looking slightly green, had nevertheless dealt with his man and was holding the head of the carthorse to stop him from bolting. Liam looked round quickly. What had happened to the fourth man?

He needn't have worried. One of the prisoners had his chains round the man's neck and even as Liam realised what was happening, the body slumped forward and fell to the ground with a thud.

307

"Hail and well met," Liam said, recognising the warrior that had reacted so swiftly. It was Dillon, a junior Captain in the Menethes Elite. Saul brought up the two warriors' horses.

"What are you thinking of doing with the cart and bodies?" he asked.

Liam shook his head. Just hide them in the woods he supposed.

"Why don't you put them in the building and open the grills," Saul suggested. "That way they'll be reduced to ashes."

Liam nodded. It was a good idea.

"What happens if no one shuts the grills?" he asked.

Finn had begun to help the prisoners down and take off their chains. Liam recognised the Spymaster and three Menethes Elite. The weakest two were unknown to him.

"The crystals would overheat and eventually crack... and maybe take the building with them." Saul grinned. "At worse they wouldn't be able to use the place again until they had replaced all the crystals."

"Then that's what we'll do." Liam decided.

Finn was standing in front of the Spymaster and Liam went over quickly. It seemed they had been waiting for him for as he approached Finn asked the question they all wanted to know the answer to.

"Have you seen anything of Emma?" and the Spymaster nodded.

"She was with us in the dungeons until about ten days ago. Pharaoh sent for her. She was to be burnt in the courtyard of his palace as entertainment for his guests." The Spymaster's voice cracked and for a few minutes he was unable to continue. "I'm sorry," he said at last. "You are too late. She is dead."

They travelled west along the line of the Great Canal, keeping to the desert and travelling at night, only venturing in towards the canal for water and any crops they could steal. Liam wouldn't let them take much from any one field. A few pilfered vegetables would go unnoticed; a lot would cause questions and perhaps pursuit. Nor would he say why they were heading west when logic would say to head north back to the Anant lands.

In truth he couldn't say why he was leading them that way. He wasn't sure they would believe him and, after listening to the little the warriors would say of the battle for Menethes Prime and after, he realised if they knew the truth they wouldn't follow him. As they travelled in silent convoy across the sands, the Spymaster using his knowledge of the stars to guide them, he wondered what they would say if he told them that Osiris had appeared to him as he was leaving the building in the woods and told him to head west. The fact that he was a Nestor was enough to condemn him in their eyes. The fact that he was Osiris, supposed Daemon Lord, would be too much.

So he kept quiet and fortunately only Finn was in any state to question his actions. The others were weakened and dispirited by their time in captivity and followed without question. Osiris had said they would be met but had not said where or when … or by whom. But for some strange reason Liam trusted him. Hadn't he warned Liam of the attack at Prime? Only Finn worried Liam. Not because he questioned Liam's judgement but because he didn't. It was as if Emma's death had left him in such low spirits he no longer cared.

Travelling at night meant they couldn't move fast. Both moons were new and gave no light at all. It was frustrating and a little frightening. The only good news was there seemed to be no sign of pursuit. After four nights of slow travel Liam estimated they had only covered about a hundred miles and the Spymaster assured him it was over a thousand from Kush Prime to the Port. At the rate they were travelling it would take decans to reach the coast and the further away from Prime they got the scarcer the farms would be. It would mean less food for them to steal and such a large group of travellers would begin to attract attention. Liam began to think that they should have headed north after all.

Abandoning his depressing thoughts he ordered Finn to scout ahead for somewhere for them to hide. It was nearly dawn and they needed to be under cover before the sun made them visible to unfriendly eyes. An hour later, as the sky ahead of them began to lighten into pale purple, there was still no sign of Finn and Liam began to get worried.

"He should be back by now," he said and Raynar, who was taking the watch as they waited, agreed.

"Perhaps there is nowhere for us to hide," he said, voicing Liam's own worry.

"Perhaps someone should look for him," Liam said but even as he began to wonder who to send Finn came hurrying back.

"Hurry," he said breathlessly. "There's a village about two minutes from here, we're bound to be spotted."

"Why didn't you tell us earlier," Liam said angrily.

"Didn't see until I was on my back," Finn said as Liam climbed up behind him. "Went the other way."

In the gloom of firstlight Liam could see he was grinning.

"You've found something?" Liam knew his friend well.

"I've been exploring the coastline," Finn said. "That's what took me so long."

"The coastline!" Liam exclaimed but Finn refused to say anymore. For once Liam couldn't feel annoyed with him. He realised there was only one explanation. "You've found a gate," he said and Finn turned his head briefly to nod. "Isn't it guarded?" Liam didn't think any of the others were in any state to fight but Finn shook his head.

"It's abandoned," he said and he led them to a ruined building only a mile away.

"Why leave it?" Liam wanted to know. "Why not put it somewhere else?"

The Spymaster answered that question as they waited for Finn to cut strips from his cloak to put round the horses' eyes.

"The Highways were put there by the Gods. No Anarian would dare move one without tarns of prayer and offerings in the temple first." He shrugged. "Maybe that was done and no favourable sign was received so they abandoned the idea."

Finn tied a strip round the last horse's head and handed the reins to Liam.

"Seems like an awful waste to me," he said. "If the Gods left these for us to use I'd think they'd want us to use them not waste them"

"Just be glad they did," Liam said and he led the horse through.

He emerged at the other gate and immediately sensed a change in the air. There was a freshness in the breeze and he could hear the pounding of waves in the distance.

"What now?" Finn asked joining him outside the derelict white stone building.

"We'll rest until it's almost dark and then go exploring... try to figure out were we are and how far it is to Kush Port."

"We could be hundred of miles from there."

"There's bound to be a fishing village somewhere on the coast. All we need is a couple of small boats. Something will turn up." Liam was feeling confident now. He had been right to follow Osiris's advice.

XXIX

Gerran shared out the fruit they had gathered in the dying hours of the previous night. It was the mid-day and there was virtually no shade. The warriors had stretched the two horse blankets between the tumbledown walls of the Gate building and it offered a little shade. Liam had taken off his shirt and sat with it covering his head and shoulders. He had his chin almost resting on his chest, seemingly asleep but as Gerran approached he raised his head and looked up. The spymaster eased himself down beside Liam and offered him what looked like a very large orange.

"It's all edible," Gerran said. "Skin and all."

Inside the flesh resembled that of a melon with a sharp, not unpleasant flavour, like that of an unripe plum. It was as juicy as a melon though and Liam was glad of it. One small flask couldn't provide enough water for all of them for the entire day.

Finn came over and sat the other side of Liam. He said nothing but ate in silence, staring over the sand dunes and occasionally glancing at the others.

"I can show you where the space craft you came in is hidden," Gerran said slowly. "With Mistress Emma dead, there is nothing keeping you here and with our Lord dead... there is nothing to keep Sarah here either. You were intending to take her with you when you escaped, weren't you?" and he had the grace not to look too satisfied at their surprise.

But then Liam surprised them both by revealing he had no intention of taking Sarah. They had no idea of what they would find on Earth. It would be safer for her to stay where she was. Only to Finn later did he reveal that he intended coming back for the others once he knew exactly what was going on. They also discussed the possibility of finding Gwydyr and their other friends from the gladiator school.

"If you're talking of gladiators," Dillon said, overhearing their conversation, "then they will have died with our Lord. The school was emptied of fighting men when our Lord broke out of Prime and marched south. Anyone who could stand was given a weapon and marched away." He sounded bitter and Liam asked him again what had happened at that final battle but he refused to be drawn.

"I saw things I never want to see again if I live to be three hundred," was all he would say.

But one of the other warriors was more forthcoming and they listened with horror as he talked of the fierce hand to hand fighting that had ensued before the Lord could break out of Prime and draw off the attacking forces south.

"Away from the direction Dolan took," Liam muttered to Finn. The Lord had sacrificed himself and his men in order to give his son a chance. Liam felt oddly stirred by the thought and also proud.

Proud to be Menethes.

Strange.

Raynar told of the forced march south, continually being harried by the Kush until the Lord had made a final stand at the mouth of a wide river.

"We could go no further," Raynar said. "The river stopped us. So we turned and faced them as the sun rose. There was a heavy mist coming in from the sea but we thought the sun would burn it off. It seemed to get thicker though." He shook his head at the terrible memories. "I don't have the skill at words to describe what it was like," he ended weakly and fell into silence.

"The Gods were against us," Dillon said and the third warrior agreed.

"There would be a cry and when you turned your neighbour had vanished into the mist," he said, "… but you would hear him… screaming… terrible screams. I came across the body of a seasoned warrior all torn apart by sharp claws and teeth. It was a matter of just waiting until it was your turn."

He too, lapsed into a contemplative silence and Finn raised an eyebrow at Liam. Clearly something terrible had happened… but were the Gods involved?

"How did you survive then?" Liam asked.

"We surrendered," Dillon said simply. "The mist lifted just before the mid-day and we saw we were so outnumbered that… when they offered terms we accepted. There were so few of us left. The rest had simply vanished."

"There were a few torn bodies," Raynar said.

"But the Gods had taken the rest… they were all gone," the third warrior said. "Lord Menethes must have gathered about twenty thousand by the time we turned at the river, not more than a hundred or two were lying in the field…. So what happened to the rest of them?"

"The Gods took them," Dillon said sombrely. "It would have been better if we had fought and died then."

"Why?"

"The Kush took ten of us and sent the rest away, including our Lord," Raynar said. "They told us they were for the Gods… that the Gods like to play with their prisoners first… If what I saw on the field was any indication, it would not be a quick or easy death."

"Not a warrior's death," breathed Liam and the other three looked at him and there was a recognition, a kind of bond, suddenly between them.

He understood.

"What are we going to do now we're at the coast," Dillon said suddenly, "Steal a boat? What if we can't find one?"

Liam gave a non-committal shrug. He really had no idea what they were going to do but he wasn't going to let anyone know that.

"We will find a boat," he said. "I'm sure the Gods are with us. Look how far we have come in a short time."

Finn was trying hard to hide a smile. Something was obviously amusing him. "A boat it is then," he said. "But we should get some rest first."

This seemed to satisfy everyone and they settled down in what shade they could find.

"What amused you?" Liam asked Finn.

"Your face," came the reply. "I get the distinct impression you haven't a clue what we are going to do."

"I haven't," Liam admitted.

"Well the sea is just over those dunes, less than a mile away... and hopefully somewhere there is Kush Port or a fishing village. You better start thinking of something." Finn rolled over and closed his eyes.

"I thought thinking was your job," Liam said and he saw Finn smile.

"When you're a Lord," he said, without opening his eyes, "I'll gladly be your Spymaster, until then I'll leave the thinking to those who can stay awake." and he yawned and put his arm under his head and said no more.

Liam didn't feel much like staying awake either. He settled down under the shade of a horse blanket and started to fall asleep. There was time enough to think about the next stage of their journey when he was rested.

Liam felt himself being shaken roughly and he was none too pleased. It had been rather a nice dream and he was reluctant to leave it. He was even more annoyed when he opened his eyes and realised the sun hadn't yet reached its highest point. He couldn't have been asleep more than two or three hours. Dillon crouched down at his side.

"I've found something," he said excitedly and Liam forced his eyes to open and he sat up. "I went to see if I could find any fresh water," Dillon said and Liam pulled a face. What if he'd been spotted but the warrior was quick to reassure him. There weren't any signs of habitation for miles. "But then I saw something out to sea a bit further down the coast so I went to have a look," and he motioned to Liam to follow him. Liam turned to wake Finn but he was already on his feet.

They followed Dillon towards the coast and then turned south along the edge of the shoreline. Keeping behind the sand dunes they followed the coastline for about two miles and then Dillon dropped to his knees and began to crawl to the top of a dune. Liam looked at Finn and shrugged and they both began to crawl after the warrior. Peering cautiously over the top Liam saw what had so excited the warrior.

A boat.

To be precise a Pirate ship.

It was Finn's turn to say it and he did so, savouring the irony.

"Please tell me you're not thinking what I think you're thinking," he said and Liam and Dillon looked at each other and grinned.

"Not even we are stupid enough to attack a fully armed Pirate crew with only two swords between us," Liam said, "but they might be persuaded to help us."

"There haven't been any Pirate attacks on Anant lands for over twenty five tarns," Dillon said. "Rumour has it they have a new Lord who is of Anant descent." He shrugged. "Perhaps his mother was captured, who knows, but if he looks kindly on his Anant cousins perhaps they will help us."

"It would be just our luck for them to be a different tribe or something," Finn grumbled.

"You should have more faith," Liam said and he stood up and began to walk down to the sea.

"For God's sake." Finn scrambled after him but Liam was unconcerned. He knew the Pirates were what he had been waiting for.

He came to halt some feet from the lapping water and waited. He was conscious of several pairs of eyes scrutinising him, not all of them visible from where he was standing. He could see five Pirates aboard the ship, which was anchored about a hundred feet from the shore. A small rowing boat was beached some feet away and as he stood waiting two men stood up from their positions beside this small boat. Liam wondered what to say but the nearest Pirate spoke first.

"Is this all of you? I was told to expect more."
Liam sensed Finn stiffening beside him.

"It's all right," he said. "I was told to come here. I knew we were going to be met." But Finn continued to eye the men warily.

"Met by us?" asked the first Pirate and Liam admitted that he hadn't known who.

"Trust Osiris," the second man said. "Always has to be mysterious."

"Is this all of you?" the first man repeated and Liam signalled to Dillon to come down.

"There are five more of us about two miles from here," Liam said and it was quickly arranged that Dillon and one of the Pirates would go and fetch the others.

"Why should you help us?" the warrior asked, proving a little suspicious even though it had been his idea.

"Our Lord ordered it so," the pirate said. "We've been waiting for the last three days. We weren't exactly sure how long it would take you."

"We have soap that will lather in the sea," the remaining Pirate said, "and clean clothes. Our Lord felt sure you would welcome it."

Liam nodded.

"Your Lord is a very thoughtful man," he said and for some reason the Pirate found this funny, which annoyed Liam and this amused the man even more.

Fortunately the idea of a bath was very appealing, even a cold sea one and Liam ignored the chuckling Pirate and quickly stripped off. By the time the others joined them both Liam and Finn were clean and refreshed and drying in the sun.

Soon the others were bathed and dressed, even the cautious Dillon. But Finn was not so easily satisfied.

"We only rescued Gerran and the others five days ago," Finn mused, "and the pirate said they had been waiting three days, not exactly sure when we would arrive." He shook his head puzzled. "But that would mean they were already here, or at least not too far away... almost as if they had been sent. But how could anyone know what we would do? We didn't know ourselves until we did it."

Liam realised he would have to tell Finn about Osiris but this only seemed to confuse him more.

"What connection could there be between the Pirates and something... you may have brought from

Urth?" Finn was shaking his head, almost as if he didn't believe Liam. "One of them did mention an Osiris earlier but…" They fell silent as one of the pirates came up.

"We have food on our ship," he said. "Mostly dried but thanks to Lord Menethes there is plenty of it," and he indicated that they should start rowing out to the ship.

"What do you mean?" Dillon asked angrily. "Our Lord would not deal with Pirates." and he squared up to the pirate belligerently. Liam quickly inserted himself between the two men and raised his hands to push Dillon back if need be.

"There are things you know nothing about," he said. "It is enough to know your Lord did work for the Gods."

"Then why did the Gods punish him?" Dillon hadn't risen to a senior post by being stupid.

Liam sighed and looked to Finn for help.

"The Gods are at war themselves," he said simply.

"Don't we know it," muttered the second Pirate and he was rewarded by a fierce look from his companion. It looked for a few minutes as if things would turn ugly but to Liam's surprise Dillon grunted and then gave a curt nod.

"There are some things that are never questioned," Finn whispered to Liam as they were rowed out. "The Gods being one."

"That looks set to change," Liam muttered ominously. "Where are we going," he asked one of the Pirates as he helped them on board.

"To Toth Prime," was the reply. The Pirate fell silent and refused to be drawn further. Liam was left to his own thoughts. He hadn't told Finn the complete story and he was beginning to wonder how much he should say now. Perhaps it would be better to say nothing until it was too late for his friend to do anything about it.

XXX

The Pirate ship had both sails and oars and the wind was in their favour. Within two decans the black walls of Toth Port were on the horizon and approaching rapidly. Only the two Pirates that had met them on the beach talked to them, the others stayed well away and chatted amongst themselves in a language that was different from Anarian yet curiously similar.

"We've made good time," Finn said and he pulled a woollen blanket tighter round his shoulders. In spite of being summer there was a cold breeze blowing across the water. Liam nodded. He was deep in thought as the Port approached. He still hadn't made up his mind what was best for them to do.

Gerran crossed the deck and joined them.

"If you are thinking of returning to Urth," he said, "I may be of some help. Most of those who went to Urth with our Lord died with him, but some of those who formed Dom's guard have the necessary experience."

"But that would leave Sarah and the boy unprotected," Liam protested.

"My Lord can be trusted," Finn said stiffly and Liam realised he had inadvertently upset his friend. "I would have to get permission from Lord Toth to leave," Finn added. "He may not welcome the loss of warriors with the threat of war hanging over us."

"It would only take six to operate the space-ship," Gerran said. "You two could easily learn how… and four others. Not much of a loss."

"We could quickly find out what the world is like now… we might not be welcomed back…" mused Finn, "and then return for any who wanted to go home."

"Let me know what you decide," Gerran said and he hurried away, back below decks.

"Emma said we had another tarn, maybe two, before we start circling the red sun," Finn continued. "More than enough time."

Liam nodded. They seemed to have decided on their course of action.

"There is spiced ale below," Finn told him. "I think I will go in search of a mug." he turned away and left Liam alone watching the black walls of Toth Port growing ever nearer.

Liam thought there might be trouble, a Pirate ship requesting admittance to the Port wasn't an everyday occurrence but to everyone's surprise the huge sluice gates were opened and the ship sailed into the port unhindered. It did create a bit of a stir on the dock and there were several groups of labourers gathered along the walls watching with avid curiosity. When Liam remarked on this to Finn, he just grinned. He had recognised some of the labourers as warriors from Prime and he had a suspicion that one or two might even be Elite.

"Your Lord isn't taking any chances," Gerran remarked. It seemed he had realised what was going on too.

They were in for more surprises. Ragnar was on the dockside waiting for them. Lord Toth was in residence at the Port with the Lady Sarah and her mother. Swift horses were waiting to take them to the Port Castle and Gerran, at least, was anxious to be reunited with his wife and daughter. Liam sensed a reluctance in Finn. He was going to have to tell his Lord that Emma was dead.

Ragnar and the guard sent to escort them all stared at the pirate ship with unease. Fortunately the Pirates refused to leave their ship. They would wait until Liam sent word. For some strange reason Liam felt responsible for them and he asked Ragnar if he could arrange for fresh supplies to be sent on board. Ragnar looked at him as if he was mad but he said he would ask Lord Toth if he would allow it.

"But don't expect him to be in a generous mood," Ragnar told him as they dismounted at the stables and handed over the horses to the care of the ostler and his lads. "Ever since he got word of Emma he's been like a wolf with a thorn in his pad. Growling at everyone and everything."

"You've heard then?" Finn sounded extremely relieved.

"Of course," Ragnar said and there was a sound of pride in his voice. "We got word from our Spymaster nearly ten days ago that you had succeeded in rescuing the Menethes Spymaster. Why do you think Mistress Judith is here? She insisted on coming once we heard that a boat had been sighted." He laughed at Liam's puzzled face. "It only takes a few hours now from Prime to Port," he said. "The Highway from Menethes Port down to Prime is no longer. We moved it. It now goes from Toth Port to Toth Secund." and he banged on the heavy metal gates of the castle for admittance.

Like Secund, the Castle at the Port was circular but there the similarity ended. The Port Castle was simply an enormous four-storey tower surrounded by a thick stone outer wall. There were no outlying buildings; everything was inside the tower. The ground floor was devoted to kitchens, storerooms and a large guardroom. A central spiral stairway gave access to a circular corridor on the remaining three levels. Half of the first floor was a huge open hall, the other half given over to oddly shaped rooms radiating off the central corridor. It was here that Judith had a room and Gerran disappeared quickly in search of her and Sarah.

Lord Toth had rooms on the very top floor and Liam and the others were shown into the first-floor hall to wait whilst he was told of their arrival. It was cool inside the tower, a welcome change from the heat of the streets but after a while they began to feel chilled and someone opened a brazier in the centre of the room.

It was sometime before the Lord appeared and servants came first with ale and food on huge metal platters. It was left on a sturdy wooden table standing against one curved wall and Liam walked over and helped himself. Days of dried meat and biscuits had given him an appetite for some decent food and ale. He was on his second helping of meat and vegetables wrapped in pastry when Lord Toth finally came down and Liam was shocked at how he seemed to have aged. Emma's death had obviously hit him hard. But then, Liam thought, warrior honour had also been involved. The Toth had lost great deal of face with the abduction of Emma. For the briefest of moments, no more than the lifetime of a heartbeat, Liam considered abandoning his plan of action and staying to help. But he quickly dismissed the thought. There was nothing he could do. And he was needed elsewhere.

"Gerran told me you want to return to Urth," Toth said sitting in a great carved chair near the open brazier. A servant brought him a plate of food but he waved it away and sat staring at the group with tired eyes. "If that is what you want then of course you must go. Tell the Reeve of your needs and he will see to them."

The Lord was interested in the tales the warriors had to tell of the battle for Menethes Prime and the sea mist that had engulfed them on that last day and he and his warriors listened in perfect silence until Dillon had finished.

"You will want to rest after your ordeal," Toth said as the tale drew to a close. "Then you can be reunited with your fellow elite to guard the Lady Sarah and her son." He looked straight at Liam. "No doubt you will wish to take some of these Menethes' warriors with you to Urth. Some of my warriors can replace them but they will be under the captaincy of Dillon." He smiled grimly at Liam. "Will that satisfy you, Gladiator?" and for once Liam didn't take offence at the name. He bowed his head. It must have taken a lot for the Toth to pass care of the Lady Sarah back to the Menethes.

The Toth sat back in his great chair and put his hand tiredly to his eyes and his Elite gathered around him. They were dismissed. Liam and Finn went out into the area around the Castle building. It could hardly be called a courtyard, merely a cobbled space between the castle and its surrounding walls. Liam sat on an upturned barrel outside the kitchens in the sun. After the cold of the hall he needed the warmth of the sun to cheer him.

"What do we do now?" Finn said.

"You can go and talk to Gerran. I... I don't think we will need any of Sarah's guard. The pirates will be enough. And then you can talk to the Reeve," Liam decided quickly. "Any requests for stores would be better coming from you, you're Toth."

"And you?"

"I will go to Prime and find Timon." Liam said.

"There were others at Prime bought at the same time," Finn said. "I know one died of plague, but the others might want to come."

"Then I will contact any one I can find news of. If the highway stretches from here to Prime it shouldn't take long," Liam said standing up. He might as well get started. "I'll go and find Ragnar. He can tell me were the Gate is and find me a horse. I'll see you in a day or two." They shook hands rather self-consciously and Liam went back into the Castle.

Finn stared after him for a moment and then went in search of Gerran. As eager as he had been to see his wife he had obviously put duty first and reported to Lord Toth. Finn sighed. He would have liked to rest himself. Liam had too much energy that was the problem.

"More like the Anant than the Anant," he muttered and he went inside himself.

Liam told Timon the whole truth and Timon reluctantly agreed to come with him. He was less sure when he heard that Liam hadn't told anyone else exactly what he was planning.

"Why have you told me?" was his only question and Liam had to stress how important a blacksmith might be.

"Apparently they are in short supply everywhere."

Timon shook his head. He would continue Emma's search for the black crystal but he suggested his assistant might be willing to go and Robert eagerly agreed

Word had been sent ahead that he was to be given every assistance and within two days of leaving the Port he was back. Finn and Spymaster Menethes had also been busy. The pirate ship had been supplied with fresh food and there was promise of more when they were ready to leave. Only Finn now worried Liam, he seemed abnormally quiet but he collected stores and shipped them down to the dock ready for loading.

Within a decan they would be ready to leave.

On the eve of their departure Liam found Finn supervising the loading of several large sealed jars that Liam had ordered specially. The pirates still kept very much to themselves. Even now the same two that had spoken to them before were on deck, the rest were nowhere to be seen. Liam hadn't seen much of Finn in the previous few days.

The people coming with them were saying their goodbyes and preparing to board the ship. Liam had a few spare clothes in his pack and had said his goodbyes to Sarah. He was tempted to tell her about the danger the planet was in but decided not to. He didn't want to worry her; they would be back in plenty of time. He just promised to return as soon as he could, kissed her on the forehead, ruffled Dom's hair and told him to take good care of his mother and then took his leave. He did not see Lord Toth but Ragnar was waiting outside to wish him good speed and a safe journey.

Finn finished supervising the loading and came on board soon after Liam. He was still very quiet and Liam wondered if he was having second thoughts about leaving.

"No," was his curt reply and he threw his bag angrily down onto the furs that would serve as his bed for the voyage. "I shall be glad to see the back of this place."

Liam sighed quietly to himself. He didn't feel like getting into a heated discussion with Finn but there was obviously something wrong and it was too long a voyage to have Finn in such a strange mood.

"What's wrong," he said. "I thought you were getting to like the place."

Finn glared at him. Liam had never seen him so angry, he was normally so placid.

"They are still saying that Ralf and Emma were having an affair. There is proof, someone saw them together," he said and he took a deep breath through gritted teeth. Liam shook his head. Such rumours were upsetting but...

"No one who knew her believes that," he said.

"Lord Toth does," snapped Finn. "He said that he understood, that he would have forgiven her." He suddenly slammed his clenched fist against the wooden partition. "Damn them, damn them all. Not dead five minutes..."

"Ragnar gave no hint of anything," Liam pointed out. "He can't believe it."

"He does. Ralf's ashes still lie in the temple at Secund. Ragnar has disowned him and denied him interment in the family tomb." Finn was shaking his head clearly deeply upset by it all.

"I don't suppose..." Liam began and then he saw Finn's face. "No, of course not." and Liam was conceited enough to consider that if Emma was going to have an affair with anyone it would have been with him.

Liam sighed. It was going to be a very long journey with Finn in this mood.

"Do you want to stay?" he asked. "See if you can somehow put things right."

Finn took a long time before answering.

"No," he said eventually. "Emma is dead. But I don't think I will ever forgive them... any of them. It just doesn't seem right"

Liam rested his hand on Finn's shoulder.

"We should get some rest," he said gently. "We sail with the tide at first light."

Finn sat on his furs but he was still brooding about Emma and the injustice done to her so Liam left him to it and went to check on the others. The sooner they were under way the better.

Once their journey had begun Finn would have other things to think about and they could all begin to forget Emma.

It took two decans to reach the Isles. The wind was in their favour all the way and they made good time. It was almost as if the Gods were favouring them. They dropped anchor in an inlet and rowed ashore in small boats. The land sloped up gently away from the shore and Liam led the way. As he breasted the small rise he stopped and gasped. In front of them was a huge white pyramid, bigger than any temple he had ever seen in Anaria. But unlike any temple its lines were not straight and rigid but flowed in graceful curves. It was the most beautiful thing he had ever seen. This was what they had spent tarns searching for and now it was ahead of them. He turned back and saw Finn gazing at it, a slight smile on his face. He looked at Liam and nodded.

"We're finally going home," he said as they started across the sand.

Robert gave Liam a long hard stare.

"Not exactly," Liam admitted. "Actually we're going to Lycia... to help an old friend."

"An old friend?" queried Finn. They had started down a small incline towards the ship and at the bottom Finn stopped and turned to face Liam. "I take it you are talking about Osiris?" He shook his head and sighed. "Liam..." He laid his hand on Liam's forearm. "Osiris doesn't exist. Emma... and *PSI Division*... both agreed he was a figment of your imagination, designed to hide your growing telepathic abilities. He was... is... nothing more than a defence mechanism."

Liam looked across at Robert standing by his side. "What do you think?"

Robert was staring beyond Finn towards the pyramid-shaped ship. "Er... Um... If that's a figment of your imagination... I'd hate to meet the real thing."

Finn twisted round on the spot. His feet became entangled and with a small cry he fell over onto the sand. Osiris extended his hand, claws carefully sheathed, to help him back up. But Finn scrambled to his feet by himself and took a step back. He was staring open-mouthed at the Nestor before him.

Osiris was exactly as Liam remembered him from the night he had come to Menethes Prime to warn Liam of the attack.

Six and a half feet of smooth fur; a flattened muzzle; golden cats eyes and a mane of hair the same colour; finally a thumb and three fingers to each hand with black claws at the end.

"Osiris." Lim stretched out his hand to greet his old friend with a typical Urth greeting. The hand grasped in Liam's felt dry and slightly rough. Just as he had imagined it would.

"So will you help me?" Osiris asked, his voice had the deep mellow richness that Liam had remembered. Liam looked at Finn. Everything depended on him now. For a moment Liam thought he was going to argue with them but then Finn shrugged.

"Our earth is long gone," he said slowly. "I suppose... I've nothing better to do. Although I don't see what help we can be."

Osiris extended his hand towards the ship, indicating they should follow him there. As they walked Osiris began to explain his need. "I have an army willing to fight and I am a good warrior, well capable of leading my men. But I am not a strategist; I cannot see every possibility, plan for every eventuality... I need someone to lead the army whilst I am... arranging other things. The Pirate Lord is too old to lead them in battle, his son is too young. They need a leader. I thought of you." He put his head to one side as if asking if they understood and Liam found himself nodding. He understood but did Finn?

"I can see why you might need Liam," he was saying, "But Robert and me..?"

"Liam's training, both on Urth and here, make him ideal," Osiris agreed, "but he will need a spymaster to gather all the intelligence we gather and make sense of it all. He tells me you are the best man for this job."

"And Robert?"

"Everyone needs a good blacksmith," Robert said with a broad smile.

They were close to the main entrance to the ship now. Finn stopped at the beginning of the ramp and frowned.

"I remember being here before," he said. "Are there... is there any one left from..."

Osiris was quick to reassure him that all the people from Urth had been revived and taken to Anaria some time before. "Your Emma was on the last but one ship," he said.

"Emma!"

"What is wrong?"

"Emma is dead," Liam said quickly. "Pharaoh had her burnt at the stake."

Osiris bared his teeth in what Liam took to be his version of a smile. "No, she is alive and on board the last tribute ship to sail."

"Then she is going to Lycia...? To Ammon?"

If it was possible for a Nestor muzzle to widen into a bigger smile, then Osiris's grin did just that.

"No, there are men on those ships who are ours. They have orders to take over the ships once they have sailed... All the Menethes warriors that your Pharaoh filled the ships with, all the weapons and armour, all the grain and horses meant for Ammon... it's coming to us!"

"Why do you hate him so much?" Finn asked.

"He took everything from me," Osiris growled. "My Lorddom, my friend, my family. Then he left me on Urth to die without honour. This time I will kill him."

XXXI

"I'm sorry. There was little we could do." The captain of the pirate ship sent to escort the last of the Tribute ships stood before Liam and Osiris with his head bowed. "They were not at the meeting place as arranged. We ventured as close to coast as we dared and eventually found them adrift just north of Menethes Port. We did what we could but the towing rope broke and the ship was swept onto the rocks." The man cast an anguished look in Finn's direction and then continued. "Some managed to scramble onto the rocks... others swam for the shore..."

"But at least half of those on board were drowned?" Finn spoke quietly and Liam felt for his friend. To have believed his sister dead, then to be told she was alive and on her way to join them... and now this. Surely the Gods couldn't be so cruel?

"She may have survived," the captain said. "Lorca took many from the sea; she may have been among those. He beached his ship and signalled we should make our way home and report what had happened."

"Emma is not dead." Osiris said firmly. "She would not have survived so much to die in this pointless way. The Gods still have a purpose for her."

"Your Gods!" Finn whirled round and strode from the hut in a fit of anger and disappointment that Liam found easy to understand. He was feeling something similar himself. He nodded to Osiris and followed Finn out but there was no sign of him anywhere in the small camp. Liam scanned the two rows of small huts and then beyond to the grove of trees where the horses were tethered but Finn had completely disappeared.

Liam closed his eyes and pinched the bridge of his nose. He could feel a headache coming on and he found himself remembering a similar headache at Kush Prime and Emma buying herbs to help him.

Emma.

If she was alive it meant she was back with Lord Toth.

But that was preferable to the alternative.

"Lord." Iolus's voice broke into his thought. Iolus was the captain of his Elite guard and had been Elite to the previous Apis lord who had died only a few decans after their arrival. "The horses are ready for Lord Osiris."

Liam indicated he was inside the hut and he waited for Osiris to emerge, partly to say goodbye and partly to reinforce to Osiris the importance of the task ahead of him.

Osiris was embarking on a most crucial mission; one that would mean the difference between success and failure in their fight against Ammon. He was going to visit his father Lord Ptah and try to persuade him to join them in their fight. Liam was hoping that if Lord Ptah opposed Ammon then more Lycian Lords would follow suit. It was Lord Ptah that had found and repaired the spaceship and then approached Lord Menethes with orders to go to Urth and bring back slaves. It was Lord Ptah who had approached the Apis Pirates to use their boats and skill in navigation to actually fly the spacecraft. It was Lord Ptah who had arranged for the Menethes to pay the Apis in food and weapons. Food and weapons that had meant the Apis had gone from an outcast tribe on the fringes of Nestor society to a tribe that was now almost ready to take on the might of

Ammon. But he had always refused to declare war on Ammon.

Liam was hoping that was about to change.

He wished Osiris a speedy, and successful, journey, raised his hand his hand in farewell and then stood watching the company as they rode south towards the Ptah homeland. He stayed, deep in thought, staring into the distance until the horsemen were no longer visible. Then he turned away intending to find Finn and offer what little comfort he could. Iolus was standing close by, waiting to see what orders Liam had for the warriors or for the camp. It was one of the Lord's duties that Liam found most irritating. He was seldom left alone for a moment. Not for the first time Liam found himself thankful that he was only a regent Lord, regent only until the last Lord's heir was old enough to assume a Lord's duties. Since the boy, Ulan, was only ten tarns old that meant Liam could be Lord for at least fifteen tarns. It was not a prospect that Liam relished. He had every intention of handing over power as soon as Ammon had been defeated.

Iolus was looking tired, his eyes bloodshot and rimmed with red. Liam told him to go to bed but the man refused.

"Then tell me where Finn has gone and then go find yourself something to eat," Liam ordered.

Iolus pointed to the last hut in a row of five. Finn was in there, he said, talking to a ranger.

Liam entered the hut without knocking. Finn was in conversation with a tall man dressed in ragged clothing that wouldn't have looked out of place on a *scarecrow*. He had a dirty leather eye patch over his left eye and his left hand was missing the ring and little finger. At Liam's entrance Finn straightened up from leaning over a map and just nodded at the ranger.

336

"This is Orestes," Finn said simply. "He has brought some bad news."

"Ammon has found our spacecraft," Orestes told Liam, looking him in the eye unflinchingly. "He has killed those that remained behind, taken all the stores and damaged the yellow crystal with fire."

"Can today get any worse?" Liam said, bowing his head tiredly. His headache erupted with volcanic force inside his head. He jerked his head upright which made things a hundred times worse but he ignored the pain. "Does Ammon know Osiris is here in Lycia?"

"Thank you, Orestes." Finn waited until the ranger had left before answering. "No. Every indication is that Ammon still believes Osiris is in Anaria, sheltering inside an Urth human.

Liam considered this new setback. Without the spacecraft they had only the boats to take them back to Anaria, a dangerous journey at the best of times and one that took too long to be of practical use. He slowly became aware that Finn was studying him intently. Obviously Finn was waiting for the right moment to tell him more bad news.

"Out with it!"

"You wondered why the Apis hadn't taken Osiris as regent," Finn said. "What it was he wasn't telling us."

Liam nodded. On their arrival in Lycia Osiris had given them the briefest of history lessons. He had explained how he and his brother Baht, Lord Apis, had supported a Lord Apophis as Pharaoh against Ammon. Osiris had maintained that Apophis had been the rightful heir. But Apophis had been defeated and destroyed and for his part in the rebellion, Osiris had been banished to Anaria. Baht and the Apis had remained in Lycia but as outcasts, dwindling in number over the five thousand tarns since then, becoming more Anarian and less Nestor with each passing tarn as their tribe became a haven for runaway slaves and outcast part-bloods.

He had told them how he had separated from Liam soon after entering the space craft, a painful process that had explained why Liam had revived and tried to escape. Osiris hadn't been able to explain why Emma had been with him in his dreams of the event but not in reality; he couldn't explain why Liam had changed his mind and agreed to stay. Osiris thought it had been something Liam had seen on the lower decks of the cargo hold, probably Emma, and Liam had agreed although at the back of his mind he had a nagging feeling that that wasn't the reason. He was sure he had been in a cubicle further up inside the ship... with all the other new arrivals. What he had seen to change his mind had been lower down... earlier...

That was all that Osiris would say. The Apis had readily agreed to Liam's appointment as Regent and preparations for battle had continued. Preparations that had included the Apis accepting Osiris's help in designing a formidable secret weapon ... the longbow... that everyone hoped would turn the tide in their favour.

So why didn't they accept him as Regent?

No one would discuss it.

Until now.

"So?" Liam asked impatiently. "How... What... did you find out?"

"The how was easy," Finn rolled up the map on the table and put it away in a long wooden container. "I got Iolus and some of his veterans drunk."

"No wonder he looked bleary-eyed this morning!"

Finn put the map in a wooden chest that was against the wall. Liam saw it was full of similar containers. Finn must have had maps covering the entire surface of Lycia. He had certainly taken his role as Liam's spymaster seriously.

"So what's the big mystery?" Liam joked but Finn's face remained stern.

"According to... tribal history..." he began.

"You mean legend," Liam said scathingly.

"Whatever..." Finn shrugged. "When the Apophis rebellion took place both sides were evenly matched. When they finally met though Apophis was outnumbered because the Thoth, that's Osiris's tribe, and the Apis weren't there. They arrived much later, after Apophis and his tribe had been slaughtered. Osiris is supposed to have claimed that he received a message sending him to another meeting place... which he passed on to Baht."

"But...?" Liam said sharply. "What does tribal gossip say?"

"That Osiris was deliberately late because he had found out his wife Nefertiri was having an affair with Lord Apophis and was planning on leaving him." Finn locked the wooden chest and then sat down on the lid, using it as a chair. "They're willing enough to let him help with new ideas like the bow, Liam. But they don't trust him to lead them in battle."

Liam didn't have to think about what Finn had told him. "Osiris wouldn't behave like that," he said firmly. "I know him too well. He just wouldn't. He talked of Ammon taking his honour. Ammon must have sent that message to mislead him. Osiris is too honourable to..."

"Did you know he had a daughter on Urth?" Finn said. "He let something slip and I wheedled the rest out of him over time. It was with his host before you. A daughter that was to all intents and purposes human but with hidden Nestor traits… what, I believe, is termed a runt for want of a better word." Finn's tone was harsh. "He seems to have had no problem abandoning her when it came time to leave. What makes you think we can trust him? The Apis don't. They don't trust him at all." Finn gave Liam a long hard stare. "What the *hell* have we got ourselves into, Liam?"

Liam refused to discuss the matter further with Finn. He became like the Apis, deaf and dumb, when the subject was mentioned. There was nothing to be gained by speculating on what Osiris had or had not done thousands of tarns ago. It would have to wait until Osiris returned from his mission. Instead Liam concentrated on training men in the use of the longbow. Everything had to be done in small groups, in small camps, so that Ammon's spies did not become suspicious. Secrecy was of the utmost importance. It was imperative that nothing of their preparations for war be discovered. Even the disappearance of the two remaining Tribute ships had to be explained, with false rumours of fierce storms and sinkings at sea being spread by Finn's rangers in the Prime cities of Lycia.

The Menethes, eager for the chance to avenge their defeat and the death of their Lord, were easily persuaded to join Liam and the Apis in their rebellion and the warriors had been spread out among the small vills that dotted the Apis lands, training small bands of Apis in the arts of warfare and battle tactics.

Summer slowly turned into winter. The leaves on the trees turned from green to russet and yellow and then fell to the ground to be blown against hut walls by an increasingly cold wind. But still Osiris did not return. Liam oversaw the distribution of their stores to all the camps, ensuring each had enough to survive the winter season. The supplies Pharaoh Kush had thought he was sending to his God came in particularly useful. Liam rather enjoyed seeing to the sharing of those.

It wasn't until winter was in its second centad that a weary and cold band of riders appeared through the trees and made their way into camp. The riders were swathed in heavy woollen cloaks, their faces hidden against the biting cold. The heads of the horses were drooping with exhaustion, steam rose from their flanks and it was clear they had been ridden hard. The riders had fared little better. As they dismounted all had to hold onto the saddles to stop themselves from falling.

"Where is our Lord?" the leader asked, his voice muffled. "I have important news." He was shown into Liam's hut, several warriors crowding in after him to hear what news he brought. Liam hadn't the heart to order them to leave. This news could mean the difference between life and death for the tribe. He took one look at the exhausted man before him and immediately ordered hot spiced wine and bowls of venison stew to be brought to all the riders that had returned. He had hoped to see Osiris but the man before him was Breon, the leader of the warriors who had accompanied Osiris. So, where was Osiris and why hadn't he returned with them?

"The Ptah have agreed to join us against Ammon," Breon said after he had been fortified with spiced wine. "Lord Ptah wasn't keen at first but Osiris persuaded him eventually. He has gone with his father to try and persuade other Lords to join us." His news was greeted by a small cheer from those close enough to hear and a whisper soon went out to those waiting outside. The Apis were heartened by the news but Liam was worried by it also. They had managed to keep Osiris's presence a secret from Ammon and now Osiris was jeopardising everything by revealing himself.

"Only to those Lord Ptah felt he could trust… those who might be prepared to join us," Breon explained. He held out two scrolls, both from Osiris. One was addressed to Lord Apis, the other to Liam personally. Liam opened the first and began to read aloud what was written there.

"Osiris says his father has agreed to join us in our rebellion against Ammon. He is sure that two other Lords will join us… the Maneto and the Bas." A murmur of approval greeted this. "Osiris has stayed behind to approach these lords with his father and he will return with news as soon as he can. He also writes that the Ptah have offered food should we need any to see us through the winter."

Liam passed the letter to Finn who began to read it for himself. Liam folded the other letter and put it in his pocket. He told Breon to retire and rest. He and his men had earned it. Slowly Liam's hut emptied until there was only he and Finn left. Finn finished reading the letter and handed it back.

"The other?" he enquired but Liam shook his head. It had been addressed to him personally and he wanted to read it by himself first.

"If it contains anything you need to know," he said, "I will tell you," and Finn had to be content with that. He said goodnight and left Liam to his letter. But it was sometime before he broke the seal. He was oddly reluctant to open it and read what Osiris had to say. He poured himself a tankard of spiced wine from a jug that had been left and then settled himself onto the furs that served as his bed. Only then did he break the seal and begin to read.

My dearest Friend,

What can I say? You seem to have all the facts. Have you made up your mind? I fancy that your Spymaster has by the look that he gave me as I left that morning. I confess I was surprised to receive your letter though. I thought you knew me better than that. What can I say that will convince you of my innocence?

But first, yes I do remember feeling your presence all those seasons ago. We must have entered the Highway at the same time and, having been physically one for so long, our minds reconnected once again. I was surprised you that you remembered me.

And yes... I did know that Imhotep and Nefertiri were lovers. Knew, accepted and forgave.
But your own experience of unfaithful wives may colour your judgement here. Will you find it so hard to believe that I could forgive such a betrayal by my greatest friend and my wife? I suspect you will.

I can only repeat that I had forgiven them. I had known for some time although I think they did not know this. I have often wondered in the thousands of tarns that have passed since then if it was the thrill of

343

secrecy that fuelled their passion? If I had
revealed my knowledge of the affair would
it have been less exciting for them. Would
their passion have burned itself out?
Would she have returned to me? At least
on that last question I have an answer that
you will believe. I would not have taken
her back! I am like you in that... or are you
like me?

I did receive a message that I believed
came from Imhotep informing me of a
change of meeting place, which I passed
on to Baht. If only I hadn't things might
have been so very different. There is
nothing more I can tell you of this matter.
The scroll carried Imhotep's seal; I had no
reason to think it was false.

As to how my father came to know I
was on Urth... it is very simple. He
believed I had died in Anaria. He had no
way to visit me. Ammon controlled the two
spaceships and the Sea Gate between the
two continents no longer worked. The two
crystals in Anaria had been thrown down
and buried by Ammon so that I and my
tribe would be unable to return. About
forty tarns ago a slave came into his
possession who spoke of Urth as some kind
of Daemon world that was ruled over by
the Daemon Lord Osiris. Eventually he
worked out what must have happened; I
had been taken to Urth by Ammon and left
there.

It was Ammon who discovered how to extend his life by existing with another. How he discovered this I do not know but he now uses the Black crystals to achieve a similar effect. It still seems appropriate that I should have survived in such a manner... Although quite how it happened I do not know for our crystals do not work well on Urth. Perhaps that is a question for the gods. But yours or mine?

You must have realised by now that I am avoiding answering the last question you asked me.

Yes, I did have a daughter on Urth with my last host. Quite how it came to pass I am unsure, but all the signs were there, she was mine. I am ashamed to say I did abandon her but not in the way Finn thinks. I left her when my last host was killed and I came to you. I meant to tell her that I had survived but it never seemed the right time. I almost told her one night in your mother's kitchen but fate intervened and I missed the chance.

Yes, she was someone you knew. Someone you knew well in fact. My daughter was Cassandra, Sean's fiancée. I am not sure how much you remember about Sean. You have never mentioned him although you did ask me once, just after I brought you to Lycia, if 'truth or dare' meant anything. So perhaps you remember more than you are saying. Do you remember what happened at Sean's funeral? She blamed you for his death, for encouraging him to become a warrior. Perhaps if I had realised how upset she was I could have done more. I should have said something, revealed my presence to her but I was more concerned with making sure you got to know Judith. I could sense Sarah was not totally of your world and I wanted to return home. May the Gods forgive me. I deserted my daughter when she needed me most. I should have realised that the loss of Sean following so closely the loss of her parents... I cannot justify my behaviour. Finn's accusation that I abandoned my daughter in my haste to return home is true.

I am to go with my father to meet with his friends. With luck I will be able to persuade them to join us. I have a feeling that, like my father, they are beginning to realise the price they have had to pay for their extended lives. Let us pray it is so. For if we are to save our world we will have to release the black crystals from their bondage and, for some, I fear the price will be very high indeed.

Wish me luck. As for the rest... I have told you the truth. You must judge for yourself.

Yours in true friendship,

Osiris.

Cassie. How could he have forgotten?

XXXII

Liam reined in his horse on the bank and stared across at the five tall ships anchored in the middle of the river. Several small boats were ferrying the last of the warriors onto the shore and ahead of him he could see the makeshift camp that had been set up to house the warriors until he arrived.

"I thought there were six ships," he said and Iolus nodded as they made their way along the riverbank and into the confusion of tents and campfires. Liam looked round him in dismay. The camp should have been better organised than this. Where were the sentries on duty that should have challenged their approach? What was Finn thinking of, letting things get so out of hand?

A tall warrior saw them as soon as they rode into the open ground in the centre and hurried over. In spite of the shock of white hair on his head Liam knew the warrior wasn't that old. He was the youngest of his elite and before that had captained one of cohorts that had regularly raided the Anarian coast. Liam strained to remember his name.

"The section commanders are gathering over by the supply wagons, my Lord," the warrior informed him, taking the reins of Liam's horse and then handing them swiftly to an ordinary warrior. He pointed behind him. "This way, my Lord."
Liam quickly looked round.

"What happened to the sixth boat...?" The missing boat was crucial to Liam's plans. It contained all of the newly trained bowmen. Ammon was in for a big surprise when they met.

"The rudder broke and it ran aground," the warrior said as he led them through the melee of tents. "Some of the bowmen were taken on board the other ships but they were already over full... the rest are coming overland. The Spymaster is with them."

There were ten warriors clustered round a map spread out on the back of wagon and as soon as Liam approached they fell back to let him through, standing erect as they did so. All saluted him with a clenched fist held against the torc. Liam responded quickly in a similar fashion and then studied the map closely. He glanced round at his captains awaiting his final orders. They had all been hand picked either by himself or by Finn and where the best the Apis pirates had to offer. He recognised one man, smaller than the rest, wearing a leather eye patch.

"Orestes!" he said with some relief. "Does this mean Finn has arrived?"

"I came on one of the boats," Finn's right-hand man explained. "He has sent word to all our spies and they can make contact with us if they can't find him. He thought it best that one of us come overland and one of us be here."

"All possibilities covered," Liam agreed. "So... where are the enemy and what are they doing?"

Orestes turned the map slightly so that Liam could get a better view and pointed to where Ammon and his allies were last reported to have been. That had been two days ago, Orestes explained and he pointed to the area where they should be now.

"They can't march fast in this direction," he said. "The land looks flat but it..." He made a motion with his right hand, "... like waves. This whole area is like that."

"We should be able to make good time," Arjen interrupted. "The land works in our favour. We can march swiftly in the depressions and intercept them... here." He jabbed at the map with his finger. "With your permission, Lord, I will issue the order to break camp. We can be ready to march within the hour."

The captains followed Arjen back into the main body of the camp leaving Liam, surrounded by his Elite guard.

"There's a group of men eager to die," Orestes said and Liam frowned.

"What makes you say that?"

"Spymaster Finn's initial intelligence said there were two hundred thousand warriors," Orestes explained. "Now, there are only one hundred. That means we're not too outnumbered if Osiris arrives with the promised men. But suppose Finn was right...Where are the missing men? It doesn't seem to worry your commander... but it worries me."

Liam agreed. It wasn't like Finn to get things so wrong. He was usually so meticulous.

"Send out more spies," Liam decided. "How long before Finn and the bowmen join us?"

Orestes circled a small area on the map with his finger.

"By the time we reach here, he should only be a few hours away."

Liam nodded and then dismissed the ranger. He looked thoughtfully at the map spread out before him. Someone had carefully drawn in contour lines to give the impression of the undulating landscape. To the north the land was flat and someone had just written the word *flat*. He briefly wondered if it had been Finn. Then he brought his thoughts back to the contour lines. If Finn's original estimate of numbers had been right where were those missing men and what were they doing? Were the dips and rises deep enough to hide a second army of a hundred thousand?

Liam turned to one of his Elite and asked him to find something to eat. He always thought better on a full stomach.

Liam decided to attack even though Finn and the remaining bowmen had still not arrived. There were at least two Apis farming villages a few miles ahead of the enemy and Liam really had no choice but to attack. Not if he wanted to protect the tribe. Every farm, every farm animal, every crop, even the humblest potato was of vital importance to the long-term survival of the tribe. Every farm had to be protected... no matter what the cost.

And the number of warriors facing them was only a hundred thousand. Most were from the Loci tribe, a neighbouring tribe that been hounding the Apis for as long as anyone could remember. Only about twenty thousand wore the red hand of Ammon on their torcs. The rest were Senu, Kephri and Baruk warriors. Liam had never seen a full blood Nestor before and not even Osiris had prepared him for the creatures that faced him across the open ground. The distance of several hundred yards between them couldn't hide the long muzzles or the fact that a full-blood was at least six inches taller than Osiris. Liam found himself imagining the sharp teeth that went with that mouth and the razor like claws. He tried to hide the feeling of revulsion that gnawed at his insides but he couldn't stop the shudder. The horse beneath him stirred uneasily as if it shared his fear.

Liam raised his hand and the warriors began to beat their swords against their shields in a steady rhythm. Slowly the massed ranks of the Apis and the Menethes began to advance towards the enemy.

351

Liam was tiring and he knew it. He swept back with his sword and struck another part-blood across the back of the shoulders. The Nestor went down but the effort left Liam with aching muscles and tired legs that were threatening to fold beneath him.

Liam saw a large group of fifty or more Loci break free of his encircling warriors and make a dash for higher ground to the east. As he checked that the fallen warrior was dead and not feigning death to spring up later and catch him unawares, Liam saw a band of twenty or more of his mounted warriors wheel off and start to chase after the fleeing Loci.

Come back, he ordered as strongly as he could. Something was gnawing at his stomach, making him uneasy and he didn't want anyone to become separated from the rest. He glimpsed the warriors reining in their horses in some confusion… The strong desire to chase down the escaping Nestor conflicting with their duty to obey him.

Iolus, tell the men to fall back to the high ground behind us. He could see Iolus was reluctant to break off the fight but he insisted again and began to order his Elite to regroup.

Liam mounted his horse and spurred it to the top of a small rise, turning to face the battlefield. It was still early morning and the Apis had the advantage of the sun behind them. The section captains were busy ordering their men to fall back and Liam saw one or two bending to help an injured man to his feet. There were a number of bull torcs that remained where they had fallen though and Liam felt a sudden pang at the loss. He bowed his head as his Elite gathered round him and waited for his next commands.

Iolus turned to Liam. "What should we do, Lord?"

There was still some fighting further down the line and Liam ordered the retreat to be sounded. Perhaps the Nestor Captain had done the same for the enemy warriors also broke away and returned to their ranks. A lone horseman trotted forward down among the fallen and carefully picked his way across the open ground until he was about halfway between the two armies. Then he stopped.

He appeared to be waiting for something.

"Iolus?"

"I think we are being offered terms for surrender, my Lord."

Liam looked round and spotted a familiar white head.

"Roman," he called. "Go and see what he wants."

The warrior urged his horse forward through the massed ranks and trotted down towards the waiting Nestor. They sat facing each other at a distance of about ten feet for several minutes then the Apis warrior wheeled his horse round and galloped back. The Nestor stayed where he was patiently waiting.

"They are asking for our surrender," Roman confirmed. "We have an hour to send him our answer."

"On what terms?" Liam asked and the warrior shook his head apologetically.

"No terms. They want our complete surrender."

"What! Surrender ourselves and be slaughtered." Iolus was only voicing Liam's own anger.

"Is that normal?" Liam asked but no one could answer that. The Apis had never been in this position before, certainly not in living memory.

"We are to submit ourselves to the will of the God Ammon," Roman said and several of the Elite guard laughed. Liam allowed himself a wry smile too.

"I think we will forgo that pleasure," he said. "But we will use the full hour to our advantage. Tell the men to get as much rest as they can."
There would be no rest for their Lord.

"Lord."

Liam had been pondering all the possible defence strategies. His hour was nearly up and he hadn't come up with anything that didn't result in complete annihilation of his warriors. Whatever the warrior wanted, it was a welcome diversion.

"I think you should come," the young warrior said and he began to lead the way towards the area where the wounded were being tended.

"Don't I know you," Liam said as they neared a grove of trees that offered some shade for the injured. "You're Noah, Ulan's friend."

Ulan was the rightful Apis Lord but, as he was too young to claim the position and had no experience of battle, Liam had assumed the title of Regent Lord. Ulan should have been safe, hidden deep in the Apis homeland, surrounded by faithful veterans. Instead Liam saw the young Lord leaning against the trunk of a tree, his arm bandaged and in a sling. He leapt to his feet as he saw Liam and looked accusingly at Noah.

"I told you not to say anything."

Liam didn't know whether to be worried because Ulan had been hurt or angry because he had disobeyed a direct order to stay behind. In the end he settled for angry.

"I came with the bowmen," Ulan explained. "Then I got on board of one of the other boats and joined the cohort under Roman, son of…"

"I know him," Liam said curtly making a mental note to reprimand the captain at the first opportunity.

"I told him I had your permission," Ulan said defiantly. "I am the Lord… I had to be here fighting with the other warriors."

Liam found it very hard to argue with him. Wouldn't he have done exactly the same in Ulan's place? Ulan was adamant. He wanted to fight beside his tribe. It wasn't his sword arm that had been injured he said firmly and it was only a scratch anyway. But Liam could be just as stubborn and Ulan was going to stay behind the front battle line. Liam refused to listen to any arguments. The boy was the future of the tribe and had to be protected.

"But they're saying the Nestor wanted our surrender so we could be used in one of Ammon's hunts," Ulan protested when he realised his arguments had fallen on deaf ears. "I'd rather die here fighting by your side than end up in a hunt. They'd empty our homeland for their hunt if we let them."

He'll empty this land for tribute.

Liam shivered. There was a whole army marching over his grave.

Pharaoh's army.

"We're not going to die today," he said. "We're going to win." He knew that some of his Elite would be relaying what he said to the rest of the men and he thought carefully about his choice of words. "We *will* win because Ra has said it shall be so."

Liam looked at the young Lord. He was going to tell the boy he could ride at Liam's side but instead he shook his head and then smiled. "And you have the important task of protecting the Spymaster." Ulan turned round in time to see Finn ride up and dismount.

"But ..."

"No buts," Liam said firmly. "If you learn nothing else from me learn this. The spymaster is one of your most important assets. Protect him at all cost. If your spymaster is taken then all your secrets are lost. Protecting him is the best way you can help your tribe today." Liam was relieved when Ulan agreed to this. Leaving the boy with the warriors Liam took Finn by the arm and led him away so they could have a private conversation.

"What kept you?"

"I thought we agreed I was going to fight?" Finn said. "I've had as much, if not more, training in combat than you."

"In the gladiator ring," Liam said but there wasn't time for further argument. Ulan had to be kept away from the fighting and Finn was going to have to do that instead. "If things go badly," Liam added. "I trust you to get him away safely."

It was a sombre faced Finn that watched Liam walk back to the battlefield to deploy the newly arrived bowmen.

"Agincourt."

"What?" Ulan turned his head from his view over the battlefield to stare at the Spymaster. He wasn't sure what the Spymaster had said. It wasn't a word he recognised.

"Agincourt," the Spymaster repeated. "It was a great victory on Urth almost entirely due to the longbow."

"When was that?" Ulan was interested in any battle that resulted in a great victory. He was going to be Lord one day. He needed to know about such things.

"A long time ago." The Spymaster frowned. "About two hundred tarns ago."

"Quite recent then."

The Spymaster suddenly laughed. It was a very strange almost bitter laugh.

"I suppose it was," he agreed. "The Toth would have not long come into his Lorddom… a minor Lordling would soon be made Pharaoh… yes, quite recent."

Ulan looked back to the battle. He could see Liam spurring his horse forward as he lunged at a full-blood Nestor who was on foot. The golden mane turned dark with blood as the Nestor went down under the Regent's blow and was trampled by his horse.

It had been a magnificent battle. The Apis bowmen had broken the might of the Nestor army in a rainstorm of arrows that had turned the sky dark and hidden the sun. Then the Regent Lord had ridden forth at the head of his warriors, the very ground trembling at the sound of the horses' hooves and the ancient war cry that had issued from the warriors as they bore down on the enemy.

"It is a magnificent victory," Ulan said and he felt so proud of his tribe that he felt his heart must burst out of his chest.

"Indeed," the Spymaster said and Ulan wasn't sure the man was agreeing with him.

"It is," he insisted.

"Will be," the Spymaster corrected. "It isn't over yet."

Ulan shrugged. It was only a matter of time.

"Was it a magnificent victory for Tuni?" the Spymaster suddenly asked and Ulan felt his cheeks burning with shame. In the excitement of the battle he had forgotten his friend who had fallen quite early on.

"Yes it was," he said angrily. "Tuni will be able to hold his head high in the Halls of the Gods among the other warriors. Sekhtet will find him worthy of a place at his table. "

"Indeed," the Spymaster said again and once again Ulan heard the strange note in the Spymaster's voice. "But he won't ever feel the warm sun on his back again or feel the grass beneath his feet. He won't ever take pleasure in a wife and see children playing round his feet. Remember that next time you are so eager to rush into battle. There is always a terrible price to pay even for a victory."

The spymaster turned his back on the battle below them and walked away towards the trees where the wounded were being tended. Ulan frowned as he momentarily forgot the battle to stare after him. Then he shrugged. Iolus was always saying the Spymaster wasn't a true warrior... that he had no stomach for battle. He turned back in time to see the Regent Lord kill another full-blood and he forgot the Spymaster's words as he raised his sword into the air in excitement.

"My Lord... look."
Liam raised his head and squinted. Bright sunlight flashed in his eyes and he put his hand up to shade them. Bright sunlight reflecting off metal shields.

"Ra's teeth." Iolus had joined the elite round Liam and he slowly stood up in his stirrups to get a better look. "Where have they come from?"

Liam counted at least forty squads, each of a thousand full-blood Nestor, appearing over the next rise. The low valley between the two pieces of high ground was carpeted with the bodies of the fallen and he could see a tall red-maned Nestor regarding the battlefield as he turned his head slowly to right and left to watch the tired warriors stumble back to their lines. A circlet of gold flashed at his brow. Could that be Ammon himself Liam wondered?

"How many arrows do we have left?" Liam said staring ahead of him at the Nestor pharaoh.

"Where is Osiris and the promised reinforcements," Liam heard one of his Elite mutter, echoing his own silent prayer. "Has he betrayed his honour again?"

XXXIII

There came a long rolling of great drums like thunder in the mountains and then a braying of horns that set the warriors' ears ringing. Out of the gathered host of the enemy came a group of riders… an embassy from Pharaoh. At its head rode a tall full-blood and with him came a small company of black and gold clad warriors and a single banner, black but bearing on it the red hand of Ammon. The company rode across the open ground before coming to the red and gold banner of the Menethes with its rampant horse. Halting a few hundred yards from Liam the ambassador looked the assembled army up and down and laughed.

"Is there any in this tag army with authority to treat with me?" he asked. "Not you at least," he mocked looking to the left of the Menethes where the banner of the Apis bull was fluttering. "It takes more to make a Lord than a few swords and a tattered banner."

A low murmur of anger filtered through the massed ranks of the Apis and swords were gripped tightly. The ambassador appeared not to notice.

"Name the terms," Liam said loudly and all eyes turned towards him.

"These are the terms," the messenger said and he smiled as he looked from banner to banner. "All that have taken up arms here today shall pay tribute to Pharaoh. All shall withdraw, having first taken oaths never again to bear arms against Pharaoh. All warriors from Anaria will pledge service to Ammon for life. They will be well treated and respected for their loyalty. All lands to the east of Ammon shall be Pharaoh's for all time. This land shall be a hunting preserve and all those who now dwell there shall return to their masters or forever forfeit their right to life."

This was directly aimed at the Apis but the rest of the terms seemed reasonable. Liam began to wonder if the Menethes would agree to them and leave the Apis undefended.

The ambassador finished and settled back in his saddle to await their answer. He didn't have to wait for long.

Manon, Lord Menethes elite captain had been put in overall charge of the Menethes warriors and his voice now came booming out from the massed ranks of his warriors who fell back to give the messenger a clear view of their Captain. "Go back to your Lord," he said, "and tell him these are *our* terms. Ammon must relinquish his Lorddom and submit to the will and judgement of Ra."

At the name of the forgotten God the messenger gave a great cry and, wheeling his horse round, galloped back to the armies of Ammon. As they went his guard blew their horns in a long arranged signal and even before the messenger was back within their lines Ammon's warriors attacked.

Out from the hillocks on either side poured the Senu and the Baruk, forces twice those of the Apis and the Menethes, ringing the enemies of Pharaoh in a sea of spear and shield. Little time was left to Liam for the ordering of his men. Upon a slight rise he stood with the Menethes under a raised banner of the bull rampant.

The first assault crashed into them. Apis arrows poured into the attacking ranks and bounced off the raised shields of Pharaoh's warriors. "We have been betrayed," Iolus shouted but there was no time to think as, from behind the shields, roaring like lions, a great company of Nestor full-bloods charged towards them.

As a great tidal wave they broke upon the line of Apis, beating on helm and shield like smiths on hot metal. At Liam's side the white haired Roman was stunned, staggering back as he fell. The Nestor that had overcome him leapt forward, reaching out a ripping claw. Liam stabbed upwards and his sword pierced through the leather armour and went deep into the Nestor's innards. He toppled forward and came crashing down knocking Liam backwards and driving the breath from his body. As he gasped, trying to stop his mind flying away into darkness, he heard someone crying out in Anarian. But what he was crying didn't make sense.

"Dragons.... The Dragon is coming..." A cry that was taken up and echoed in Apis and Menthes in their own language.

Over the low hills horns were sounding. There upon a ridge behind Ammon appeared a warrior, clad all in white with a trim of gold that shone brightly in the sunlight. Behind him, hastening down the long slopes were ten thousand... fifty thousand... Nestor on foot, their swords in their raised hands.

"Osiris," Liam shouted in relief. "Osiris has come."

A roar went up from the Apis that even the dead in the halls of Ra could have heard.

"Lord Ptah has come."

The host of Ammon roared, swaying this way and that. Again a horn sounded as down the slopes charged the Apis and the Ptah, the Bas and the Maneto, the Hapu and the Menethes... all the army that Osiris and Lord Ptah had gathered. From behind the host of Ammon leapt Osiris, the white warrior, the Nestor leaping sure footed over the bodies of his enemy.

The terrified Ammon and their allies broke ranks and began to flee, many cut down before they realised what was happening. Liam saw a banner of the Red hand swaying in the breeze as it, and all that was left of Ammon's army, fled eastward. Everywhere Nestor warriors were laying down their arms and pleading for their lives.

Ammon had escaped. Liam had his warriors searching for Pharaoh's body but it was not there. Somehow he had eluded the pursuing warriors, fled the field of battle and disappeared. He was nowhere to be found.

Nowhere in Lycia.

"He must have used the second spacecraft to flee to Anaria and sanctuary with Pharaoh Kush," Liam said as the victorious Lords sat around a huge campfire toasting their victory with looted wine from Ammon's own stores. "We know he must have had access to one to visit Anaria so easily. That must be how he found our craft and was able to surprise the guards we had posted."

"We should have thought of that possibility earlier," Finn said gloomily.

"Why the long face?" Lord Ptah asked. "We have won." He was a full-blood Nestor but the resemblance to Osiris was uncanny. Both had a full mane of golden hair although Lord Ptah's was streaked with grey and both had the same golden brown fur.

"If Ammon has escaped to Anaria he can have had only one plan in mind," Finn said. "He intends to raise another army and take back all that we have won here today... all and more besides."

"Can he do that?" Liam wondered and he was worried by how quickly Finn nodded.

"He has at least sixty thousand warriors somewhere. I suspect they are in Anaria preparing to help the Kush in their fight with the Anant. If the Anant are defeated then Ammon will be able to call on the combined forces of the Anant and the Anari to fight us." Finn sighed. "Plus any warriors that he took with him today… a formidable army."

"Formidable indeed," Liam agreed. "And there is nothing we can do. Without our space ship we cannot get to Anaria in time to be of any help. And the Apis don't have enough ships to sail even a tenth of our warriors across to Anaria." Liam suddenly felt depressed. It had all been for nothing. Ammon would come back at the head of an even greater army and the warriors who had died fighting that day would have died for nothing. Already the Menethes were asking when they would be able to return home. Liam felt too tired to think about all the problems that faced them now. Things would look brighter in the morning. He bade the remaining Lords a good night and went in search of his blanket and space under a canvas sheet. He had barely had time to roll himself into his blanket and close his eyes when he heard someone shouting his name. He covered his ears with his hands, hoping he wouldn't be noticed but it was no good. Iolus took hold of his shoulder and shook him until he admitted he was awake and stood up.

"Forgive me Lord, but the Spymaster thinks you need to hear this," Iolus said.

"Can't it wait until morning?" Liam grumbled.
It seemed it wouldn't. Iolus led him back to the dying campfire. He wasn't the only Lord that had been woken and there was quite a group of warriors jostling for a place in the warmth. An Apis warrior was talking with Finn and Lord Ptah to one side of the fire. As Liam approached they stopped talking and waited for him to join.

"What's all the fuss?" he asked.

"There may be a way for us to get to Anaria," Finn said excitedly and he nodded towards the Apis warrior. "This is Lorca. He has just arrived from Anaria... with news."

Liam looked at the warrior. Although exhausted it was clear this man hadn't been involved in the day's fighting. His exhaustion came from a long journey... from the state of his boots, one undertaken on foot. Finn nodded again, prompting the man to begin his tale.

"I was the captain of one of the ships that was meant to accompany the last of the tribute ships," Lorca began. "After we had pulled several survivors out of the water I ordered the boat to beach. I'd gone in too close to shore, the wind was blowing something fierce and I didn't want to end up on the rocks myself. As we hit the shore there was a terrible sound as if we had hit rock. I thought the boat was holed for sure."

Liam glanced at Finn. Where was this tale going and why did Finn think it was important? Finn merely frowned and gave a curt nod in Liam's direction. "Tell our Lord what was uncovered later," Finn prompted.

"Crystals... really tall creamy white crystals... curved in at the top," the man said excitedly. "When we left Toth Port at the end of winter they had been erected on the cliff top just south of the city."

Liam must have been more tired than he realised for he still couldn't see what point Finn was making with all this. "So?"

"I saw the same crystals here in Lycia," Lorca said. "We got blown off course and ended up far to the north. I saw the same crystals on a cliff top there. I think it is a gate... a gate between here and Anaria." The man looked at Liam hesitantly. "I... I thought you would want to know."

"The sea gate, Liam," Finn said. "The one Osiris mentioned in his letter."

"The private letter you aren't supposed to have seen," Liam pointed out but he couldn't be angry with his spymaster. If Finn hadn't read that letter he might not have realised the significance of Lorca's report. "Find Osiris... wake him if he has retired." Liam suddenly felt a surge of energy run through him. "If any one will know if this is the sea gate to Anaria he will." He grinned at Finn and the surrounding Elite who were looking puzzled at their Lord's sudden change of temper. "Ammon thinks he has us caught in Lycia like rabbits in his trap," Liam gloated. "Maybe... just maybe... we can trap him instead."

There was a faint cry from the front of the marching column; a cry that was repeated down the lines of tired warriors. Liam looked ahead, squinting into the setting sun. For a moment he saw nothing then two pale monoliths came into focus, curving inwards to form an almost complete circle. At least thirty foot high the creamy white crystals stood out against the deepening purple sky like an *angel's* halo. Liam's spirit lifted at the sight of the sea gate. It really did exist.

Finn twisted in his saddle to face Liam. "Doesn't it strike you as odd..." he said, pausing as if he was trying to gather his thoughts into a coherent sentence. "I mean... just when we need a miracle this turns up. Lorca runs aground and finds the crystal. The Toth has the foresight to erect them even though he can't have a clue what they are for... and then it is Lorca again who is blown off course and finds the same gate here in Lycia... Who else would have recognised it as the same as in Anaria?"

"Your point being?" Liam asked but Finn could only shake his head.

"I just thought... maybe... it's as if someone is guiding everything."

"You're not telling me you believe that some God or other has a hand in all this?" Liam laughed.

Finn shrugged, a little red faced and embarrassed. "Oh... I don't know. It would be nice though... Maybe then Osiris would be right and Emma is alive because the Gods still have some task for her."

"They're not gods," Liam muttered. "Just some form of 'other dimension aliens'," and they rode on in silence.

"All the answers lie through there." Liam pointed ahead as they drew closer to the crystal gate.

Finn grinned happily. "It feels good to be going home."

"Home!"

"I meant..." Finn paused. "Yes... I meant home. But Liam, this planet is still in danger."

Liam shook his head. "There is an answer... we've just not found it yet."

The first of the Menethes warriors passed between the crystal monoliths and vanished.